SECRETS
THE
WALKERS
KEEP

Secrets the Walkers Keep
By J. Morgan Michaels

Publisher's Cataloging-In-Publication Data
(Prepared by The Donohue Group, Inc.)

Names: Michaels, J. Morgan.
Title: Secrets the Walkers Keep / J. Morgan Michaels.
Description: [Middletown, Connecticut] : [Tribeless Publishing], [2018] |
        Series: [Casters of Magic]
Identifiers: ISBN 9781732714700 (paperback) | ISBN 9781732714717
        (hardcover)| ISBN 9781732714793 (ebook)
Subjects: LCSH: Family secrets--Fiction. | Magic--Fiction. |
        Retrocognition--Fiction. | Self-realization--Fiction.
Classification: LCC PS3613.I34432 S43 2018 (print) | LCC PS3613.I34432
        (ebook) | DDC 813/.6--dc23

Library of Congress Control Number: 2018955886

SECRETS THE WALKERS KEEP

J. MORGAN MICHAELS

To crashing thunderstorms, star-lit skies, and the person who taught me to enjoy them.

I love you, Mom (even though you lost my skis).

JM

Chapter 1

Cheering filled the room as my cousin Paige walked through the run-down doors of the hole-in-the-wall bar that we frequented all too frequently.

"I have arrived," she said, flopping herself into my arms for a hug.

She grabbed my glass and took a long sip from the small straws sticking out of it. "You want one of your own?" I asked her, trying to pry it from her hands.

She shook her head and laughed before finishing my drink completely and pushing the empty glass across the bar. "Sure."

"Two more, please," I said to the bartender.

"Another one?" a man near me asked. "How many cousins can ya'll have?" He was leaning uneasily against the wall in a futile attempt to stop himself from swaying.

"Enough to start our own soccer team," Paige said, noticing that I was already ignoring him.

That night was like too many others—my family drinking and talking in the feeble light of a bar with cheap drinks and scant virtue. At some point, someone had playfully nicknamed

1

those nights 'Cousins & Cocktails', and I had started attending them long before I was old enough to drink.

"I don't think I've met you before," the man said to me, cheap beer spilling down his already dirty hand.

"That wasn't really in the form of a question, so I don't have to respond, right?" I asked Paige, still not turning toward the man.

"His name's Manhattan," she said, scurrying off to join our other cousins by the pool tables.

"Yeah, thanks for that," I said to her back.

My cousins loved doing stuff like that to me. My name was just too peculiar not to spark conversation from people who had never heard one like it. And it was always, *always* a conversation I didn't want to have.

"Really?" the man asked.

It was our favorite bar, our own little corner of the world, but it had its price. It was always infested with pickled old drunks like him, a constant reminder for those of us in our twenties of what we didn't want to become someday.

"No. Not really. She was kidding. My name's Bob. Excuse me," I said.

I moved away from my new friend and through the small crowd to find my cousins. "I still can't believe she named her Rain," I said, picking up an earlier conversation. "What the hell is that?"

"I know, I mean, seriously," Paige said. "What kind of person gives such a beautiful baby such a stupid name?"

"My sister. Who else?" my cousin Damon said. Rain was his older sister's new baby, and the first person in the family to have a name worse than mine.

Not unlike family dinners, it was customary during Cousins & Cocktails to partake in some light family smack talk, mostly about those who weren't there but sometimes about those who were. That was just something we did, but we knew never to say something about someone that we wouldn't say to their face if they asked. I'd like to think that's because we were just that honest, but it's probably truer that we were a family of talkers, and you could assume anything you said to someone was fair game to be repeated.

"Do we know who the father is?" Paige asked over the chatter of the others.

"I'm guessing her boyfriend, but who knows with her. I can't even remember if she ever mentioned his name," Damon said with an indifferent shrug. His sister wasn't exactly known for staying with the same man, job, or hair color for very long.

"Rain Walker?" Paige shook her head. "Could your sister be any more of a hippie?"

"Are we sure it's Walker?" Damon asked, and everyone laughed in response. Women in our family hadn't changed their last name with marriage since long before it was socially acceptable. Their children always carried the Walker name too, despite what anyone had to say about it, including their fathers.

"Another?" Damon asked me from the bar.

I moved closer to the bar. "Kettle One, on the . . ."

"Yeah, I know. That's what you always get. That wasn't my question." He waved to the bartender and pointed to our empty drinks.

"So, where's your girlfriend tonight?" I asked.

"No idea," Damon said. "We broke up yesterday."

"Oh. Sorry. What happened?"

"Who knows? My mom thinks she couldn't deal with the family, but it's more likely that she caught onto the fact that I wasn't that into her. She kept saying things like 'let's move into together', and I was saying things like 'let's spend less time together.'" Damon handed me my new drink and clinked his beer bottle against it. "Clearly I'm broken up about it."

Another one bites the dust, I thought.

No one could understand what they were getting into when they started dating a Walker. Few families were as large as us. Even fewer were as close as us.

It seems most people have cousins, but they're the definition of distant relative. You see them at a wedding or a funeral, and you call yourselves family, but you're otherwise unattached and any real interest you have in each other is contrived and a bit brittle. In the Walker family, however, the word cousin was interchangeable with brother or sister, and you could easily use it in a sentence five or six times and be talking about different people. After all, there are eighteen of us.

That night carried on as they always did. The laughter got louder, and the drinks seemed to evaporate all on their own. The room filled with more family as a few others joined us, and before long it was well after midnight. The outdated jukebox looped through the same set of songs, at the mercy of the only people paying into it—us.

"Hat, get your ass over here," Damon yelled to me a while later, holding up shots.

I took a shot from him, brought it into the air to match the others waiting there and asked, "What are we toasting to?"

Damon shrugged and then looked around and said, "To the dirtiest goddamn bar in all of Providence."

I downed the frothy shot and looked at the clock on the wall.

1:17 a.m., the last thing I'll remember clearly.

And it was.

Songs from the jukebox were still playing in my ears as I tenderly lifted my head off the pillow. "Ugh," I said aloud, realizing I had slept in my contacts and hadn't bothered to shut the lights off.

How did I get home? I wondered, fishing through my wallet. Judging from the receipt with the exorbitant tip I couldn't afford and my illegible signature, I must have taken a cab.

No one does Thursday nights quite like us.

"Damn it, Cat!" I yelled, as the memories of the night before drifted together into one large, throbbing headache.

My cat jumped off the table and ran swiftly into the closet to hide under a pile of unused luggage. On the table, he left an empty fishbowl and a lifeless fish in a pool of tepid water. "Again?" I yelled at him.

That was the third goldfish I had bought in two weeks. I didn't know why I even bothered. I was never home to look at the damn thing, and the people at the pet store were starting to look at me funny when I went in for replacements.

I rolled my eyes as I scooped the fish into the trash can. Cat never wanted to actually eat them. He just sort of treated them like toys. Unfortunately, he hadn't learned, or hadn't learned to care, that once his toy was out of water, it would die.

Cat had a real name once, of course, but it was something silly and hard to pronounce. That's what happens when you tell your five-year-old nephew he can name the stray you found. His breed made him deceptively smart. His disposition made him funny and just plain devious.

A half hour later and running late, I made my way to the door. My sunglasses were already on to shield me from the sun's attack, and my mug was full of coffee, the only thing that made getting up make sense most days. I closed my front door and leaned up against it.

It was an abnormally warm morning—the last of the hot summer days encroaching on the city before the season would shift away without warning. I took a deep breath, summoning the strength to push through my hangover, and took my first step into the new day . . . only to be pulled back and slammed against the door. I hadn't noticed that I had caught part of my shirt in it as it closed.

Lovely.

My phone buzzed with a picture Paige took of us all the night before. All I needed was for it to pop up on someone's Facebook page. Cousins & Cocktails was supposed to be a secret, from our moms at least.

"Morning!" my semi-new and habitually chipper mailman said as I crossed the street to my car.

I smiled but didn't say anything back, partly because I couldn't spare the energy and partly because I never liked forced pleasantries. I wondered if the hint of a circular tattoo peeking out from his chest was professional or not. Then I looked down at myself—unshaven, disheveled and dehydrated—and thought perhaps I shouldn't judge others when I lived in my own very fragile glass house.

My trip to work was foggy at best as I drowned myself with as much coffee, water, and aspirin as my stomach could handle. I made it through the doors of my office and to my desk without any unwelcome early-morning conversation and was slumped in my chair fishing through a pile of unopened mail before I bothered to pull my sunglasses off. When my head involuntarily laid down against my two-year-old desk pad, I lied to myself, saying I would stop drinking on work nights.

"Die!" someone shouted behind me.

I jumped a little from the volume of it, but I didn't bother to turn around. Whoever it was, they were trying in vain to pull a piece of crumpled paper from the gullet of our office printer. It was an evil piece of middle-aged machinery that had been around so long we had come to call it Sadie (short for sadistic). Sadie played by her own rules and it wasn't uncommon for her to decide she was done working by Friday. She always liked long weekends.

A steaming cup of coffee appeared above my head and I lunged for it.

"You can thank me for this later," my coworker Talia said. "Wow. You look like I feel."

If she felt as bad as I looked, she was doing a wonderful job hiding it. Her smooth, dark caramel skin was as flawless as ever, and there wasn't a hair in her full, straight black mane that was out of place. If she hadn't been the one to bring me the coffee, I might have considered throwing it on her so she could look as bad as she claimed to feel.

Talia was probably the closest thing I had to a friend outside my family. Something I'd always struggled with. Sometimes it felt like we were bred that way, to have our closest friends be bound by blood. It was easier in some ways because no one understood the impact of a family our size. It was harder it other ways—like trying to figure out who you were without your family. I cherished my non-Walker friendship with Talia more than I could explain to her over a cup of coffee.

"What's this?" I asked, reaching for the excessive stack of papers she was trying to slip onto my desk unnoticed.

"Just some stuff that needs to be pulled . . . from storage. Sorry."

I don't really think she was sorry. 'Storage' was a rat-infested chamber of death, a low-rent building we kept in the seedy south side of town to store all of our archives. I was the most qualified person to go there, because I was the only person who didn't know how to say no.

"It's alright," I said, "I'll have them by Monday."

There was nothing normal about Cartwright & Company, a quality that was both aggravating and the key to its success. It marketed itself as a "full-service client management company," but we were actually a conglomerate of dozens of different services. Basically, if a client wanted it done, we did it. And if a client wanted something shitty done, I did it.

That day, I spent hours in a stuffy copy room. The copier was hot with exhaustion by the time I pushed the big, green start button for the one trillionth time. The task at hand, the one that required my overpriced college education, was one thousand and one copies of one thousand and one different documents. The room had not nearly enough ventilation, and it didn't take long to become a toner-scented steam bath.

I love my life.

They called me a 'project assistant,' which loosely translates from corporate vernacular into 'paycheck slave who learns fast'. That meant I got the jobs no one else wanted or knew how to do. I had done everything from running papers around Rhode Island and fetching piles of fresh, free-trade coffee, to managing complex databases and restructuring business plans.

But those are just some examples of the more glamorous tasks I got to do. I had also cleaned bathrooms, babysat excessively unruly children, and once had to put on a gorilla costume and hand out fliers outside one of our client's stores. It was 97 degrees out that day, and the costume smelled like mulch and peppermint disinfectant.

The first happy thought I had all day was when I checked my cell phone and saw a text message from my mother.

"Dinner on Sunday. I'm making turkey. If you make it on time, you get dessert," it said.

My mom was funny and loving, in equal measure, which made it so easy to have her be part of my everyday life. And I knew I was lucky to have a mother like that, one I didn't dread hearing from. As if she knew I needed it, her Sunday dinner announcement was going to be enough to get me through the rest of the day.

After about six or eight more gallons of water, I started to feel more like a normal human being again. I was dangerously close to finishing my copying jobs when Talia slipped into the room carrying a messy blue file folder and sticking out her chest a bit. When she fluttered her eyes at me, the fermented stench of trouble filled the room.

"Why do I have the feeling you bring me bad news?" I asked.

All beautiful women are guilty of trying to use their beauty, and all the features that come with their beauty, to get what they want out of men. And Talia was no exception.

"You caught me," she said, handing me the folder. "Some of the files you had were wrong, or I gave you the wrong ones, something like that. Anyway, they have to be re-copied. I'm sorry."

To the passerby, Talia was a sultry and somewhat striking woman with perfect nails and a large enough investment in shoes to finance a year-long world cruise. But to those of us that knew her, she was chronically absent-minded about everything except her appearance; a quality you would try to convince yourself was endearing until something important got lost in the bedraggled hole of her mind.

My job wasn't the kind you had because you loved it, it was the kind you had because you needed to eat. I finished college a little early—early enough to realize how much debt I was really in. Broke, frustrated, and a little lost, I returned home to Providence. Talia was dating Damon at the time, and she pushed me to apply at Cartwright & Company. With all the numbers in my bank account preceded by minus signs, I was in no place to decline any job. I don't think I even asked her what I would be doing, just when the first paycheck would arrive. I loved Talia for getting me this job, and I hated Talia for getting me this job.

By lunch time, my destruction of the rain forest was complete. With arms full of paper, I was ready to make my way out of the copy room. But it was a long walk back to my desk, and the thought of having to talk to anyone about anything was about as appealing to me as socks are to a child at Christmas. Call me dramatic, but I popped my head out from the doorway to scope the hallway, super-spy style, and made sure no one was coming. Then I practically ran against the walls, dodging office windows and ducking behind the stacks of paper in my arms to avoid eye contact with anyone that walked by.

It was a successful run, and I was just a few feet away from my desk when someone coughed from behind me and said: "I'm going to kill you."

Chapter 2

I spun around, and too fast, too, because all the copies I was holding spilled out of my hands and onto the floor. Standing behind me with a confident smile and two cups of coffee was my cousin Charley.

"Well that was graceful," she said.

"If you're going to kill me, do it now before I have to pick all this up," I said.

Charley sat down on the floor cross-legged next to me, pushing aside some of the papers to make room. My eye twitched a little as I watched her casually sip her coffee and avoid helping me. Then I laughed. I couldn't help but love her for everything she was and everything she had been since we were kids.

"Why didn't you tell me you were going to Cousins & Cocktails last night, bitch?" she asked.

"Because I go every week, hoe?"

Our relationship was, at best, unorthodox. It sat on a foundation of quick-witted quips and harsh terms of endearment that to anyone else would sound offensive. By all rights she was my cousin, but my mom started taking care of her when we were little kids, so you wouldn't have known her as anything but my sister.

"Let's go get lunch," she whined.

"I can't."

"Why not?"

"Mostly because the thought of eating anything right now makes me sick."

"Fine, fine. Then just come outside and get some air with me. I have this coffee for you . . ." She taunted me with one of the cups she was holding.

Outside, the skies were clear and the sun was shining. It was dreadful. Sitting on a worn bench outside my office, I put my hand to my forehead to cover the exposed area above my sunglasses as I sipped on the coffee. It was cold and tasted like it was about as old as I was, but bad coffee was better than no coffee.

"I'm quitting my job," Charley said, sitting down next to me and pulling her hair into a ponytail. She was unique, both in personality and beauty, and I always thought of both as soft and stern. Her feminine brown hair and devious smiles complimented the slant in her nose, and her strong stances surely intimidated others.

"Why this time?" I asked. "Did someone look at you the wrong way?"

"It's not like that, butt face. I just fucking hate it."

I took a long sip of my coffee and leaned back on the bench.

"Aren't you going to say anything?" she asked.

"We had exactly the same conversation last week. I think we were even sitting out here drinking coffee then too. So I was just waiting for you to remember what I said to you then."

Like all of us, Charley was trying to make her way through the world, finding a destination without a map or even a clear idea of what that destination looks like. She tried college a few times without any success to speak of. She did a short stint in the military, until she realized that following rules wasn't her thing and keeping her mouth shut wasn't possible. Since then, she's flit from crappy job to crappy job in search of something that would light a fire in her soul. She wanted passion, for something or someone, and just couldn't find it. And she did nothing to hide her impatience with the whole process.

Just then, both of our phones starting buzzing uncontrollably. My sister, Sydney, had sent a message in our overused family group text and a sea of smiling and heart-shaped emojis followed. Her kids were like my own, and I loved seeing pictures of them even though I was with them several times a week. What I didn't love seeing was the constant barrage of messages that group text produced.

Ten years old. That's how old I was the last time I could remember not seeing or talking to anyone in my family for more than a day. Our mom used to send us to an overnight camp for a week every summer and that year Sydney was too old to go and Charley was too young. I spent five whole days without my family, and it hadn't happened since.

"*So cute,*" Charley wrote back to the group.

"I thought the two of you weren't talking," I said.

The dynamic between Charley and Sydney was interesting to say the least. One minute they were best friends, not spending a moment apart. The next, they'd scream or send horribly blunt text messages to each other. The shift happened so frequently and so suddenly, that it was impossible to keep up. Maybe that's what sisters are like.

"We weren't, but then she called me because she got a flat tire, and I told myself to get the fuck over it," Charley said.

And so it goes. Sydney calling Charley because she needed help invoked the Walker's Golden Rule. It went something like this: take care of each other, no matter what and without question. Our family had plenty of rules, and even more expectations, but the Golden Rule was drilled into us in the womb. And it's one you could be hung for breaking.

"So what do I do about my job?" Charley asked.

"I love you like a hooker, but I don't think it makes sense for you to keep jumping jobs until you figure out what it is you want to do. Otherwise we're going to be having the same conversation next week. Or tomorrow. You should spend a little time looking around, take a class or something, I don't know. I just don't think jumping to another job you'll hate is going to help."

Charley was silent, mostly because I was right. I knew she wouldn't take my advice, but that wouldn't stop her from asking the same questions again in a week or two. And it wouldn't stop me from giving the same advice until she listened to it. She was vacillating in a perpetual cycle that only she could break.

Who was I to talk, though? I was in a job that tested the acceptable boundaries of personal dignity. I drank too much. I was totally addicted to coffee. And there wasn't one thing in my life that brought me a sense of purpose. They say that those who don't do, teach. Well, those that don't have their shit together give advice to other people on how to get their shit together. At least I had that.

* * * * *

When I got back to the office, Father Time's grandmother was waiting at my desk. She was some sort of real estate manager for Cartwright, with a silly nickname too juvenile for her age, and one that I intentionally never remembered.

"I went through your research on the Szela account," she said, as she hovered over my desk. All she owned were pant suits from the eighties, with big shoulder pads and pants that were tight against her bony hips. Her suit that day was pea green and the overly narrow points of her blouse's collar poked out of her jacket as she made robotic gestures with her hands at me.

"Uh huh," I said, drinking what was left of my coffee and tossing it into the trash.

"I checked out all your numbers and they all came out perfect," she said. She felt she needed to check every spreadsheet I gave her with her "trusty calculator." She was old, so I tried to be easy on her; the transition to a calculator from the abacus was probably harder for her than I realized.

"Okay," I said, breaking my own rule and finally making eye contact with her.

I often wondered why someone whose first vote was in the Herbert Hoover election would bother to get a face-lift. Her glossy skin covered her face much like a queen-sized sheet fits a king-sized bed. The constant surprised look she had from her eyebrows being raised two inches above their natural height made her difficult to look at, which is why I rarely did.

"I'm going to go type up some notes for the Board to review tonight. I think they will be very excited," she said in her helium-inflated voice. When she said 'type up,' she literally meant on a typewriter.

"Wait . . . why would they be excited?" I asked, the words from her grating voice finally processing in my weary mind. "My research said that they shouldn't put their processing plant there."

"Manhattan, I reviewed it and everything will be fine," she said. She had one of those old-person, permanent head bobs, where even when they weren't doing anything their head naturally shook. She looked like a bobble-head, stuck to the dashboard of a Dodge Dart, driving up a dirt road.

No, it won't be fine, you . . . relic.

My face started to develop what I liked to call "smushy mouth syndrome." It's caused when different parts of your brain fight for supremacy over your facial expression. One part wants you to flare your nostrils, roll your eyes and let a tiny "pfft" sound blow through your lips. The other part wants an insincere smile to mask your true feelings, accentuated by a subtle crane of the neck toward the recipient. After four or five milliseconds of being caught up in the battle between the two parts of your brain, your face ends with your lips inverting and a flat, forced line appearing across your mouth (smushy mouth). It's enough movement to be considered a smile but not encouraging enough for them to believe you meant it.

"Um . . . I'm not sure it will be. Even if the local government will allow a plant that produces hazardous waste to be built in their town, the building Mr. Szela wants was declared a historical landmark last year. We'd have to look at it more, but I'm not sure that he can make the structural changes to the building he would need before it can be operational. The cost of the permits alone for the build-out will probably outweigh the tax savings of having it there in the first place."

"I'm sure we can get them to speed up the permit process. Their unemployment rate is so high," she said waving her hands like she was waxing a car.

Whatever. Ask the town to let you pollute their water too, I don't care.

"Okay," I said.

I picked up my desk phone and dialed a series of fake numbers. She waited a bit, but eventually got the point and walked away. I sighed and wondered why I couldn't ever just say what I was thinking—what really needed to be said.

"Hat, buddy, what's going on?" my boss, Graham, said as he breezed over to my desk later. He was just short enough to lean comfortably on the monitor of my computer as he looked at me with his chocolate brown eyes.

It shouldn't surprise you that my job annoyed me in ways that sand in your underwear couldn't, but for some reason, I could never take it out on Graham. I really liked him, and he made the sincerest effort to be a good boss to me and everyone else there. He was the CEO, a job he landed when he was just twenty-six. Even though I knew him to be smart, I never did understand how someone that young landed a position like that, and maybe I was a little envious of him because of it.

Graham rubbed his chin with a uniquely curved dimple in it, and asked, "Plans tonight?"

"I don't think so," I said. "I think it's just a lay-low kind of evening." As soon as those words came out of my mouth, I regretted saying them.

"That's too bad, really. I have this friend that I'd love you to meet," he said.

One of the joys of being on such good terms with Graham was his predisposition for setting people, namely me, up with other people. One of the joys of also being his employee was the sense of obligation when he did it. He was a self-proclaimed cupid and found it his life calling to 'find me a good woman.'

Never say you don't have plans until they explain why they are asking. You know better.

"That's okay, thanks though," I said.

Graham's previous three (yes count them, three) fix-ups had ended badly. I think the last one's name was something like Aubrey, or Audrey, or Jane; some name like that with an 'A' in it somewhere. Anyway, she was still leaving me messages three months after our alleged date. I say alleged because it was no more than a half-hour long, it was only coffee, and she spent the entire time rambling on about her pet tarantula. I don't even think I got the chance to say another word after "hello." I left by way of the emergency exit next to the men's bathroom.

"Come on, it'll be fun."

So would standing on my head and asking Cat to scratch at my face until I bleed.

Admittedly, I wasn't the greatest dater, but I firmly believed that anyone who could use the words "baby," "wedding," and "spider," multiple times in a short, thirty-minute conversation should have police caution tape conspicuously displayed around their person at all times.

"Thanks for the offer, but I really need a night in."

He stared at me for a moment, then shrugged and turned to walk away. I knew him too well to believe that he'd give up that easily, so I made a mental note to have amazing, couldn't be canceled even if I wanted to, plans the next time he asked what I was doing.

"Wait," he said, turning back to me but looking at his phone.

Quick, Hat. Think of an excuse. You can just say you forgot about it. Maybe someone is in the hospital. No. That's bad karma. What about Charley? Maybe I can say she needs my help with something. How about . . .

"Bad news, my friend," he said, reading through a message on the phone. "It's our infamous friend, Ms. Monica. She needs me to send someone over tonight."

I looked over at Talia's desk and she was staring back at me with her pointer finger on the tip of her nose, and the other hand's finger pointing at me, the classic "you're it" signal. In response, I pointed a different finger at her.

"It's okay. I can do it, I guess," I said.

Ms. Monica, or so she preferred to be called, was the most demanding, demeaning, and dimwitted client we had ever worked with. Whenever she was short a server, she'd email Graham and one of us would have to suit up and be her server on-demand. And demand she did. The tips weren't bad, but working for her while she treated us like indentured servants was. I had no idea how much she had to pay to have that kind of service from us, but it made me feel a lot like a prostitute. My body, my choice . . . except at Cartwright & Company.

Chapter 3

Ms. Monica's restaurant was a classy joint. It was maybe a notch above bad diner food, but not by much. She tried to fix that by making it look upscale, but at best it looked like a themed restaurant, if the theme was Tacky '70s.

The servers wore extremely unflattering red, collarless shirts over red velvet tuxedo pants. My pants were a size too large and without belt loops to use to hold them up, they would constantly slide down my body and force me to hold them with one hand. That's not ideal for a profession that requires balancing heavy trays.

In the company locker room, I rushed to get dressed. The restaurant didn't start getting busy until well into the evening, but I think Ms. Monica enjoyed making us try to get all the way to Warwick in afternoon traffic. I finished tying my plastic-looking, non-slip dress shoes and looked in the mirror. In the full outfit, I looked a lot like an uncooked burger, one that a child ate and then threw back up.

Once, a man came into the restaurant after completing a gig as a clown for a child's birthday. He still had half his make-up on and was swimming in the checkered, high-water pants that hung ungracefully on suspenders from his shoulders. He took one look at me when I came to his table and laughed . . . at me for looking ridiculous.

It was 5:17 p.m. when I screeched into the sequestered parking lot of the restaurant. I fumbled to pull myself together, digging through the messy backseat of my car for my apron, hoping that I was clever enough to leave my pens and name tag in there from the last time I was sentenced to a shift working for Ms. Monica.

"Ya late!" Ms. Monica bellowed to me from the hostess stand as I tried to slink into the restaurant unnoticed.

Ms. Monica was a large, obtrusive, woman with a loose grip on the English language and a tight grip on any biscuit within an arm's reach. Her clothes were always much too tight, contorting around the unforgiving bulges of her body, and her lower lip was either naturally plump or grew to be that way from her incessant yelling. She was also utterly unaware of the megaphone-like volume with which she spoke.

"Sorry, Ms. Monica, it won't happen again," I said. That wasn't true and we both knew it, but it always made her feel better about my tardiness.

"Fix ya nametag, it's crooked."

She said crooked like "crocked," but in either case it was the least of my worries and should have been the least of hers. It looked especially nice with my name mistyped 'Manhettan' on the flimsy, fake gold plastic. The edges were curling, and the letters had a dingy yellow tint from too much time spent in a greasy kitchen.

I sighed. I never hated my name more than when I was working at the restaurant. It just invited too much conversation with customers for my own liking. Whether my parents had given me my name because that was where I was conceived or because it was my father's favorite drink, both of which were possible, was unbeknownst to me. I had always made a conscious effort never to ask.

But neither of those stories went over terribly well with customers, so I resigned myself to use a made-up story each time I worked. The trick was to find something just boring enough that it wouldn't spark additional discussion. "It was my great-grandfather's middle name," I said to my first table when they asked.

A shift at the restaurant always had a very predictable dance about it. I brought customers food, customers tipped me, and I pretended that the whole interaction didn't make me want to end my own life with a slotted serving spoon. It was a slow night of hours that felt like days. By the time the TV above the bar was on the ten o'clock news, Ms. Monica had disappeared into her office to devour an unsuspecting cheesecake and I started my end-of-the-night cleaning with little fervor.

Only one more hour, I thought, trying to pep-talk myself into making it through the last bit of my day. *You've got this, Hat. You've got this.*

I was laying on the floor cleaning the cooler underneath the salad bar. The restaurant was emptying but the bar still had plenty of people waiting around for nothing. I was only half-listening to the overly starched and hair-sprayed reporter on TV talk about things I didn't care about until she nearly shouted the word "Murder."

It was loud enough to make me jump, which is a problem when you're working under a dozen ill-fitted salad dressing containers. The containers slipped off their designated track and poured directly on my head. The smell of the night was Italian . . . oily, zesty Italian.

Customers stepped over me as they made their way to the exit, not stopping to wonder why a pair of legs sticking out of the salad bar were crying "uncle." I sighed loudly and closed the cooler doors, leaving the mess hidden and pretending nothing happened.

On the TV, they were still talking about the body they found on the south side. It wasn't something you needed to pay much attention to; dead people were always showing up there. Providence was a great city, safe for the most part, but it had a dark side like all other cities I suppose, an arcane danger that swam beneath the surface of the otherwise still waters.

* * * * *

Have you ever felt like you didn't fit into your own life; like you're doing what you're supposed to do by going through the never-ending motions, but at the same time you feel like you're just pretending it isn't all meaningless? That's all I could think about as I made my way out of the restaurant that night. I was one big, bloated square peg trying to fit into the ever-narrowing round hole of my life. Though I tried never to let myself slide too far down that slippery slope of thoughts, because who knew what was at the bottom of it. Not me.

The frustration of my thoughts and my iron-fisted efforts to forget them had wound me up into an edgy second wind. It was fed with the kind of energy that you get when your body enters a complete sleep and nutrition-deprived state, some sixteen hours after you've woken up. I decided against my better judgment to take a small detour to my local twenty-four-hour gym.

Running water over my head in the locker room's small sink was both cold and refreshing. But for some reason it didn't do anything to get rid of the smell of Italian dressing. To the passerby, I probably looked homeless, or peculiar. Maybe both.

I looked up into the mirror as water dripped down from my thick, light brown hair and splashed over the t-shirt I had changed into. Nervously fingering through my hair, I looked for more grays to pluck. I shouldn't have had any, but I'd already found six in the months since I had turned twenty-five. I stood on my toes and leaned toward the mirror to look at my teeth.

Shit. Lettuce. Fucking fantastic. I don't even remember eating lettuce today.

The treadmill at the gym was my sanctuary. It was the best way I knew to untangle the knots my mind got into. It was a point of control in my life, maybe the only point of control. I always knew I could set the speed and that would be the speed it went. It may be silly, but I enjoyed the consistency of it.

That night I cranked up the volume on my cheap headphones and slammed my worn sneakers down on the perpetually spinning belt. Angry music from my phone revved up in my ears, screaming words I shied away from saying in my own life, and I tapped the controls of the treadmill to a higher speed.

"Push it," I said out loud to myself. The faster I could run, the better I would feel, this much I knew from experience. I was always convinced that if I ran fast enough, all the crap from my life would just fall into the distance behind me. I just wasn't sure if I would ever reach that speed.

The treadmill's speed ramped up again, demanding that adrenaline flood my body with a purpose it lacked otherwise. I walked around my life like a has-been, without actually having been anything. And I knew it. Sometimes I would just sit somewhere, anywhere, and watch people. I'd study how they interacted with each other and with the world around them. I'd contemplate their existence and my own in relation, and I'd wonder: *Do they feel as unsatisfied with their lives as I do?*

Most people, my family included, gave me this dismissive snicker whenever I talked about feeling this way. The kind of snicker that seemed to imply "what more do you expect out of life?" In short, my answer was "a lot", I just hadn't been able to define what that meant yet. Years of trying without success made me unsure I ever would. What's worse, complacency was starting to set into my life like a vexatious disease, the kind that isn't fatal but still dampens your experiences and holds you back on the brink of fulfillment. Every day I felt more like a prisoner of my own life and the chains I carried were getting heavy.

Deep in my thoughts, it was a while before I fell out of my trance. Short of breath, I lowered the treadmill's speed as sweat poured down my body and mixed with the faint smell of Italian dressing and copy toner that still lurked on my skin. It was late, with only the handful of people willing to work out past midnight left.

My eyes wandered downstairs where a man was leaning up against the entrance to one of the classrooms. He was holding a white towel around his neck and staring up at the balcony. He had a perfectly toned body, the kind that you only get from divine intervention or relentless hours at the gym. I secretly hated guys like him—the ones who looked like they'd been lightly airbrushed in real life, giving them a year-round natural tan.

His gawking quickly become a distraction. I attempted to inconspicuously peek behind me to see who he was looking at and judge whether they were worth all the attention. Doing so strained what little balance I could ever speak of. And with pure, undeniable finesse, I slipped, twisted, and fell onto my beloved treadmill, ass-first. The shock from the fall was short-lived because the high-speed belt flung me, now head-first, two feet behind the machine.

The only other person left upstairs was a woman I didn't know, and she quickly dug her head into the magazine she was reading to avoid any eye contact. I ignored the urge to get up, choosing to stay sprawled out on the scratchy industrial carpet in defeat, laughing to myself (or at myself). I didn't have the mental capacity to feel any more embarrassment.

"Are you okay?" someone asked from the staircase.

I propped myself up on my elbows and looked over at them. It was him, the gawker.

Great, he saw that.

I lowered myself back down to the ground and closed my eyes. "Yeah. I'm fine. Thanks," I said to the ceiling. After I realized he wasn't going away, I gave a gritted smile. "I wish I could say that it was the first time that's happened."

My cell phone was at his feet, as it had flown to the other side of the room during my gymnastic demonstration. When he crouched down to pick it up, he kept his eyes on mine and smiled.

"I teach martial arts here if you're interested. It could help you with your balance . . . or lack of balance." He chuckled. "Maybe you should stop by sometime for a lesson."

He was tall and handsome, with dark brown hair that skewed intentionally in every direction. I was sweaty from my run and knew that my hair, which had never done anything intentionally, ever, was matted to my head in the most unattractive way possible. Being a solid three or four inches shorter than him meant I knew he would notice. Even in his baggy gym shorts and sweatshirt, he looked better than I did on my best day. I hated him.

I took my phone started to walk away. "Yeah. Sure. Maybe," I said. "Thanks."

"Max."

I looked at him like he was speaking some new language that consisted of only clicks and whistles. "Huh?"

A terribly perfect, if not naturally coy, smile stretched across his face. "My name . . . it's Max." He reached out to shake my hand.

In order to shake his hand, I had to shift my phone from my right hand to my left. It went well. I dropped it again, and then smacked my face on his knee when we both bent down to get it.

Max laughed and wiggled his pointy nose. "Long day?"

"Yeah . . . sorry. Thanks." I was already halfway down the stairs before I looked back and saw him still staring at me with an entertained smile. Clearly, he'd never seen a hot mess in its natural habitat before.

Fuck!

Apparently, I did have some capacity for embarrassment left.

Still smiling, he called to me from the top of the stairs. "What's your name?"

"Everyone calls me Hat," I called back.

"Like the kind you wear on your head?"

"Do you wear yours anywhere else?"

Staggering through the parking lot, it was clear to me that I was in no state to multitask as I tried to force my phone to turn back on. It was used when I got it, and never worked all that well. Dropping it eight or nine hundred times didn't help either. I was collapsing into my car when my phone came back to life.

Three voicemails?

With my proclivity for ignoring voicemail messages, even my excessively large family knew not to leave me one. Something wasn't right. I was starting the first voicemail when an incoming call from my sister blinked across the display. From the moment I saw her name, my stomach boiled like I had swallowed a handful of burning embers directly from hell.

"Sydney? Is everything okay?" I asked as I answered.

They say you can hear in someone's voice when they're smiling and it's true. You can also hear when they've been crying, and even without sobs, I could hear my sister's loud tears on the other end of the phone.

"No. You need to come to my house," she said.

"Syd, what's wrong? What's going on?" My stomach couldn't handle the embers any longer, it boiled like a kettle abandoned on the stove and I fought back the choking urge as unsettled acid crept up my throat.

"It's Mom, Hat. She's dead."

Chapter 4

In that moment, death made me forget how to breathe.

Time continued without me in it. I couldn't have told you if seconds or hours had passed from when Sydney first called me. I was there, in my car, motionless and staring at my phone, trying to remember how to breathe.

I must have driven to Sydney's house, because the next thing I remember I was standing outside her condo with my phone still clutched in my sweaty hand.

Breathe.

I can only describe those moments as a waking dream; you watch it all unfold and look at everything as if it's real, but don't believe any of it is. You can't believe any of it is. Except that time there was no waking up. There was no sitting up in bed and clutching your pounding chest. There was only the door to my sister's condo, separating my waking dream from the reality that just couldn't be real.

When I finally opened the door, a sadness exploded from the room and rushed over me. I looked into my sister's cracked, red eyes from across the room and had no words. She looked back at me with hopelessness and said nothing either.

Before I could close the door, her daughter Zoe was wrapped around me. She sobbed uncontrollably into my shirt, and her tears soaked through and dripped directly onto my heart. I stood in the doorway and rubbed her head, still having to remind myself to breathe. I was either unable or unwilling to take another step into the house . . . another step toward reality.

"Hey, you," Paige said to me from the exposed kitchen, the wisps of her short blond hair covering her swollen eyes.

Sydney, Charley, and our younger brother Finn, all looked up at me, waiting for me to say something.

"Hi, family," I said back with no feeling. Part of me, that inner-child that never fully grew up or lost his naiveté, was waiting for someone to tell me I was dreaming and that once I woke up it would all be okay. But no one did.

With Zoe clinging desperately to my arm, I walked over to my sister and hugged her. The world spun just a little slower around us as we held each other, like we had demanded time itself to stop so that we wouldn't have to experience the next moment it would bring.

Paige pulled a sniffling Zoe back to her room and soon the only sound left was that of Sydney's lips sucking slowly on the end of her cigarette.

"What happened?" I asked, finally breaking the silence.

Sydney started to talk, but her tears and trembling voice suffocated all her words. Charley moved to sit on the arm of her chair, hugging Sydney from above.

"They said it was a heart attack," Charley said while rubbing Sydney's shoulders.

"What? That can't be right," I snapped back.

"Hat." Charley's lips folded inward as she spoke.

"How could she have a heart attack? She was healthy. Right? I mean, she told us she was healthy," I said. If I fought it hard enough I thought I could prove to them, and myself, that it wasn't true. Then everything would go back to the way it was just a few hours before. Everything would go back to normal. I would be able to breathe again.

"It happens." Sydney grabbed my hand and squeezed it. "It happened."

Charley went into the bathroom and I sat down next to Finn, letting all my weight fall against him. He pushed his weight back, and we sat there, eyes on the floor, leaning on each other for the support that neither of us could provide. Charley started crying, and the sound of it echoed down the hall at us. She was the toughest among us, so hearing her break down made the whole situation feel graver.

"When?" I asked.

"Earlier," Sydney said, lighting another cigarette. "I . . . I went to the house and she was just . . ."

"Can I have one of these?" I asked her, reaching for her pack of cigarettes. I quit after college, but at moments like this, what did it matter?

"We're going to the funeral home tomorrow to make the arrangements," Sydney said as she wiped the tears from her face with her sleeve. Even in death, my family never waited for anything. "You're going to come, right?"

Is there an option? If there was, I wasn't going to go. *She's the big sister, she can handle this. I'm still not sure I'm breathing.*

"Yes," I said instead. "We'll meet you there?" I looked over to Finn and he nodded.

Okay. We have a plan. Plans are good. Plans meant you had control and that you knew what was going on. Breathe.

Sydney was crying harder than I had ever seen, intense waves that crashed against your heart and stuck to it like cement. Our mom used to say that her crocodile tears were infectious, and that you could cry just from looking at her. I wanted to fix it—to make it better, for her and myself. But our mother's death was out of my control, and I hated things out of my control. So, I simply looked away to avoid getting infected by those tears.

"Paige said she'll call the aunts . . . and they can call everyone else. I . . . I don't know who else knows yet," Sydney said in between waves of tears.

Right, the aunts. Good. They'll tell everyone. We won't have to talk to anyone. We have a plan. Plans are good. Breathe.

Charley returned to the room with a red face and wet eyes, and eventually we all found ourselves bunched together on the couch in silence. There was nothing left to say. Between the four of us, we barely made up one functioning brain, one functioning heart, and one functioning soul.

The hardest part about that day was not that our mother had died, but that she wasn't there to help us get through it. She was a Walker's strength incarnate, and in times like these she would swoop in and make everything and everyone better, even when it didn't seem possible.

She wasn't a rock, because a rock fends off water. She was more like a leaf, floating peacefully on the surface of the water no matter how violent it got. She showed you how to take on the uncertainty around you, and without her we were drowning. We remained huddled on the couch, knowing that together we were strong, or at least stronger.

Paige left, and within minutes phones were buzzing and ringing all around us. Walker cousins, aunts, and uncles had been alerted and the unofficial, yet unstoppable, family phone tree had been activated.

Sydney was the first to break our Walker stronghold; she could never leave a phone unanswered. She pushed the wildly curly hair she inherited from our mother away from her face and lowered her big eyes as she answered. Even though she was already the shortest of us, she looked even smaller somehow—doll-like, with a stiff face that helped her talk about all the things none of us wanted to say.

I was shutting my cell phone off when Zoe came out of her bedroom and shuffled over to us. "I can't sleep . . . I just can't," she said.

I looked up into her sad eyes, so much like her mother's. Of anyone in the room, Zoe must have felt the most helpless. She was old enough to be told what was happening when it was happening, but younger than she should have been when losing her grandmother.

I opened my arms and she joined us on the couch. Charley lovingly rubbed her head and she dozed off in my lap. I couldn't imagine what was going on in her mind; I didn't even know what was going on in mine.

Sydney was answering her phone for the fifth or sixth time when the burning feeling in my stomach returned. My mind was broken; a record stuck on repeat. "It's Mom, Hat. She's dead," my sister's voice kept saying in my head. It was a sentence that changes your life forever, and I knew I'd never be allowed to forget it. Over and over it played like one of those mercilessly bad songs that never go away, even after you turn it off.

I gently moved Zoe's head to Finn's lap, who had fallen asleep next to us, and made my way toward the door. "I'm going home to shower and whatever. I'll see you in the morning," I said to Sydney over whoever she was talking to on the phone, not realizing that it was already morning.

My legs buckled as I walked to my car, making each step unnecessarily taxing. It could have been the lack of food or sleep. Or it could have been the emotional hangover from being in that room. No, it was probably because someone I adored in my life was no longer in it and my body couldn't handle the emotional weight of it.

You've got this, Hat. You've got this. People's moms die all the time. This is normal, I tried to remind myself.

When I finally made it home, I collapsed into my over-stuffed armchair and covered my stinging eyes with my arm. Cat jumped on top of me and kneaded my body with his prickly paws. If he was a talking cat, I'm sure he would have asked, "What the fuck?"

If he had, I wouldn't have had an answer to give him. But somehow my furry friend sensed that, too. Instead of talking, he just purred his way up my chest and lay so his body was wrapped around my neck like an airplane pillow, tickling my ear with his whiskers.

It's Mom, Hat. She's dead.

The soundtrack was still on repeat. For the first time since I heard those words, a few tears escaped the fortress of my face, but I wouldn't let go completely. I couldn't be sure they'd ever stop if I did. The tears dripped off my cheeks and into Cat's fur as I let his light breathing, with just a hint of a purr, sing me to sleep with its peaceful rhythm.

A few hours later, light from one of my few windows started to tease my eyes open. Cat was a real trooper in my time of need and hadn't moved at all. There was a moment, the briefest of moments, where I looked around and everything seemed normal. Before the memories could attack me, my mind fantasized that I'd just woken up from a bad, twisted dream and everything was actually okay. But it wasn't.

I opened my phone to see ten missed calls and a few text messages, all from Walkers. I closed it without responding to anyone; there was nothing I could say. No words could answer their questions of how I was without making the whole situation a lot more real than I was ready to let it be.

One of the text messages was from Charley telling me I was already late to meet everyone at the funeral home. I changed into the first clothes I saw, splashed mouthwash on my face instead of water by accident, and rushed out the door.

Okay. Funeral home. That's normal, right? That's where people go when someone dies.

It's Mom, Hat. She's dead.

Fuck.

The funeral home was bright and cheerful, which I found morbidly oxymoronic. If I was in a better place, maybe I could have understood why a business like that would need to have artificial cheerfulness to combat the unhappiness and loss that fueled their revenue. If so, maybe then I might have appreciated the sun-filled windows, the stuffed flower boxes, and the bright shades of canary yellow on the walls outside.

I entered through thick, wooden double doors which made too much noise when they opened to try to slip in. Sydney was in the corner talking to a tall man in a dapper blue suit. Charley and Finn sat on a church-like bench nearby watching them, averting their eyes to the showroom full of caskets. The man in the blue suit was addressing someone else, too, someone I couldn't fully see from the door.

"I love it," that someone said in an uncomfortably high squeal and I saw Charley roll her eyes. Then I realized who it was. It was her mother, my mother's younger sister Camille. You know, the one that had dumped Charley on my mother's doorstep and never came back.

"Manhattan, is that you?" Camille barked from around the corner. "You're late."

I didn't bother responding. Camille wasn't a bad person, per se, she was just a lot to handle. If you didn't know her well, you'd think she was vivacious and adventurous. Well, she was those things, but if you had to spend as much time around her as I had, you'd know she was also selfish, aloof, and an all-around pain in the ass. My mother had never, and would have never, said she didn't like Camille . . . but my mother didn't like Camille either.

I was introduced to the funeral director, the man in the blue suit, whose name I forgot immediately. Nothing in his world was real to me yet, including him. "Ms. Walker and I were just discussing the casket with your sister," he said.

I rested my chin on Sydney's shoulder from behind, wrapping my arms around her and looking over her at the flip-book of caskets. The funeral director had a small notepad next to it and at the top, my mother's name written. Amelia Walker.

I can't believe this. Are we seriously shopping for a big box to bury our mother in? Wait.

"Camille, Mom wanted to be cremated." I came out of my fog long enough to form and communicate a full thought. What were we even doing there? My mother has explicitly told me, told all of us, that she never wanted to be buried in a big box.

"It serves no purpose," she'd said on many occasions. "Why should you kids go through all the hassle of staging me in an expensive box and then dropping me into a big hole? I'll already be dead; I promise I won't care."

"Oh, Hat. I don't think anyone really wants to be cremated. It's just sort of something you say, like 'you look pretty today,' or 'sure, I'd love to babysit.' I think she just didn't want to be a bother. No, it will be better if we buried her next to our dad." She reached out and cupped her hand around my face and patted me like I was a small child. Maybe it was meant to reassure me. But, reassure me it did not.

Sydney shifted her eyes away from mine, confirming my suspicion that Camille had already bullied her into this decision before I had gotten there. She was the big sister. It was her job to take care of this, to do what Mom wanted. Not mine. I made pleading eyes at the younger two, Finn and Charley, but they strained themselves to keep from noticing.

In an unprecedented act, I decided to enter the arena against my narcissistic aunt. I put my hand over the book of caskets and started, "Camille . . ."

"Now, listen. Auntie will take care of everything." She turned her back to me and said to the funeral director, "We'll have the wake here on Monday, followed by the funeral at St. Albert's cemetery on Tuesday morning. Oh, Mia wasn't really Catholic, though. But who is these days? The boys went to school there, I'm sure that's enough. It'll be fine."

There was a foreign taste in my mouth, blood maybe, as I clamped my tooth down on my lower lip. I was screaming inside my head, and the growing ulcer in my stomach was slowly bubbling up, taunting me for my habitual complacency and my seemingly genetic inability to stand up for myself or anyone else.

My mother wasn't Catholic, and she wouldn't have wanted any of what they were planning. I may not have had the nerve to stand up to Camille any further, but I knew who would.

I ran outside and took my phone out. Dismissing four new missed calls, I scrolled to find and dial a familiar number.

"Hello?" a warm voice asked from the other side, "Hat?"

"Yes, Auntie. Hi."

"How are you?" my Aunt Gloria asked. If she was upset, she wasn't going to let me hear it.

"Um . . . I'm okay, but . . . do you think you could come down to the funeral home?"

"Sure, honey. What's going on?"

"Well, Camille is here, and she's . . . ," *being an intrusive, controlling bitch,* ". . . well, she's kind of making all these plans, and they aren't what Mom wanted. I don't know what to do."

"I'm getting in the car now. I'll be there in seven minutes."

Gloria was my mother's oldest sister and being the matriarch of our family was no easy task, I'm sure. But she was good at being in charge, and she was good at handling people, most especially her sisters. She may have been the tiniest of us, but she was irrefutably the strongest of us and everyone in the family relied on her to lead them because of it.

When she arrived, she bypassed the parking lot completely and drove up on the lawn in front of the funeral home doors, taking out a stone cherub by the walkway's gate. She stopped long enough to kiss me on the cheek and say: "I'll take care of it," before storming through the doors like a four-foot-five, fifty-something-year-old knight without her sword. But anyone that knew her also knew she didn't need a sword to get what she wanted.

A few minutes passed and the voices inside the funeral home got louder. Charley and Finn escaped to join me, and the angry voices flowed behind them as the doors shut. It wasn't the first time any of us had seen Gloria and Camille go head-to-head. Gloria always won, but at the cost of much civility.

The voices stopped, and the doors swung open again. Camille fled past us without a word and slammed the door to her car as she got in. She paused only to check her makeup and hair in the rearview mirror before speeding off.

Gloria followed with a sobbing Sydney attached to her arm. "I figure we'll have a small get-together tomorrow at your mom's house so that everyone has a chance to have a proper goodbye," she said. "We'll say a few nice things, maybe me and one of you kids, and then everyone can just hang out and enjoy each other's company. How does that sound?"

The relief of not having to make any decisions was welcomed by all of us. With the next gust of wind, Gloria was in her car with her Bluetooth headset over her ear as she activated the family phone tree again.

"You kids make sure to get the house ready. I'll take care of the rest," she said over her phone conversation. She backed off the lawn without looking, running back over the fallen cherub she'd hit on her way in and smashing it into a thousand pieces.

Chapter 5

It was not uncommon for the Walkers to host services that close to a loved one's death, despite what others had to say about it. We were not known for convention or conformity anyway. But when it was my mother we were pushing so fast to say goodbye to, it was the most unwelcome of customs. Soon, everyone in my life was going to be in front of me asking me how I was doing. I couldn't answer that because it was only just starting to feel real.

Our home was in the historic and beautiful Blackstone section of Providence, a neighborhood with roots in working-class families like ours. Our mother decided to stay there, wrapped in the memories of our childhood, long after we had all moved on. But without her there it felt hollow, even though it was still full of her belongings. I guess that's what she meant when she said that material things were just that—things.

"You can always replace things," she used to tell us, "but you can't replace people."

Her house usually had a warmth about it; this rich, embracing warmth that just kind of hugged you when you walked in. Entering it without her there made me realize that the warmth had disappeared with her, and her house had become nothing more than a large wooden box full of things.

Commander Sydney, who had packed up her tears temporarily to take out her bullhorn and whip, assigned me our mother's bedroom. I wasn't sure I could stand to move any of her things. It would make the situation all too real. That child deep inside me was clinging to the idea that she was still alive and all this talk of her being gone was a prank, or some misunderstanding that had gotten out of control. I wished that kid was right.

Our mother was a habitually clean person, so it didn't surprise me when I found the room immaculate. The only thing in it that appeared out of place was a small, leather-bound book that sat atop her perfectly made bed. I picked it up and the deep, musty leather smell filled my nose. It wasn't much larger than my hand and looked much older than my hand. From inside the leather on the back were four darker leather straps that pulled around each side of the book and shut it tight with a lock. The odd thing was the lock had no keyhole.

That's weird. I'll have to remember to ask her about that. Wait, she's dead. I can't ask her anything.

There I was, looking through her things and it was all getting to be a little too real. Her room—she'd never be in it again. That book—she'd never open it again. She was dead, and I had to accept it.

I slowly sank to the floor, sitting with my back against the bed. I had to let a few tears slip out before the building pressure of them crushed my insides. It was just a few though. Just enough so I wouldn't burst, but not so many that I wouldn't be able to close the flood gates again.

Sydney appeared in the doorway a while later. "You okay?"

"I don't know," I said. My eyes were sagging low on my wet cheeks as I looked up at her. "I know it's dumb to think like this, but I just keep hoping if I don't believe she's dead it won't be true, and everything will go back to the way it was before."

Sydney gave a sympathetic head tilt and then lowered herself to sit next to me on the floor. "It's not dumb, Hattie. It just is. We'll get through this," she said, pulling my hand into hers and intertwining our fingers.

I closed my eyes and rested my head on her shoulder. "I know. I just don't want to have to."

I must have fallen asleep at some point because the next thing I knew, Sydney was gone and I was laying on the floor next to the bed. The colorful quilt our mother made from a collection of our baby clothes was draped over me. I unfolded my body from the tight, anxious ball I had curled into, and lightly slapped my cheeks to remind myself of where I was.

It's Mom, Hat. She's dead.

Keep breathing.

How long would that last? Would it be my first thought every time I woke up, forever? I had to get out of that house. There was nothing for me to do there but stew in sadness. I ran down the stairs, out the door, and into my car without telling anyone where I was going.

The house was a mile behind me before I started to even consider where I was actually going. Home? Going far away, much further than that, had an appeal to it. But I knew no matter how far I ran or for how long, my mother would still be dead at the end of it.

A car stopping abruptly in front of me showed me how little attention I was paying to the road. I slammed on the breaks and made it to a stop just inches from its back bumper. In the narrow miss, everything in my car shifted and flew forward, including the book I had found on my mother's bed.

Did I take that with me?

* * * * *

The next day, I got to my mother's house early by my standards, but not early enough for the sibling vote on who'd have to go up and speak in front of everyone, and it was unanimous that it would be me.

Super. What the hell am I supposed to say to all these people? "Hello everyone. We're here today to celebrate the life of my mother, Amelia Walker, whose life was unfairly taken from us just a few short days ago. I'm shaken, and broken, and a lot of other things that I can't even express. And how are you?"

While that may have been the truth, it wasn't what people wanted to hear. They needed me to get up there, talk about what a great woman she was, how sad we all were that she was gone, and how she would have wanted us all to celebrate her life in lieu of mourning her death. And those things were all true, because that's the kind of woman our mother was, but I didn't care what they needed. I needed her to be alive and if I couldn't have what I needed, why should I have cared what everyone else needed?

People started to arrive, and I withdrew to sit in an isolated chair with my back to the door. I kept my eyes on a picture of my mother, my siblings, and me at a weekend vacation on the beach. You could see our smiling faces, but we were all holding up our hands showing a finger to the camera. No, not the finger you're thinking of. It was our pinky finger.

"This is how you know you're really a Walker," my mother said to me once when I was a child, showing me my noticeably crooked pinky finger.

"But how come it has to be different than everyone else's?" I asked.

"Because you are different from them, Hattie, but you're the same as me and the rest of the family." She showed me her crooked pinky finger. "But who wants to be normal anyway?" she said in a reassuring voice I would never get to hear again.

My hands were shaking at the thought of having to talk in front of everyone. Not because I was afraid of talking in public, but because I was afraid of what I had to talk about. As if my heart had hardened and fallen into my stomach, I was reminded that she was more than just my mother, she was my siblings' mother, an aunt, a sister, and a close friend to so many. And for a moment I was sadder for them having lost her than I was for myself. I knew if she were there, she would have been the first to tell me to stop being so damn selfish and be there for my family when they needed me most.

Damon found me a little later in a corner sitting in the raggedy rocking chair my mother refused to get rid of. "Hey," he said, sliding onto a small table across from me.

I didn't look at him. "Hey D."

He leaned in to hug me and his crisp white dress shirt crumpled around my face. "How are you?"

"I'm okay, I think. I'm sorry I haven't called you back."

"It's fine. But, how are you?" Damon asked again.

Damon was like the big brother I never had, and he knew me well. Too well, probably. We had shared a bedroom for a while when we were kids, in the aftermath of intersecting divorces too complicated for us to understand at the time. We made a deal way back then and it was simple: no bull-shitting each other. With our fathers suddenly absent from of our lives and our respective sibling relationships tense because of it, we just couldn't handle any more bullshit than we were already dealt. It was a passionately serious pact, sealed with the shaking of crooked pinky fingers, and it afforded us the license to push the other when we felt they weren't being forthright.

"Not good," I answered. "I'm holding it together, though."

"Hey boys, we're getting ready to start," Gloria said. She walked with me through the crowd, and past a still-indignant Camille without acknowledging her. Two of my younger cousins had just finished setting up a makeshift riser, and Damon's purple-haired, punk-rock younger sister was plugging in one of her practice microphones and a small amp.

"Do you want me to go first?" Gloria asked.

"I think I should. That way, if I fuck up or don't know what to say, you can take over," I whispered.

She handed me the microphone. "Okay. Let's get goin'."

I got up on the riser and tried to hold the microphone steady in my shaky hands. "Hi, family," I said meekly. No one stopped talking.

"Hi, family," I said again, trying to project my voice into the microphone. I only succeed in amplifying a large thud, the sound of my teeth smacking into it. At least it got their attention.

Silence fell over the room. I tried to swallow but my throat was dry like someone had poured flour down it when I wasn't looking. Slowly, I scanned the faces of the audience: family members, friends, friends of family and even more people who I didn't know looked back at me.

"Hello again," I paused and looked over to Damon. 'Hello' was pretty much all I had planned. He nodded his head toward me in encouragement. "Thank you for coming. It's great to see you all . . . even with . . . even under these circumstances."

Stay positive, Hat. Stay focused. Say something good.

More flour in my throat.

"I wish my mom were here," I said. "Not only because I miss her, but because she loved you all so much that she'd really enjoy seeing you together." A bit of nervous laughter shot out my mouth, through the microphone, and over the heads of the silent room. Damon's hand appeared next to me, holding a glass of water. The crowd stirred uncomfortably as they waited for me to drink from the glass.

Okay, Hat, get it together. You've got this. You've got this.

My siblings had moved closer to the riser and were looking up at me with supportive eyes. Charley and Sydney flanked Finn, all three holding hands and waiting to hear what I would say next. It was sweet, but I wanted to throw the microphone at them for making me stand there by myself.

"So, this sucks," I said.

A mixture of laughter and throat clearing filled the room. I knew only my family would appreciate my candor, the rest probably found it inappropriate given the circumstances. "I'm sorry, but it does." I drank more water and handed the glass back to Damon. "I wish we weren't here. We lost a great person . . . actually, a great person was taken from us, too soon. I'm not just saying she's great just because she's . . . dead, and that's what people always seem to do in situations like this, right? They stand up and talk about how great someone was, even if they weren't. But she was . . . she was great every day and to all of us."

Okay, bring it back now Hat, get it together. You've got this.

"I don't know what to say, except that you've probably noticed today is not a wake, or a funeral, or anything else like that. My mom . . ." I looked over to my siblings again, ". . . our mom was someone who liked to celebrate life. She wouldn't want us all here being sad for her because she'd think it was a waste of time. She always told me she was so loved that she couldn't be anything but thankful for every moment she was living, and that when she died, she'd die surrounded by people that loved her, and how could you be sad about that?"

Tears filled the room as everything got a little more real than anyone was prepared to handle. "And . . . and those of you who knew her well know that she always said death only sucks for the people left living. I know she's here somewhere, smiling at you all and sending the comfort and support that . . ."

It's Mom, Hat. She's dead.

My body could no longer hold back. My stomach started contracting and tears streamed down my face.

"I guess that's all I have to say. I love you . . . we love you and . . ."

The contractions and tears became so violent that I couldn't take it anymore. I tossed the microphone to Gloria, jumped off the stage and rushed through the crowd to lock myself in a nearby bedroom.

"Hat was right," I heard Gloria say into the microphone as I leaned up against the bedroom door. "This does suck." The crowd laughed a little again.

"As many of you know, this is not the first time I've been up here, looking out at all of you. Mia is the third sibling to leave us, and her death saddens me in ways I can't express to you. She was often my source of advice and comfort, and I miss her so much. Today, I try to accept the loss of a sister, a friend, an ally, and . . . a pretty wonderful woman."

She paused briefly as one of my cousin's babies started crying hysterically and then giggled a little to herself.

"Speaking of babies . . ." Gloria continued over the noise, "I was only about seven years old when Mia was born, but I remember the day our parents brought her home from the hospital so clearly. She was smiling and happy then, too. Just like she was for the rest of her life, Mia's presence as a baby was . . . all encompassing, and the rest of us would always look at her in such awe. She hardly acted like the middle child she was born to be. She was electrifying . . . strong-willed . . . a leader, and she loved her children and her family more than anything else in this world."

There was a long pause and a sniffle from my aunt that I could hear even behind the closed door. "This family always takes care of each other, and we'll handle this sadness together just like every other challenge we've ever faced. Mia will be missed, but if she was here she'd be yelling at me from the back of the room telling us to stop crying over her and to have a good time. So, in honor of her, that's what we're going to do. We always listened to Mia in life, but now we must listen to her in death. Celebrate. Enjoy your time together. That is all."

A knock at the bedroom door followed a few minutes later. "Hat, you have some people here," Paige said.

By then, I had mostly composed myself. And by composed, I mean I shoved all signs of emotion down so deep you'd need a drill, a hammer, and a circus contortionist to get it out. I re-emerged from the bedroom to see Talia, Graham, and a few other people from work standing by the door.

"Hey, handsome," Talia said, wrapping her arms around my neck.

I gave a forced laugh and reached my hand around her to shake Graham's. "Thanks for coming, you didn't have to."

"Of course we did," Graham said.

When Talia moved away, he came close to me and put his arm around my shoulder. "Listen buddy, if you need some time to rest, recoup, whatever . . . you take as much as you need. Paid. Whatever you need, really."

"Thanks, that's really nice." I shifted underneath his lingering arm and looked at Talia. "Wait. How did you hear about this?"

"Um," Talia's eyes widened and looked around the crowd, "Damon."

Of course, Damon. Those two could never seem to stay away from each other very long.

The crowds started to thin out, and my obligatory acceptance of condolences was becoming sparse. I was watching two of my cousin's kids fidget anxiously and I couldn't help but feel bad for them. While both were well-behaved, they were too young to be so somber and still for that long a time. Everyone moved so mechanically around us, and I don't think they knew how to act. Having never lost a parent before, I had no idea how people were supposed to act around me, and certainly had no better of an idea on how to act around them.

Fake laughter was what brought me out of my quiet observation. I turned and watched as Camille flirted shamelessly with a tall and handsome man with salt and pepper hair. Regardless of her surroundings or the situation, Camille considered flirting, and all the things that came after flirting, in good taste. Her bedroom had seen more men than a barbershop, yet she was the only one of my mother's sisters to never marry. She also loved leftovers, and I was fairly sure that the man she was talking to had been around before with at least one of her sisters.

I stole a cigarette from Sydney's purse and walked outside to light it. Camille's cackling was an uninvited guest in the already overfull ravine my mind had turned into. Loving people in your family is natural, but liking them—that takes work. And it was just too hard that day.

"Let me know if you need anything," Damon said to me quietly as he was leaving. He and my mom were close, and if I could have stepped outside of my own head for a few minutes, I might have noticed that her death was hard for him too.

Self-centered, party of one, your table is now ready.

At least he wasn't leaving alone. Talia said goodbye to me and walked with Damon down the street, stopping for a tender kiss and a long hug. Then they moved slowly through the pockets of cars, and passed someone I couldn't see at first, who walked unhurriedly toward the house.

Fuck! I thought, when I realized who it was. He was the last person I wanted to see, but it was too late to hide from him; he'd already seen me.

Chapter 6

"What's up, Fattie?" he asked as he approached the door. I leaned in for an uncomfortable hug, but he pushed past me into the house without saying anything else. My eye started twitching, something it only ever did, but usually always did, when he was around. I bit my lip and followed him back into the house.

"Hat," Sydney called to me before rushing over from the kitchen as I was grabbing my keys, "You're not leaving just because he's here, are you?"

"No, I'm just really tired," I said, kissing her on the cheek and then making my way back to the door.

"Hat," Sydney yelled behind me. The door was closed behind me before she finished. One second with Victor Walker, older brother or not, was one second more than I could handle.

* * * * *

Sleep that night was onerous. I tossed so barbarically that my sheets somehow ended up wrapped around my neck. Poor Cat didn't know what to do with himself as he tried to find a spot on the bed free from my constant movement. When I did fall asleep, it was brief, and I'd wake up only to remember the events of the prior two days.

It's Mom, Hat. She's dead.

Each time it happened, it was like I was experiencing it for the first time. After a while, it just wasn't worth trying anymore. I decided that if anything in my life was going to start feeling normal again, I had to force it back to normal. That's what people do right? That's how they move on? It had to be better than reliving those days over and over again.

People were surprised to see me in the office so soon. Their eyes roamed cautiously over me as I tried to sneak to my desk unnoticed. If I was going to have a normal day, I couldn't spend it listening to people tell me how sorry they were for me.

"Hat?" Graham yelled from his office when I walked by it later with my third cup of coffee.

"Hey," I said without lingering near the door.

"Come in here for a minute. We need to talk."

All my life, whenever someone said, "We need to talk", something in me snapped, and a survival reflex would prompt me to immediately start scoping out an exit plan. It was like the alarm that sounds at the fire station: fierce, absolute, and impossible to ignore. No one ever said, "We need to talk", and then followed it up by telling you how nice their day was, or how much they enjoyed the shirt you were wearing. It was always, always, a way to start a conversation I didn't want to have. It was the trumpet announcing Confrontation, my arch-nemesis, before he entered the arena to battle me.

I slipped into Graham's office and shut the door. "What's up?"

"I thought we decided you were going to take a few days off?"

"I just needed to be somewhere, doing something. I'm fine. Really," I said, slowly sipping from my coffee cup.

"I don't know if I believe that you're fine, but I guess I understand."

The door opened and Talia peeked her head in. "Ballari's on the line," she said to Graham.

"Got it. Buddy, I have to take this, but just try to take it easy. Okay?"

"Sure," I said, escaping his office and closing the door behind me.

Talia followed me back to my desk, shaking her head. "I cannot believe you're here," she said, taking my cup of coffee from me and sipping from it. She was wearing what I liked to call her reporter outfit: a crisp collared shirt and a long gray skirt that gave her an extra-sharp look, especially with her dark-rimmed vanity glasses and her hair up in a tight bun.

"Yeah, I just couldn't stay away," I said. "I needed to get out, get moving, you know. There was too much time to think at home."

"I get it. It's been a rough couple of days for you. I can distract you . . . if you want. I went home with Damon last night."

"So I saw. How'd that go?"

"Good," she said playfully. "I don't know. He was sad. I was sad. I figured a good fuck would do us both some good." We both laughed a little at the truth of it. "I gotta get back to work, more on this later."

As she turned to walk away, her skirt got caught on the rough corner of my metal desk and ripped a little. "Damn it!" she screamed.

"It's okay," I said, looking at the rip. "It's only a little rip. I bet it'll be easy to fix."

"No, it won't. It's ruined," Talia said, tears forming in the corners of her eyes. Even after having known her for a few years, I couldn't say that I really understood what went on in that head. One moment she was calm and collected, and the next, something small like that would tip her over the edge and she'd become nearly apoplectic.

"Talia . . ."

Talia shook her head eccentrically and then smiled. "You're right," she said, "it's just a little rip. No big deal."

Women.

Okay, Hat. It's a normal Monday. Everything is normal. Time to do some normal stuff.

I picked up the phone and work continued just like it always did. Despite how I felt about my job, there was something comforting about knowing that a bomb could blow up the city, and aliens could enslave the surviving population, but Cartwright & Company would still be open, business as usual.

When I turned back to my computer screen, an instant message from our receptionist was waiting for me. "Someone is here with a package, but he says that you have to sign for it yourself."

In the lobby stood an overweight and damp looking courier from my mother's lawyer's office. "Just some paperwork. Sign this here," he said. He wiped his greasy forehead, and then used the same hand to give me a clipboard stuffed with crumpled papers.

Lovely.

"Thanks," I said insincerely. I opened the envelope slowly as I wandered back to my desk. The first word that peeked out was "estate," and quickly I shoved it back in the envelope.

The word "estate" was almost funny. Like my mother was some kind of socialite heiress. It more likely was that she had little more than her house, and I would have traded it, and anything in it, to have her back. It was weird to think about her having an "estate" at all, a term you only seemed to hear when someone died. She was really dead, and I didn't know if I would ever get used to that.

"Hey, can you help me?" a woman's voice asked from behind a large box.

"Oh, sure." I dropped the envelope and took the box out of her hands.

"It's Manhattan, right?" she asked.

"Yeah." I balanced the box between my desk and my hip so I could shake her hand. Her handshake was assertive, but her skin was soft and smooth. "You can call me Hat, or whatever."

"Okay 'Whatever', call me Liv—well, call me Liv if you want me to answer. Listen, I have to bring this stuff and a bunch more to a house I'm working on and I could use some help. Do you think you could come along?" She gracefully brushed a piece of blond hair out of her eyes. Her naturally golden locks were in a constant state of flux around her pleasant, almost familiar face.

Dear god, yes . . . get me out of here. "Sure," I said.

I had seen Liv around the office from time to time, but we had never officially met. She was Cartwright's interior decorator and usually worked alone off site. On the rare occasion that I would hear about her, it was usually eavesdropping on some new guy trying to figure out if she was seeing anyone. She was indeed beautiful, so their interest wasn't surprising. If her charmingly slender body and bright blue eyes weren't enough to make a man instantly fall in love with her, then her hair was. That hair. It smelled like a tropical forest, and it went on forever.

"Thanks for coming," she said as we rode in her sleek BMW SUV to the job. "There's just so much to do."

I wiggled in my seat. "No problem."

"Was it your mom who just passed away?" she asked bluntly as she steered through lunch hour traffic without bothering to use her blinker.

Please don't make a big deal about it. Please don't make a big deal about it. Please don't make . . . "Um . . . yeah," I finally said.

"Well that sucks," she said.

I laughed a little. "My thoughts exactly."

We arrived at a large home off Federal Hill, and you could tell that whoever lived there spent a lot of money to keep it looking nicer than the houses around it. Liv haphazardly examined various paint chips, fabric squares, and carpet samples while I unloaded the boxes from her SUV.

"This is the third time I've redecorated this house in two years. This woman gets bored easily," she said as she flipped through a wallpaper booklet. "I just can't even be creative in here anymore. What do you think of this?" She held up a green and yellow pin-striped wallpaper sample.

I squinted at the paper. "It's nice," I said. I turned away from her and continued to stack more boxes in the corner of the room.

"Ugh, please. That's not what you really think, is it?" She took a couple steps closer to me and stuck the sample in my face.

"What? No . . . no, it's fine."

"No, it's fine, huh?" She turned her head and leered at me through one eye. "Why don't you tell me what you really think?"

I took a deep breath and exhaled. "It looks like baby vomit."

"See, that wasn't so hard, was it?" She laughed a little and dropped the book on the couch. "And you're absolutely right; it's awful." She jumped backward onto the couch, stretching out her arms and letting her stylish, brown suede boots land on the antique coffee table.

"I bet there's hope for you yet," she said as she idly fingered the little gold plate necklace that fell over the short-sleeved, tan dress she wore.

After I finished bringing in all the boxes, Liv sent me to the kitchen to fetch some waters. Doing so made me feel a little like an uninvited guest fumbling around the house of someone I didn't know. Apparently though, that four-bedroom, two-and-a-half-bathroom palace with a massive solarium was just a summer home. Can a house with a solarium qualify as just a summer home? But what did I know? I lived in a four hundred square foot hovel underneath a Colombian fish market, and regularly found emptied purses and wallets tossed aside, post-crime, on my stoop.

I walked into the kitchen and grabbed two water bottles out of an otherwise empty fridge. As I looked around, I started to get dizzy and lightheaded. A cold sweat slithered down my spine and my mouth dried out completely. I started chugging water, spilling it all down myself and onto the floor. But the more I drank, the drier my mouth seemed to get.

Then it all began.

My stomach churned as the room started to waywardly rock and spin around me. Everything in sight decayed into a blur. My eyes widened as I fought to focus on anything that could steady me. There was nothing. What was left of the light was bitter and harrowing, and each shard carried with it a thousand indiscernible images.

Breathing became arduous, and the harder I fought the sensations the worse they got. Spasmodic noises followed, howling at me from every direction. Each carried a unique, and equally potent, emotion with it. Mixed together, they ran through my veins like a barreling train, desperate to find an escape and leaving wakes of spasms throughout my body.

I was rattled. Confused. Scared even. In the deepest of those moments, I held my breath, certain that it would be my last. Whatever was happening, I had no control over it, and it owned me completely.

Just as my grip on sanity started to slip, salvation came, and the lights and noises slowly faded away. Left in darkness and the silence, I was alone. I felt almost weightless as I oscillated between perception and reality, reason and truth. I had been stripped of every internal defense and left to deal with the magnitude of my situation, exposed. With that, however, came a calmness and clarity that I had never before achieved. I had been forced to the primal depths of my soul and was surprised by the serenity that waited for me there.

As my sight started to return, I could see I was still in the kitchen, but something wasn't right. It felt different. I felt different. Still wobbling from the experience, I reached for the counter to steady myself, but I couldn't see my hands. Panicked, I looked down and realized I couldn't see the rest of my body either. I wasn't really there; I didn't exist. There was no time to put the pieces together, though, because a scene unfolded before me.

A woman walked into the empty kitchen. She had an ostentatious blond wig covering her thinning hair, which poked out inadvertently below it. Oversized and overpriced jewels sparkled all over her, as if to distract you from the expensive, yet ugly, fur-lined shirt and leopard print, skin-tight pants that covered her aging body. Her glory days were long gone, but she used copious amounts of money to clutch onto what little youth she had left.

"Luz," she yelled.

She couldn't see me flinch, because I wasn't really there.

"Luz! Where are you? I'm ready for my afternoon cocktail," she yelled again, standing next to a crystal martini glass and a half drunken bottle of vodka. She longingly stared at them, waiting impatiently for Luz—apparently the only person in the house who knew how to lift the bottle and pour it into the glass.

Luz, or the woman I assume was Luz, finally came into the kitchen, dressed in a maid's uniform. She silently ignored the obstinate glance she got from the other woman and began making a martini.

Past the fur-lined woman's insufferable demeanor, something screamed sadness to me; her eyes were glossy and mellow, and her lips curled downward in the corners, almost unnoticeably. I wished she could have seen me so I could have told her that no amount of liquor, jewels, or clothing would make her feel whole.

And just as quickly as it came, it left—whatever it was. The weightlessness returned for the briefest of seconds. Then the lights and noises, swallowing me whole and pulling me from that scene. I closed my eyes and held my breath again, and when I could no longer keep it in, I exhaled sharply and opened my eyes. It was over and I was back, in full form, in the empty kitchen.

What the hell was that? A hallucination?

Whatever it was, I was still caught up in it. Sensations of extreme nausea crept up from my stomach, and I reached the trash can just before I started dry heaving uncontrollably. Who knew how long my head dangled in that trash can, as I tried to regain control over my gagging, and tried even harder to make sense of what I had just experienced.

"You alright?" Liv asked as she walked into the kitchen, dropping a set of binders loudly on the counter.

"I'm not sure," I said, pulling my head from the trash can and looking out the kitchen door. I'm not sure who I expected to find, Luz and the other woman maybe.

"Who are you looking for?" Liv asked, giving me a 'you're crazy' smile. "No one's here except us."

"I don't know. I thought I saw someone." I ran my hand from my forehead to my cheek to check my temperature before resting it on my neck.

I'm losing my mind.

Feeling normal was not a sensation I was familiar with anyway, but I had never questioned my mental stability before that day.

"Perhaps a ghost?" Liv asked, giggling.

"Yeah. A ghost." I finished wiping up the spilled water on the floor and made my way to the door. "Never mind; I guess I just need to have them increase my dosage." Telling Liv about my hallucination crossed my mind, but how could I? It was only going to make me seem crazier than I already appeared to be.

"Hey, it happens." Liv shrugged. She pulled an apple out of her purse and bit into it, casually leaning back against the counter.

It happens? Sure, it happens—to mental patients who steal their guard's keys, break out of the hospital and wander around the city, petting their scarf and asking people if they've seen their talking garden gnome.

Liv was either used to being around people who regularly questioned their sanity, or she had already called the 'nice men in the lab coats' to come get me. "Are you going to that client mixer at Graham's house tomorrow night?" she asked.

I threw my head back to my shoulders and let out a moan. "Fuck! I completely forgot about that. He roped me into it last week before . . . before everything else." I took a deep breath. "I guess I have to."

"Meh . . . maybe it won't be so bad." Liv's mouth was still full of apple. "We'll dress up, maybe have some tequila . . . make a night of it."

There wasn't enough tequila in Mexico to turn a client mixer into a good time. Mixers were like trying to iron your shirt while you were still wearing it, but Graham thought they were fun and considered client facetime invaluable. I hated the thought of forced socialization with people I didn't know and cared very little about. I avoided the thought and went into the living room to finish unpacking.

When we were ready to leave, I bent down to close the last box of Liv's stuff and noticed a lone picture on an expensive end table. In it was the woman from my hallucination, maybe a few years older than how I had seen her. She stood at the base of a dock, a fleet of boats in the water and a flock of birds in the air passing by behind her. Although she was smiling, she looked just as sad as when I saw her in person.

I must have seen that earlier, I told myself. Seeing that woman in the kitchen was some kind of daydream, or hallucination, caused by restless sleep and disharmony of mind. Wasn't it?

Chapter 7

A wet pillow soaked from a sad and fitful night's sleep woke me the next morning, hours before I had to be at work.

It's Mom, Hat. She's dead.

I sat up and opened my phone, dismissing a day's worth of missed calls and text messages from my ever-persistent family. I appreciated their love, but I wasn't ready to engage with them yet. Everyone would have the best intentions when they peppered me with questions about my well-being and whether I lied or told the truth, but I couldn't answer without being reminded of my mother's death. It landed me in a small boat within that heavy storm, and I always did get seasick a little too easily.

I wasn't ready to see anyone yet, either. Each of my mother's sisters, in their own way, reminded me of her. One liked to wear the same kind of clothes. Another one crinkled her face in the same way when she smiled. Camille was the hardest; her hair was identical to my mother's, and from behind you'd be certain it was her. I couldn't stand that brief moment of hope that it would be my mother when she turned around.

Through it all, though, I did wonder about my siblings. If I could have pulled myself out of my own cloud of sorrow, I could have found out just by asking. I was a bad brother, but I had to let myself do the only thing I could do: survive and let my world carry me forward.

I curled up in my favorite chair with Cat and pulled out the package from my mother's lawyer, debating whether or not I could handle looking at it. When I finally did open it, a heavy ball of tissue paper rolled out onto my lap as I shook out the stack of bound papers. Cat immediately began sniffing it, cautiously pawing at the paper with his claws.

Why do I have this?

I ran my fingers over my mother's necklace, pulling it free of the tissue. I'd almost forgotten about the necklace, its memory lost in the bottomless pit my mind had become. It was probably meant to go to my sister or one of my aunts when she died; but having it meant I had my very own piece of her.

Remembering what it was like to look at it when she still wore it, I studied the necklace closely. The stone itself was an erratic mixture of intense blues, greens, and turquoises, and if you looked at it hard enough you could almost see the colors move. It sat at the center of the necklace with six mesh metal petals blooming out around it like a flower. My mother claimed it was much rarer than any stone you could buy at a store, an heirloom in a family that rarely had anything of worth to pass down besides love.

I missed her so much in that moment, more than any moment since she had passed. I wanted to call and talk to her. I wanted things back the way they were. Most of all, I wanted her not to be dead.

Tears started, and then subsided just as quickly as I slipped on her necklace. Despite its feminine features, I liked having it draped over my chest, close to my heart, where she was still fully alive. I fell asleep with Cat in my lap and my hand pressing the necklace firmly against my chest.

* * * * *

"Welcome!" Graham said as he ushered me into his home that night. His eyes were already sparkling; he was always in his element when he was entertaining.

"Go . . . go mingle!" He handed me a glass of something fizzy and hurried off into another room.

Graham's townhouse was in one of the posher neighborhoods on the east side of Providence. It had a strict industrial feel, but with splashes of lavish and abstruse accents. The wall's exposed brick was the highlight of the room, and the most pristine, light cherry wood floors below them could have been laid just days before. Calm but oversized metal lighting fixtures extended down from the ceilings ribbed with exposed beams. Fresh flowers filled vases atop every available surface, and open-air shelves displayed their colorful contents proudly. You could practically smell money float through the air as you moved through the rooms.

But that was Graham. He was professional, polished even, but also a little flashy. He'd have a new, exorbitantly priced car every few months, and he told me once that all of his suits were custom made. He believed in spending lots of money and making sure everyone saw him do it.

"Hat, you know Mr. Szela, right?" Graham asked later when I walked by him. "Frank, this is Hat Walker, one of our best assistants." Graham pushed Frank toward me and walked away again.

I threw on my best client-friendly smile and pretended to look interested. "How are you tonight?" I asked.

"Just fine," he said. His eyes didn't move from a waitress' small ass as she sashayed past us. The extra-large ice cubes in his glass clinked as he sipped on his drink. The whiskey was so strong that as it drifted up my nose it almost knocked me over. He wasn't acting like he wanted to talk business, so I wasn't surprised when he followed the waitress into the kitchen without saying another word to me.

"He's sleazy," Talia came up to me and said, "I caught him looking down my shirt at the two ladies earlier."

"Well, that's just lovely," I said.

"I better go in there and watch him before we have another sexual harassment case to deal with." She downed the rest of her glass of champagne and disappeared into the kitchen.

Liv was in the corner talking to another client, an older woman who owned a small boutique dress shop in the financial district. That woman had no use for our services, she just had more money than most small countries and not enough things to spend it on. I met her briefly once, when I was sent to her shop during a food truck festival. My job was to chase birds away from her stoop. And I did. I spent twelve hours in the beating sun getting shit on, and not figuratively.

Liv nonchalantly ended her conversation and walked over to me. When I dropped my eyes, she ducked a little to force me to look at her. "So you made it?"

"Yeah. I guess we didn't have much of a choice though, right?"

"There's always a choice." She grabbed my glass and placed it on a nearby serving tray. "Besides, I kind of like these things. Let's get you a real drink."

She took my hand and guided me through the crowd. An elaborate bar was set up in the game room, complete with bartenders better dressed than I was. I ordered a Kettle One, on the rocks, with a few splashes of pineapple juice and leaned up against the bar to wait for it.

On the other side of the room, a tall crystal vase filled with lilies caught my attention. I found it gripping, maybe because it was something my mother would have liked, or maybe because the lilies were the most brilliant shade of purple I'd ever seen.

As I walked over to it, a cold sweat formed and trickled down my spine. Breathing became hard and my stomach churned. I was taken hostage by another deluge of lights and noises. My stomach flipped inside my body in every direction as the vibrations of my internal struggle shook every inch of me. The brief moment of weightlessness and serenity came, but only after my world had been extracted of any control I once had.

When I opened my eyes, I was still in the game room, but no one else was. I looked down, and just as shocked as the first time, I realized I wasn't really there either. Just then, Graham walked into the room.

"Can we please have a drink and talk this through," Graham asked someone. He walked past an empty crystal vase and sat near the pool table.

A stocky Indian man followed him into the room, shuffling quickly behind with his short legs. "You know I don't drink," he said with a deep voice. It had just a hint of accent, but I don't think it was Indian. "I don't think you understand what you're asking me for," he said, folding his arms and leaning up against the pool table.

"Of course I do," Graham said, a sly smile opening up his mouth.

"We're talking a lot of money here. A lot, a lot of money. I just don't think it's worth it."

*"Look around you," Graham said, scanning the
room with his eyes. "Does anything here look like it
was cheap? That table you're leaning on was nearly
$50,000 and I don't even play. Now imagine what
I'm willing to pay for something I'm actually going
to use."*

Breathing heavily, I opened my eyes. Liv's hand touched my
shoulder, and I jumped . . . at least a foot into the air. I wasn't
sure that the hallucination was over.

"Jumpy?"

"Yeah, sorry," I said, looking around nervously to see who
else had noticed.

"Come here," she said, grabbing my hand again.

She pulled me out of the room and through the house. We
passed by a string quartet in tuxedos, a double set of bathrooms, and a library that was bigger than my entire apartment.
We moved beyond the heart of the party to the end of a long
hallway, just in time to see a red-faced woman charge out of
Graham's study. A short and apologetic-looking man ran after
her, carrying two coats.

"That didn't look good," I said, as Liv locked the door
behind us.

The study didn't even have a computer, which led me to
believe it was more for show than anything else. The large
metal desk blended in against the slate colored walls. The
only non-neutral color in the entire room was a small, bright
red couch that sat in a low loft next to shelves filled with
untouched books.

"So, what was that about?" Liv asked. She moved aside a
few decorative bottles from the desk so she could lean on the
corner of it.

"That couple just now? No idea."

"No, not the couple," she put her hand to my chest and playfully pushed me. "I'm talking about whatever happened before in the game room."

"What?" I asked. "It was nothing."

"You don't have to hide from me. I know something . . . special happened. I could feel it when I came up beside you. I know what you did and you know what you . . ." She stopped for a second to look at my blank expression, pushing her tongue up against the back of her teeth and giggling. "You don't really know what happened, do you?"

"I have no idea what you're talking about. Maybe I should just go," I said, moving toward the door.

"Shhhh. Wait. I have something to show you," she said, pulling me toward the door.

"Why do you have to pull me around everywhere? What are we doing?"

"Have you ever heard the saying 'if these walls could talk?'"

I nodded.

"Okay . . . well, what if the walls can talk and you just need to know how to listen?"

"You know, I think I am going to go." I tried to move toward the door, but she held onto my shirt and pressed her hand against my mouth to keep me from saying anything else.

"Just go with me here." She took the two dangly earrings she was wearing out of her ears and handed one to me. "Hold this in your hand and press your ear up against the wall."

I laughed under my breath at the ridiculousness of it all and shook my head.

"Do it, come on," Liv said.

My ear scraped against the wall's texture as I pressed up against it. Its thick coat of slate-colored paint reflected light from the fireplace in its grooves, illuminating Liv's face is the most flattering way. She swung her head to move her golden hair away from her ear and joined me against the wall. We looked silly.

She started whispering to herself and there was a certain cadence in her voice, even though she spoke so softly that I couldn't make out the actual words. Her chant was slow at first, but then faster and faster. Then I started to hear voices coming from the wall.

"Don't be such a snot!" a young man's voice said. "These people are from my office. We have to be polite, ya know?" His voice was so clear that he had to be standing on the other side of the wall.

"Don't call me a snot; these people are the snots," a female voice shot back. I shuddered at the thought of the scene they were creating and everyone from work watching it unfold. "I've been trying to make all kinds of good conversation with these people and no one's been givin' me the time of day." Her voice boomed with anger and hostility, but you could still hear the undertones of hurt in it.

"Baby, I'm sorry. I know they can be kinda stuck-up some-times, but it's work and they're the ones who pay me, so . . ." he cleared his throat, "maybe you could just calm down a little and we can try to get through it."

"Calm down? You want me to calm down? You're such a prick!"

The voices stopped, but the sound of an angry doorknob turning and high heeled shoes walking away took their place.

"That didn't look good," my voice said.

I jerked away from the wall and dropped the earring on the floor. It was my voice I had just heard . . . but it hadn't come out of my mouth. Liv flashed me a triumphant smile before bending down to pick up her earring. "Well?"

"What the hell was that?" I opened the study door and looked out at an empty hallway.

"What are you looking for now?"

"People," I said, closing the door again. "I don't understand what that was." I plopped myself down on the plush leather couch next to the desk, scrunched my eyes, and ran my fingers nervously through my hair.

"Am I gonna have to lay this out for you?" She sat down on the couch and put her hand calmly on my knee. "Okay," she jingled the earring in her hand, "that was us listening to what just happened in this room before we walked in. Are you with me now?" She playfully bumped her shoulder into mine. "It's a cool spell, right?"

"It's crazy that I'm listening to you like this is real. People don't cast 'spells' Liv," I said, throwing my fingers up into full-on air quotes.

"Some do," she said before leaning in and giving me a gentle, smooth kiss on my cheek. "Sorry, I didn't think that was gonna be such a shock for you. I had a feeling you were like me when we first met, and then I was pretty sure that whatever I saw in the kitchen had some magic to it. I thought me showing you that spell might make it easier to open up to me, but I can see now this is much newer for you than I thought." She patted me on the knee and got up.

"I still don't understand what just happened."

"I know you don't." She walked toward the door and opened it. "You will soon, but I think you've probably had all you can handle for tonight."

"Wait!" I rushed to stand. "What happens now?"

She leaned against the wall and her beautiful locks of hair fell around her face. "What are you doing Friday night?"

"No plans yet, why?"

"You've got plans now. Meet me at Sweaty Betty's at nine, we'll go from there. Oh . . . and dress to impress, please." She gave a confident wink and walked away.

"Where are you taking me?"

"You'll see," she called without turning around.

Chapter 8

The rest of week continued without much sleep as I obsessively replayed the events of that night over and over in my head. Who was Liv, really? Were spells real? If so, would that mean my hallucinations were real too? There were too many questions, and yet, somehow, it didn't matter what the answers were. They kept my mind occupied and unavailable to think about my mother's death, and any relief from that was welcome.

Sweaty Betty's turned out to be the nickname for a local diner on the north end. Thanks, Google. It was a small little joint, carved into the corner of a major street. When I got there on Friday, I circled the surrounding blocks in my car for a while until I found a space behind a dumpster in another business' lot.

"Hey, hey," Liv said when I finally entered the diner. "You're late." She was already eating a too-healthy looking salad.

"I know. You didn't mention that there's nowhere to park here." I signaled to the waitress, or the biker posing as a waitress, as she passed by us. "I'll take whatever she has. And a water, please."

"Do you like tofu?" Liv asked me, holding up a white chunk of something on her fork.

"Yeah, actually, can you make that with chicken?" I yelled to the waitress as she entered the kitchen. "That's right. Chicken."

"Your loss, it's good," Liv said.

"This place is kinda dead," I said.

"Yeah, it's more popular during late night, but I wanted to get a quick bite before we head out, so I figured this would work."

When my salad arrived a few seconds later, my hopes that it was "fresh made" dwindled away. I figured I'd settle for no bugs. I fished through it with my fork, pushing the zesty Italian dressing off to the side.

"Am I dressed impressively enough?" I asked, tugging at my dark blue, collared shirt. "Where are we going?"

"It's this place I hang out at a lot. I think you'll like it."

"Oh yeah? Why?"

"You'll see. It's a surprise."

What isn't with you? I thought.

The surprise was actually when she turned down a nearly deserted road behind the mall. I regretted leaving my car back at the diner as we passed the string of boarded-up factories and abandoned construction projects.

Isn't this how horror movies start?

We pulled into a narrow alley between two tall, dark buildings. Passing the buildings exposed a huge parking lot that you couldn't see from the road. It was packed with cars, spanning from the two buildings we'd just passed to the train tracks on the other side.

"Where are we?" I asked.

Liv didn't answer. She parked, and we walked up to a windowless door on the far side of the lot. All the building's windows were painted black so you couldn't see in, and there were no signs telling me where we were. Waves of bass from music inside shook the brick walls, and the closer we got to the building, the clearer the music got.

Sex club? Underground dog fighting ring?

"Nothing like that, relax," Liv said, looking back to me.

Had I said that out loud?

"Welcome to Equinox," she said, holding the door open for me.

It looked like a normal bar, and that was weird to me. There was no reason why I shouldn't have known about a bar that popular, one that could be full on a random Tuesday night.

On our way to the bar, we passed a set of carpet-lined stairs going up to a glass-enclosed room on the second floor. The glass room overlooked the bar on three sides, and the stairs up to it were guarded by a living "do not enter" sign—a giant man with a shaved head and biceps bigger than most people's heads, including mine.

The bar itself was massive, wrapping around the entire right side of the room and underneath a balcony attached to the glass room above us. A modest stage, flanked by large speakers and lights, lay dormant in the back of the room with its tattered curtains closed. The same type of curtain ran up all the walls, blocking every window in the old building.

"Kettle One on the rocks, with a few splashes of pineapple juice," I said to the bartender. "What do you want to drink?"

"I'm good," Liv said, taking out her phone. She leaned against the bar and eagerly typed out a message.

"You're not drinking?"

"I will in a bit, don't worry."

We sat down at a small cocktail table in the middle of the room and I started sipping on my drink. "So, this is nice," I said.

"Yeah, I like it." She tilted her phone from the table to look at the display. It was hard to hear her over the loud music and the crowd, who cheered enthusiastically at some sporting event plastered on the twenty or so TVs around the room.

"How come I've never heard of this place before?"

"I don't know. It's one of those places you just have to know about, I guess." She leaned back in her chair and crossed her legs. "They've got great bands and the drinks are cheap. He doesn't advertise, so you just kind of find out about it from someone. Speaking of . . ."

Liv turned to watch a man in an arresting black shirt walk up from behind her.

"Hello, beautiful," he said before hugging Liv. "How are you, Love?"

"Hey, you. I'm good. Meet my friend Hat," Liv said.

"Interesting name," he said, extending his hand. "Cooper here." His voice had a hint of a British accent. His newish looking jeans and expensive sneakers made him appear relaxed, in a completely controlled way. His product-less black hair was a sight—curly in some places, straight in others, and unkempt allover. It was long enough to cover his eyes, but he had pushed it back, and shorter wisps stuck out behind his ears. It was so messy that it made it hard to guess his age. Liv was just a few months shy of thirty; maybe he was around the same?

"Hi," I said, shaking his hand nervously.

Cooper looked me straight in the eyes when he shook my hand, as if he were giving me the five second evaluation. I wondered if I would get a copy of the report after. He was taller than me and had a small scar under his right eye, the kind that had healed over years ago but would forever distinguish his face from others.

"Alright," he said, letting go of my hand and turning to Liv. "So, where you been, Love?"

"Oh, you know. Life and things." Their bodies were so close as they spoke that I felt conspicuously left outside the conversation.

"Of course, you know I would invite you upstairs, but . . ." he nodded slightly in my direction.

Oh right, but this kid isn't cool enough.

Liv stood on her toes and whispered something in Cooper's ear. He looked at me over her shoulder while she talked, scanning me again with his inquisitive eyes. More details for his report.

This isn't awkward at all.

"Come on then," Cooper said to me, as he wrapped her arm in his to pull her along.

I downed the rest of my drink and shuffled quickly behind them. Cooper blew past the large man at the foot of the staircase, disappearing into the glass room above the bar. Liv was waiting in the middle of the stairs for me, but the man was entirely too large for me to pass without him moving, so I stood passively in front of him, waiting for either a meteor to fall from the sky and kill me, or for him to move. His nostrils flared at me and he crossed his arms. Air lightly whistled from his cave-like nostrils as he continued to block my path.

"He's good," Liv said to the large man and he finally moved.

The glass room that made up the second floor was an elaborate lounge-style area with a private bar and separate bathrooms. A few unfamiliar faces turned to look at us as we entered and the feeling in the room was . . . less than welcoming.

"Everyone, this is Hat," Cooper said, grabbing my shoulder and shaking me in a friendly way, "and you all know Liv." A few of them waved or said hi, to Liv, not to me. The rest turned and went back to whatever they were doing before we walked in.

"This is Justin, my right-hand man," Cooper stepped back and pointed to a younger man on his right. He was maybe twenty, with fair white skin and flat blond hair. His jeans couldn't be described as tight because, although small, they still hung off his slim body, and his long-sleeved graphic t-shirt was at best a child's medium.

I extended my hand toward Justin. "Hi."

"Hey," he said, turning around and walking toward the couch without pretending to notice my hand.

Okay then, not feeling the love.

"This is the always-ravishing Elle," Cooper continued, pointing to the woman on the couch. Elle had thick, jet-black hair that made waves from her head to her shoulders. Her backless, fire-red shirt and black leather pants complemented her precise make-up, and together they made her look like a rock star (or maybe a groupie). A clump of shiny silver bracelets that dangled off her wrist jingled as she tossed her hair over her shoulder, exposing a small, four leaf clover necklace with diamond accents that hung delicately from her neck. It was the only subtle thing about her.

When Cooper noticed that no one else was coming forward to be introduced, he said, "Alright then. Justin, grab us two more, would you?"

I sank into a large chair in the middle of the room. All the furniture looked like it came from someone's living room, albeit someone rich's living room. Two leather couches and another chair surrounded a frosted glass coffee table with metal hardware and a variety of fresh drink rings imprinted on the top. The bar had a few stools, and there were some small cocktail tables and chairs strewn about the room.

Justin roughly handed me a glass full of a clear blue liquid, and I tilted it against the light to try to figure it out. It looked more like mouthwash than any liquor I had ever seen, but there was also something serene about it. It was clearer than the Pacific Ocean off the coast of Hawaii and the ice cubes almost sounded mellow as they clinked against the side of the glass.

"Try it. You'll like it," Cooper said with a confident nod.

I took a quick sniff over the drink before putting it to my lips.

Wow.

"It's vodka and pineapple," I said, sniffing it again.

"For you," Liv said. "Mine tastes just like our favorite California wine." She held up her glass to Cooper's. I suspected that it wasn't the first time they'd shared a bottle of their favorite wine, although it might have been the first time they had shared it with their clothes on.

"What is it?" I asked, taking another sip.

"It's called Blue Ice," Cooper said, sipping his own glass of the mysterious mixture. "It can taste like whatever you want it to taste like."

"How?" The drink was so spellbinding that I didn't look up from it when I spoke.

"What do you mean, how?" Cooper asked with a laugh. "Don't worry yourself with how. Just think about what you want to drink, and drink."

Was it that simple? I was suspicious, but I took another sip and thought about beer, which I hated, and immediately stuck my tongue out.

Definitely beer. Gross.

"It's the house specialty," Cooper said. "Ingredients are top secret though, so don't ask." He held his glass up to mine, clinking them together before taking another sip. "Best part though, no hangovers."

"And no calories," Elle added.

"Right. The birds always love that part. But keep it all under your . . . hat, yes?" Cooper said.

I would have laughed if I wasn't so distracted by the drink, and if that was funny.

"All we need is for the police to start rummaging around here again, looking for something they wouldn't understand if it bit them," Cooper said.

It didn't take long for the group to completely lose interest in me. Cooper and Liv landed in a deep conversation, one that I wasn't being invited to join, their animated faces only inches from each other as they spoke. But it didn't really matter, because I was still wrapped up in trying to explain Blue Ice to myself. I finished my drink, to the taste of vodka and not beer, and saw that there was a pitcher of it sitting on the bar.

"Do you mind?" I asked Cooper, holding up my empty glass and gesturing toward the bar.

"Go on then," Cooper said, waving at the bar without turning to look at me.

A woman sitting at the bar in a sleek white dress and matching headband lit a cigarette as I approached to pour myself another glass. "Can I bum one of those?" I asked her. She handed me one without responding. "Thanks. Wait, we can't really smoke in here, can we?"

"We can do whatever we want in here," she said, wrapping her redwood-colored lips around the cigarette and getting up.

These people love me.

"So, Hat, tell us about your powers then?" Cooper asked when I returned to the sitting area. His hand was resting securely on Liv's thigh.

I looked at Liv and took an uneasy sip of my drink. Everyone was watching me and waiting for a response to a question I didn't understand. A few more seconds of silence and Cooper asked, "Are you sure he's a Caster?"

Liv left me in my discomfort for a few more seconds before finally laughing and saying, "Oh, he is. He's just new, and he doesn't know what that means yet."

"Oooohhh," Elle cooed in a low voice and sat on my lap. "How innocent . . . it's like you're a virgin."

"No, I'm not a . . . ," I started.

"It's okay baby," she said, putting her arm around my shoulder and leaning in to kiss me. Her lipstick was sticky and left a noticeable residue on my cheek. "I think it's cute."

"But I'm not a . . ."

"Justin," Cooper yelled over me. Justin came and sat on the arm of the couch. "Give our new friend here a little show, eh?"

Justin rolled his eyes and scoffed before holding out his hand with his palm flat, facing the ceiling. Slowly his fingers separated and curled, and as they did, a tiny bead of light appeared, floating unaided above his hand. As it grew, it looked more and more like the flame from a candle, glowing red light above a darker blue light. It started to swirl, slowly pulling in more light and getting larger until a softball-sized sphere of fire hovered above his hand. He moved it closer to me, and the heat from the fire brushed against my speechless face.

Holy shit!

Then with one quick motion, Justin closed his hand and extinguished the fire, leaving only small strands of smoke that seeped out from between his fingers.

"How's that?" Cooper asked.

"Impressive," I said, trying to hide my amazement.

Everyone jumped back into their own conversations, like nothing that had just happened was unusual, and left me to stew in my seat. My lip, caught underneath my clamping tooth, might have betrayed the image I was trying to portray: that I was completely unaffected by what I just saw.

"So what's a Caster?" I asked Cooper as he handed me another glass full of Blue Ice.

Even Liv snickered at that question.

I felt like the new kid at school who went to his first health class, weeks after it started, only to ask "what's a condom?" and have all the kids look at me with shock and condescension. "You don't know what a condom is?" the other kids would ask, laughing at me. I'd slink down in my seat and pretend I had never asked the question, and continue going on thinking that condoms were the plastic packets that ketchup and mustard came in at fast food restaurants.

"We've been called lots of things over the years," Cooper said, "witches, wizards, enchanters . . . and all sorts of other things that are less kind."

"Devil worshipers," Liv said. "Heathens."

"That's probably my favorite one. I can't say it's ever mattered to us what term they use, though. It's just their way to classify us; names to call people that have something they don't."

"What's that?" I asked.

"Power," he said. He leaned back comfortably on the couch and put his arms behind his head. "Caster is a term that's a little bit more . . . modern, I suppose. In any case, we like to keep our distance from the rest of them, so that's why I've built this area of the club—so we could enjoy ourselves without worrying about the rest of the world." He raised his hand to present his adult clubhouse.

"How many people are like you?" I asked.

"Like us, you mean? Who knows? We aren't exactly kept track of by census, are we?" He laughed at himself. "I've got to go check on a few things downstairs. I'll be back up in a bit."

Liv chugged the rest of her Blue Ice and stood up. "We should probably get going anyway, I have an early day tomorrow."

"Well, Love, try to come 'round a bit more often then," Cooper said, kissing Liv briskly on the lips, "and bring your new friend."

Elle came up beside me and slapped my ass playfully. "Oh yeah, definitely bring your friend."

"He's only just gotten here, Elle, take it easy on the boy," Cooper said, reaching for my hand again. "Don't worry about the others. They're a skittish bunch, but they'll come around eventually."

"So, what'd ya think?" Liv asked when we got back to her SUV.

"You're definitely full of surprises," I said. "They didn't seem overly interested in me though."

"I've known them for a while, except maybe Elle, and they're a little tough on new people but they'll get used to you."

"Why'd you bring me there?"

"Because it's fun?" She laughed. "I think it's good for you to meet other people like us. This is all going to sink in soon, and when it does, you'll want to be here with us."

When we pulled up to my car, I fished through my pocket for my keys. Liv watched, then tilted her head at me and smiled. As I went to say goodbye, she leaned over and kissed me, her soft lips running smoothly across mine.

I pulled away and coughed in surprise. "Wait. What about Cooper?"

She held onto my shirt and pulled me into another kiss. "What about him?"

"I . . . I thought . . . I guess . . . ," I stuttered, leaning as far into the door as I could to get away from her.

"I think you might spend too much time thinking, and too little time actually doing."

I pulled back. "What does that mean?"

"It means you should try living a little more and worrying a little less. Passion and sex are only complicated when you make them complicated," she said with a whisper-like laugh.

I sighed.

"I promise, when you embrace who you are, things are going change for you. I mean, if you want them to. Do you like the way things are, or do you want to get everything you possibly can out of your life?"

There were a few uncomfortable seconds posing as hours before I finally said: "I want everything."

She casually moved back into her own seat and fastened her seat belt. "Good," she said. "So, want to follow me back to my house and we'll live a little together?"

Chapter 9

"What the hell is wrong with you?" I asked myself out loud when I pulled into my driveway, after having not followed Liv home. Offers like that didn't come every day, at least not to me.

There weren't many women to speak of who had seen my bedroom, or me theirs. I just had such a hard time connecting to anyone like that. Each time I tried, the encounter would end with little fanfare and a gnawing sense of emptiness. I'd lie in bed, staring at nothing on the ceiling, and wish to feel something more than I just had. Something fulfilling. Something to make it worth doing it again. I don't know what was missing. Love maybe. Or passion. But something was definitely always missing.

In my mind, that something came from the perfect woman, and she was a lot like Liv: bold, beautiful, smart, a little mysterious, and a whole lot more take-charge than I ever was. Yet after being kissed by that seemingly perfect woman, I was still waiting. Maybe that something didn't exist, or maybe I wouldn't know what it was when I felt it. Or maybe Liv was right, and I needed to live more and worry less.

✳ ✳ ✳ ✳ ✳

The next morning, I came out of the locker room at the gym and passed the stairs that led to the treadmills. Casters, spells, Liv, and everything else from Equinox was running through my head. They were wild thoughts, surreal even, and they took up so much space in my mind that I couldn't dwell on the one thing I had done nothing but dwell on for days. But they also worked me up into a healthy anxiety about a world I couldn't comprehend yet. As much as I loved some quality treadmill time, I knew it wasn't going to cut it.

'Max McKay, Owner/Instructor' a plaque posted on the wall in front of one of the gym's classrooms said. Above it was a framed picture of Max in a commanding martial arts pose. He had white pants on and a black karate belt tied tightly above them, but his t-shirt looked more like something you'd see in an Old Navy commercial. The door to the room was propped open, and I could see him moving around inside.

An ancient-looking stereo was attached to a shelf in the corner of the studio, blaring out an odd mash-up of techno and classical music. Max was alone and working through what looked like an intense martial arts routine. His forceful but almost effortless movements were entrancing. Hesitant to interrupt him, and eager to see what he could do, I leaned against the doorway and quietly watched the dance-like movements unfold.

He threw strikes into the air with his hands, followed by sweeping kicks with his feet. He'd kick low, and without putting his leg down, he'd kick high. His eyes and head would shift in new directions just before a strike was unleashed, and I could almost see the imaginary attackers he was fending off. Block, block, kick. Block, kick, punch. The routine was picking up its pace and despite the flushing of his face, he never lost a step. Hissing sounds from his disciplined breathing came with each move and certain strikes, the ones that exerted enough power to knock imaginary attackers over came with a coarse roar.

The fabric of his white pants made a sharp snapping noise with each flawless kick he executed, and each new movement stretched the material of his clothes enough to remind me to be jealous of his body. And that body moved in ways I didn't know were possible, and in ways that my body never had, nor would.

His foot soared into the air again, whipping off a series of kicks. His other foot, planted firmly on the ground, slowly rotated so the kicks made a complete circle in the air, knocking down any invisible enemy attacking. A series of flat-handed strikes followed when both feet were back on the ground, before one last kick jettisoned into the air. His other foot followed, lifting his entire body above the ground. The striking foot had made a full crescent while he hovered in the air, twisting his entire body. Steadfast and sturdy, he landed on the ground, took a quick breath, and then bowed respectfully toward the flags hung on the wall.

I was already clapping lightly before he turned to me. He grabbed a towel from a bench against the wall and dried his face. "Hello there. Come for your balance lesson?" he asked.

"Sorry for staring," I said. "But that was crazy. I mean . . . like incredible crazy, not 'try to lick your own elbow' crazy."

"Haha. Thanks, but don't praise me too much, I missed the mark on one of those jumps," he said. By then, the smell of fresh sweat was encroaching on me as he stood uncomfortably close.

"Right. I can't pick up a pen without toppling over, but you missed the mark on that jump. That's the same. I guess I'll stop admiring you then."

"I didn't say that." He threw his wet towel in the corner and turned down the stereo. "So what do you think? A balance lesson, you know, so you can at least pick up a pen?"

"Um . . . I was kind of in the mood for something a little bit more . . . aggressive."

He laughed a little and said, "We can do that." He started to walk away but then hesitated and turned. "Listen, your cousin was in here earlier and told me about your mom. I'm really sorry to hear about that."

"This is probably going to make me sound like a jerk, but do you think that we could not talk about that? I mean, thank you and all that good stuff, but I'd really rather be hitting something then talking about that."

"Right. Done." His bare feet thumped against the padded floor as he walked to the back of the room. He pulled some padded gloves off a shelf and slipped them over his hands. "Okay. Why don't you try hitting these for a bit? I'm going to watch your form and balance." He held out his hands unevenly and nodded for me to start.

The gloves expanded like catcher's mitts, with a large round pad on each. Had they been a real attacker, I wouldn't have done much more than make them laugh as I slapped them. After only a minute, my hands hurt from the sandpaper-like material of the gloves, but the release felt good nonetheless.

He started moving backward in a circle, forcing me to follow him with my attacks. He kept the gloves in constant motion, moving them back and forth and then up and down.

"Okay good. Now when you're hitting, make sure to keep your thumb tucked underneath your fist," he said. I tried to do what he said, but he just shook his head. "No. Don't hold it in your other fingers."

He dropped his arms, presumably to show me what he was talking about, but I was already mid-punch. Luckily, he was a lot stealthier than me and moved away from my fist long before I would have hit him.

"Okay," he said with a little chuckle. He took off the gloves and grasped my arm with his strong hand. "Hat, relax your hand." He pulled at my fingers and like they were made of clay, molded them into what, to me, felt like an unnatural fist.

It turned out that "tucking" your thumb meant to pull it underneath your other fingers, to shield it from the impact. "If you don't keep your thumb here, when you punch something other than those pads, you'll break it," he said.

That can't feel good.

For someone who could punch and kick with such aggression, he had a surprisingly gentle touch. "Are you tired now or do you want to try again with your new and improved fist?" he asked.

He slipped the pads on again and taunted me a bit with funny faces. I loaded my new fists by my chest like I knew what I was doing and starting swinging at him again.

"Come on! Is that all you've got?"

He was dodging around me, making me flail about after him. I couldn't seem to hit the pads anymore; he was either making the game more challenging or I was just getting worse at it. My elbows were starting to get a little sore from my jerky punches and within a few more minutes of the cat-and-mouse game, I was panting uncontrollably with sweat dripping down my tingling arms.

Mental note, work out arms more often.

"Okay, let's take a break. That was pretty good for your first time," he said. He tossed the pads on the floor and patted me on the back as I hunched over with my hands on my knees. He was good at being reassuring, but for someone who, only minutes before, was spinning in the air like an Olympic gymnast, I doubted he was at all impressed by me.

"That was harder than I thought," I said, rubbing my knuckles.

He handed me a bottle of water and we sat cross legged on the floor. "Learning a good punch is helpful, but if you're ever in trouble, go for the eyes, the throat, the groin—anything that you can imagine hurting like hell if someone did it to you. You don't even need a fist, look," he said, tightening his fingers and pushing out the palm of his hand. "Drive this into someone's nose. It'll probably break it and distract them long enough to get away. You ready to try a lesson in balance?"

"Sure, I haven't made an ass of myself even once today."

"Great," he said, totally ignoring my joke and getting up. Instead of standing up like me, you know, like a fumbling old man with bad knees, he flipped from the ground in one easy motion. He leaned back quickly, and as his back touched the floor, he bent his legs up to his chest and flung them forward, taking his upper body with him as his legs soared into the air before landing securely on his feet. The entire ordeal took less than a second.

Show-off.

"Alright, what I want you to do is stand right here, feet shoulder-width apart, knees bent slightly, eyes closed."

Okay. Shoulder-width apart. Shoulder-width apart. I should be able to figure that out, even with my eyes closed.

He came up behind me and kicked my shoes with his bare foot, pushing my legs wider. 'Shoulder-width apart' feels a lot wider than you'd think it would.

"Ah!" I yelped a little when he touched my lower back.

"Ticklish?" he asked in his deep voice. He was running his hand up my back and pressing gently to get me in the position he wanted me. "Now keep your eyes closed and slowly lean backward. Remember to keep breathing and don't move your feet."

In my mind's eye, I looked something like a flamingo trying to master yoga as my back arched. I thought surely my head was only inches from the floor and my newly-developed Gumby powers had me ready to try my first back-handspring. I was positive he'd show me that next.

"Good. Now bring yourself back up, straighten out your back, and take a deep breath."

"So, what kind of karate do you teach?"

He pinched my arm. "Shhh. Concentrate. I want you to try the same thing again, but this time, try to really stretch yourself out and go back further."

Maybe my head wasn't as close to the ground as I thought before. I stretched backward and I could feel him close behind me. He placed a sturdy hand under my back and another on my chest. The hand on my chest was pushing down lightly and the hand on my back was steadying me, but not holding me up.

"Good. Just relax and concentrate on your sense of balance."

What sense of balance?

His hands guided me past my comfort zone and I worried that if he removed them, I'd be stuck in that position just long enough for the paramedics to arrive and take pictures. A shadow moved across my face and I tilted toward the door to see what it was, nervous that someone was watching the spectacle. It only took another second to realize just how important concentration was, because when I no longer had it, I fell backward and took Max with me.

My body made an awful smacking sound as it hit the padded floor. Max fell right on top of me and his arm got trapped behind my back. That poor guy, he didn't see my clumsy ass coming when he offered to teach me about balance. He could jump and kick into the air, and land flawlessly, but ten minutes and a simple breathing exercise with Manhattan Walker and he was down for the count.

We were in a full-on fit of laughter at the situation after we landed. I had managed to release his mangled arm, but Max was still on top of me, holding his torso up with his strong arms on either side of my neck. Our laughter gradually turned into amused breathing, and I became more and more aware of the position we were in.

Why is he still on top of me?

The mix CD in his prehistoric stereo ended and silence took over the room. Still trapped under the weight of him, I could only look up into his eyes as they hovered above me like two sky-like gray saucers. I should have looked away, or pushed him off me, but I didn't. His arms bent slowly, lowering his upper body onto mine. And when he didn't stop, our lips met.

I distressfully cleared my throat and pushed him off me.

"I'm sorry," he stuttered, standing up and holding his hand out to pull me up.

I ignored his hand, rolled over, and stood up like an old man. "No, it's fine . . . I didn't . . ."

"I guess I thought you . . ."

"I'm not." I started heading for the door.

"Don't leave," he stuttered a bit again. "I guess I got carried away. I'm sorry."

"It's fine, really. I have plans, so I need to get going anyway."

"Oh." There was a hint of disappointment in his voice. "So maybe we can try this again sometime?"

The kissing or the balance lesson?

"Yeah. Sure," I said.

Before he could say anything else, I was gone.

Chapter 10

Liv and I made plans to meet up on Sunday morning, and I knew I had no idea what I was in for. Her house was nestled in a quiet corner of Pawtucket, just north of the city. As you'd expect, the inside was beautifully decorated with bright tones of blue cascading across the walls and heavy tan drapes framing the sunny windows. There was at least one life-like, panoramic painting in each room; the living room's being a huge wood-framed portrait of a barren birch forest in winter. Nothing looked out of place, even if its place was intentionally askew, and the whole house was naturally lit and warm like Christmas morning.

We sat around eating Chinese food and watching bad reality TV for a while. My distaste for the manufactured drama of the program made it hard to focus, so I kept lazily eyeing everything in her house. Pictures tilted in every direction sat atop one of her side tables in diverse, artistic frames. One of them, a picture of her and Cooper, sat openly in front of the others, enclosed in thick glass and a brown frame. Studying the picture, I tried to figure out how long ago it was taken, and how long they had been (not) a couple. The more I focused on it, the more everything else around me just started to drift away, until only that picture was left.

Shit.

I could feel it happening again. The cold sweat, the churning in my stomach, the harsh lights and noises. I struggled, hoping that if I fought it hard enough, it would just go away and leave me be. But as everything decayed into a blur, I knew it was once again out of my control.

> *"It was an accident," Cooper said to Liv in an otherwise empty room above his club. He was using a damp cloth to wipe down what looked like an already clean table.*
>
> *"No, Cooper," Liv snapped. Her forceful words were laced with anger. "An accident is unintentional, this . . . you had a choice, and you did it."*
>
> *"Love, it just happens sometimes, you know that. I can't always control it, so isn't that the same thing?" He reached out to touch her arm and she pulled away.*
>
> *"I don't think I can ever trust you again," Liv said, walking toward the door.*
>
> *"Don't leave, not like this. Don't let one stupid mistake throw everything we have away."*
>
> *"I'm not," she said over her shoulder, shrugging. "You are."*

"Damn it," I said. That hallucination made me dizzy. As I stood, I tried to steady myself on the table, only to knock into it. The picture I was looking at fell off and broke. "I'm so sorry. I'll clean it up."

Liv let out a little laugh. "Don't be. And leave it. I'll clean it up later," she said. "It just happened again, didn't it?"

"What?"

"Whatever happened at Graham's too. Where do you go?"

"I don't know. It's hard to explain. I'm actually kind of worried that there might be something wrong with me."

"Just tell me about it."

"It's sort of like a hallucination, I guess. I lose control and start to see things. They're like memories, but they aren't my memories. I don't know."

"So, like a vision?"

"Hallucination. Vision. Is there a difference?" I asked

"Sure. Hallucinations aren't normal, but visions are, at least to people like us."

"Do you get them too?"

"No, that's all you," Liv said with a laugh. "Your visions are what my dad would call an innate gift. It's like magic that's just sort of always there, without casting a spell or anything. We all have them, and wish we didn't sometimes, but it's all part of being a Caster, I guess. I think the Universe gives us our own specific talents to help us focus. It makes sense, right? There are so many things to do with magic that it would take us a thousand lifetimes to learn everything."

She moved to the ottoman in front of my seat and forced her face in mine so there was nowhere to look except each other's eyes. "I think it's time we work on this. I'm going to help, but to be honest I'm not a great teacher. I'm actually kinda surprised you even need to be taught—you're the first person I've ever known to be this old and just figuring out they had powers. It's weird."

"Yeah," I said, "*that's* what's weird here."

"Whatever. I guess I was lucky. I had my mom and dad around to show me how to do all this stuff, so maybe you learn earlier that way. I don't know."

"What if you have it all wrong with me? I could just be losing my mind. Or it could be a sequence of coincidences."

"Meh. I don't believe in coincidences. But for arguments sake, let's say that you weren't like me, or like everyone else you met at Equinox the other night . . . even if you weren't like us, just the fact that you've already started to see what we're capable of means it's real. So, knowing that, shouldn't you be able to trust that I'm right about you, and that this is part of who you are?" When I hesitated, she smiled and jumped up off the couch, throwing her half-eaten egg roll in an empty container on the coffee table. "Exactly. Come on, help me move this."

We moved her coffee table to the side of the room and she shut off the TV, directing me to sit on the floor with my legs crossed. She placed incense in burners around the room and lit them, closing each shade as she passed by. Then she handed me a tall white candle on a small plate with a flowery pattern on it. "Light it," she said, handing me a lighter.

"It's about to get all kinds of supernatural up in here," I said, lighting the candle and putting it down in front of me.

She dimmed the lights and sat down on the couch behind me. Her voice had changed from its usual playfulness to one of seriousness. "I wouldn't call magic supernatural; it's as natural as the sun, or the trees that the sun beats down on. Casting magic is nothing more than connecting with the Universe's energy. It's a force that's everywhere. It's woven into everything and everyone. To me, there's nothing more natural than that."

I closed my eyes and inhaled the sweet, yet slightly overpowering, smell of the incense.

"The only difference between us and everyone else is that we have the ability to tap into that power. If you're going to be able to do that, you have to give yourself up to the Universe's energy—believe in it and let it become part of you." Her voice started flowing in a hypnotic tone. "Now, stare at the flame of the candle while I talk. Relax and don't fight your thoughts. Let them enter your mind and exit without causing you to pause."

"What if I have to pee?"

"Shhh." She threw a fortune cookie at my back and tried to keep herself from laughing. "Just relax, Hat, and listen to me while I read this to you." She turned on a small sound machine from the side table and subtle sounds of a rain storm trickled out.

Speaking softly, she said, "Feel the ground beneath you, the rock of the Earth, holding you so steady that you know you could never fall. Hear the sounds of the rain, and picture it falling down around you, your constant connection with the Universe in its most illustrious form. Smell the incense as it's carried by the wind past you, a breeze so much like love; it's always there, but rarely able to be seen. And know the fire in front of you, an everlasting flame and symbol of your power, the power of a Caster, to affect the things around you with your will alone. Earth, water, air and fire—these elements combine into the fabric of desire. They are ultimate and unwavering, and a gentle reminder that few things are out of your reach."

"Could I use it to bring my mother back?" I asked sadly, breaking the hypnotic vibe she'd cast into the room.

Liv joined me on the floor, pulled me into a hug, and kissed me softly on the cheek. "If Casters had the ability to cheat death, the world would be filled with people we just couldn't let go because we loved them too much. It's intentional, I think, that we don't have the power to alter everything."

"I don't think I can do this," I said, trying to push the thoughts of my mother out of my head.

"Sure you can. It's in your blood," she said simply. "Just don't force it. Relax. Just be. The connection will come easily if you let it." She stood up and returned to her seat behind me.

The smell of incense started to give me a headache, and the more I focused on just the candle, the less relaxed I felt. Liv started talking again, telling me more about magic in her soothing tone, and bringing the hypnotic waves back into the room.

Then, for a moment, I let myself just be. I started to ponder each flicker of the candle, letting its gradient light dominate my focus. Its flame would sway, and my body would sway with it. As it burned, the wick let off little sparks into the wax, getting louder until it eventually drowned out the sound machine, Liv, and my own breathing. The room around me was insignificant, and any thought I had that wasn't about that candle floated through my mind untouched.

A warm energy washed over me, pouring down from above and touching me at my core. It was in my veins, pumping life through me like it pumped life through the Universe itself. It was pain and it was beauty. It was infinitely mysterious, yet immediately familiar. I was at peace, accepting the Universe for being both chaotic and orderly; kind and equally cruel, just as it accepted me for everything I was, and more importantly, everything I wasn't.

A familiar cold sweat returned, like someone was melting an ice cube on my neck and letting it run down my back. It was just a little easier that time, maybe because of the meditative state that Liv had put me in. I was aware and connected to my body, the vessel that contained my power, in ways that I never thought possible and at the same time, comfortable letting the vision pull me away from it.

My stomach still churned as I was bombarded with all the lights and noises, but the less I fought it, and the more I realized that it was real, the less I worried it might actually tear me apart. I let it toss me, turn me, and ripple through me until I reached that moment of weightlessness and serenity.

"Shit, this hurts," Gloria said to my mother, sitting down next to her and pointing to a cut on her hand. Her light blond hair and freckles glowed in the sun of the day. It was summer and they were relaxing on Gloria's deck—probably their favorite place to be together. My mother looked beautiful in her sunflower-patterned dress, and sipped on a large cup of coffee, feeding an addiction she and I shared.

"Let me see it." My mother took Gloria's hand in hers and examined the cut. "And this is why you shouldn't put small razor blades in your junk drawer, Gloria."

"Ouch," Gloria yelled as my mother pinched her cut closed and cupped her hand around Gloria's. My mother closed her eyes and a light smile washed over her lips. When she pulled her hand back, the cut was gone.

"Nice," Gloria said, examining her hand where the cut once was. My mother just smiled and shrugged, modest and serene as always.

From the other side of the deck, I appeared. I vaguely remembered that day, or at least I remembered my mother in that dress. The only way I can describe how it feels to watch yourself, in third person, move around in a vision is that it's like watching a home movie.

"Hey, there," I said, kissing both of them on the cheek as they swung lightly on the deck's swing.

"Hey, son. How are you?" my mother asked. I missed hearing her voice every day so much.

"Eh. Good. Going to get some coffee. Want any?" They shook their heads and I made my way into the house, but my vision stayed with them.

Avoiding my mother's glance, Gloria said, "Don't."

"I didn't say anything," my mother said.

"But I know what you're thinking, and we aren't having this conversation again."

"You're right, I know. Just sometimes I wonder if all we did was postpone the inevitable," my mother said. The knuckle from her free hand's pointer finger was grazing over her eyebrow, her classic tell of inner turmoil.

"Is that part of the conversation we aren't having?"

My mother sighed as she watched me through the window as I made coffee, oblivious to a world that was paralleling my own in secret.

"Mia, stop torturing yourself. We did what we had to do for our family. They're safer this way."

"Maybe. Or maybe they would have been safer if we just let them become whomever the Universe decided they would be, not what we decided we wanted them to be."

My aunt crossed her arms and lowered her voice. "I can't believe it's been almost thirty years and you're still questioning this. Do you really want that life for our kids? All the sacrifice. The hiding. The pain. No, it's enough already. That's why we took their powers. It ends with us, that's what we all said."

The flame of the candle in front of me had died out on its own by the time I came back from that vision. I looked around sensitively, still sunken in a deep fog, and rubbed my temples. The lights and noises that carried me to and from those visions had lingering aftereffects I still wasn't used to.

Was that real? I wondered. Could my mother have been a Caster too? I closed my eyes tight, desperately trying to hold onto the image of her. But the woman I was looking at, the one I thought I knew so well, had just shown me how little I really knew.

Chapter 11

That afternoon, I passed my street without even considering going home, and aimlessly tried to make sense of my new world. I drove around the city in circles and thought about all the wild things that had happened to me in the past few days. I couldn't stop wondering if when my mother and Gloria took that piece of my life, an important piece, it had forever made me feel fragmented and unsure of who I was. It was as if nothing I experienced before I met Liv was real, like everything in my life before was a lie, or the least fulfilling part of the truth.

For the first time, not feeling normal felt like the most natural thing in the world to me. Could that mean that Liv was right and being a Caster was part of who I was, or who I was supposed to be? In the nonsense, things were starting to make sense. I felt different, like a part of me that was empty had been filled, and I liked it.

At one point, I passed St. Albert's, a large Catholic church with a small private school extending off the back. I knew both places well; I had attended that school through the sixth grade.

I hated that place.

I tried closing my eyes as I passed it, but only succeeded in nearly hitting the mail truck parked on the street in front of the church.

Good one, Hat.

Eventually, my drive took me out of the city. I was far enough out that the houses had space for lush trees around them and bigger backyards behind them. The air had turned crisp and the year's first light frost was glazing over the green grass of the neighborhood lawns.

Gloria had a modest home there, and I circled her block four or five times before finally parking. Her perfectly manicured lawn rolled up and down the sides of the cobblestone pathway that wrapped around the house. When I rounded the corner, I found her sitting there on her deck, wrapped in a large fleece blanket and reading a book.

"Coffee?" she asked without looking up at me.

"Sure," I said with a happy nod. For a brief moment, it felt like nothing was different. It was like my mother hadn't died, there were no secrets dwelling in the air between us, and she was the matriarch of our family whom I trusted implicitly. But none of that was true anymore.

Two of her well-groomed cats scampered past my feet as I sat down at her kitchen table, poured some sugar into my coffee, and leaned back against the glass picture window that encased the nook. A picture of my mother and my aunt, one I'd never seen before, was sitting on the edge of her table. I picked it up and smiled. They looked so happy.

Gloria sat down next to me with her own overflowing coffee mug. "I miss her, too," she said.

"I know."

Gloria let out a long sigh. "Do you think there is any chance I can convince you to forget what you know so far and go back to your life before?" she asked.

"How could you even know what I came here to talk to you about?" I asked.

"It doesn't matter how I know." Gloria reached out and gently touched my face. "But I know."

"Did you really think you were going to be able to keep this from me forever?" I asked.

"Well . . . we have for over twenty years, so yes. That was the plan at least. I'm sorry you had to find out this way, or at all. It shouldn't have happened like this," Gloria said, before sipping her coffee.

I rubbed my eyes as the contacts in them had dried out from too many hours of wear and said, "And what was your plan for when I found out I had powers?"

"You don't understand, you shouldn't have ever gotten powers. We cast a spell when you all were young, this sort of suppression spell, that should have meant you never had to deal with this. We were trying to remove magic and all the problems that come with it from our family entirely."

"What changed?"

"I wish I knew, Hat. I really do. We didn't want this life for you."

"I can't believe this," I said. I wasn't sure I wanted that life for myself either, but if she'd had it her way, I wouldn't have even gotten the choice.

Gloria's eyes were heavy as she filled her mug with more coffee. "I'm sorry you're upset, but nothing about this is as simple as you're making it sound. This is the way it had to be to keep you safe."

"Safe from what?"

Gloria sat down in the chair closest to me and took hold of my hand. "Being like us, Hat—having the ability to use magic—it's an amazing gift, beautiful really, but it can also be dangerous and a tragic burden. We cast that spell so that magic wouldn't ruin your lives."

"But you took away my right to choose," I said, shaking my head. "I could have been a totally different person. Maybe I wouldn't be normal, but hell, I might have been happy. You don't know. You didn't even give me a chance to find out."

"That's not fair. Magic has always been part of who this family is, and it wasn't an easy decision to get rid of it. But technology was advancing so fast that it was becoming impossible for people like us to keep our identities a secret. Our family was changing too, we kept getting bigger and bigger, and it was getting to be too hard to protect all the children. And there were just so many things we had to keep you safe from."

"But Mom regretted that decision. I know she did. I saw it."

"She was with us when we cast those spells, Hat," she said, without looking at me. "We all made the decision together, even though it was hard, and we stuck with it. Did your mom question it sometimes? Of course. I think we all have at one point or another. But it didn't matter because the safety of this family was our first priority. And there isn't any use in us fighting over a decision that was made a lifetime ago. What matters now is what happens next."

"No, I think what matters now is that the two people I trusted most out of the whole world lied to me about who I was for my entire life. Now my mom's dead and it's like I never knew her, or you for that matter. I wish I could describe how terrible that feels." I crossed my arms, doubting nearly everything I'd ever believed about my family, doubt that I could see stung Gloria worse than anything else I could say or do.

"Listen to me. You have a right to be mad. You have the right to be a lot of things. Hate me for it if you have to. I can take it. What I can't take is worrying that you won't be alive long enough to forgive me. You have to promise me you'll keep yourself and this family safe by keeping this all a secret."

"What does that mean, exactly? I just forget what's been happening to me? I go back to being normal? Or, not even normal, I go back to being me—whatever that was. I don't know what's happening, but I do know that I've spent my whole life searching for something that I thought was missing without knowing what it was. And now, maybe for the first time ever, I feel like I might have found it. I might for once be where I'm supposed to be. And I don't want to give that up."

"I know how easy it can be to let yourself get sucked into this world. I really do. Magic can make you feel like a whole different person, like you can stand on the top of the world and name yourself the king of it. But it comes with a price and it's not a fair trade. Trust me that there are things going on out there that you don't see. Dangerous things. I can't even begin to tell you the number of threats that are waiting out there for Casters, the number of people who would kill us for just being who we are. If you expose your powers, you're not just risking your life, your risking all of our lives. The only way to keep this family safe is to keep everything you know a secret."

There was a long silence as I tried to process everything she was telling me, or not telling me. Could I trust that anything she was saying was true after what I'd found out? "Are secrets the only solution?" I finally asked.

"Secrets hold this family together."

* * * * *

Sleep was like gold, and I had not enough of either. My habit of tossing and turning had gotten so bad that Cat openly refused to share my bed anymore. That morning, there was still an hour before my alarm would go off and I just laid in bed, staring up at the ceiling, and wishing I could sleep.

My phone started ringing. It did that a lot these days. I loved my family for caring enough to check in on me . . . constantly, but I still wasn't ready to talk to any of them in-depth about anything. Looking at the screen, it said, 'Unknown Number.'

"Yeah, pass," I said aloud.

I'd learned that unknown numbers usually meant the person waiting on the other side was a bill collector. Who knew for what, at that point I had stopped keeping track of them. Despite my extreme work schedule at Cartwright, and the regular shifts at the restaurant, my student loan debt was still crushing me.

It didn't matter though. As a master of avoidance, I had already set up a prerecorded voicemail message, with a nasally voice saying: "This number has been disconnected, please check the number or try your call again later. Code 6759." The message repeated itself about three or four times, just long enough so that the caller wouldn't notice that it dumped into my voicemail eventually. When that tactic stopped working, I'd change my number again.

I gave up on the idea of sleep and shuffled toward the kitchen. I filled my coffee pot with water, the brown stains in the glass not bad enough to make me want to replace it, and dumped it into my overused coffee maker. It made horrible noises as it started, and for a second I contemplated how devastated I would be if it stopped working altogether.

I never slept with a shirt on, so when I walked into the bathroom and turned the harsh overhead light on, the titanium-like metal of my mother's necklace glistened in the mirror.

Wait.

Something looked different, but then again, everything usually did until I put my contacts in. I settled for shoving on my glasses and pulled the necklace up to the mirror to study it. I had seen the necklace on my mother at least a thousand times, and the stone was the same, of that I was certain. But the setting, the setting was different.

Am I crazy? Is it a different necklace?

The mesh petals that had once delicately held the stone in place around my mother's neck were gone. In their place, five solid flames surrounded the gem, erupting out from behind it. The chain was different too; it was shorter and thicker, and it pulled the setting closer to my neck. It looked like something I would have picked out for myself, like it was made just for me and wouldn't look good on anyone else.

What is this? I wondered. Why had it changed? How had it changed? Why was it that every time I looked at it, the pattern of colors seemed to be just a little different? I dropped the necklace, and rolled my neck, trying to jump-start my brain and wake up a little more. Its magical transformation was remarkable, but also maddening as yet another secret my mother had kept from me came to light.

Then, a coldness that even the deepest of New England winters couldn't bring crept from the stone and onto my skin. A shallow glow formed below the stone, with the lightest tones of turquoise juxtaposed against a darker blue and green background. It created a jagged texture in the stone like sand wet from tears.

The colors started moving freely as the cold spread to the air around me. Each calming breath I took produced visible condensation in the air and did nothing to calm me. Was the necklace alive? The temperature, the glowing, the movement of colors—they were all superficial. Beyond them, beneath them, the necklace was connecting with me. There was power in it, and I could feel the energy weave through my body, fusing itself to every molecule within me.

The energy grew, moved from the stone into me, and then exploded out into the world. I watched as it destroyed my bathroom. Anything that once stood erect was knocked over. The mirror shattered slightly in the corners. The faucet turned on. Even the shower curtain and the rod it was attached to came crashing down.

I ran from the bathroom, pulled the necklace off my neck and tossed it into the chair. Just as I did, the door to my apartment swung open and my landlord barreled in with a large package from his fish market.

"Hey, Hat. Just some stuff I thought you might like," he said, dropping the package on my kitchen table. He was a nice enough guy, and often gave me free fish to make up for the fact that he couldn't do anything about the house always smelling like it. But right then, as I faced a necklace with a life of its own, I couldn't have cared less about him, fish, or eating ever again.

"Thanks. You can just leave it there," I finally said.

If he saw my panicked look as I stared at the chair, he didn't say anything. Instead, he just smiled and left. But I hardly noticed because I couldn't keep my eyes off that necklace. It had stopped glowing, but even though it wasn't close enough to touch, I could still feel it with me.

A final gust of cold air brushed by me. With it were voices in the distance. They sounded further away than I should have been able to hear but had taunting clarity.

"Murder," they said.

Chapter 12

"*What is that doing there?*"

When I got home from work on Friday, my mother's locked book sat in the middle of my favorite chair, a place I hadn't put it before I left. Cat was sleeping on top of it and had his face pressed firmly against the leather. He gave an ungrateful hiss when I picked up the book and sat down with it.

"Did you put this here?" I asked him as he repositioned himself at my feet.

With everything else that had been happening, I had forgotten all about that book. That locked book. That locked book that didn't have a keyhole.

Is this what my life is now?

Scissors, a knife, a screwdriver, a lighter, unabated pulling and swearing—nothing would break those straps. They were thin and didn't look all that special, but they took a beating for over an hour and didn't even fray at the edges. After another hour of continued failure, I grumbled and fell into my chair in frustration.

I spent the rest of the weekend scouring every corner of the internet to try to find a way to open it. There was nothing to show me how to open a lock without a keyhole, but I did learn everything you never wanted to know about the lock-making process.

The best bet I could make was an antiques dealer I read about on Wickenden Street. He sold old clocks, locks, and socks. No, seriously. That's what it said.

Later in the week, I snuck away from work to find him. Wickenden Street was in a funky area of the east side that had every assortment of eccentric stores within it. The antique shop sat on a misshapen side street with a carved wooden sign above the door that read, "Oddities" in a thick script text. The sign was at such a bad angle that you would have never seen the store if you weren't looking for it. It could have been intentional.

The storefront was small. If you took a normal store and cut it in half, Oddities was no larger than that store's closet. Shelves hung from every open space on the walls from floor to ceiling, with random knickknacks, clocks, books, and dusty wooden figurines filling every square inch of them. Nothing said "antique" to me, unless it was meant in that pleasantly derogatory way people call old junk "antiques."

The room was so tight that if you stood squarely in the middle, you could touch the shelves on either side with your hands. It was dark, too, the only natural light coming from behind the dirty shade on the door. The door tapped a bell above it when I opened it, but only made a thud. It looked like the clapper had either been removed or had just fallen out from old age, but its string still dangled uselessly inside the bell.

An old man with small, round glasses and patchy pockets of white hair around his ears didn't bother to look up when

I entered, nor did he say anything as I approached his tall wooden workbench. Small pieces of metal were strewn about around him, and his miniature hands were working to solder two of them together. He sat atop a wobbly stool, which poorly concealed his considerable lack of height.

"Yes?" he asked curtly when I'd gotten closer to him. He still didn't look up.

"Um . . . I was wondering if you could help me with something."

He adjusted his glasses and continued working on his scrap metal. "I'm not here to help. I'm here to sell. You buyin'?"

"I have this book," I said, putting my cell phone in front of him. A picture of my mother's book was zoomed in on the display. "It's locked and I can't I figure out how to open it." When he didn't look at the phone right away, I slid it closer to him with my finger.

"Have you tried using a key?" He dropped his metal project and held a small pane of stained glass up to the light, squinting into it.

A key! Why didn't I think of that? "That's the thing, it doesn't have a keyhole."

That got his attention, and he finally looked at me before inquisitively picking up the phone to examine the picture. "A lock without a keyhole, eh? Interesting." He pulled his head back so he could look at the phone through his glasses on the edge of his nose without moving them, his bushy white eyebrows curving around his biting eyes.

"Have you ever seen something like this?" I asked.

He put the phone back down and picked up another piece of glass without looking at me. "Nope. Can't help ya."

"Are you sure? I've been trying to find something online about it but haven't had any luck."

He muttered something under his breath and then said, "I doubt you'll find anything about that lock on one of those damn computers."

"So, you do know what it is?"

"Listen kid, that book isn't yours, and I won't be the one who helps you open it." He got up from his stool and went into the corner to look at something under a large magnifying glass.

"But," I looked to the cash register and read from the small nameplate on the front, "Mr. Withers, the thing is, it was my mother's, and she's . . . she passed away recently."

He looked up again, tilting his head and peering into my eyes. "Hmmm."

He made his way toward a door at the back of the store, behind the workbench. "Most things are locked for a reason, kid. Better to just keep them that way."

"Oh . . . I understand," I said as I tip-toed toward him, "sorry to bother you . . . I'd read you were sort of an expert on these things. I didn't think you wouldn't know how to open it."

He stormed around his workbench, threw his foot up on a lower shelf, and pulled himself up to my height. "If I told you it was a blood lock would you even know what that was? No, you wouldn't. Don't come here and tell me what I do and don't know, when you clearly know nothing. So fine, it's called a blood lock. You happy now?"

"What does that mean, a blood lock?" I asked, taking a step backward and hitting the shelves behind me.

He hopped off the shelf and went back to his bench. "It's exactly what it sounds like, kid. The blood of the person who sealed it is the only thing that can open it. Good luck with that."

"Seriously? Can you step back over here into reality with me for a moment, please?"

He jumped off the stool again and wobbled on his tiny legs to the back of the store, grumbling before disappearing behind the door and slamming it shut. Things were being thrown around aggressively from the other side of the door, and I could hear them bounce off the walls and even break from where I was standing.

"Do you have this in blue?" I yelled to him, holding up a tattered leather bag from one of the shelves.

* * * * *

"What . . . the . . . fuck," I said to Cat when I got home from a grueling day on Friday. He was sleeping on my bed, on top of my mother's book, where again, I hadn't left it. This time, the necklace was placed neatly on top of it. Last I checked, that was still in the chair after I refused to put it back on.

Resigned, I put the necklace back around my neck and sat down on the bed. "What do you want from me?" I said to the necklace as if it could respond. "The damn thing won't open."

I stroked the course leather of the book and thought about my mother, and how very little I actually knew about her. Her powers, the necklace, that damn book. "I guess if you wanted other people to open it, you would have opted for a regular lock," I said to no one alive.

Shit. Not again, I thought, as that cold sweat started dripping down my spine. I tried to let it just wash over me again, and my lack of fighting made it a bit easier. The lights and noises were almost manageable, and for the first time, I could barely feel the churning in my stomach. By the time I had gotten to a place of serenity, a new vision unfolded.

"I think it's in my book," my mother said to her brother Kevin. She couldn't have been much older than eighteen. She was in someone's kitchen and her hands were stained green as she messed with a heap of herbs and leaves in a big bowl.

Kevin slammed the small leather book I couldn't open on the table and grunted, *"Mia, the book's locked."*

I had never met Kevin—he died before I was born. He was a few years older than my mother, so was maybe twenty-one, twenty-two in that vision. His chocolate brown eyes, which everyone said were like my grandfather's, twinkled from the sunlight in a nearby window.

"Calm down, will ya? You're so impatient," my mother said, rolling her eyes. *"Besides, you were with me when I bought it. You know how to open it."*

"So you want me to cut you to get some blood?" Kevin smiled and said, *"Done."*

Kevin passed by the knives and rummaged around the kitchen for something smaller to cut with. As he bent over a drawer, the necklace he was wearing slipped out from under his shirt. But it wasn't just any necklace . . . it was my necklace. Or my mother's necklace. Or whoever's necklace. In any case, it was the same necklace, but it was in a completely different setting. His setting was all gold, with a flat back that wrapped around the stone like talons.

"Cut yourself!" my mother said, moving away from him. *"You're family, your blood is as good as mine."*

"You'll still love me when I get committed, right?" I said, reaching down and rubbing Cat's back as I came out of the vision.

He paid little attention to me as he played with something in the carpet. "What is that?" I pushed him away and picked up a small sewing needle. "Seriously? Where did you even find this?"

You talk to your cat like he'll respond way too often.

I pricked my finger with the needle and pinched it to let the blood drip out slowly onto the plate that locked the book. Nothing happened.

That didn't make me feel stupid at all.

I brought my finger to my mouth and sucked the last bit of blood off it and used the sleeve from my other arm to wipe the blood off the book's lock. As it spread around, I heard a clicking sound and four buckles popped out from below the plate, loosening the four straps. I eagerly tugged at the lock, and it pulled off easily, but anticlimactically so, because the book was nearly empty.

"Are you freakin' kidding me?"

On the first page, one line of text in my mother's familiar handwriting said: "Test not the force of a Caster's power, but the reach of their heart."

Seriously, Mom? I thought as I continued to flip through it, hoping to find something else written. All that trouble for one line of text. The only other things in the book at all were a few pictures stuffed in the back.

One of them was of a little girl, maybe three or four, sitting on my aunt's deck, with a big hat blocking her face from the bright sunlight. It could have been Charley or Sydney; they looked so much alike when they were babies. I turned it over and the year written in the corner meant it had to be Charley.

Damn it.

Another sweat formed, despite the last not even being gone yet, and I was tumbled into another vision.

> *"What do you want, Camille?" my mother asked in a scathing tone. Her sister was in the doorway with a toddler-sized Charley asleep against her chest. They were both wet from the rain that poured down relentlessly outside. My mother had an abnormally large stomach, something all the Walker women faced when they got pregnant. With Charley there, it meant my mother was pregnant with Finn.*
>
> *"So you're still mad at me?" Camille asked, pushing herself into the house.*
>
> *"Does it matter? It doesn't change anything."*
>
> *Camille laid the sleeping and still wet Charley down on the couch and sat next to her. "I'm sorry, Mia. Really. I am. I was just in a bad place and I guess . . ."*
>
> *"What do you want, Cam?" my mother rubbed her stomach, "I've got a lot of other stuff going on here."*
>
> *Camille squeezed her wet hair and let it drip onto my mother's floor. "I want you to forgive me."*
>
> *"Okay. Fine. You're forgiven. Is that all?"*
>
> *"You don't sound like you mean it."*
>
> *"That's because I don't mean it, Cam. You slept with my husband while we were still married, and then you lied to me about it for years. Then, only after he walks out on my family do you decide to clear your conscience and tell me about it." She lowered herself onto her favorite rocking chair with*

a grunt. "Now your conscience is clear, so you can go and leave me be."

"I'm sorry."

My mother didn't respond. It was rare that she'd talk when there was nothing to be said, but her eyebrows were ragged and thin from worry.

"I need you to take Charley for a while," Camille said.

"Wait. What?"

"I just can't handle her right now with everything else that's going on."

"You're seriously trying to leave your child here with me right now? After everything? I . . . you've got to be kidding. You will seriously never change."

"Please Mia. I wasn't supposed to be a mother. I'm not good at it."

"Then you should have been less good at laying on your back."

Camille walked back to the door, leaving Charley on the couch. "She should be with her brothers and sister."

I was only about five when the events of that vision unfolded. Back then, I woke up one morning and Charley was sleeping in Sydney's room. A few days later Finn was born. Charley never left, and that became life as we knew it. The identity of Charley's father had always been a mystery to all of us, including her.

"Cat, call Jerry Springer."

Chapter 13

"Wait, so she's your sister and your cousin? That's awesome," Liv said that night when we walked into Equinox. "I had no idea big families were like this. I have a brother, but both my parents were only children. I always thought we were screwed up, but you Walkers are so . . . delightfully twisted."

"That's us, twisted like a Twizzler but usually not as sweet," I said.

"Look," Liv pointed at the stage as we started walking up the stairs. A small crew of men were scurrying around, pulling cords, and turning on lights. "They're setting up for some live music. I bet it'll be good."

"Hey kids," Elle said from the bar as we walked into the lounge. She swayed over, Blue Ice in hand, and wrapped her arm around my waist. "We didn't scare you away?"

"Not yet," I whispered into her ear and smiled. Liv rolled her eyes, flopped herself onto one of the couches next to Cooper, and started talking to him.

Elle was saying something to me, but I was distracted by Cooper, who I watched intently over her shoulder. I didn't remember noticing the first time we met just how slim and well-proportioned his body was, a feature he hardly kept hidden underneath his tight shirt. His broad shoulders and rounded jaw line made him look like someone who should be in magazines rather than running some little bar in Providence. It was also impossible not to see as he sat next to Liv what an attractive couple they made.

His eyes moved to mine and I didn't look away fast enough. "Everything alright?" he asked, raising his eyebrows.

"Yup. Great," I said. My face felt crimson with embarrassment, and I knew there was no way he didn't notice it.

Did I just check him out?

Justin, who I elected president of my unofficial fan club, was at the bar when I fled there to get a drink. I started to say something, but he walked away without acknowledging my existence. My subconscious need to have people like me took over for a second and I thought about chasing after him and bartering for his friendship, but before I could, the lights went dim and music began to emanate from the stage.

I joined the others on the balcony to enjoy the view; not only the great view of the stage, but of the less privileged people, packed together in the main room of the bar like teens at a boy-band concert. By then, the overhead lights had gone out completely, and the only movement or sound came from the dark shadows of the band shuffling into their places on the stage.

The band started and the crowd roared in anticipation, including all of us on the balcony. Their sound was unique; combining spurts of flute with solid rock and an addicting tempo. The flutist, the only girl in the band, also sang, creating a harmonic, truly original sound with the lead singer.

"What band is this?" I asked, yelling as loud as I could but barely hearing myself over the music.

"They're called Bluish," Cooper yelled back. "The lead singer is a friend of mine from school."

Everyone was in high spirits as the band electrified the room with its sound. They were so captivating that they had already played a half dozen songs before I noticed that my drink was empty. So I ducked back into the lounge for more Blue Ice.

As soon as I closed the glass door behind me, I could sense something was wrong. An unusual, but distinct smell like burnt paper and starch was in the air. One of the small cocktail tables next to the bar was tipped over and a chair next to it broken. At the end of the bar, where the counter angled and anchored itself into the wall, I saw a clear liquid pooling and slowly flowing out into the room.

A spilled drink?

Instinctively, I grabbed a dry towel from one of the cocktail tables to clean it up with, and continued my cautious stride toward the bar. The closer I got, the more of it I saw, and in turn, the slower I walked. The puddle's origin came from behind the bar, and slowly washed out onto the floor. I moved closer, and my unwelcome suspicions were confirmed, it was blood. A lot of blood.

It took everything I had, and more that I didn't have, to pull myself up on the unsteady stools and peer behind the bar. There was a body. God how I wished it wasn't a body. Justin was lying on his back, his lifeless eyes rolled up into his head and his limbs bent savagely in different directions, like a doll that had been thrown carelessly on the bed.

His shirt was pulled up to his chin, revealing his skinny, pale body. And the worst sight yet was the unsteady asterisk carved into his chest, just above his stomach. The small folds of flesh from the wound were serrated and black ash colored. They were so deep that you could see the bone of his ribcage reflected back from deep inside the wound against what little light was coming from the stage in the other room.

Horrified seems like such a mild word compared to how I felt. I didn't know whether to yell or run, pass out or throw up. I jumped off the stool and around the bar, splashing into the blood on the floor. I took hold of his wrist to check his pulse, and even though I had never seen a dead body outside of a casket, or checked anyone's pulse for that matter, I knew he was dead. Who can survive when the contents of their skeleton are exposed and all of their blood has spilled out around them?

From inside my shirt, I felt my necklace start to grow cold. The air around us was chilling, and a wind blowing directly from the necklace wafted over both of us. I pulled it from my shirt and watched the stone closely as the colors began moving freely again, uninhibited by my movements or my observation.

My hand was growing numb and when I exhaled, my breath frosted, and floated in front of me. The colors started moving faster, shifting erratically like hyperactive organisms under a microscope. They would clump together and move around each other for a moment, only to break apart, shift, and start all over again. The mellow glow followed and danced delicately behind them, a dance that moved to the hollow beat of weather-torn wind chimes in a rough winter blizzard.

"What happened?" a voice beside me asked.

I turned around and there was Justin . . . again. His body was still immobile on the floor, the position you'd expect any dead person to stay in, but his fully formed ghost was also standing next to me. His ghost looked so alive that if it weren't for his corporeal body beside me, I wouldn't have even been able to tell he was dead.

"Justin? How . . ." I didn't know what to even ask.

The music downstairs was still so loud I could barely hear anything Justin said. But it didn't matter. As the cold of the necklace ran through me, the powers of it made it so I could feel everything Justin felt. The necklace was tethering me to him, passing all the thoughts and emotions from his ghost back through it.

His confusion was overwhelming, especially as it magnified my own. It flowed into me with smatterings of fear and anger and tears started to form in the corner of my eyes.

"What happened?" he asked, looking around.

"I don't know," I said. "I'm sorry. I just found you . . . I'm sorry."

The feeling of someone else's emotions overriding your own was purely uncanny. And the dislike I always thought Justin had for me became blatantly clear with our connection. He didn't care about me, why I was there, or what I was doing. He just felt so damn confused about his death, and I was nothing more than a spectator.

"Where is he?" he asked, looking around again.

"Who?" I asked.

"The man without a face."

"What?"

"The man without a face," he yelled while looking at his dead body. "He did this. He came out of nowhere and did this. The man without a face."

"What does that mean? He didn't have a face?"

Justin's confusion melted into more anger: anger at me, anger at a man without a face, anger at a life that he had just been robbed of. It intensified, sending shockwaves through the necklace and into my arm. The sensation was so acute that I started shaking.

Then images I had never seen started appearing in my head. Justin as a happy child. Justin's first kiss. The first time Justin met Cooper. In under a minute, a lifetime's worth of memories flashed through my mind. It was so fast it was impossible to process, and I felt like I could implode at any moment just from the weight of them.

I yelled, pulled the necklace from my neck, and threw it across the room. It clanked against the wall and fell to the floor. When I looked back, Justin's ghost was gone. I was still crouched next to his body, shrouded in disbelief at what had just happened, but our connection had been severed.

"Oh my god," Elle yelled from behind me. "What did you do? Hat? What did you do?"

"It wasn't me," I yelled back, pulling myself up out of the pool of blood, "I found him like this."

"Justin!" Elle screamed to him, pushing past me to fall to the ground and shake him. "Come on baby, wake up."

"Elle . . . he's dead."

"Shut up! Just shut up," she yelled back to me, crying hysterically and holding Justin's head in her lap. "Not like this. No. Not like this. Come on Justin, wake up." Her screams rose to a volume that rivaled the band's, loud enough to signal the others to come rushing in from the balcony.

"What's going on?" Cooper asked calmly. He looked down at Justin, then at me covered in his blood, before shaking his head.

"I found him like this!" I said.

Cooper turned to Liv and nodded at me. She walked toward me, and her heels sloshed through the blood. Without a word, she grabbed my chin gently but firmly with her thumb and first two fingers. Her eyes locked on mine, and they squinted, shifted, and widened in repetitive succession.

"What are you doing?" I asked.

"Shhh. This will be easier if you just relax," she whispered without breaking eye contact.

Pressure started building in my temples and I could almost hear Liv rummaging around in my head, like someone who's cleaning out the attic while you're asleep in the room below it. It was unsettling, and violating, and completely out of my control.

"Stop fighting me," Liv said, except she didn't say it out loud. I could hear her voice inside my head. "Just let me see what happened."

The pressure increased until I winced. I couldn't tell what she was looking at, but it was like she was reaching out at me with her mind to tear open my consciousness and explore my thoughts. A few minutes more of silence and she finally broke eye contact and turned to Cooper. "It wasn't him," she said.

"I told you it wasn't me," I said, pushing her hand away and shooting dirty looks at all of them.

"We had to be sure," Cooper said.

The giant with the shaved head who guarded the door came up the stairs and Cooper turned to him with little expression and asked, "What do we do with him?"

"I'll take care of it," the giant said.

"What does that mean?" I yelled.

"Don't worry yourself over it," Cooper said, turning to whisper something to the giant.

"This is ridiculous. Beyond ridiculous. What's a word that's beyond ridiculous? That's what this is. I can't believe we're standing over a dead man's body and you're telling me you're going to 'take care of it.' We have to call the police, or an ambulance, or someone."

Liv pulled me into the private bathroom off the main room and started stripping me of my bloody clothes. "We can't stay here," she said. She ran paper towels under warm water and washed some of the blood off my arms. I was too shaken up to care, or notice, that she was seeing and touching my naked body.

"What did he mean when he said he'd take care of it?" I asked.

"I don't know exactly."

"Liv, this is serious. We have to call the police."

"They can't do anything with this, Hat. And even if they could, it's dangerous for them to know who we are. We just have to let Cooper handle it however he handles it." She wrapped me in a short blanket that usually hung off the back of one of the lounge's chairs and stuffed my bloody clothes in a plastic bag.

We came out of the bathroom and most of the Caster crowd was gone. The giant was moving Justin's body, and Liv handed the bag of my bloody clothes to Cooper. He looked at me, but said nothing more.

"Do you want this?" Liv asked, holding up my necklace as we walked toward the exit.

I hesitated. After what the necklace had done, after the way it made me feel when it connected me to Justin's ghost, I wanted nothing more than to leave it for someone else to find. Maybe then I could pretend I didn't know what it could do and forget what had happened.

Instead, I said a quick "Yes" and took it from her.

We left the club through the back entrance minutes later, saying nothing to anyone. We may have left my bloody clothes, a lifeless body, and the truth behind, but the dark veils of death danced with us even after we were miles away.

"It's not right," I said as Liv's SUV sped through the city. "He was just murdered in there and they're acting like nothing happened. What happens when it's me next, or you? Are they just going to toss our bodies in a car and dump us somewhere?"

"I don't know," she said.

Chapter 14

There was nothing to say, and we sat in silence as Liv steered us through the dark side streets of the city. Justin was dead, and the gruesome symbol carved into his chest would forever be carved in my memory. My hand still felt cold from holding the necklace, and my insides felt cold from the emotions his ghost left behind.

When Liv dropped me off, my street was darker than it should have been. Broken street lights in an area of the city that few want to live in were of very little concern to people who matter enough to get them fixed. They made it impossible to see the shadow-like figure hunched over on the house's stoop, until I walked past it and it let out a raspy cough.

"Jesus, Auntie," I yelled, jumping and trying to hold on to the only thing covering me, the blanket.

Gloria unwrapped the bundle of scarves her face was hidden beneath. "Sorry Hat, but we need to talk," she said. "Where are your clothes?"

"It's late and I've had a really rough night. Can we do this tomorrow?" I started to walk down the driveway toward my apartment. If she agreed, I'd avoid her for as many days as possible, hoping she'd forget what she wanted to talk to me about in the first place.

Gloria followed me down my driveway and her feet dragged along the cracked pavement. Even in the darkness I could see her eyes burn with worry. "No," she said.

Super. So we're doing this now.

I fumbled through the dark to find my spare key, buying time before we had to start the inevitable conversation. "Let's go inside," I said. I started a pot of coffee and went into the bathroom to find clothes to put on.

"I'm really worried about you, Hat," Gloria yelled to me. "You can't keep hanging out at that club."

"How do you even know where I've been hanging out? Are you stalking me now?" I asked as I came out of the bathroom and tried to pull my sweatshirt down past my head.

"It doesn't matter how I know, just that I know. Those kids there, they act like this is all a big game or that magic is just some toy to play with, and it's not. I don't want you to pay for that carelessness," she said.

I poured us two cups of coffee and after shaking a nearly-empty container of milk to listen for chunks, I placed it next to the cups on the table. "A Caster was murdered tonight," I finally said.

"I know," she said.

"How could you possibly know that if they didn't call the police?"

"It doesn't matter how I know, just that I know."

For someone I loved so much, and had always had such high respect for, Gloria was certainly pissing me off. "Huh. Well. What it must be like to know everything. Well, did you know that when I found Justin . . . that's the guy that got murdered . . . when I found him, his ghost started talking to me?"

"No, I didn't. What did he say?"

"I'm not really sure. Something about a man without a face. But you're missing the point. I had a fucking ghost talking to me tonight."

"And you're still missing my point, Hat. Someone got murdered at that club and that is exactly why I don't want you there. Something's going on out there, something big, and whatever it is, it's coming quickly, and I don't want you to get caught up in it when it gets here."

In that moment, I was getting caught up in something else. A cold sweat misted down my back and pulled me rougher and faster than ever into a new vision.

> *"Hurry up," a voice said. The room I was looking at was dark, lit only by the glow of a dim flashlight. There were three, maybe four, men scurrying around the dark room, but I couldn't make out any of their faces.*
>
> *"I don't see it," another voice said.*
>
> *"It has to be somewhere in here," the first voice said. "I didn't just take out those two guards so we could look through her collection of pottery. I want that mask." They spoke in such a hushed tone that I could barely make out the words.*
>
> *"I've got it!" a new voice said, dumping a box of someone's prized possessions out on the ground. He handed the first man a golden mask, which was the only thing in the room I could see clearly. It was petite, almost feminine, with small holes for eyes and a few solid gold beads sporadically decorating it. From the forehead, eccentric gold panels sprouted*

out and formed a headdress above the mask. It looked like it was two pieces with the headdress floating above the mask as if they were unattached.

"Yes!" the first voice said. "That's it. Give it to me." He reached for the mask and pulled it over his face before I could see what he looked like. "Hidden in plain sight," he continued, "with the Mask of Apate."

With his simple words, the mask began to glow brighter than the only flashlight in the room. He removed his hands, but the mask stayed attached to his face, casting clouds of dust up from the ground until nothing could be seen anymore.

When the dust cleared, so had the mask's form and that man's identity. His face was blank. You could still see the contours of it, his nose poking out and his eye sockets sunken, but it was like it was all covered with thin white fabric. He was a breathing blank canvas, and with each movement of his face, wayward charcoal shading would darken those contours as if he was being drawn upon. Then the shading would fade away as quickly as it came, taking with it any defining feature; a sketch erased by its creator.

His hair was full, straight and piercingly white, almost ultraviolet. It framed the mask from forehead to chin, and because I couldn't see him before the mask took over his face, I had no way to know if his hair was naturally like that or if it too was an effect of that mask. Whoever he was, the powers of that mask were keeping his secrets well.

"Let's go," he said.

"What was that?" Gloria asked me when my breathing finally returned to normal.

"It doesn't matter."

"What I need from you right now is a promise, Hat. You have to promise that you'll keep yourself safe by staying away from that club. I'm sorry for all the secrets, but it's the only way."

"Oh? You want to talk more about secrets? Sure. Just how many more little family secrets do I have to look forward to?" I asked.

"What is that supposed to mean?"

"It means that I feel like every other day I find out something more you all kept from me, and I'm sick of it."

"Like what?" Gloria asked, shaking her head.

"Like my dad and Camille."

She coughed into her coffee as she went to take another sip. "I don't know what you're talking about."

"Does Charley know? Does anyone else?"

"I'm not saying that I know what you're talking about . . . because I don't. But if I did, I would say that no one except your mother and Camille knows about that. I'm not even sure your dad knows about it."

My father was a man who had many talents—like being evasive, unpredictable, and sometimes invisible, but being perceptive was never one of them. It wouldn't have surprised me if he had several kids he didn't know about. Usually, *I* felt like a kid he didn't know about.

"I would think you, of all of his kids, could appreciate your mother not wanting to inflict his paternity on anyone else," Gloria said.

"Maybe before I could have, but now I just feel like it's one more thing on a long list of secrets I really wish I didn't know. I can't believe you two would keep that from Charley either. Doesn't she have a right to know who her damn father is, even if he is a jerk?"

I reached up and rubbed my temples. They had begun throbbing with growing intensity as the conversation went on. All I could think about was that if they did explode, at least it would mean I wouldn't have to deal with my family anymore.

"I'm going to tell her," I said.

"Hat, no, you can't."

"Why? Because secrets hold this family together? I don't think that's working as well as you think it is."

"Hat . . ."

"Or are you worried that if I tell that secret, I won't be able to hold any of them in."

"No, I'm worried that you won't be able to handle the secrets you don't know about yet."

* * * * *

The next morning, my phone buzzed itself off the night-stand, waking me up from the first straight hour of sleep I had gotten all night.

"Where are you?" a text message from Sydney asked.

Shit.

I was supposed to be at my cousin's football game. He was in some all-star championship something-or-other game that was advertised as a big deal. I still didn't like the idea of throwing myself into a crowd of Walkers, but it was unquestionably better than sitting around thinking about what had happened the night before. I jumped out of bed and threw on the first clothes I saw.

Cheering roared from the bleachers as I approached the game. My cousin maneuvered around the field in his bright white and grass-stained jersey, dodging the smaller children from the other team as he ran with the ball.

He was the youngest of my first cousins and the last still in high school, but on the bench with his team was another cousin's kid, just a year or two behind him in school. They were victims of what we called the "Walker Effect," where generations naturally overlap and blend together so much that you can't tell where one starts or the other ends. Gloria and her mother, my grandmother, were having kids right around the same time, so Gloria's oldest son was actually a little older than my youngest aunt. Confusing, right? Anyone who wasn't in a big family like ours, which was pretty much everyone, thought so too.

It was always easy to find the Walkers in a crowd. While no one would have stopped us if we wanted to sit in the bleachers with the normal people, we tended to form a pack off to the side in the grass. And that's where I found them, in a sea of folding chairs, coolers, and unnecessarily large blow horns.

The other families, the smaller families, hated us when we went to those games. We were large, loud, and completely unapologetic about it. We'd been attending various sporting events at that field for as long as I could remember, yet we always remained *that* family, the one everyone knew but pretended not to.

"Hi, family," I said as I sat next to Sydney.

"Glad you could make it," Sydney said, throwing me a soda, or more accurately, throwing a soda at me.

"Aww, Syd, don't be mean, I had a crazy night." I kissed her on the cheek.

"Whatever, Hat. We haven't seen you in forever." She was right, it was the first time I had seen any of them since the service. I was a bad brother.

"Uncle!" a cute little voice yelled. Sydney's youngest jumped into my lap and we had a long, in-depth conversation about the salamander he'd found on a nearby rock. He might have been the only Walker who wasn't annoyed with me, so I took full advantage of his attention.

"Where's Charley?" I asked, hoping for some thawing of the cold shoulder I was getting.

Sydney kept her eyes on the game. "Don't know."

Alright then. If you're going to be a bitch, I'm going to leave. I stood up and put my nephew back on the ground with his salamander and his very dirty face.

"Wait," Sydney yelled. She reached into her bag and pulled out a manila envelope. She handed it to me, and its official logo reflected the sunlight; it was from our mother's lawyer, with the same emblem as the envelope the necklace was in.

"I need you to sign these papers before you leave," she said, throwing a pen at me.

"Why do these papers have Charley's name on them?" Victor asked as he emerged from the crowd, his head buried in a similar legal packet. "What's up, Fattie?" he asked, bumping into me as he passed and poking my stomach with his pen. "Looks like you're getting chunky again, kid."

Victor had a way of bringing a sour flavor to my life. The guilt from disliking someone I loved was irksome, but usually tempered by how good I felt whenever he wasn't around. I had gotten used to him not being around. I missed him not being around. Even his name had an acidic taste about it, Victor.

Sydney stood up and massaged her neck. "What's the problem, Victor?"

"Charley," Victor said. "Why's her name on these papers?"

"Because Mom left the house to all of us," Sydney said.

"What do you mean all of us? There's only four of us," Victor said. The ends of his slightly crooked teeth were peeking below his lip as he scowled at her.

"Vic, come on, she's lived with us from the time she was three; she's practically a sister," Sydney said.

Victor chucked the packet onto an open chair. "She's not our sister and this is bullshit," he said.

My eye started twitching and I fantasized about a giant, cartoon-like anvil falling from the sky and smashing Victor into the ground. After what I had been through, after seeing someone murdered, his pettiness around our mother's house was trivial and infuriating.

"It's Mom's house," Sydney said. "She can leave it to whoever she wants."

"It *was* her house," Victor said, before taking Sydney's seat and turning his attention back to the game.

Such an insensitive prick. Victor had only ever been good at two things: mooching from other people and being absolutely nowhere to be found when anyone needed him. So I did what I was good at—I walked away.

"Hat, wait!" Sydney called after me. "Are you seriously going to take off already?"

"I'm sorry, Syd, but I just can't handle this," I waved goodbye to the pack of Walkers, "not right now."

"You know, you're not the only one who lost her."

"I know," I leaned in and gave her a gentle hug, "I'm sorry."

"Don't be sorry. Be here, with us. We need to stick together to get through this. You know that's what Mom would say to you too."

"Or she'd say 'stop being such a damn bitch and just sit down and watch the game,'" Victor said, chomping on a sandwich he'd undoubtedly stolen from someone else's cooler.

"Vic, stop," Sydney said as I started to walk away again. "Hat, wait, I need you to sign those papers."

I tossed the packet over my shoulder, leaving them to soak in the damp grass.

Chapter 15

"Another one," someone said, as they dropped a box off in the copy room. Something had gone wrong with a client's legal case, and the lawyers needed someone special like me to go through hundreds of boxes and find a few missing documents.

At that point, I was already twenty boxes in and still hadn't found it. There were so many boxes stacked in the room that I could no longer see the exit. It was comforting to be surrounded with mountains of paper, with no fire extinguisher, and an exit you can't readily get to.

"Hat, are you in here?" Graham asked from behind the boxes.

"Yup, I'm here," I said, raising my hand so he could see it above the mess.

Graham navigated through the box maze to get to me. "How's it going?" he asked.

I closed the box I was working on and opened another one. "Going as fast as I can," I said.

"No buddy, I know you are. I was just checking to see how it was going. I'm trying to see if there is anyone else that I can pull in to help you."

"It's fine Graham," I said. "I don't have any plans tonight anyway, so I might as well spend it here."

Graham frowned and sat down on a box. "Everything okay?" he asked.

I stopped shuffling through the papers long enough to look up at him. "Everything's fine. Why?"

"You haven't really been yourself for a while now, and I was just wondering if there is something I can do to help."

The edge of a stack of papers gave me a paper cut and then slipped onto the floor as I jerked my hand back. "It's nothing, really. I'm sorry if I seem distracted, I just have had a lot on my mind."

"Hey," he held down the lid on the box I was trying to open, "I'm not asking as a boss who's trying to increase your productivity. I'm asking as your friend who's trying to make sure you're okay. You can trust me, you know that, right?"

"Yeah. I know. It's really nothing though," I said, pulling the box's top open. "I better get back to all this or I'll never finish."

It was already almost 7:00 p.m. when I got to the fiftieth box. I tried to tell myself I was making progress, but for every box I went through, the paralegals dropped off three more. The boxes and I were packed so tight in the copy room that I couldn't even see the screen on my phone when it rang.

"Yes," I said, pushing the Bluetooth headset in my ear.

"Sorry . . . I'm looking for Manhattan Walker?" a man's voice said.

Digging through the piles, I found my phone and read "Unknown Caller" on the display.

Fuck. If this is a bill collector, I'm going to kill someone. No exceptions. No apologies.

"Yeah, this is Hat."

"Right. This is Demarco Sterling, your mother's attorney."

I let out a sigh of relief.

"Listen, I'm sorry to bother you, but did you happen to sign those papers for your mother's house?" he asked. The visual of a large pile of unopened mail on my desk, including the envelope from his office, came into my head.

"I haven't yet. I'm sorry."

"Right. I know things are hard right now, and I certainly don't want to be the one to rush you, but your brother, Victor, keeps calling me and asking if they've been signed so we can start the process of selling the house."

Of course he is.

Mr. "The World Owes Me Something" was waiting for his payday. Harassing the lawyer of our dead mother was probably a lot easier than getting a job.

"Sorry, Mr. Sterling. I'll sign them first thing tomorrow."

"Again, I'm sorry to bother you with this during what I'm sure is a difficult time," he sounded sincere, "but I need to also inform you that Victor has requested a copy of all your mother's legal papers, including her will. He wants to contest your cousin's portion of the inheritance."

What an asshole.

"Can he do that?" I asked.

"He certainly can try, but I'm the one that drew up those papers with your mother after her last divorce. They're solid, and there's nothing there to contest."

Shit.

The phone slipped from my hand and dropped to the floor as that familiar cold sweat appeared and guided me into a new vision.

"Mia? Are you here?" Demarco's deep voice filled my mother's house in a lighthearted tone.

"Hey, good-looking," my mother said with a smile, appearing from another room. "You look very handsome."

"Well, I knew I'd be taking out a beautiful woman tonight." He smiled back and held up a bouquet of sunflowers, her favorite. "Ready for your celebratory dinner?"

"What are we celebrating again?" she teased.

"Hmmm . . . I do believe, Ms. Walker, that we're celebrating the anniversary of your divorce."

"Oh yeah!" she said in between giggles. I had never seen my mother flirt that openly with a man before, and it was both amusing and discomforting at the same time. "Why is it I have more fun celebrating my divorce with you than I ever did celebrating my wedding with him?" She put the sunflowers down on the table and reached up to wrap her arms around his neck, standing on her toes to reach him.

"Maybe you should have just said yes when I asked you to marry me the first time. Then we could be celebrating our wedding," he said. As he bent down to kiss her, his expensive suit tightened across his broad shoulders.

"Mmmm . . . ," she said into his lips. "Maybe we should skip dinner." They both laughed, and she grabbed his hand to pull him over her as she laid down on the couch.

"Ah, ah, ah!" I yelled and cringed while picking up the phone and shaking myself free of my vision before it showed me things that would scar me for life.

'Things I Didn't Need to See My Mother Do,' for one hundred, Alex.

Demarco was calling into the phone as I brought it back up to my ear. "Manhattan? Hello?"

"Sorry, the phone slipped," I said. Talking to him got a whole lot creepier after that vision. "Listen, I want to transfer my portion of the house to Charley."

"Okay, I'm not going to advise you on how to handle your finances, but I should tell you that the house is pretty much all of the inheritance there is, and it's worth a sizable amount in its current condition. It would behoove you to . . ."

"Just do it, please," I said to the man who had slept with my mother on a couch I grew up watching TV on. "Send whatever you need me to sign to my office, and I'll sign it as soon as it gets here."

That ought to piss Victor off.

"It'll take a little time to get everything switched around, but I'll take care of it."

"Listen, before you go, can I ask you something?"

"Of course."

"That first package of paperwork you sent me had my mother's necklace in it. Did you put it in there?"

"No. We were not in charge of any of her smaller personal possessions. Really just the house and some of her accounts. Perhaps it came with something else?"

"No, it was definitely with that paperwork. You know what necklace I'm talking about, right? She wore it all the time. Did she ever tell you anything about it?"

"She didn't. I'm sorry." Demarco's voice got a little higher. "She was a pretty private person. I mean, your mother and I were . . . well, we were close, but . . ."

"Sure! That's all I needed to know. Please do not finish that sentence," I said, holding my free hand over my eyes as if it would help me forget where that vision was headed before I checked out of it.

"Shit." I jumped when I removed my hand and saw a man standing beside me. "I've got to go," I said to Demarco, hanging up the phone before he could say anything else.

"You didn't really expect that lawyer to know anything, did you?" the man said, moving a little too close for my comfort.

"Who are you?" I asked, taking one giant step back.

"You don't recognize me?" He asked, rubbing his fingers along his chin. "It's okay, I guess. We've never actually met."

He was lively-looking, young, and handsome. There was something familiar, and warm, about him. He reminded me of someone else I knew, many other people I knew. Then it hit me. "Kevin?"

"Well, Uncle Kevin, if you want to get technical."

Dead Uncle Kevin would have been most accurate. "What are you doing here? No, wait, how are you here? No, you know what? Answer both," I said. If he really was dead, he certainly didn't look it. Like when I saw Justin's ghost, he was as whole-bodied as you or I on any given day.

"How isn't important, I don't think. But why may be. I'm here to help you if I can."

"So, are you a ghost or something?"

"Or something." He started walking toward me, a soft scent of sulfur drifting up around him.

"Is this normal?" I asked. "Seeing ghosts all the time?"

"Has anything really been normal since you found out you were a Caster? I'm here because of this," he said, tapping the necklace through my shirt. He didn't feel dead, either.

"I saw you wearing it once, in a vision I had," I said.

"The Opalescence."

"What?"

"That's what it's called. The Opalescence."

"Do you know how I got it?"

"From your Mom, sort of."

"How? It came with documents that would have only been sent after she died."

"I'm going to have to give you a bit of a history lesson in order to explain that. The story, at least as how it was told to us, was that the Opalescence has been in our family for a long time. The first Walker to have it saw what could happen when it got into the wrong hands. She made a promise to keep that from happening ever again and bound that promise in a spell with her blood. And with that, she didn't just commit herself to protecting it; she committed all of the Walkers that came after her, including me and you. She wasn't just idealistic, she was smart, too. She knew that death couldn't be allowed to interfere, so with her spell she made it so that if the person wearing the Opalescence dies without giving it away first, it'll send itself to another Walker."

"What is so important about this thing?"

"Do you remember what happened with you and that dead Caster? How it connected your spirits together?"

"Are you kidding? Of course I do. You don't forget something like that."

"Well . . . that's just the beginning."

"Of?"

"Of its power. Has it done other things yet?"

"It trashed my bathroom once, if that's what you mean."

"Ha. Yeah, that's what I mean. The power to move objects with your mind is just one of the many things it can do. Even after having it myself, I still don't know everything it's capable of. And I've heard from others that it changes with each person. The easiest way anyone ever explained it to me is to think of it like a sponge. It absorbs energy, holding onto some of it, growing or contracting some of it, or changing some of it altogether. At its best, it can be wildly impressive. At its worst, it can be . . . explosive."

"I've got more than enough going on right now. I don't want that kind of stress."

"None of us did, I don't think. But it's sort of a necessary burden—a destiny thing. And it's just your turn, I guess."

"But why me? I mean, it could have gone to anyone else, right? What about Gloria? She can take it. If she and my mom knew that it would send itself to another Walker after she died, why would they suppress our powers?"

"I don't have all the answers, Hat, and I was long gone by the time that decision was made. All I know is that having the Opalescence is serious, and it's yours now. When I saw that you got it, I worried that without anyone to explain it, you might not understand why you had to keep anyone else from getting their hands on it. And after that murder, maybe I worried too that you'd walk away from it, not knowing that doing that would put everything in jeopardy."

"Are you really trying to lay some sort of cosmic duty on me here? What if I do just walk away from it? What if I just say no?"

"That's not an option, I'm afraid."

"It's always an option, Kevin. And I have to tell you—it's looking pretty fucking appealing right now after what this thing did when Justin got murdered."

"I'm sorry you had to see that, to feel that. I know it's not easy. None of this is."

"Hey look, you're my family and I love you because of that, but you were dead before I was born. Don't come to me and act like you know what I'm feeling."

"I'm not just being sympathetic, Hat," Kevin said to me. "Once you're connected to the Opalescence, you're connected forever – and that connection doesn't end with death. I can feel it always, just as I can feel you and ever other person who has ever worn it. You will too, with time."

"But I don't . . ."

Kevin stepped forward abruptly and grabbed both of my shoulders. A cold sweat followed and pulled me into a place of weightlessness as another vision appeared.

> *A woman with bobbed hair and a colorful, ankle-length dress with sleeves stood on a hill overlooking a small town. She was holding the stone of the Opalescence and its powers spilled out of her hand and swirled, creating a vortex around her.*
>
> *Streams of murky light protruded from the vortex, attaching to and pulling at the life force of anything alive. The trees around the woman were dead, the bark stripped, and the branches barren and rotting. The grass under her feet was brown and limp. Even the clouds overhead lost their opaqueness and descended from the sky before disappearing completely into the vortex.*
>
> *Dead bodies littered the hill and the road to the town. The town itself was ablaze, and as people fled from it toward the hill, their bodies connected to the vortex's streams of light. It wrenched at them, taking everything they had.*

First to go were their cries, ripped from their throats and pulled into the vortex until they were mute. Then their strength, slowing them from a run, to a walk, to a crawl, and finally to nothing. Then skin turned a pasty yellow as they fell to the ground. The last thing to go was the color in their eyes. The vortex easily pierced and drained it, pulling it into its center until their eyes turned hollow.

Everything around the woman was at risk as she commanded the power of the Opalescence. The pain she was inflicting was unbearable—I could feel it from the people but also from nature itself. The desolate vortex ate at all life and didn't show any signs of stopping.

All the suffering, all the pain, and all the devastation stayed with me as I stumbled out of the vision. "What . . . what was that?" I asked.

"The end . . . or as close as we've come to it. That's what happens when the wrong person gets ahold of the Opalescence. Its power is not just scary, it's catastrophic."

I circled around the boxes in silence with my eyes on the floor.

"I know this a lot to take in, and the responsibility of what I'm telling you is heavy," Kevin said. "There's nothing fair about dealing with the Opalescence, especially for you since you've been kept in the dark about magic for so long. I'm sorry for that, but it's not something you or I can change."

"What am I supposed to do now?"

"Nothing. Really. The best thing you can do, the safest thing you can do, is just keep it a secret. Don't tell anyone, including the family, that you have it. Go about your life , try to ignore its powers when you can, and silently hope that no one comes after it."

"And if someone does?"

"Then, well, you'll have to protect it. If you're lucky, you won't have to die for it like I did."

Chapter 16

I laid low for the next few weeks, from my family, from Liv, from everything. What Kevin had told me was major, more major that I could process at the time especially given Justin's murder. A break was well warranted. I did miss Liv, though, and despite what happened the last time I was at Equinox, I craved the comfort and excitement that came with hanging around her and her friends. I was starting to feel out of place in my own life again, and with each awkward interaction I had with anyone I couldn't be myself around, I yearned to go back there just a little bit more.

A text from Liv on an otherwise quiet Friday afternoon tested my resolve, and I failed quickly.

"Nine, tonight. Be ready, I'll pick you up," it said.

"Equinox?" I replied.

"Negative. We're going to the playground."

Another one of Liv's mysteries. *"Where?"*

"Be intrigued," was all she wrote back.

Without any hints about where we were going, I got in Liv's SUV that night. We were somewhere in North Providence when she pulled into the driveway of a small, one-story house. It had dingy green vinyl siding and a four-bay garage that was almost larger than the house itself. Every window was obstructed by a drawn shade from inside, but with its long driveway and bordering hedges, you couldn't see any of the neighbors anyway.

Several other cars were already parked around the yard when we got there. "Where are we?" I asked as we got out of the SUV.

"The Playground," Liv said, facing me as she walked backward toward the house. She held her hands up on each side as if to impressively introduce the very unimpressive house.

"You made it," Elle yelled ecstatically as she opened the door for us. She let the door close behind her and jumped from the doorway straight into my arms, wrapping her legs around my back and kissing my cheeks rapidly.

"Back off, Man Trap," Liv said, trying to pull Elle off me.

"Don't be jealous because he likes me more than you. Besides, it's not like he'd be the first guy we've shared," Elle said to Liv. She ogled me with her sultry eyes, and her audacious black hair tickled my face. She leaned in to kiss me, only to back off and jump away right before our lips met. "It's cute when you blush," she said to me, playfully slapping my arm.

We followed Elle into the house, and the front door led directly into a long, narrow hallway. It had no windows, nor any other doors except the one positioned at the other end. It was painted a flat shade of green, almost like a muddy olive, and it got darker as the hallway went on, giving it the illusion that it got smaller the further you went. I caught myself crouching; my head knew that the walls and ceiling weren't closing in, but my eyes didn't. I tried to focus on Elle as she confidently walked in front of us.

Elle's body was tight, yet curvy, and undeniably sexy. Her tight denim skirt with its low waist and thick, brown leather belt highlighted each of her curves as she walked, with her hips swaying from side to side in time with the sharp click of her heels against the granite floor.

Half looking back to see if I was watching her, she pushed her hands out to either side of her body and separated her fingers. Vibrantly colored silk-like ribbons flowed from her fingertips into the air, brightening the dismal space and leaving me awestruck in their wake. Blue at first, the ribbons swirled effortlessly behind her as she walked. I reached out to touch them and felt nothing more than air before they dissipated as effortlessly as they had appeared. The ribbons turned red next, rippling through the air like brilliant flags on a windy day. Yellows, greens, and purples followed, until we reached the door and she pulled her hands back to her hips and blew an air kiss at me.

"Impressive," I said.

Liv pushed past Elle and walked through door. "Please, it's nothing you couldn't see for twenty bucks in Vegas."

The door at the end of that odd hallway dumped you right into an outdoor courtyard that sat at the center of the house. It was warm, like it was the start of spring, and so unlike the burgeoning cold weather outside. Flowers in full bloom scattered themselves around a blanket of lush green grass that had the aromatic hint of being freshly cut. They were interrupted only by the oversized tree trunks that shot up from below them and draped the area with their green, leafy branches.

Past the opening of the courtyard's ceiling, you could see that any of the trees' branches that weren't directly over the courtyard were either barren or holding onto the last of their colored and dried-out leaves, much like every other tree in that late New England autumn. Like an idiot, I kept walking without letting my eyes leave the mystery of those trees and stumbled directly into a chair.

Stone walkways extended from four doors on each side of the courtyard, one of which we had just walked through, and met in a patio area at the center. Music streamed from large speakers attached to the house on two of those walls. Half empty carafes of Blue Ice, a stack of glasses turned upside down, and a big bucket of ice were on a wicker bar by one of the doors.

The whole crew from Equinox was already there, including a few people I still hadn't been introduced to yet. They were all casually sipping on Blue Ice and waiting for Cooper to finish cooking on the large built-in grill in the corner.

"All right?" Cooper asked, extending his hands to present the courtyard. "What do you think?"

"It's warm," I said, looking around for heaters. "And what's the deal with the trees?"

"Ah . . . all part of the wonder that is The Playground," he said, smirking at the others.

"Are we all just going to hang out like nothing happened?" I asked Liv as she was pouring us drinks at the bar.

"What do you mean?" she asked.

"Justin, Liv. I mean Justin. Does anyone else even remember what happened?"

"Of course they do, but this is what our life is like sometimes. Justin wasn't the first Caster to die, and I wish he hadn't, but he did. It sucks, but we'll stick together and move on from it."

"He didn't just die, Liv, he was murdered."

"He wasn't the first Caster to be murdered either," she said, walking away.

"Hat," Cooper called to me. "Have yourself a look in here."

He was standing next to a large telescope, but the lens was pointed at the wall and not the sky. "But . . ."

"Go on."

The moon, full, bright, and in all its glory, was in perfect view from the telescope. "Holy shit," I said. I looked up into the sky, which was covered in clouds and the moon nowhere to be seen.

"Like it?"

I studied the craters of the moon from a view I had never seen before, and then its backdrop of amazing stars. "How?"

Cooper leaned in close to me and whispered. "You can see just about anything."

"Like?"

"Like anything. Just think about what you want to see."

I thought about Providence first, and the panoramic view you can sometimes catch from Prospect Park when it's a clear day. The telescope blurred then refocused and the city at night filled my view. It was higher than you would see from Prospect Park, with the lights of the buildings creating a glow around the few tall buildings in the downtown area. I thought about my apartment next, and slowly the telescope started to zoom in. It passed over the buildings, and into my ghetto neighborhood, before stopping just above my block. The neon sign for the Colombian fish market above my apartment was just close enough to be read.

"What is this place?" I asked.

"It's whatever we want it to be. It's our place to be what we are; something we can't do out there in the world very often," Cooper said.

The tension and memories that I carried with me into The Playground drifted away, and I played with the telescope for a while, having it show me all kinds of amazing things. Cities I had never been to, the rain forest, Antarctica, and even the earth, from as far away as I could imagine.

Around me, everyone freely exposed their powers to each other in playful but somewhat reckless ways. They looked liberated, happy even, and I wondered if theirs was a life I could let myself be drawn into and really be a part of. It was a whole new world for me, one that clearly flew in the face of my aunt's wishes, but that night was the most phenomenal night of my entire life. The world had presented itself to me on a silver platter, waiting for me to take a bite out of it.

"Try to loosen up, mate, you're all tense," Cooper said to me later when he found me leaning against the bar watching the others.

"I'm good. I'm just still taking it all in, I guess. It's still sometimes hard to believe that all this stuff was happening around me my whole life and I had no idea."

"That's the story of the centuries, isn't it? Some people see magic, by accident or whatnot. But they choose not to believe. They choose to stay in their little worlds believing little things," Cooper said. He filled my glass with Blue Ice and then his own. "Perhaps part of your problem is that you still think of yourself as one of them looking in at us, rather than one of us looking out at them."

"So you've got me all figured out, is that it? Maybe it just takes me some time to process things. I've always been more of an observer anyway."

"I suppose you probably mean pushover."

"What?" I asked indignantly.

"It's alright; there's no judgment from me on that. You were born into a world that taught you to play by the rules, to ask for things nicely, and to be okay with it when you don't get them. This," he looked around, "this can change that. It makes you realize that maybe you don't have to live in their world anymore. That's why our world tends to scare them a bit."

"And who is this 'them' you keep talking about?"

"Everyone else. The average man. Whatever you want to call people who don't have powers like us. I hate to say it like this, but they are two very different worlds, and it's difficult for us to live equally in both. Doesn't it feel good though? The liberation of it all. The freedom. Being more than them."

"I don't know that I ever wanted to be more than anyone else. More than what I was, maybe. But doesn't this all seem a little too easy? I mean, twitch our noses and poof!—the world is an easier place?"

"I didn't say easier," he leaned in and whispered. "Better perhaps."

"Alright, boys and girls," Cooper announced to the group. "It's time for a little fun." He walked over to the patio table and dumped out some stones from a cloth pouch.

"Didn't we learn our lesson with these the last time?" Liv asked.

"What are those?" I asked.

"They're called honesty stones," Cooper said to me. It was pretty clear from everyone else's face that they had seen them before. Each stone had a colored symbol on the top, a combination of circles, lines, and triangles. He flipped them over and mixed them around the table. "Alright then." He picked up a stone and hid it in his hand and watched as everyone else did the same.

The stone I picked had a deep purple circle with two bent lines extending unevenly from the middle like wings. "Looks like you're mine," Cooper said, showing me his matching stone.

Everyone else paired off and went to separate areas of the courtyard. I moved my chair in closer to Cooper's and asked, "What do we do?"

"Just push your stone up against mine." He placed his stone on the table with the symbol facing up. "Once the two stones touch, you're bound into the spell until you give an honest answer to the other person's question. It's sort of like magical truth or dare."

"Great. I'm not sure that . . ."

He put his index finger on the stone. "Don't be a wanker. Just do it."

I slid my stone slowly across the table until it touched his. As they connected, there was a jolt that zapped my finger. I tried to pull it away, but it was as if it was glued to the stone and the stone was glued to the table. The space around us got dark. The music and the voices from the others faded into the distance and we sat alone in a space of our creation, a tiny tear in reality.

"Go on then, you start," Cooper said.

"I don't know what to ask."

"Ask anything," he said. "It's just a game, don't over think it."

Game or not, I wasn't going to waste the opportunity to ask the one question I really thought he wouldn't answer otherwise. "Don't you . . ." I swallowed hard and started again. "Why doesn't it bother you that Justin was murdered at your club?" My eyes sank away from his, unsure of how he'd respond.

He looked around and took a deep breath. He was either going to explode all over me or brush it off completely.

"It bothers me," he said, the volume of his voice shallower than I'd ever heard it. "It bothers me a great deal. He was my employee and my friend. But you don't know me particularly well, do you? I'm the type of person who needs to focus on the future, and Justin's death, no matter how much it bothers me, is in the past. Death and murder are unfortunately not uncommon for people like us. There isn't a person here tonight who hasn't lost someone they love because of magic. It's a part of our life, and we have to accept that or else we'd do nothing but mourn."

"But, don't you think that . . ."

"Sorry," he cut me off with a smile, "you only get one question." His natural volume had returned and he pulled his finger from his stone. "My turn. Let's see . . ." He probed me with his eyes before leaning back in his chair. "Do you think you'd like to shag our girl Liv?"

"I don't know," I said before trying to pull my hand from the stone. My finger didn't budge.

"Not good enough," he said, tapping the table. "It only releases you when you're honest."

"I was being honest," I said. "I really don't know. I mean, look at her. Who wouldn't want her? I do, or I think I do, or I think I want to," I said.

If that answer wasn't good enough, I'd have to be locked in that spell forever. I was being honest; I didn't know how I felt about Liv, but I did know I wished I felt more. I also kind of wished that she would look at me in the same way she looked at him. But that wouldn't have been fair—how could I ask her to be more into me, when I wasn't sure I was into her at all?

Another light shock came from the stone and I was finally free from it. Cooper was still smiling at me when the light and sounds around us normalized and the tear in reality sealed itself up.

"Good game?" Liv asked as she wrapped her arms around Cooper. "What did you guys talk about?"

"Hey," Cooper barked at her, "you know the rules. That's between me and him, right?"

"Oh yeah, definitely," I teased Liv, trying not to remember that she had the power to get that information from me if she really wanted it.

A muffled but loud noise came from inside the house and Cooper darted his eyes between us. "Have another drink and maybe we'll try the stones again," he said before slipping in a door to the house and locking it behind him.

Chapter 17

The weeks were starting to pass by quickly, and when I wasn't working, I was spending my time at Equinox. The memory of Justin's death had been pushed to the recesses of everyone's mind, including mine, and I had forged a new kind of "normal" for myself there.

Cooper, Liv, and the rest of their band of free-spirited Casters continued to show me how to live in the moment and what it meant to have powers like ours. With them, there was always magic around, and that was comforting, exciting, and a little unstructured—all things I needed in my life at the time. It was the only thing helping me to move on from my mother's death, something I was starting to feel like I was finally doing.

The first snowfall didn't blanket the city streets until well after a dreary Christmas. Even though we were a devoutly unreligious family, Christmas had a special place in my mother's heart, and ours by extension. The first holiday season without her seemed devoid of purpose, with none of us willing or ready to bring any holiday cheer too close to our hearts. If it hadn't been for Sydney's kids, we probably would have just skipped it altogether.

"Are you coming to New Year's?" a text from Paige asked after I skipped the traditional post-Christmas Walker get-together that I was sure everyone else had attended.

For the first time since I was born, the Walkers were not regularly appearing characters in the story of my life. They were once what made me everything I was, and yet I was wholly disconnected from them now. My world had built a path for me to walk down, and I knew my tight-knit family couldn't come with me, nor could they understand why. Even if I wanted to share it with them, I wasn't sure it was safe or that they would believe me.

"Of course!" I wrote back.

Paige had been doing the family's New Year's blowout bash at her house since I was eleven and I had never missed it. New Year's was on a Friday this year, a recipe for an extra-large and extra-extravagant party.

"Good (or else I'll break your fingers)," her reply said. That was Paige's not-so-subtle way of letting me know that while everyone had been lenient about my habitual absences recently, they weren't going to be forever.

New Year's was one of those events that the Walkers considered mandatory. You needed a doctor's note, a rare disease, and a plane that was broken down in a foreign city to consider missing one of them, and even then, it would never be forgotten.

"So, party at your cousin's this weekend?" Talia said, sitting down on my desk.

"Isn't there always? I can't believe it's already New Year's."

She grabbed my cup and took a sip of coffee. "You have been missing in action a lot lately. Damon keeps asking me if you're still alive."

"Yeah, I suck." I pulled my coffee back from her. "Are you going?"

"I think so."

I leaned on my desk and looked up at her. "Does that mean you guys are officially seeing each other again?"

"Not sure. I guess it's just one of those things that's convenient and comfortable. I like him, I'm just not sure where we stand."

Damon's relationship with Talia, if you could call it a relationship, seemed both destined and doomed. They continued to float aimlessly in and out of each other's lives like rafts on a rapid river. When they'd cross each other briefly, they'd hold onto the other's raft to see if either was anchored in place for once. But neither ever was, so they'd float further down the river together, unanchored, and eventually let go and drift apart, waving goodbye until the next time their rafts met.

"You're totally going to end up marrying him and being my cousin-in-law," I teased.

"Yeah, because you need more of those. Hey, what's that?" she asked, reaching toward my head.

"What's what? Ouch!" I yelled, grabbing my head as Talia removed her hand. "What the hell?" It felt like she had ripped out a chunk of my hair.

She purposefully contorted her lips into a pouty face and stuck out her chest slightly at me. "Sorry! My ring got caught. You had some lint or something in your hair and I was trying to get it out."

Looking for a bald spot, I patted my head and hissed at her. "Was that your way of trying to distract me? It didn't work, by the way. How long are you two going to go on like this?"

"You know I love him, it's just that we're never in the same place at the same time. It's hard because we get along so great, and he's so sweet, and he's . . . really good in bed."

"That's just too much information."

"You asked. See you at the party." She strutted back to her desk with an overmodest smile and my coffee cup.

✳ ✳ ✳ ✳ ✳

Friday came quickly and I drove to Paige's, even though she only lived a few blocks away in the nicer neighborhood of Mt. Pleasant. The driveway was stacked with cars, so I parked on the street; a set-up for a quick getaway. I could already hear the beats of party music bouncing down her lawn as I got out of my car, and laughter and shouting trickling down behind it.

Charley and Paige greeted me from the porch. "Hat!" they both said.

"You better get in there, everyone's been asking about you," Paige said, tossing back the last of her drink and jetting into the house.

"I thought I might have to come get you," Charley said. "I'm so happy to see you that I won't even give you shit for never texting me back."

"Hi!" I gave her a rough hug, lifting her off the ground. "Is Victor here?" I whispered as I put her down.

She smiled at me. "Nope, thankfully." He tended to be as equally odious to her as he was to me, so she always understood why I didn't want to see him. "I think he's at your dad's house for the night."

Our dad actually, but we'll have to get to that later.

"Did you hear that he was having a fucking fit about your mom leaving part of her house to me? As if I asked her to. What an asshole."

"Agreed. Hey, did your Mom show up to this thing tonight?"

"Yeah, she's chatting up that guy that Aunt Gloria used to date."

Shocking.

"I know. Classy, right?" Charley said, rolling her eyes. "She hasn't even said hello to me yet."

From room to room, I progressed through the house in an obligatory lap to say hello to my family. I pretended to remember the names of the other people I encountered, sure that I had been introduced to them at some point. In a family as large as ours, there are always a plethora of people who come and go and come again, and it's nearly impossible to remember who is who, especially when you don't care that much. Ex-boyfriends and ex-girlfriends. Ex-husbands and ex-wives. We weren't strangers to exes, but despite not wanting to be related to us anymore, some of those exes just never wanted to leave.

Most of my mother's siblings had been married at least twice, and her youngest sister skewed the average with six marriages to five different men. My generation wasn't on track to do much better. Five of my cousins were either on their second marriage or just ending their first; the rest of us wouldn't be far behind. If the Walkers had to stick by that whole "till death do you part" thing, we'd die a whole lot sooner than we seemed to already.

"What are you doing over here?" Damon asked when he found me in a corner later. "Come on, your sister is looking for you and driving me crazy in the process," he said, yanking on my arm.

Damon got distracted by new arrivals to the party and I broke free from his grasp. Across the room, Finn was standing with some girl I had met before at some point. It might have been that girl who lived above the pizza place on the East Side, which I was sure was the main reason he was dating her at all. I waved and started walking over to him when Sydney stepped in front of me.

"Gonna avoid me all night?" she asked, putting her hands on her hips.

"No Syd, I wasn't avoiding." I leaned in and kissed her cheek. "I just got here and was just looking for you."

"Liar. Listen, I had the lawyers mail those papers to your office again, because we never see you anymore. You need to sign them and send them back, ASAP."

"Sure. Whatever you say, sis." I smiled. Charley slipped past us and handed me a drink without stopping to interrupt a conversation she wanted no part of.

"No, Manhattan, I'm serious. We can't do anything with the house until you sign those papers." She grabbed onto my shirt and pulled me down a little, closer to her height. "Sign . . . th e . . . damn . . . papers."

"Wow. Full name and everything. Okay. I promise I'll sign them on Monday. But I can only do that if you don't kill me now. Right?"

When I was able to escape from her, I made my way back to the bar. It was clear it was going to be my favorite place that night.

"Hey there," a familiar voice said.

"Oh, Max, hi," I said. "What are you doing here?"

Max laughed a little. "Uh, I was invited?"

"Oh. Right. Sorry. Of course you were invited. That made me sound like a total ass, didn't it?" I finished my drink quickly and started making myself another.

"I was hoping I'd get to see you around the gym, you know, for your next balance lesson." He leaned casually against the bar with one arm and watched me avoid looking at his striking gray eyes.

"Oh yeah," I said, trying to act casual but spilling vodka all over the bar, and myself. "I guess I've been busy."

He leaned in closer to me. "Life-stuff busy, or avoiding me busy? I thought maybe I saw you in there a few times. You're not avoiding me because of what happened last time, right?"

I stepped back a bit to put some space between us. "What? No . . . no, of course not. Just . . . busy. That's all . . . with stuff."

"Okay?"

"So, who'd you come with?" I asked.

"Your cousin."

"Ha. You're going to have to be a bit more specific in this family."

"Damon. I've known him for years. He invited me the other day and made it sound like the kind of party you can't pass up. I didn't have any plans, so here I am."

The look I shot Damon was full of daggers, but his back was to me, so I don't think he noticed.

"Lame, right?" Max spoke into his drink.

"What? Oh, no, it's great. It's always a good party." I bit my lip and watched the others float around us. "Have a good time. I guess I'll see you later?" I nodded politely before walking away and adding him to my list of people to avoid that night.

An hour or so later, I was back at the bar taking shots with Talia and Damon when Max appeared again. He came up behind me and reached under my arm to steal one of the shots slotted for me. He giggled a little as he felt me stiffen in front of him, trying to not turn around. Although they were several shots ahead of me, both Damon and Talia noticed.

"I'll catch up with you guys later," I said.

"No, you won't," Damon said. "You'll stay right here and talk to us. I never get to see you."

"Do you know Max?" Talia asked. By the look on her face, I could see that she already knew the answer to that question.

"We've met," I casually nodded again. "He owns the gym I go to."

We were all getting steadily drunker, and the two of them continued to kill any and all attempts I made to break from the group. Several cousins floated by being introduced to the "guy from our gym," and I pretended to be much more sober and much less interesting than I was to avoid talking to him.

I said I was okay with what happened at the gym, and I guess I was—but that didn't mean I wanted to talk about it or think about it. Max had this penetrating forwardness about him when he spoke, which made me both uncomfortable and envious. I found myself fidgeting nervously around him, even when his big gray eyes weren't watching me.

The crowd got rowdier as it approached midnight, the time by which I'd told myself that I would escape. I planned to duck out under the cover of darkness, and drunkenness, while the rest of the party cheered and kissed during the ball drop.

Talia and Damon had taken to openly making out in front of us, which left me standing silently next to Max, who might have been getting at least some joy out of watching me squirm. We continued in silence for a bit, with me playing the shifty-eye game, looking at him while trying to look away before he looked at me, so it didn't look like I was looking at him. Usually, it's funniest when both people are playing, but Max didn't have a problem staring me down each time I tried to look at him.

The next time I looked to see if he was looking at me still, Max openly sighed, rolled his eyes, and grabbed my shoulder. "Enough. Come over here," he said, pulling me toward the basement door. Damon and Talia were watching me let him pull me away, and I hoped they had both drunk enough that neither would have any memory of it the next day.

"I'm just going to grab another drink," I said, jingling the ice cubes in my otherwise empty glass.

"Shut up and come down here." He opened the basement door and pushed me through it.

"Get ready for the countdown," someone yelled from the living room.

There were still a few people lingering in the basement, but they were mostly people I didn't know. When I got to the bottom stair, Max opened the adjacent closet door and pulled me in with him. Its only light came from the stairwell, and I stumbled into bins of empty bottles and folded cardboard boxes as I walked through the blackness.

When I turned around, Max gently pushed me up against a shelving unit. The array of back-up liquor bottles pressed against my back and clinking from the impact. "So, are you being all sketchy because I kissed you the other day?" he started forcefully, and continued before I could respond, "Because I apologized for that."

"No, no, it's fine. I mean, it's not a big deal," I said.

The crowd started yelling out the countdown above us. "Ten! . . ."

"If it's no big deal, then you're being weird because . . . ?" Max leaned in a little closer to me and flashed his perfect smile.

"Nine! . . ."

"I'm not . . . I'm . . . I'm just . . ." I mumbled.

"Eight! . . ."

"You're just what, Hat?" He was a little closer and his voice softened as he looked down at me.

"Seven! . . ."

"Well?" he whispered.

"Six! . . ."

Silence between us. I was staring up at those big sky-like gray saucer eyes of his again, and he moved a little closer, his firm chest pressed against mine.

"Five! . . ."

More silence, his breath and mine colliding in what little space was left between us.

"Four! . . ."

What am I doing?

"Three! . . ."

He smiled.

"Two! . . ."

I smiled back.

"One!"

By the time "Happy New Year" was resonating through the house, our lips were locked again. This kiss, unlike our last, was intense, with his hand holding my head, and my hands clutching the shelves behind me. When he didn't feel me pull away, he continued with a gentle but firm fury that pulled us closer together and pushed the rest of the world farther away.

I tried to remember a kiss, any kiss, that was better than that one. It might have just been the booze, but I relished the way he pulled a little on my lower lip with his teeth when he moved away only to release it and move back in for another kiss. For once, I let go of the worry, the questions, the contemplation, and just lived in the moment.

The overhead light startled us when it flashed on and time unfroze.

"Oh shit, sorry!" Paige slurred, her eyes widening as she realized what was going on. She giggled to herself for a second, before turning around and stumbling back up the stairs.

Heat radiated off my flushed cheeks. The moment I was living in was over, and my mind turned to judging me for my impetuousness. Another second passed and Max tried to lean in again, but I held him back with one hand, nervously scratching the bridge of my nose with my other. When he took a step back, I slid through the growing space between us and rushed up the stairs and out of the house without another word.

Chapter 18

A foghorn tore me from an alcohol-induced slumber the next morning. Okay, it wasn't so much a foghorn as it was the message alert sound on my cell phone. But they sounded remarkably similar in my throbbing head.

I pulled myself up unsteadily and chugged the cup of stale water I still had on my nightstand. One eye was blurry and scratchy from having left one of my contacts in, and the sweatshirt I wore the night before (and the one I collapsed into bed in) smelled a little like vodka and Max.

Cat had finally agreed to sleep with me again, and he stretched wildly before jumping off the bed with a groan when I reached for my cell phone. He was annoyed that I woke him up at an unacceptably early time.

"And how are you this morning?" a text message from Damon said.

"Ugh. Hungover." I replied. I hadn't realized until then just how used to Blue Ice, and its lack of aftereffects, I had become.

"You disappeared after midnight. Go home alone?"

"Yes. Did you?"

"I stayed at Paige's . . . but not alone. I hear you had an interesting night," another message from him read.

"No idea what you're talking about." I was always glad in situations like these that the other person can't hear my voice in a text message.

"Hmmm. Sure about that?"

"Ugh." It was futile, but I held onto the hope that the conversation would end there.

"So?"

"So, what?"

"Don't be dumb. What's the deal?"

"I don't know. It just happened. We were drunk."

"I think Max really likes you," Damon's next text popped up quickly, giving me the impression he hadn't even waited for my last response.

"Eh, maybe not so much after I left."

"Pussy." Damon's texts were coming in faster. *"He's a good guy. You should give him a chance."*

"What? No. It was just a stupid drunk night. Blame Kettle One." I texted back.

"Blame whoever you want, you're the one making out with dudes."

"Shut up! It's not DUDES . . . plural, it was just DUDE, as in one. Obviously, I didn't plan on it. It just kind of happened."

"A drunk man does what a sober man is thinking," he wrote back with one of those annoying emojis with a kissy face.

Wondering who else Paige told about my little supply closet indiscretion, I started a few responses to Damon and then deleted them. It was good ten minutes before I had one I could bring myself to send.

"Do you think I'm gay?"

His response was too quick. *"Yes,"* it said.

"I'm not." I wrote back. Or at least I never thought I was.

"I think Max would disagree with you."

"Whatever."

"Hat—seriously. What does it matter if it was with a guy or not? Did you enjoy it?"

"I'm not gay."

"You're not gay like Malcolm X wasn't black. Just do him. You'll feel better after . . . I promise."

I took the battery out of my phone and threw the pieces across the room before sliding back down into bed and covering my face with my blanket. Nothing about that night made any sense to me. My eyes were shut, and I was drifting back into my coma-like sleep when incessant knocking shook my front door.

"No . . . ," I groaned into my pillows loudly. "Go away."

The pounding knocks continued, growing louder and closer with each interval. Whoever it was knew I was home, and I was more likely to find a thousand-dollar bill under my pillow than I was to get back to sleep with that noise. I stumbled through the dark room, digging my dried plastic contact from my eye and tossing it into one of my apartment's dirty corners.

Charley was standing on the other side of the door, leaning her head heavily against its frame. Her oversized sunglasses covered her eyes, and a she had a cup of coffee in each hand. "Bitch, I know you didn't think I would stop knocking," she said. She handed me an iced coffee, pushed her way into the apartment, and flopped loudly on a kitchen chair.

"And Bitch, I know you didn't think I'd let you in if you didn't bring me coffee," I said, sipping on the icy goodness she brought me.

Sunglasses still on, Charley laid her head on the table, trying to drip coffee into her mouth without lifting her head back up. "Make me food, woman," she cackled.

I took inventory of my fridge aloud: "wilted grapes, some soy sauce, an empty bottle of Kettle One, and a half gallon of milk that I don't remember buying. Looks like we're eating out. And you're buying 'cause you woke me up."

She lifted her arms at me, but not her head. "Carry me!"

* * * * *

"This is so good," Charley said around a mouthful of food. We were at our favorite diner, inhaling a standard post-drinking healthy breakfast of extra cheese omelets, sausage links, and french fries smothered in ranch dressing.

I stretched and yawned. "Since when do you get hung over? Did you even drink last night?" I asked.

"I got caught talking to Sydney's date and his brother for most of the night." She chugged her third glass of water. "What a fucking tool. He kept telling me how sexy he thought I was and I kept telling him to fuck off, but he wouldn't. He thought I was joking, but look at this face. If I gave you this face, would you think I was joking?" she asked, scrunching her face to make the most unattractive look I had ever seen on her, or anyone else.

"What's his name?"

"As if I'd remember." She waved her empty glass at the waiter. "Just leave the pitcher," she said to him when he came over. "I doubt I asked his name," she said to me.

"Did he finally get the hint?"

"No!" She held up a clean butter knife to check her teeth. "They left and then like fifteen minutes later he called my cell and left this disgusting drunk voicemail. I'll have to remember to thank Syd for giving him my number. You have to hear it. He sounds like he's playing with himself while he left the message."

"Ew. I'm all set. Thanks."

"I know," she yelled again, startling the people at the table next to us. "Like I'd want that midget anyway. He was not attractive at all, and I couldn't stop staring at his freakishly large nose. I mean, come on. You could see his brain with those nostrils. Besides, he looked like he had a small penis." She stuck her straw in the water pitcher and finished it off, then reached around to snatch a pre-set water from the table behind us. "Now him," nodding at the waiter as he walked by again, "him I'd take home. I bet he'd look good with my bedspread."

"Slut," I whispered into my coffee as I sipped it. The people at the next table were already blushing because of Charley, and I didn't think they needed to hear me be vulgar too.

"Oooooh." She turned back to me. "Speaking of sluts . . ." She tilted her head down and peered at me over the rims of her scratched sunglasses. "Let's talk about you."

Shit.

I put my face in my hands. "Was there anyone that Paige didn't tell?" I said through my fingers.

"I don't know, but that's not who I heard it from."

"Super. I'm glad to be the source of such juicy news. Maybe we can just post it on Facebook."

"Maybe I will later. So, what's the deal?"

"Did you see that Damon is back with Talia?" I asked.

"Yeah, yeah . . . when is he not? Tell me about this guy."

Maybe I should tell her about her real father . . . that would change the subject.

"Just so you know," she leaned back in her chair and pulled her leg up to hold it near her chest, "I don't have to work until Tuesday, so I can sit here and wait this out for a long time."

I gave a small, nervous laugh. "I don't have anything to report."

"The hell you don't. I saw his sexy self last night," she said. "He was one hot fucker. If you're not going to jump him, I will," she said before making a loud "mmm, mmm, mmm," noise and throwing her dirty napkin at me.

"You know, not for nothing, and I'm not pretending to be the subject matter expert in this kind of thing, but . . . isn't your family supposed to, I don't know, freak out when they catch you making out with another guy—tell you it's wrong or something?"

"In this family? Bitch, please. We're a bunch of black pots standing in a glass house waiting for some kettles to throw stones at. No one can say shit to anyone about anything. Plus, let's be real here for a second, it's not like anyone cares that it was a guy. I think I would have heard about this even if it was a girl you were tongue wrestling with. It's so rare for you."

"I know. But still, I don't . . . ," I grumbled and hurried through my words. "I don't want to talk about it."

"Tough shit. We may be loud, never know when to get the hell out of each other's business, and say things we probably shouldn't, but we're supportive. Hell, I'm supportive, and that gives me the right to hear all kinds of lewd details. Now get on with it, slut."

"I don't know. It was a stupid drunken night. It just happened," I said, shaking my head.

"You're way too uptight about this. Why do you care that it was with a guy?"

"I don't know what the hell I'm saying. Maybe I don't even care that it was with a guy. I just never thought about it before. I thought I wanted . . . I don't know. Please can we just change the subject?"

"Hmmm . . . denied. You're overthinking this whole thing. Maybe you just never met a guy worth exploring it with. Come on. Give me something good that I can hold against you later."

"You suck."

"Now if you had said that to him last night, this could have been a totally different conversation." The glee from her sadistic words spilled out all over her.

"Shut up," I yelled, throwing my half-eaten piece of toast at her. We were turning into the kind of customers that the waiters would curse about after we left, and dread ever seeing again.

"He looks like an amazing kisser. And, I hear you guys were really going at it . . . ," She took her phone and snapped a picture of me. "So, was he?"

"What was that for?"

"Just something to remember this moment by."

"Please?" I begged, covering my face with my hands. "I'll give you one hundred dollars in cash, right now, if we can talk about anything else."

"Get real. This is the best thing we've had to talk about in months and you've never had a hundred dollars on you in your life." She slapped my hands away from my face. "I'm not letting you leave until you tell me how that kiss was. And

I drove, so unless you plan to walk home, start being chatty, Cathy."

I took a couple of deep, annoyed breaths. "Fine. It was great. Okay? Probably better than great. But don't go analyzing it. I still have no idea how I feel about it, and I'm really, really not looking to figure it out right now."

"Sure, sure. But can I just say one more thing before you go all 'Hat Walker' about this, like you always do, and avoid it, and pretend we never had this conversation?"

I nodded reluctantly.

"Okay. How do I say this? So, you know how sometimes you see someone with lettuce in their teeth?"

I ran my tongue over my teeth.

"No, no," she said. "But you know what I mean, right? You see they have lettuce in their teeth, everyone else sees they have lettuce in their teeth . . . but they don't see they have lettuce in their teeth?"

"I have no idea what the fuck you're talking about," I said, shaking my head.

"Okay, okay. I'm landing this plane, I swear. The point is, no one ever says anything, you know, except for me maybe, because they figure that person will eventually look in a mirror and figure it out for themselves." Her voice was getting louder. "Do you get what I'm saying now?"

I'm sure she thought the extensive hand movements and extra emphasis on certain words was helping her analogy, but it wasn't. "No," I said.

She rolled her eyes and scoffed, "Hat . . . you have a gay man in your teeth."

Chapter 19

"I'm making breakfast," Liv said when I arrived at her house the next weekend. She tugged on the faded pink apron she was wearing and smiled at me. "Come in."

"Oh yeah?"

"Chocolate chip pancakes seemed fitting with the crappy weather," she said, as I followed her into the house. "But I got fruit too, if you're feeling healthy."

"I love this painting," I said as I passed a portrait of Cape Code on the wall in her kitchen, complete with a classic New England lighthouse glowing in the distance at dusk.

"Mmmm," Liv said, having just taken a bite out of a huge strawberry. "I painted it. Touch it."

"Really?" I asked. I didn't know much about art, but I did know you weren't supposed to touch it.

"Uh huh. Touch it."

My hand slowly moved over the grainy, textured paint on the canvas and magic flowed from the painting into my fingers, taking me through a wave of new sensations. I hadn't left Liv's living room; I was still there looking at a motionless painting on her wall, but all my other senses went wild, helping me experience things a simple painting alone couldn't have.

My stomach fluttered for a second as my ears filled with the sounds of squawking seagulls overhead, and waves crashing in the distance. My feet sunk into the sand, and the faint scent of seaweed at high-tide and suntan lotion brushed past my nose. A cool breeze tickled my skin as it carried salt from the ocean through the air, almost enough that I could taste it on my tongue.

"Wow . . . ," I said, removing my hand from the canvas. "How'd you do that?"

"I figured out a few years ago that with a combination of some enchanted paints and a special brush, I could do a lot more than just paint a picture."

"Incredible," I said, touching it again.

"There are so many cool things that magic can do." She moved back to the stove and flipped a batch of pancakes on the griddle. "Will you hand me that butter?"

Watching her cook, I couldn't keep my mind from wandering. Before me was this beautiful and talented woman, and she was making me food. I was standing in a place that a million guys would kill to stand, yet the only person's lips I could picture against mine were Max's—and that wasn't a thought I was comfortable with. I could admit that there was some kind of attraction there, but one I didn't understand and one I was trying to pretend I didn't want to pursue. But I knew pursuing it would change my life forever, and it had already changed so much.

"What?" Liv asked as I came up behind her. She was scooping up the last of the pancakes and putting them on a flower-printed plate near the stove. She turned toward me, and I leaned in to kiss her.

She put the spatula down and wrapped her arms around my neck, and we kissed like that for a few moments. Her lips were so soft and I tried to relax and enjoy that, but it all felt forced and stiff. I started to get angry at myself for not wanting her the way I wanted to want her. It felt so unfair to be given what you've always asked for, only to realize that it still wasn't right.

Liv pulled away when she noticed me twitch, placed her hand gently on my cheek and said, "You still think too much. Come here." She grabbed my hand and pulled me into the living room with her.

Does she actually know what I was thinking?

There was a brief moment of panic in my gut when I thought she'd want to continue what I started in the kitchen. In a new world where my relationship with my family was different, and I had so few people I loved and trusted, I worried that going any further with her would be a line we couldn't uncross later.

"Just relax," she said, pulling her feet up on the couch. "Sit up here with me."

Facing each other on the couch, she grabbed my hands and held them in hers. "Close your eyes. Take a deep breath and relax," she said.

An image of her emerged from the darkness in my mind and started walking toward me. A soft glow illuminated her face and she was the only thing I could see. "Can you hear me?" she asked.

"Yes," I said aloud.

"You don't have to speak; I can hear your thoughts up here," she said within my head. Looking down I could see myself there with her as she grabbed my hand and led me into the darkness. "It's okay," she said, pulling me closer to her, "you're safe."

"Where are we going?" I asked. A few more steps and a torch light appeared next to her. She picked it up off the wall it hung from and moved to light another nearby torch with it. As she did, a dozen other torches, placed in a circle around the room, lit themselves, illuminating everything.

Out of the darkness came a library, with shelves stuffed with books, stacked higher than the light would reach. It had no doors and no windows, but it did have a lingering smell of old leather and musty paper. "This is so weird. Where are we?" I asked.

"Deep inside your mind."

"Who knew my mind would be so . . . dusty?"

"Magic's funny like that. It doesn't always show us things as they really are. A lot of the time, things will appear how you want to see them, or how you need to see them."

"And here I thought you were just a mind reader."

"I catch people's thoughts now and then, whenever they're close and they're being a little too loud with them, but I think that's just a side effect of my real power. I can connect with someone's mind in ways even they can't. My dad used to call it 'mind walking'. It's a really intimate place, a person's head. I don't do this with just anyone, or all that often with those I do, but I was here briefly without you that night at the club, and I wanted to show you what it's like to be here yourself."

I let go of her hand and picked up a book off one of the shelves. Inside was an image of me, my siblings, and a few cousins, all playing in the yard outside my mother's house. I remembered that day clearly; my mom had gone to visit Gloria at the hospital after some kind of kayaking mishap the night before and left us with my father. I was only about five at the time and had fallen out of the half-completed tree house, breaking my arm in three places. My father, unsure if I had actually broken it, told me to "sleep on it and see if it feels better in the morning." Kids heal fast, and the next morning it did feel better, but my arm was completely mangled—having set itself in an unhealthy and unnatural position. My mom was furious, but not as mad as me—the one who had to go to the doctor's office and let him re-break my arm. The picture I was looking at in the book looked like it was from right after I'd gotten home. Everyone was signing my cast, except for Victor, who was trying to draw a penis on it with a pink marker.

"They're like photo albums of my life," I said to Liv, showing her the next picture. It was of Damon moving his stuff into my bedroom. That was after my father left, the second time. His mom and dad had gotten a divorce too, and he moved into our house with his sisters. As expected of any child in the same situation, I remembered being sad when my father left. But I also remembered how much fun it was having Damon living with me, and how nice it felt to have a big brother who preferred making forts out of sheets and staying up past bedtime over pushing me down stairs and locking me in closets like Victor.

"Haha . . . look at this one!" Liv said, holding up another book. It was me at my college graduation. I was whiter than fresh snow and was carrying more bags under my eyes than any airline would have allowed on board. My cousins and I had partied a little too hard the night before, and I wondered if Liv would find a picture of that night, because I hardly remembered it, and would have loved to have seen it for myself. "Whose horse is this?"

"Oh," I said, tilting the book so I could see it better. "My mom's. That's her with her brother Kevin. They used to spend a lot of time with that horse before Kevin died."

Seeing your life in front of you like that is a bizarre experience. Some things I remembered, others I didn't, and even more that I wished I didn't. When I opened another book and saw a picture of St. Albert's on the first page, I closed it quickly and returned it to the shelf.

"Who's this?" Liv asked, holding up another page in her book.

"That's my cousin dressed as a girl for Halloween. If I remember correctly, the week before that was taken he'd cut his sister's hair while she was sleeping and my aunt decided that would be his punishment." He didn't look very happy at all, especially when, in the next picture, his sister Paige was applying a fresh coat of lipstick.

The next book to catch my eye was bigger than any other in the library of my mind. It was wedged in the shelf between a book that had three interlocking "O"s or zeroes on the binding. It was made entirely of red leather and it creaked as I pulled it free. The cover was adorned with gold-colored stenciling and words too worn to understand. It was so heavy, I could barely lift it.

Liv leaned over to look at it with me, and as I opened it, the library around us started to shift. Even though we weren't physically there, I could feel sweat start to form on my spine. Noises and lights swirled around us until we landed in a place of weightlessness together. A vision unfolded within the book, showing us something I couldn't have remembered because I had never seen it. It was another dead body.

> With lips seven shades of blue, her face was so pale that it made the body almost look fake. Her eyes were closed, but it was unmistakably my mother, my dead mother, lying on the floor of her house. Standing over her body was a man I had seen before. The man without a face.

"Murder," someone said, but I couldn't tell who.
Liv's eyes were wide and her jaw dropped slightly as
she looked at me. "Murder," the voice said again.

The book slammed shut and the noise of it echoed off the walls of the library like metal hitting metal. Back and forth the sound roared, growing louder with each hit. The floor bent and tilted. Books fell from the shelves and doused torches rattled together as they rolled around on the floor. The ground was shaking, causing the bookshelves to crash together from the force of it all.

There was no up or down anymore. Everything contorted around us, as the fingers of that sound kneaded our constructed reality like sourdough. The books created from my memories decomposed into heaps of indecipherable sludge, and with one final, earthquake-like rumble, the illusion shattered and threw us both from the depths of my mind.

"I'm so sorry, Hat" Liv yelled, holding her head like we were still surrounded by the deafening echoes. "Nothing like that's ever happened before. It's like one of your visions took over in there. I didn't realize that could happen. I'm sorry."

"It's not your fault." I shot up and paced the room, hoping that if I shook my head vigorously enough I could toss out the sight of my mother's dead body from it.

She didn't get murdered. She couldn't have been murdered. Not her too.

A spinning dizziness robbed me of all my balance. Breathing heavily, I tried to sit and missed the couch, landing harshly on the floor. The whole thing was one, large emotional punch in the gut. Murder. What a terrible word to know.

With heavy tears, I told Liv about everything that had been happening to me since we met. The Opalescence. Kevin. Seeing Justin's ghost and the vision I had of the man without the face stealing the mask we saw him wearing over my mother's body. Gloria and her explanation of why I shouldn't have had powers. All of it. I couldn't hold back. I didn't want to. I needed someone to know everything, someone I could trust with everything. And I needed that person to tell me that what we just saw wasn't true.

Murder. Every cell in my body began to burn up, like scalding water had been splashed against my skin. Anger, grief, sadness; those were all just words and they couldn't do justice to what I was feeling, nor could they carry any significance next to the unendurable word. Murder.

It was awhile before I had the strength to ask Liv the one question I couldn't handle the answer to. "Do you think what that vision showed us is true?"

"Yes, I do," she said.

Chapter 20

The weeks that followed that vision were filled with torturous nights of sleep. In my dreams, I'd see myself standing on the edge of a cliff, looking over a rocky beach. My mother would pass in the distance, walking barefoot along the enormous rocks and looking away from me at the violent ocean. When I opened my mouth to call out to her, the word murder, in a dark, lurking whisper would come out. I knew I was sleeping, and I could even feel my body sprawled atop my lumpy bed in the conscious world, but I was powerless to wake up from it. Soon she would walk out of sight, but the whispers would continue in a voice that wasn't mine. They'd grow louder each time they spit out that word until they were so loud they overtook the sounds of the waves crashing against the rocks.

When the voice became too much to bear, I would jump off the cliff to escape it, but just before I hit the rocks my eyes would open, and I'd be awake again. Over and over that sequence played out, with the same non-ending each time. Eventually I would stop trying to sleep, but the voice would walk with me the entire day, never letting me forget it was there waiting for me whenever I closed my eyes. I was like a mouse running around blindfolded in a maze, hoping I'd find the exit before I died of starvation.

Nothing with my newfound knowledge about my mother's death was normal and there's an unfair twist when murder is involved. You don't just have to deal with the pain of saying goodbye, you have to struggle with the daunting question of why. Was she murdered for the Opalescence?

That damn necklace was such a conspicuous question mark of its own, and I hated feeling burdened by it. Why had she left it to me if her whole intention was to keep me out of that world?

I wanted to approach Gloria with those questions, but I couldn't be certain of how it would turn out. If she did know that was why my mother was murdered, then it could explain why she was turning into the antithesis of everything I had known her to be. If she didn't, she'd use it as one more reason I needed to make everything about myself a secret. And how could I be the one to tell her that her best friend and sister had been murdered?

The sound of a large crash below my feet was followed by applause all around the restaurant. "Manhattan!" Ms. Monica shouted from the door of the kitchen after I dropped the plate. "That's the third one tonight. They comin' out your pay." She retreated to the kitchen and I followed her with a tray full of broken plates.

The kitchen was a messy, odd-shaped room that was set up so you had to yell for everything. When you walked in or out, you had to yell "In" or "Out," preferably matching whichever direction you were actually going. If you needed more bread made, you had to yell "Bread," and so on. I think the whole point of that system was to get people to pay attention, or to make it less noticeable when Ms. Monica yelled at you about something trivial, like dust collecting on the top of an unused tea caddy.

Either way, you developed an immunity to it all, especially in the kitchen. You'd be waiting to load your food up on a tray, yelling for a "side of veg!" as all the cooks ignored you. "Side of veg, please!" you'd beg.

The space between the servers and the cooks had an invisible layer of soundproof glass, but only when you needed something from them. Then, five minutes later, when your food was getting cold, and the horribly outdated kale and orange slice garnish you had to put on the plate was withering away under the heat lamps, the head chef would look over, yell an obscenity, and shoo you back to the dining room . . . still without your side of veg.

"Manhattan! Time ta lean is time ta clean," Ms. Monica said, breezing past me a few hours later. I loathed that expression, even more than "bang for your buck", which to me always sounded like a hick's haiku.

It was my turn in purgatory and it was slow—slow enough that I had to wonder if Ms. Monica was keeping me there just for her cruel amusement. I had to be costing her at least ten times the wage of a normal sever, so it didn't make good business sense for her to keep me—not that I ever mistook her for someone who had any business sense, let alone good business sense.

I tried to focus on her discount customers, whose job it was to inhale copious amounts of food in her low-class cafeteria while simultaneously trying to suck a little more life out of me, but I couldn't. Despite everything else that had been happening, for some reason my mind was drifting to my gym, or better yet, to someone at my gym.

That was the first time I had let myself think of him since I saw him at New Year's. I gazed into the nothingness of the restaurant, past the chintzy decorations, fake brass accents, and caricature sketches on the walls, and let myself wonder what it'd be like to kiss him again.

My apron buzzed me out of my day dream, and I ducked behind one of the room's giant, splinter-wood support poles to check my phone.

"Equinox, 10:00 p.m.," a text from Liv said, speaking directly to my need to disconnect from my mind.

There was no way that the Wicked Bitch of the West was going to release my soul from her talon-like clutches until at least eleven, but I desperately needed to be anywhere in the world but there.

Time for an out.

I walked over to one of the server stations. Ms. Monica had perched herself on a tall stool behind the hostess stand a few feet away. My stomach started to slowly gurgle, and the back of my throat sank. At first, the convulsions were light, almost like a cough to stop the tickle in the back of your throat. Soon, with the aid of the rotting fish smell from the garbage, and my hand pressed against my stomach, the gagging noises started. When I finally heaved what was left of my barbeque burger dinner into the trash can next to me, all heads turned to look at me.

Covering my mouth, I ran past Ms. Monica and into the bathroom. I cleaned myself up and flushed the toilet a few times for good measure. I splashed a bit of water on my forehead and exited the bathroom holding my stomach, worriedly wiping the water off with a paper towel as if it was sweat from my brow.

Ms. Monica pushed her way through a pack of customers over to me. "What's wrong with you?"

I looked at her through innocent eyes. "I don't know what happened. I just couldn't keep it down. I don't know if it was something I ate here or what," I said a little too loudly, and the group of customers next to us started stirring.

Ms. Monica was the type of person who, after you'd burnt yourself severely on a coffee pot, would hand you an ace bandage and some ointment, and then tell you to pick up your table's food from the kitchen and get back to work. I did know her pretty well though, and not only did she not have the stomach to see or smell vomit, she'd recently gotten busted by the health department for knowingly keeping a waitress on her shift after she'd gotten sick.

"She'll take your tables then. Get outta here," Ms. Monica said, pointing to another waitress before fleeing into her office holding her stomach. I gave the sincerest apology to the other waitress that I could, although I was neither sincere nor sorry, before bolting for the exit. As I was opening the door, seconds from freedom, Ms. Monica emerged from her office and screamed at me. "Manhattan, make sure you go ahead and tell Mr. Graham that I'm gonna need both of you on Friday. We got ourselves a big party and I need hands."

You also need brains. Fuck.

"Sure thing, Ms. Monica," I said, still projecting my best queasy voice. It would have been Talia's turn to take the next shift, but Ms. Monica had completely puked all over that plan by demanding both of us. I waved meekly, with all the strength a sick person like me could muster.

Eh . . . that's Friday's problem.

Pushing through the crowds at Equinox later that night, I made my way up the private stairs and smirked at the commoners who were without that luxury. At only ten minutes late, I considered my arrival time a personal record. A crew of men was setting up the stage in the back of the room. The bar was packed full of people waving cash and shiny credit cards in hopes of getting a drink, and the bartenders practically sprinted back and forth behind the bar to accommodate all of them. Cooper was there, standing near the corner in the server's station, talking closely to another man I didn't know. The older man handed Cooper a picture with a piece of paper stapled to it and Cooper looked at it closely as they continued their quiet conversation.

"Hey Coop," I said, coming back down from the stairs and walking up behind the man.

Cooper quickly stuck the image in his pocket and reached for my hand around the other man. "'Ello."

The other man looked annoyed when he turned around to face me. "We'll talk later then," he said before walking away.

"Didn't mean to interrupt," I said, shrugging.

"No worries. We were done anyway."

When Cooper and I made our way upstairs, Elle handed me a full glass of Blue Ice and kissed me on the cheek. Everyone appeared to be in extra high spirits, bouncy even, with the prospect of another exciting evening ahead, full of doing whatever they damn well pleased.

"What's that?" Liv pointed to my neck when I went over to say hello. A glob of ketchup from behind my ear came off as I wiped it with a bar napkin. "Ew," she said.

"I know. I was working at that dump of a restaurant when you texted me, and I didn't have time to shower after I made my escape."

"You didn't have to bag out of work."

"Trust me, I don't mind. I'm sure they can keep working on that cancer cure without me for tonight."

"We're about to start, Coop," one of Cooper's employees said, trying to get his attention. He had pulled Elle to the couch and they laughed to one another seductively, stopping only to sip from their glasses of Blue Ice.

"That doesn't bother you?" I asked Liv, looking over to the couple in dire need of getting a room.

"Them? No. Should it?" She reached into her pocket and unfolded a tiny mirror to look at herself. Her eyes were smoky and sculpted, with long lashes that framed her beautiful blue eyes, and her lips were an extra-luscious shade of pink. Her hair shimmered against the lights of the room, and every piece of clothing she was wearing was just a step above sexy and stylish. Everything was different about her that night.

"I don't know . . . I thought you two had a history," I said.

"So?" She pulled herself in closer to me. "Being like us is about more than just the magic, it's a state of mind—an attitude. We live in the now and own every moment because it's ours to own. Live more and worry less. Remember? Try letting go of the past and just let yourself be, Hat, like him," she whispered intensely into my ear. "Do what makes you happy, when it makes you happy, and don't apologize or regret it."

"Equinox is proud to welcome back Providence native, Olivia Vanguard," the announcer yelled into a microphone from the stage. Liv broke away from me and ran down the stairs to meet him, pushing through the crowd and jumping on stage to take the microphone before signaling the band to start.

I ran out onto the balcony. "She sings?" I asked, pushing myself up next to Elle.

"She sings good . . . ," she said. "But don't tell her I told you that."

The drums started first, and then lights illuminated the stage behind Liv. The crowd cheered unabashedly. She brought the microphone to her lips and the words from her song rebounded off the walls, bringing a euphoric energy to the room. Her body moved to the beat of the song and no one, including me, could take their eyes off her.

You could lose yourself in her lyrics. And each time she touched her hip or shrugged her shoulders as she sang, it was like she was reaching out and kissing your mind with hers. But she didn't need magic for that. Her voice touched every part of your body all at the same time. It is hard to describe, but when you can close your eyes and hear someone's voice singing from inside you, you know that their music has touched you in ways that no music has ever touched you before.

"She's amazing! Why is she singing here and not off recording records somewhere?" I asked to no one in particular.

"Are you saying that she's too good to sing at my club?" Cooper asked. His smile was like that of a small child's who had just put a bug in your pocket when you weren't looking. "She's done a couple of tours regionally, but I do think she's pretty happy to just be a big fish in our small pond."

Liv joined us during the band's break, reeling off the high that she had sung everyone into. She was still in the 'zone', something she'd later tell me was a hyperactive yet almost spacey place she went to in order to bring herself in front of all those people. And performing, that was her way of living in the moment.

Looking at Liv, I thought about what an extraordinary woman she was. If, in her words, I should just be, then why couldn't I just be with her? Then I remembered the last time I finally let go of my need to control how I felt, and how freeing that was. I finished the rest of my drink and headed for the door.

"Hey, where are you going?" Liv called behind me as I walked toward the stairs.

"To own my moment."

Chapter 21

The road to the club was disappearing into my rearview mirror as I sped down the streets of Providence. My hands were wrapped tightly around the steering wheel as I refused to lose my nerve to do what I really wanted to do. There was only one possible destination.

I walked confidently into my gym, breezing past the main desk and not bothering to stop and swipe my member card. Max was standing in gym clothes by the door to his classroom, washing the interior window. I picked up my pace and rushed toward him with a passionate, if not urgent, fearlessness that I had never before experienced.

He turned to silently watch me walk toward him; his beautiful gray eyes the only thing I could see. He tried to say something, but my lips were already over his before he could get it out. I refused to think of or focus on anything except for that moment. No internal debating, no questions, and no hesitation. I was living more and worrying less.

Eagerly, I continued to kiss him, gently holding the back of his neck with one hand and using the other to press him up against the wall. He moaned playfully at my aggression and wasn't able to hide a smile as he kissed me back. I bit his lower lip on the next kiss, running my hand up his shirt and feeling his hard stomach.

Then Max pushed me away a little. "Hat . . ."

I wouldn't listen; I just went back at him, kissing his neck and pulling at his shirt. Before he could protest further, his shirt was over his head.

"Hat . . . ," he said in between kisses. "Wait . . ."

His shirt was on the ground by then, tossed aside with my inhibitions.

"What?" I finally asked with a growl, when he held me back again. He gave a breathy laugh and looked out past me at the rest of the gym. With eyes shut tight, I dropped my head onto his bare chest. "We're in a room full of people, aren't we?"

His chest bounced up and down against my forehead as he laughed harder. "I wouldn't say full."

Smooth, Hat. Really smooth.

"That's so not how I thought this would happen." If given the option, I would have taken a guillotine dropping from the ceiling and chopping off my head rather than having to turn around and face the room of people.

Max grabbed my hair gently, pulling my eyes up from the ground and said, "My office. Now."

We never did leave Max's office that night. The whole experience was surreal, exciting, and almost never-ending. By the time we finally laid still on his daybed, sweaty and exhausted, the early morning gym crowd was already congregating outside his office. Unable to fully catch my breath, I laid my head against his stomach and he absentmindedly played with my hair.

The intense and warm ecstasy we shared that night was everything I had always been looking for, but never found. I never expected to find it with another man, but somehow in that tiny office, just before the sun came up, it didn't matter who it was with. Something inside me changed and I let it. He was what I'd been looking for, I just didn't know it until now.

My inexperience certainly didn't seem to bother Max or stop us from diving off the deep end of each other. Reflecting on the short hours we were together, I couldn't help but feel sad . . . not because of what happened, but because being there, in his arms, was the closest thing to a perfect moment I'd ever felt, and I was sad that we'd have to let that moment go at some point.

I sat up and stretched. "I have to go," I said groggily, looking around for the remains of my clothes.

He rolled over and pulled the blanket around his shoulders. "Don't rush off."

"Rush off?" I laughed. "I've been here all night. I need to shower before my sister's birthday party." I feared showing up at Sydney's house smelling of gym mats and sex. One of my cousins was bound to notice. "And if I don't go home and feed my cat he'll murder me in my sleep tomorrow."

I was forcing my shoe on, unwilling to expend the energy to actually untie it, when Max pulled me back into the bed playfully by my shirt. He put his arm against my chest and used his weight to hold me down. "I'm not letting you up until you say you'll go on a date with me."

"A date?" I asked with a flat grin. "Hmm." Even if I had wanted to say no, I knew those big gray eyes would have been enough to stop me. "Wasn't this a date?"

He leaned in and kissed me, still holding my chest down with his strong arm. "I could keep you here all day," he said, still just inches from my face.

"Alright, alright . . . I submit." I grabbed his phone on the nearby desk and put in my number. "You're better off texting me, I don't usually answer calls."

Max still didn't have any clothes on when I opened his office door, which opened up behind the front desk of the gym. I pulled it shut quickly to shield him and it slammed, causing the chipper five-a.m.-ers, who stood around waiting for their ridiculously early spin class to start, to turn and stare at me.

My shirt was untucked, my hair was . . . well, inexplicable, and since I hadn't bothered to put my underwear on, it stuck out a little from the pocket where I had stuffed it. I gave a gritted-teeth smile and slowly made my way through the hordes of spandex-loving spinners with their fluffy fresh towels and reusable, green-living water bottles. None of them made any effort to move as I struggled to get to the door, knocking into their stuffed gym bags as I walked along what I'd always remember being the longest walk of shame ever.

"May or may not have just had sex with Max," I wrote to Damon in a text message before starting my car.

I got to my house just in time to cross paths with my landlord as he opened his store. I slid meekly past him with a small wave as he pulled up the metal gates covering the main door and windows. He gave me an odd smile, as if to say 'I know what you did last night . . . " and 'don't come anywhere near my daughters.'

If he only knew.

I was all the way past him and almost in my apartment when I noticed that my shirt was not only untucked, it was also on inside-out.

"About damn time," a text from Damon said.

* * * * *

When I arrived at Sydney's house, it was filled to the brim with cousins, siblings, aunts, and even one uncle for good measure. In total, I hadn't gotten more than a few hours of sleep in days and would have rather poked my eye with a rusty nail and walked around for the rest of my days with an eye patch (complete with the pointing and laughing of small children) than face the Walker clan that day. But I also didn't want to take it out on Sydney. It was her first birthday without our mom and I knew that would be hard.

"Uncle!" My plan to slip into the house undetected was thwarted when my nephew jumped into my arms loudly from a nearby chair. Zoe followed, attaching herself to my side. I picked her up too and pretended that I was strong enough to hold both of them up. We fell into the couch and they laughed at me for being a silly adult.

"You made it," Sydney said, as the kids left to cause trouble where everyone would least expect it.

"Wouldn't have missed it," I said, kissing her on the cheek. "Happy birthday, sis." She was still giving me *that* look, the one our mother always gave us, and the same one she had been giving me each time I saw her since our mother's death. "What?" I asked.

"Nothing," she said, leaving me in the living room and taking the empty iced tea pitcher to the kitchen.

She had every right to her feelings about me though. We hadn't been nearly as close as we once were, and I was even more distant since finding out the truth behind our mother's death. I didn't want to be like our mom and keep secrets from her and everyone else, but how could I be the one to tell them she was murdered? And even if I did, how could I rationally explain knowing it was true?

Later, I was trapped in a conversation with one of my aunts' insanely boring boyfriends. I never figured out which aunt, because he was too new to know that when he said "your aunt," he could have been talking about nearly a dozen different people. He also had no idea that talking to him was like talking to a beige chair. Actually, I would have rather been talking to a beige chair. I was only catching every other word he said, just enough to "uh huh" and "sure" in the right places and maintain the illusion of a conversation.

"That makes sense," I said without any idea of what he was talking about. My phone buzzed in my pocket and I pulled it out immediately, pretending it was much more urgent than it could ever be to cut off his attempt to continue the conversation.

"I'm not going to let you forget about that date," a text message from a number I didn't have saved said. I slid my phone back in my pocket, unanswered. Waiting a little while for my response wouldn't kill him.

"Sorry, can I borrow Hat for a second?" Damon said to my aunt's boyfriend. "I need to show him something."

"Excuse me for a second?" I tried to leave him with an expression on my face that implied I might actually come back, but I had no intentions of doing so.

"Thank you, I owe you," I said to Damon as we ducked into the empty hallway. "No Talia today?"

"She's here, somewhere. No Max today? I'm surprised you're rested enough to be here . . ."

I rolled my eyes. "Touché. So, how's it going with you two?"

"Fine."

"So, how's it going with you two?" I asked again with a smile.

"I don't know, good I guess. The same probably. We keep looping around in the same way we always do. You know? We break it off, then she appears in my life and there's definitely this connection, but then something will happen and she pulls away. She's a hard chick to figure out and it gets old after a while. But enough about me, tell me about last night. How did it happen?"

"Look it's Talia," I said as Talia walked out of the bathroom. "Hey Talia! How good to see you."

"Uh, yeah, thanks," Talia said, shunning my fake friendliness and giving Damon a confused look. She took a sip of something orange-colored in her glass and wrapped her arm around Damon's waist.

"Cousins & Cocktails this week?" Damon asked.

"Yeah, maybe," I said.

My eyes shifted to the playroom where all the kids were crowded around Zoe, clapping, laughing, and watching her every move. Much like her mother at that age, Zoe had a commanding persona, one that easily made her the alpha cousin. I slipped quietly into the room and when one of the other kids noticed me, he signaled to the others and the room went silent as the group looked to Zoe to lead their alibi.

"What are we up to?" I asked them. They weren't old enough yet to understand that I was their age once, and I had done the same thing with my own cousins when caught by one of the adults. "Alright, what trouble are you causing?"

"Nothin' Uncle, we're just talking," Zoe said factually, nodding at her brothers and cousins in silent instruction for them to agree with her. In her hand was a key chain with her cousin's name on it.

"Zoe's doin' tricks," one of the kids blurted out.

Bending down to eye level with the group of children, I asked, "What kind of tricks?" From the corner of my eye I could see Zoe start waving her hands around and mouthing something to the rest. I moved my body to block her from the others.

There was a natural order with the Walkers, the same as in any other family I suppose. The children tried to keep secrets with one another, and the adults used their experience, having once been children themselves, to pry those secrets out of them. I couldn't judge the kids, though, because as I had recently learned, adults keep secrets too.

"She's tellin' us when we got stuff," Zoe's youngest brother said. He had already lost interest in the conversation and was pushing a dump truck around on the ground.

"Hey, I think they're bringing the cake out," I said to the group, pointing to the other room. They scattered and stampeded over me at the prospect of a mid-day sugar high.

"Not so fast," I said, grabbing Zoe's arm as she tried to follow the rest out of the room. "Tell me about your trick."

"Ugh. It's n-b-d," Zoe said, rolling her eyes.

"If it's no big deal then show me," I said, brushing off her real world use of text message lingo. *I'm not THAT much older than you, little girl.*

"I don't know . . . I just pick stuff up and I can tell you where it came from."

I reached into my pocket and pulled out my cell phone. "Okay, David Copperfield, show me," I said handing it to her.

"Who's that?"

I groaned. "Just show me."

She closed her eyes and slowly rubbed her hands around the screen. "You got it last summer. It was hot that day, but you had to get a new phone because you dropped your old one in the parking lot at work and it broke. Hmm." She stopped for a second, twitching her face. "You went with Auntie Charley. She thought the case was ugly, but you got it anyway. Then you dropped it as soon as you got out of the store and that's how it got this crack." She opened her eyes and handed the phone back to me.

That was no trick. Everything she said happened, just how she said it did, right down to the crack. "How'd you do that?"

"I dunno," she laughed, folding her lips over her braces, "it just happens when I touch stuff."

"Is it like you see it happening in your head, like a picture or a movie?"

"Ugh. No. I don't know. It's like someone told me a story about it a long time ago, and when I touch it I remember what they said."

"Did someone tell you the story about me getting this phone? Auntie Charley maybe?"

"No. I don't know. It's hard to explain. I just kinda know. You don't believe me?"

I looked into her bright, grass-green eyes. "No Zo, I do. It's a pretty cool trick . . . but can you do your uncle a favor?"

She flipped her hair to the side and crossed her arms. "What?"

"Can you keep it a secret?"

"Why?"

I didn't have a good answer to that. "Because."

She rolled her eyes at me and tossed her hair again. We both knew that she was too old to accept "because" as a valid reason for having to do anything.

"Can you just trust me on this? Please? Are you old enough to do that; to just trust me because I'm your uncle and I'm asking you to?" I didn't have any other way to explain it to her. How do you tell an eleven-year-old that you need her to keep her magical powers under wraps until you've figured out whether or not it's safe for her to use them?

"Yeah, whatever," she said.

"Promise?"

She did promise, and I believed her, or at least I believed that she wasn't planning to tell anyone. As she walked out of the playroom, she passed Talia looking over us. "Everything okay?" Talia asked.

"Yeah, it'll be fine," I said, turning away from her and looking out the window. There really wasn't anything she could have done to help, even if I had a way to ask her for it.

As I sat alone in the playroom, I pondered the implications of Zoe's powers, feeling more isolated from my family than ever. I couldn't explain any of what was happening with Zoe to her mother without explaining everything else to her. It was another unfair rift in our relationship and things were already so rocky between us. It ate at me a little to hold it all in, but until I could be sure they'd be safe knowing the truth, I'd have to keep that from them too. In the meantime, I had to hope that an eleven-year-old's promise to keep a secret would last long enough for me to figure that out.

To ward off the ever-watchful eye of my enlarged family, I pretended I was watching TV as I inched my way slowly toward the door. There were just too many thoughts running around in my head, thoughts I couldn't talk about with anyone there, and thoughts I couldn't stand pretending I didn't have any longer.

Just as I was about to reach for the doorknob, someone poked the back of my head. "Looks like someone's got a little less hair to brush in the morning," Victor said, his eyes blood-shot and his breath reeking of pot.

"Mm hmm. Thanks," I said.

"Don't start crying about it, I'm just saying."

"Right. I'm actually on my way out, I'll see you later," I said, finally grabbing the door knob.

"Wait," Victor said, holding the door closed. "Did Syd talk to you about the paperwork for the house?"

I released a deep breath and let go of the door knob. "No, but I signed everything last week and sent it back to the lawyer. He should have it soon if he doesn't already."

"You don't have to get all huffy about it. She told you we can't do anything with the house until you sign off, right? I've got some stuff coming up and I need the money."

"Yup. Don't you worry, you'll get your money."

"What the hell is your problem?" Victor asked, moving between me and the door.

"You mostly," I said, looking around cautiously to see who might be listening. "I hate the fact that the only thing you care about is selling her house, and the only thing I hate more is the fact that I wasn't expecting you to act any differently."

"It's not the only thing I care about, fuck head. But yeah, I want the damn thing sold so I can go about my business. What good is it to us until it's sold anyway?"

"You're right, I'm the asshole."

"Don't get indignant with me because I refuse to make this family my be-all-end-all like the rest of you. And I love that you act like I'm the one that treats the family like shit when you're the one who's never around."

Did you ever think that you're the reason I'm not around anymore?

Chapter 22

"*Neither will I,*" I wrote back to Max as I walked to my car.

His next message lit up my phone quickly. "*So when?*"

I smiled, but he couldn't have known that. "*You tell me.*"

Planning a date was a lot easier once you'd already slept with the person. There was simply no pressure to be had. You already established whether or not you'd be willing to see the person again if you were still in their bed when they woke up the following morning. It was the only way to plan a first date.

"*Is tonight too soon?*" his next text asked.

It wasn't too soon for me. We decided to meet at a restaurant downtown called Brickhouse. They had great food and were always just busy enough to where you didn't have to shout to talk or wait for a table, but you also weren't sitting there in an empty room.

Max was perched at the bar waiting for me when I walked in. He wore a sharp black, fitted dress shirt over jeans and a light leather jacket. He looked great.

When I walked up to him, he leaned in and kissed me, completely unfazed by anyone who may have been watching.

He smelled like leather and fresh cranberries, a combination I admit sounds odd, but will also admit smells incredibly sexy. In contrast, I smelled like two cups of a coffee and a stale muffin, the only things I had allowed in my body that day.

"Glad you could make it," he said, handing me a full glass of wine.

He looked too good for me to tell him that I didn't like wine. "Yeah, you know, I had some free time and this cute guy I know texted me earlier." I took an obligatory sip of the wine and placed it back on the bar. "So I figured I'd come for dinner with you before I had to meet up with him."

Max tightened his lips, gave a fake scowl, and touched my knee. "Don't make me show everyone in this place just how hot you are for me," he whispered into my ear, his hand running up my leg.

"Um," the skinny and short hostess interrupted us apprehensively from a distance. "Sir, your table is ready if you'd like."

Dinner was perfect, and I don't remember a thing I ate. Talking to Max was a lot like talking to myself, and that made me uncharacteristically calm. I never had to worry about saying the wrong thing, because he acted like everything I said was the right thing. He was slowly showing me that a date, unlike all the dates I had ever been on, didn't have to be painful or uncomfortable.

We talked about everything, like my affinity for architecture, and his one guilty pleasure (or the only one he admitted)—old country songs. He liked hearing my crazy stories about Cartwright & Company or my family, and I was enthralled by his ambition. He opened his gym when he was just twenty-six, and only two years later it was wildly successful and growing more popular by the day.

Max wasn't what I pictured when I thought of a gay man. He was strong and confident, manly, and had never hung a rainbow-colored flag anywhere on his person, ever. He didn't swish, he had no desire to wear makeup, and he played football in a league avidly and aggressively every season. I was unintentionally holding onto a lot of stereotypes about a man who sleeps with other men, even after I'd done it myself. I knew if I let him, Max could help me change all that.

It was liberating to have a conversation with someone where you could say anything. Well, anything except for the obvious; that I sometimes could see the past, that my mother was murdered, and that I had some mythical necklace too powerful to understand. Other than all that, I was totally an open book.

"What?" he asked at one point when he caught me getting mesmerized by those big gray eyes.

"Nothing. Just thinking about you."

"But I'm right here."

"So?" I asked, laughing.

The night continued with more wine, which I was starting to change my mind about, and a lot of laughter. He was captivated when I spoke, even when what I was talking about was frivolous or stupid. We were so deep in our own world that it took our waitress pulling the salt and pepper shakers from our table for us to sit back and realize that the restaurant was empty, and that all the chairs had been put up on the tables, except for ours, in preparation to close.

Max grabbed my hand as we left the restaurant. "Wanna go for a walk? I don't think I'm ready to let tonight be over yet."

It was crisp and cold that night, an easy excuse to pull close together as we walked. The winter winds blew through the tunnel-like streets of Providence's financial district, knocking us around and chilling our exposed flesh. It was quiet, all the other businesses were closed by that time of night and there was hardly anyone left in the streets.

We turned down one of the short alleyways, and Max pushed me against a brick building. He kissed me, his lips full of life and growing more accustomed to mine. "You could kiss a thousand people in your life and never feel like this," he said when he pulled away.

"Is that your way of telling me you've kissed a thousand people?"

Normally, I'd find a statement like that a little too gushy, but the manly and genuine way he said it made my stomach jump a little instead. He grabbed my hand and pulled me along through the alley. His hands were strong and comfortable to hold, and he made me feel like nothing else in my life mattered; all that mattered was us, in that moment.

The sound of metal rapping against the building behind us startled me. We turned around to see two muscle Guidos moving down the alley toward us, like two stone towers sliding across a chess board. A third Guido, a near-replica of the others, appeared from around the corner at the other end of the alley, boxing us in. Max's nose flared a little as they started to close in on us.

"What's up, fags?" one of the Guidos said with a snort. He was still dragging the thick metal pipe along the building as he walked, leaving white streaks of brick dust behind him.

This can't be good.

"What's this?" Max said to the pipe-wielding Guido. He pushed at my chest gently, moving me behind him.

"What's what? We just thought we'd talk," Pipe Guido said back to him.

The Guido with the goatee, the one on Pipe Guido's side, had a menacing look on his already grim and scratchy face. He didn't look smart enough to form his own sentences, but he did look strong enough to beat on you until he got his point across. The third Guido, the one with the popped collar, was shuffling in closer behind us.

"Who needs a pipe to talk?" Max asked calmly. He moved his left leg out in front of him, steadying his stance and bending his knees slightly.

Pipe Guido lowered his head and looked to his side at Goatee Guido, giving him a nod. When he'd lifted his head back up, he lunged at Max without warning, pulling the pipe above him in preparation to strike.

Max lifted his arm and stepped forward into Pipe Guido's path gracefully, blocking his arm before the pipe could make its way down. In one, uninterrupted move, Max's hand opened and wrapped around Pipe Guido's wrist. He pulled at the man's arm, forcing it to stiffen. Max's other hand quickly came up from his side, striking Pipe Guido's stiffened elbow with the inside of his straightened hand.

Pipe Guido's face contorted in pain as his elbow popped out of place, but Max was already striking him again with the same hand, this time just below Pipe Guido's ribcage. Pipe Guido bent over involuntarily with a grunt, using his good arm to hold his side.

Max used Pipe Guido's brief submission to swing both of their bodies around and force the pipe in his hand to hit Goatee Guido, as he came up on their left. Using Pipe Guido's hand, still clasped around the pipe, Max struck Goatee Guido, first in the knee, and then swiftly at the base of his neck on the other side. The loud cracking of his bones resonated off the walls with each blow, and with a large thud, he folded to the ground.

Collar Guido, who had been standing idle behind Max until then, watched the action and waited for his moment to enter the fight. Pipe Guido had regained some control over his pain-stricken body and had reached around to grab at Max's clothing with his free hand. Like a puppet master, and still holding his bruised arm, Max twisted Pipe Guido's arm to his will, forcing him to his knees in pain.

Goatee Guido was still heaving on the ground, holding his battered knee, when Collar Guido took his opportunity and jumped onto Max from behind, completely avoiding me in the process. He was able to land a powerful strike with his knee into Max's back, with just enough force to make Max release Pipe Guido.

Pipe Guido sprinted forward out of Max's reach. Max had his hands on his knees, his back still in pain, but it was short-lived. As Collar Guido sprung at him again with flailing, unskilled fists, Max executed one perfect back kick to his stomach. The air exploded violently from Collar Guido's lungs, and he slowly bent over, coughing. Then Max spun his entire body and pulled the heel of his foot into his hand by his head, and then released it with a tremendous force against the back of Collar Guido's bent neck, sending him face-first into the ground.

The other two had recovered when Max turned around again. They circled him and tried to pretend they weren't still in pain. Max looked at me long enough to throw me a wink.

Is he enjoying this?

Collar Guido leapt at Max with a pathetic battle cry, but Max caught him mid-air and, turning into his jump, effortlessly tossed him into the nearby trash cans. His landing tossed them all loudly around the ally, forcing rats to scamper out of their winter hideouts and past our feet. Unfortunately, Pipe Guido saw his opportunity, and with both hands, he hit Max squarely in the stomach with the pipe like a baseball bat.

Spit and a little bit of blood shot out of Max's mouth as he fell backward onto the ground, landing on his back. Goatee

Guido was already on his feet, lifting his large boot in preparation to kick Max in the face.

"No," I yelled shortly. The Opalescence went cold and tingled against my chest. Like it was telling me what to do, my hand shot up and raw, untamed power shot out flinging Goatee Guido at the wall. He bounced off it like rags in a hamper before landing on the trash cans.

Luckily, Max was too occupied to see me use those powers. Pipe Guido had made an unskilled attempt to kick him once he'd stood up, but he easily blocked it. Max's right leg came up and struck Pipe Guido in his kidney with the flat top of his shoe. Then he pulled the same leg back to his body and without putting it down, he launched the bottom of his foot directly at Pipe Guido's face.

"Enough," Collar Guido yelled, holding his bloody nose with one hand and pulling a small knife out of his pocket with the other. He pulled back to regroup, and Pipe Guido stepped behind him.

"Shit," Max said as they both approached him.

My heart stopped as the knife sliced through the air at Max. At the last second, he somehow managed to dive into the open space between the two men, landing nimbly on the ground behind them. As he twisted around to get back up, Max pushed against his back and drove both his feet into the rear of Collar Guido's knees, forcing him to land hard on the ground. Collar Guido screamed out, as both his knees popped and slammed against the pavement.

"Max!" I called out, throwing him a broken broom handle from one of the trash cans. It hurtled through the air and, as if the make-shift staff was an extension of his own arm, Max caught it and the force of the weapon followed through to spin around his body. The splintered end landed first across Pipe

Guido's face, drawing blood. The other end caught up quickly, striking him across the back of the head.

Max followed through and used the end of the broom's solid tip to poke Collar Guido's jugular. Hitting someone there doesn't require a lot of strength, as I saw by Collar Guido falling to the ground and struggling to breathe. One brilliant strike after another with the staff, the sound of wood against bone rattled off the brick walls at us. A cracking noise was next, as the staff struck and broke Collar Guido's nose.

Like an instrument, Max continued skillfully using the staff in the symphony of their defeat. Watching him was entertaining, so much so that I didn't see Goatee Guido get up and come at me from behind. He threw himself on my back, reaching his hand into my shirt and pulling the Opalescence off. "Ha," he yelled into my ear.

"Is this what you came for?" I hissed, throwing my elbow into Goatee Guido's stomach, pushing him backward. Then I turned and thrust the palm of my hand into his nose. He set his arm to throw a forceful punch, but before he could hit me, my foot shot up between his legs.

I grabbed the back of his swaying head with both of my hands and thrust it down upon my waiting knee. His eyes were closed before he hit the ground, unconscious and bleeding. I slipped the Opalescence back over my head before Max had finished with the other two. Pipe Guido ended up in a crumpled mess on the ground, and Collar Guido escaped, limping down the alley.

Max came over to me, dropped the broom handle and kissed me softly. I could taste blood from his split lip in my mouth. "You okay?" he asked me.

"Is this what you do on all your dates?"

Chapter 23

One early morning, months later, I was sleeping in Max's heavenly, oversized bed when the light sounds of one of my favorite songs tickled me awake. Max sat on the edge of the bed wearing only a tight pair of trunks and a guitar. I rolled over and wrapped his fluffy white comforter around my naked body and gave him a sleepy, content smile, with my eyes still half closed.

He continued his song and I was drowning deep inside his sound as his fingers danced over the guitar strings. His voice was both invading and inviting. It was like standing at the base of a waterfall and letting its warm, fresh water pour over your head and down your body. I hummed the song along with him, swaying a bit from side to side. Each movement of the strings was like a movement in my heart, another happy moment I'd be sad to leave.

When he finished, he laid the guitar at the foot of the bed and climbed back into the covers with me. He forced his head onto my pillow, kissed me, and stared into my eyes. "Good morning, handsome," he said. He smiled and the spot where the doctor had stitched his lip a few months before was still a light shade of pink, reminding me what a dead sexy hero he was.

"How come I didn't know you could sing like that?" I asked him.

"I don't know. I guess it's not something I just give to anyone."

"What's that on the side?" I said, pointing at the guitar.

"My dad's signature. He and my mom were really into music when I was younger. I think my sister and I learned how to sing before we learned how to talk. We didn't even have a TV growing up, just a piano. Sometimes I really miss him, and his guitar makes me feel better—like I have something of his to stay close to. Is that silly?"

I laughed. "Definitely not." I held up the Opalescence, the only thing I was wearing, and showed it to him. "This was my Mom's."

"What was she like?"

"Amazing. I know everyone says that about their mom, or I guess people who like their mom say that about their mom, but she really was. She was gentle, and warm, and so full of love."

"Hmmm," he hummed into my ear, "it sounds like someone else I know."

"Yeah?" I laughed and pretended I didn't know who he was talking about. Then I kissed him deeply to change the subject.

Time was helping me heal, but Max's overly inquisitive nature, combined with my complete comfort in telling him anything, meant we could too easily fall into a sand trap of questions that I couldn't answer.

"So why don't you sing more often? For me more often. I liked it," I said.

"I guess I have to be inspired."

"And you're inspired this morning?" As he went to speak, I covered his mouth quickly with my hand. "I swear if you say some dribble about me inspiring you, I'll have to vomit all over your nice sheets."

He yanked my hand away and we both laughed as he leaned in to kiss me wildly. I liked kissing him enough that it didn't even bother me that he had morning breath, or that the stubble on his face was scratchy as all hell.

"It's not like these sheets are all that clean after last night anyway." He laughed, slapped me on the thigh, and got out of bed. "What do you have going on today?"

"Ugh. I have to go into the office for a couple hours and get ready for some big meeting that's happening this week. Exciting, right?"

"I guess it's exciting if you make it exciting. You going to stop by the gym after?"

"Maybe."

He looked like he might have been a little disappointed when I said that, but if he was he didn't say it. "Come on, you're getting so much better with your balance, and I still can't believe how fast you've picked up some of the blocks and strikes I've been showing you."

"I learn fast."

"Oh yes, I know." Mr. Gym-body was already dressed and ready for his workout. The only workout I was planning that morning was several reps with my full coffee mug.

"Do you have plans tonight?" he asked me.

"Just hanging out with some friends, you?"

"Work. But nothing after." He lifted his eyebrow. "When do I get to meet these supposed friends of yours?"

I laughed and dragged my feet over to the coffee pot. "When I'm ready to share you."

Being with Max made everything else that happened in my life a little easier to digest. He grounded me from the intense spinning of the world around us. He made me feel good about myself; so good that keeping him away from Equinox and the people there got harder as time went on. He hadn't met any of my family either, at least not in the context of us being together. The connection I once had with all of them had yet to repair itself, which was the only thing Max ever thought was suspicious about me.

"You talk about your family a lot. They seem like such a huge part of your life, but you never see any of them," he said to me a few weeks after we first started dating.

I brushed it off as being busy, with him, and work, and everything else. I couldn't have begun to explain to him that my detachment from them was about my exploration into a life that I couldn't share with them, or him for that matter. Knowing them as well as I did, and knowing that they knew me as well as they did, it would only be a matter of time before one of them forced my hand.

My family's size and closeness already created a dynamic that was too hard for Max to truly understand. No matter how I said it, there was no way to explain to him what the change in my relationship with my family was about, not without risking what we had.

"Okay, so tonight's taken by your friends. When do I get a piece of you?" Max asked as he chugged a protein shake.

"You got a piece of me just last night, Mister," I said. "Tell you what, this Sunday, you and me. I'll cook."

"Oh yeah? Since when do you cook?" Max came up behind me as I poured my coffee and wrapped his strong arms around my stomach. "What are you going to make?"

I turned around tilted my head back to look at him. "Something fast and something we can eat in bed. Maybe eggs."

"I love sex and eggs," he said before kissing me. "You have a deal."

With coffee in hand, I went to the window and tightened Max's terrycloth bathrobe around my waist. He was so much taller than me that the tail-end of the material dragged behind me on the ground as I walked. His condo had an amazing view of the Providence River, and his window was just high enough to be able to see the surrounding streets start their lazy movement. I pulled my cell phone out of the robe's pocket and looked at the time, 10:00 a.m.

Okay, so maybe it's not so early.

It wouldn't be the first time I was late to work because of Max.

I was only on my second rep with my coffee when Max ran past me with his gym bag. "Late. Gotta go," he said, reaching in and kissing my neck. "Stay as long as you want, just lock the door when you leave. Or . . . you could call out of work and stay in bed until I get home."

"Bye," I said, throwing a packet of raw sugar at him as he walked out the door.

* * * * *

The fleeting months of winter had somehow landed me in a normal cycle, if normal was ever something you could describe my life as. For the first time since I found out my mother was murdered, I felt like I was moving forward. I would never forget what happened, but like the cut above Max's lip, I was slowly healing and accepting that life goes on.

The inherently relaxed environment at Equinox made it easy to not dwell on that or any of the other things that pulled at me from the past. Without any visions, ghosts, or gangs of thugs to remind me of my obligation to it, the Opalescence became more like a piece of inherited jewelry, and less like a burdensome duty with powers I didn't understand yet.

"You got another message from your sister," Talia said to me when I got to work the next morning. "Are you going to call her back?" The pink message paper she handed me was crumpled up and in the trash can before Talia even finished speaking.

Victor was still floating around Providence, which didn't do anything to ease my discomfort around my family. After I finally signed those papers, they were able to put my mother's house on the market. They'd gotten a few low-ball offers, but none they were willing to accept. Knowing Victor, he would never leave town until he got his cash. Knowing me, I would spend a lot less time around all of them until he did.

"Damon was asking about you the other day too," Talia said as I scrolled through my email. "He said he hasn't seen you since your sister's birthday party."

"Yeah, I know. I've been busy."

"With Max?" Talia asked, sitting on my desk.

I kept reading through my emails, or more appropriately, deleting emails without reading them. These days my focus was rarely on my job.

"Hello? What's going on with you?" Talia asked, waving her hand in between my computer and my face.

I sighed and turned away from my email. "Sorry. What did you say?"

"What the hell is wrong? Did I do something?"

"What? No. Of course not."

"Then why don't you ever talk to me anymore?"

So much of my life involved magic these days. Keeping it a secret meant sacrificing close relationships with those that weren't in that world, like Talia. And it meant I had to be more guarded than usual.

"I'm sorry," I said to her. "It's not you, it's me."

She shrugged and pouted a little. "Is it because I'm dating Damon again? I know things have been weird between you and your family, but if that's it, I won't tell him anything you don't want him to know, I promise. I just want things with us to be like they were before, you know . . . best friends forever."

That was not a phrase I had ever used in my life, with her or anyone else for that matter. "I swear it has nothing to do with you, or Damon. I've just been in my own little world. And yes, I've been spending a lot of time with Max."

"How's that going?" Talia asked.

My feelings for Max grew every single day we were together, and we had been together a lot in the last few months. He was patient with me, so patient, as I slowly figured out who I was and freed myself from the reclusive thoughts that had dominated my life before him. He never once pressured me to do or say anything more than I was ready to. I had never experienced feelings at that level for anyone before, and I didn't know how to express them to him, or myself. I spent so much time just allowing myself to be happy that I hadn't really thought about how to put words to it all. The only thing I did know was that it no longer mattered to me that those feelings were toward a man, especially a man I found as captivating as Max.

"It's been really . . . exciting," I said, smiling as I thought more about Max. Just as Talia started to say something else, an

IM popped up on my screen. The receptionist was informing me that my sister was in the lobby, and she refused to leave until she talked to me. "I have to go take care of this. I'm sorry."

"Wait," Talia said, as I walked away.

"What's up, sis?" I asked Sydney when I got to the lobby. She was standing in the middle of the room with her arms crossed and eyebrows pointed.

"Can we talk somewhere?" she asked.

I brought her into a nearby conference room and pulled out a chair for her, but she didn't bother to sit down.

"I just want to say that I think it's really shitty that you haven't called me back," she said. "Fifteen messages. That's how many I've left. What if it were important? What if one of the kids were hurt and I needed you?"

I panicked a little. "What happened? Are the kids okay?"

"They're fine. I'm just saying, it could have been that."

"Okay, fine. You know I never check voicemail. So, what's up?"

"What's up? You want to know what's up." She started pacing the room. "Okay, well, my mom died last summer, and since then my brother has decided to completely abandon me and the rest of his family."

"Come on," I said, trying to hug her. "I didn't abandon anyone."

"No. You can't just hug me and think I'm going to forgive you. I'm trying to hold this family together, Hat, and I have to tell you, I'm not doing a very good job of it."

"What do you want me to say?"

"I want you to say that you'll stop hiding out. You know I understand how you work. You avoid things when they get rough, and I tried, or I'm trying, to be patient about that. But you can't do it forever. Not with us."

"Syd . . ."

"I can't figure out if you're just being selfish, or if you think we don't all know about that boyfriend of yours. Oh god, please tell me that he's not the reason you're hiding out. Trust me, no one cares who you sleep with . . . and it's not like it was a huge surprise to anyone anyway."

"Thanks, that's sweet," I said, rolling my eyes.

"I'm serious Manhattan. I feel all alone out there. You're not around, Finn is about as much help as he ever is, and Victor is . . . Victor. I had to tell him, you know, about what you did with your share of the house. He exploded all over me about it. Me. He exploded all over me about something you did. How fair is that?"

"You're right, it's not fair at all. I'm sorry."

"That's it? You're sorry?"

"What do you want me to say? Things have been . . . I've just been . . . I don't know. Things haven't been the same. I haven't been the same, and I'm trying to figure it all out. I'm sorry. I'll try harder."

"How about at all?"

"Syd, I said I was fucking sorry, what more do you want?"

"I want my brother back."

Chapter 24

$\mathcal{S}$ ydney left with little interest in goodbyes. She had come for a reason, and she had spewed that reason all over me. Was she wrong? No. But she didn't really know everything else that was going on, did she? And throwing Max in my face like that, that was low—the kind of blow only a sister can execute effectively.

"What happened?" Talia asked me as I got back to my desk.

"Oh, you know, just getting berated for being myself. Nothing new," I said, turning my attention to my phone.

"Spring Fever Party. Tomorrow night. Meet at The Playground at 7:30 p.m.," a text message from Cooper said.

March was coming to an end and most of the snow had finally melted away. Saturday morning had already started off warmer than usual, and I knew that the entire city would be rushing around for some much needed winter release. When I got to The Playground, the entire crew was waiting outside, sipping on soda bottles filled with Blue Ice.

"I'm not late," I yelled as I got out of my car. It was warm enough to finally wear shorts, something we were all taking full advantage of.

"Yeah right," Liv yelled back to me. "Let's go already." She jumped into the back of Cooper's topless jeep.

"Shotgun," I called, jumping into the jeep as another car full of Casters took off.

Cooper gave a half smile as he floated past me and climbed into the driver's side of his jeep without opening the doors. "Fancy a bit of fun?" he asked.

Elle climbed in next to Liv, and Cooper took off fast. By the time we were on the main road, the music in the jeep blaring, I raised my arms high and let the warm wind run through my fingers.

There was a certain high that came from hanging out with them. Their world, our world, was liberating, and it made it so easy for everything else to just fade into the distance.

Liv and Elle, who were usually oil to each other's water, were dancing close, enjoying the spirit of the day. Each had one hand holding their drink, and one hand clutching the roll bar of the jeep. A short song was on repeat and in full force when we pulled off onto a route toward the shoreline. I left my maturity in the wind and found myself dancing and singing along with the rest of them. The crowd yelled the lyrics again as the song started over, just as we passed a cop waiting in the bushes.

"Shit," I yelled, leaning forward and watching the cop pull out behind us from the side mirror. "Quick, sit down," I yelled to the back.

Cooper shifted the jeep roughly and it screeched through the next light. We were easily over the speed limit by twenty miles, and he gave no sign that he was going to slow down. The cop's lights came on and his siren blared after us. Cooper still didn't stop.

"You have to pull over," I yelled to Cooper. Part of me was completely panicked at his disregard for the law, yet the other part of me was electrified by his 'I'll do what I like' attitude.

"Relax. It's all under control," Cooper said. He smiled and looked in the rearview mirror. "Elle, love, care to take this one?"

Elle sat and rubbed her palms together. Cooper had turned off onto a side street and the cop followed, gaining speed. Elle grabbed the jeep's roll bar with both hands and smirked at me as I tried to figure out what she was doing. We made another sharp turn and Cooper dropped his speed to an almost dead stop.

The police car whipped around the corner behind us, sirens louder than ever, but then passed us completely. The cop glanced back at us briefly before hitting his accelerator and curbing around the next corner.

"How did you just get out of that?" I asked.

"You want to see what he saw, baby?" Elle asked in my ear, holding her hand out to me.

When I grabbed her hand, a bright light exploded over my eyes, like the flash from a camera. When I could see again, I looked around the jeep and it had turned into an old, rusted, champagne-colored sedan. The four of us, myself included, looked like little old women, riding carefully along the road with purses in our laps and perfectly chiseled white hair surrounding our wrinkled faces.

Elle released my hand, our likeness returned to normal, and everyone laughed. "I can't believe you did that," I said.

"Sure you can," Cooper said. "Come on then, who's better than us?" He reached into the back and pulled Elle toward him. "Brilliant babe, simply brilliant," he said before pulling her into a kiss and ignoring the road in front of him.

The three other grannies and I ended up at a bar on the beach near Newport an hour later. The town was dead, as it typically was in the spring. Cooper said he had a friend who owned a bar where "the waves literally come up and hit the doors," and he always had a party to celebrate the start of the season.

"It's just nearest and dearest," Cooper said when we got out of the jeep. "Nearest and dearest" translated into over two hundred people dancing and drinking around the outside bar. Loud dance music blasted over the speakers, and shots were flowing down large ice towers at the ends of the bar.

As soon as we walked past the bar, an unknown man handed the girls a drink and they continued to the dance floor. "Coming?" Elle asked me, walking backward to keep pace with the Liv.

"No way." I waved my hand. "I don't dance."

She stopped, looked at me with a seductive smile and then pulled my arm toward her. "You do now." She finished her entire drink in one gulp and slid the glass onto a table without looking. She pulled my hand over her head and onto her shoulder, dancing in front of me as she pulled me further and further into the dancing crowd.

"No, really," I said.

"You still don't get it," Elle said. She grabbed a drink from a man's hand and downed the entire thing.

"What don't I get?" I asked over the music.

She leaned in close. "We're like rock stars, and just because we can't tell these people why, it doesn't mean we can't still act like it." The dance floor was packed, and the beats of a rhythmic reggaeton song bounced over everyone's body. Elle fingered her long hair with both hands and swung her exposed sides to the music.

"Loosen up your hips," she said, putting her hands on each of my hips and forcing them to move. "Yeah, you're getting better. Now put a little attitude into it," she snapped her fingers and giggled.

Elle motioned for another man to hand her his drink, and he did so without question. Maybe she was right, maybe we were like rock stars. Cooper certainly thought so too, but it didn't make me feel any less like a dorky kid at his first middle school dance.

A handful of shots appeared, and we finished them off, tossing the empty plastic cups onto the ground and pushing our way through the crowd to a coveted spot near the DJ. More shots. Elle rocked me around that dance floor, amazing everyone around us with her sexy and perfectly spontaneous moves. Each round of shots seemed to taste more bitter, and I longed for the custom taste of Blue Ice.

She continued to ride me like that for a least another hour, becoming progressively more drunk as she did. "Mmmm," she cooed at one point after falling into me. "You're still so innocent. Untainted. I love that about you." She gently but unsteadily ran her hand down my cheek and I looked into her eyes. They seemed dimmer than before, lacking the boldness and luster that once pulsated from them.

"My turn with him," Liv said, dancing up behind us and shooing Elle away. "Having fun?" she asked me.

"Yeah, I am. You?"

"It's nice to be outside." She wrapped her arms around my neck and we danced slowly together.

"What is it?" I asked as she stared at me.

"Nothing. It just seems like you've fallen in pretty well with the group."

"You didn't want me to get along with them?"

"No, I did . . . I guess it's just . . . you know what? Never mind, it doesn't matter."

"My turn again," Elle yelled, pulling Liv off me. Liv continued to stare at me for a while before disappearing completely from the crowd. The women in my life were so complicated. Was she jealous of Elle, or did she just not want me to get so cozy with her friends? I wish I had her powers to be able to tell what she was thinking.

"Careful mate, she'll dance your shit off," Cooper said when I collapsed next to him at the bar. "Need a drink?"

"I need two," I said, wiping some of the sweat off my face with a bar napkin. "She's a trip . . . I'm exhausted."

Cooper ordered us a few drinks and we sat quietly and watched everyone.

The Spring Fever Party was in full swing and Elle captured another man on the dance floor and kept going at full speed. The bar's owner came up and patted Cooper on the shoulder. "My man, Coop. How are you?" he asked.

"I'm excellent. Top notch party, my friend," Cooper said.

The bar owner reached into his back pocket to pull out a folded envelope. As he handed it to Cooper, I could see the name Oddities in the corner. "Here's what we talked about," he said.

"Good. I'll take care of it," Cooper said before the man walking away.

"What was that?" I asked.

"Nothing mate," Cooper said, signaling the bartender again, "just a little business."

I was still sweating from my time on the dance floor, so I didn't notice it at first. But when the lights and noises changed, I knew I was being overtaken by my first vision in months. I fought it at first, having no desire to see horrible things like I did the last time. But the more I fought it, the more violent it got—tossing and turning me into submission before landing me in that place of weightlessness.

Black candles, hundreds of them, littered a dank basement room. Elaborate symbols were methodically carved into the wax of each, and their flames roared with unusually dark colors.

In the center of the room, light bended, creating ripples in the air like gas from an exhaust pipe. It quickly became more pronounced, contorting the light and forming a shape. It all happened in less than a second, but when it was over and the ripples were gone, there stood the man without a face, holding an envelope just like the one Cooper had.

The blank canvas of his face crinkled slightly as he breathed under the mask, and his fierce white hair reflected the light of the candles back at me. He unzipped his sweatshirt and exposed his thin frame. Then, he picked up a random candle and, without flinching, extinguished it by thrusting the flame into his bare chest.

"And we begin," he said to no one. His voice was muffled under the mask and with each word, charcoal-like smudges would appear on and then disappear from his face.

The untamed flames of every candle burned higher than before, and melted wax dripped over their cryptic symbols. The symbols glowed deep from the core of the candles, and then the flames doused themselves. Like creepy jack-o-lanterns, the symbols cast the only light into the room.

"It's time," he whispered.

The symbols pulsated with orange light, a majestic color that snaked into every corner of the room. And with each beat the symbols would pull themselves further and further from the physical attachment of the candles, until they drifted independently in the air around him.

Currents of sound followed, like wind thumping against hollow trees. They were slow, intense, and unnerving, and somewhere underneath them speech formed in a slithering whisper.

"You must be patient," the voice said.

"I have been patient! I've been nothing but patient," the man with no face said. "It's time to take what is mine."

The symbols started swarming clockwise around him, unbounded magic at the command of its master. Then three of the symbols met in the air and collided, their misty colors fusing together into an image. Like the reflection from my own mirror, they showed him the Opalescence, me wearing the Opalescence.

"You have already failed once," the voice told him.

"I didn't expect that boyfriend of his," the man with no face said. "You should have just let me use magic in the first place."

"I meant with his mother. It doesn't matter. His visions are unpredictable, and that charm you're using doesn't guarantee he won't be able to see who you are. We can't let him know that yet."

The man started to say something else, but another symbol in the air passed between him and my point of view. Like it knew I was there, it let off orange sparks of sizzling light, and the man without a face turned to watch as the symbol forcibly pushed me from the past.

My return from the vision was turbulent with my emotions, and I nearly fell off my chair when it ended. The attack in the alley wasn't random. It wasn't a robbery. And it wasn't the last time it was going to happen.

To be hunted, that is a feeling I know. The man who had killed my mother wanted the Opalescence. Fear of what was to come and anger for having to deal with it detonated deep inside me, surging the Opalescence's power outward and shattering four glasses on the bar.

"What's wrong then?" Cooper asked, looking around nervously to see who might have noticed my outburst.

"What was in that envelope?" I asked Cooper, my voice uncomfortably low.

"That, mate?" he asked, nodding over his shoulder at the man who was long gone. "Like I said, it was just some business. Nothing for you to get worked up over."

And yet, I was worked up. The vision was different this time. Maybe I was finally starting to understand how they worked. They were invasive, at best, but they showed me things that were happening around me that I couldn't have seen otherwise. And they were triggered, by a place, an object, or a person. There was always a catalyst to their entry. This time, something with Cooper's shady business dealings were the trigger.

"Do you know who he is?" I asked.

Cooper grunted and pulled me away from the crowd and toward the parking lot. "Will you calm down? I haven't the slightest idea of what you're talking about. Who?"

"The man without a face. The one that killed Justin."

"What? Of course not. I would have already handled that if I knew who he was."

"Then why did I just get a vision of him with an envelope just like that?" I asked.

"I'm certain I have no idea," Cooper said patting my shoulder again and guiding me into the parking lot. "I'm going to need you to relax."

"Tell me what's in it!" I screamed.

"You're losing it a bit, aren't you?" Cooper asked. He pulled the envelope out of his pocket, ripped off the top and dumped a stack of papers into my hand. "Here. Go ahead then. There isn't a thing in there about that man, or anything else you'll find interesting."

I flipped anxiously through the pages and it was only a stack of financial statements for a bunch of companies I didn't recognize. Was it related to the man without a face? I couldn't tell. But I had gotten that vision for a reason. He was coming for me and I had to do something about it before I was the next person he killed.

I handed the papers back to Cooper and walked away without saying anything else.

"Hat," Cooper yelled after me. "Where are you going? Hat!"

Chapter 25

My visions were trying to help me navigate through a dense thicket of forced destiny. I didn't ask for the Opalescence, but having it meant I could be killed. I had been exiled from a normal life that everyone else took for granted, and suddenly I was the naïve prey, being hunted by a man with no face who wanted what I had and had already killed for it once.

Murder.

That word started making its rounds through my mind again, growing louder and louder. I could practically hear the fear bubbling up beneath the surface of my sanity. I was right when I said my mother's murder was like the cut above Max's lip. But like that cut, my wound was delicate and vulnerable to being reopened. It was gaping, and the blissful thoughts of moving on were lost as I wondered if I would be next.

"What are you doing here? Go away!" old man Withers said to me when I entered his store that morning. "There's nothing for you here."

"I need your help," I said, shutting the door.

"And what kind of help is it that you think I can give you, hmm?" he puffed at me. "Go away and leave this old man in peace."

"Peace isn't an option anymore," I said flatly. "Do you know anything about . . ."

"Pfft. I know a lot, and I know all about you, Walker," he interrupted.

"And?"

"And you Walkers are always more trouble than you're worth. Hmm. Walkers are a lot like this piece of rope," he said, holding up a piece of thick, tattered boat rope, "twisted and staunch . . . almost impossible to break, and usually impossible to untangle yourself from."

"Fine. Think whatever you want about me, about us, I don't care. What I do care about is the man who has no face. Do you know what I'm talking about?"

"I don't know anything about that," Withers said, as he started to walk toward the back of his store.

My heart jumped, pounding rapidly and irregularly into my ears. My vision blurred. Rage was weaving itself around my ethics, darkening my morality, and testing the confines of my humanity.

For the first time, I could consciously feel the Opalescence power at my command. I lifted my hand into the air harshly, my palm facing Withers. The door to his office slammed shut from the Opalescence's power with such force that it rattled his worthless knickknacks and junk right off their shelves and onto the floor.

Withers whipped his head around and glared at me through his round glasses. "Oh, you think you're powerful, is that it?" He threw the piece of rope on the ground and stormed over to me. "You're just a scared little boy running around with powers you don't know enough about, in a world you know nothing about."

"Then tell me about it," I yelled down at him.

Withers scratched his head and scowled. "A temper only a Walker could muster. For a family that people claim is wrapped up with such great purpose, there is darkness that lurks within you. Pfft. All the sooner you'll leave me be I guess."

He walked to the front and turned his store sign from 'open' to 'closed,' leaving it crooked in the window before pulling a blind down behind it.

"For the past year or so, I've been hearing rumblings about a man with the power to shift himself in between places. At first, they said he was just collecting things, special spells, potions he couldn't have made himself, enchanted objects—anything he could get his hands on. No one thought much of it. There always seems to be some new, power-hungry child running around trying to harvest as much power as they can. I didn't even give him a second thought . . . until the deaths started."

"Who is he, behind the mask?" I asked.

"Look kid, I can see where this is headed. So before you go on thinking I'm some kind of coin-operated swami, here to answer all your questions, let me clue you in on something. It doesn't matter to me who he is as long as he stays away from me."

Withers felt around under his desk before pulling out a box filled with multicolored bottles sealed with tiny pieces of cork. The glass that shaped them was wavy and imperfect, like you'd find on a stained-glass window, and each had a symbol molded into the front, an asterisk.

"I've seen this symbol before," I said, pointing to the bottle. "It was carved into a man's chest after he was murdered. What does it mean?"

"That symbol is from a wretched spell used to steal a Caster's power before they die. These are called Bottle Robbers, they're what you use to hold the power after you extract it, so it doesn't return to the Universe like it's supposed to. There's a whole ungodly ritual that has to be performed in order to absorb it afterward. These aren't exactly something you can just pick up at the grocery store. The glass has to be enchanted in a perfectly corrupt way, and that's not a skill most people have. They're expensive too . . . too expensive in my opinion. And right before the murders started, an antiquities dealer I know in Brazil phoned to say that someone here placed an order for them. I've since heard that the recipient of that order is the one who stole the Mask of Apate and wears it to conceal his identity."

"It just doesn't make any sense. If he wanted Justin's powers, he could have attacked him at any other time, or in any other place. Why risk doing it where he could have been caught by any one of a room full of other Casters?"

"First of all, it's doubtful that he's the only one willing to rip power from another Caster, no matter how indecent of an act that is. So, it's purely my speculation that this was him, but I've been around the block long enough to know that power-hungry people like to flaunt what they acquire. So if he killed that man with other Casters around, he did it intentionally. He's not just killing for sport. He's making a statement; telling you and everyone else there that he's more powerful than you, and that he can kill whoever he wants, and steal whatever he wants."

"How do I find out who is behind the mask?"

"Why do you care? What, would you go after him if you found out? Pfft. That kind of stupidity is what gets Casters killed." He stopped, looked down at something below his work bench, and a sly smirk took over his wrinkled face.

"Hmmmm . . . I don't think that murder is the one you're worried about, now is it? This is about Amelia."

"It's about a lot of things, but yeah, it's about my mother too. Did you know her?"

"Don't be ignorant. Who do you think sold her that blood lock, eh? And this man without a face, you believe he killed her?"

"Yes. Don't you?"

"It doesn't matter what I believe. I try not to get involved in the dealings of Walkers anymore. And it was going all too well until you came around."

"How do we find him?"

Withers caught me off guard by hitting me in the back of the head with his open hand. "We aren't finding anyone! You can just go ahead and keep me out of this. I'm not your little teacher, or your therapist, or your friend. I'm not here to help you understand the past or to hold your hand while you figure out the future. You're lookin' at the one person in this world I care about. And if you were smart, you'd learn to just stay out of the way of people like that."

"Then what?" I yelled back. "I just stand around and wait for him to kill me next? What if the next person he kills is someone you love?"

"Love? Love? Is that what you think matters? Pfft." He pulled himself up onto his work table. "In this world, kid, everyone you love will disappoint you, everything you believe to be true will be a lie, and no one is ever who they appear to be."

"Fine," I said. "Don't help me. I'll just wait here then until he shows up. Then it can be your problem too."

Withers grumbled and then rummaged through a box on the floor until he pulled out a well-worn notepad. He ripped a page from it and wrote the words 'The Trials of Truth.'

"Here. If you want to know who he is, use this spell. The Mask of Apate is a special piece. It doesn't just hide his face, it completely obscures his identity. There's no basic magic that's going to reveal who he is to you. You need to go further and this spell will take you there."

"This is it? Just these words are the spell?"

"You are quite stupid, aren't you?" Withers raised his eyebrow. "You still haven't figured out the blood lock yet, eh?"

"No, I did, but there wasn't really anything in the book."

"Your mother showed me the Trials of Truth spell once. I'm certain it's in that book."

"And I'm certain that in the entire book there was only one line written. The rest was blank. Maybe it was a different book."

Withers started laughing and shaking his head. "I can't tell if you're a novice, or just an idiot. Did you trying reading what was written, boy? It doesn't matter. You're clearly not experienced enough to handle that spell anyway."

"I can handle it," I said.

"Hmmm. Really? Well, have at it then. But the reason a spell like this is so exceptional is because it takes you beyond this place, to a higher plane of existence. There's a journey to get there and it comes with the greatest risk—fail and you'll be sacrificing part of yourself. People come back from that journey changed. It's going to change you."

"Then I'll have to change."

"That damn Walker stubbornness is going to get you killed one day."

* * * * *

"Test not the force of a Caster's power, but the reach of their heart," I read the words from my mother's book quietly out loud when I got home.

A soft bell rang in the distance from nowhere and when I looked back at the book, one large word dominated the page above that line, Walker, written in large black letters.

The book itself hadn't changed. The word hadn't just appeared out of nowhere, either. It was like it was written in invisible ink and saying that short spell gave me the ability to see what was always there.

"Damn, you were tricky," I said to the sky.

I flipped anxiously through the book again to find that each page was filled edge to edge with handwritten notes, clippings from other books, random sketches and a few pasted pictures. Some notes were written like recipes, instructions for different kinds of potions. Others were written like reference books, with information like the best use for each color candle, or how the phases of the moon can affect a Caster's power. There were all kinds of spells, too, with notes scribbled in their margins, mini-accounts of how the spell had worked, or how it hadn't.

On the second page, was a small passage outlined by thick marker.

'To give us strength, the Universe gave us family.

To test that strength, it gave us misfortune.

In that misfortune we found our path to peace.

In peace, we came together with our family.'

The passage was beautiful, and so indicative of how my mother felt about her family, a feeling she spent her whole life instilling in her children. Above it was a note in my mother's handwriting which said: 'Nothing in this world is more powerful than the love of a family.'

A page in the middle was haggardly earmarked, saving the spot of a spell with a name I couldn't pronounce. It was long and had complex instructions that I didn't totally understand, but according to the notes it was meant to protect a Caster by suppressing their powers and the powers of all those born to them.

The first step had some kind of long emulsification process with sweet almond oil and okra. Then it said you had to bless the result of that with cinquefoil. I had no idea what cinquefoil was, or how one would bless anything. After that concoction sat in direct light from a full moon next to something called a hag stone, the disgusting next direction was to mix in nail clippings of the Caster.

It said if the spell was successful, before the full moon was gone, the concoction would disintegrate into white-colored ashes. As if it weren't an elaborate enough spell already, those ashes had to be buried next to a tree until the next new moon, where it would somehow unearth a totem of an ancient Irish god with powers of protection.

At the bottom of the page was a list of all the Walker children, myself included, and the date when the spell had been cast on each of us. I was looking at the spell that had suppressed my powers and changed my life forever.

Near the back of the book, I found the spell Withers told me about, The Trials of Truth. A brief description with it said it would take the Caster to a place where the truth exists, uninhibited. The instructions looked simple enough, but it required a second person. I'd need help.

Written in red ink and all capital letters on the bottom of the page was a warning: 'The truth hurts.'

Chapter 26

"Pat, hey," Liv said from behind her propped open front door that night. "What are you doing here?"

"Sorry, I should have called." I held up a large pizza. "Hungry?"

She twitched her lips at me a little and then let out a little sigh. "Come in." I followed her into her dining room, and we attacked the pizza.

"So, what happened to you in Newport?" she asked. "Cooper said you wigged out and then just took off. How'd you even get home?"

"I had another vision . . . it was big," I said.

Liv chomped down on another slice of pizza and kept talking. "What was it this time?"

I paused and slowly chewed on my slice of pizza, trying to figure out how to explain to her everything that ran through my mind since that vision. "It was the man without a face. The one we saw in my mind. He's coming for me. For the Opalescence." I handed her a piece of paper with the instructions for The Trials of Truth written on it. "I need your help."

"Where did you get this?"

"From some of my mom's stuff."

"It's . . . an ambitious spell, I'll say that. Do you think you're ready for something like this?"

"It doesn't matter if I'm ready to or not," I said.

"It does to me, Hat. It's not that I mind helping you with this, but spells aren't always black or white. There's a really big grey area and sometimes there's just no way to tell what you're gonna get out of them. I've seen spells like this before, and they can be really scary."

"I can't just sit here and wait for him come after me, not after what I've seen. Not with what I know. If he gets the Opalescence . . . it'll be bad. And, I don't want to die over this thing. If you've got other suggestions on what to do here, don't hold back. But if not, this is all I have to work with. I'm sorry to ask, but you're the only person I can trust with this."

"It's okay," Liv said, cleaning off the table. "Let's just do it."

She got up to shut off the rest of the lights in the house. We took a cross-legged seat on her floor in the living room, and she lit a circle of candles around us.

"The spell calls for a small tree at the center of our circle," she said, holding out a cactus. "This was the best I could do on short notice. It said it needs to be tall enough to cast a shadow." She held it up against the light of the candles and watched the shadow move across the wall. "This should work."

Then I started to read the spell aloud.

"Wait," Liv said, "you can't just read the words," she looked at me like I was stupid, "you have to connect first. Remember before? That connection to the Universe, that's what gives us the ability to cast spells and makes us different than any random idiot reading words off a piece of paper."

"Did you just call me an idiot too?"

My eyes closed, and my thoughts drifted to the first time I had made that connection to the Universe. I lacked some form of discipline or experience to be able to readily find that place on my own, but something about Liv's presence, and the scent of her ocean breeze candles, brought the waves of power through me again, faster than I expected.

Liv brushed her thumb against my forehead, smearing a drop of oil against it. "A good spell is a lot like good sex," she said softly. "You need to put your whole body into it. Give me your hands."

I put my hands in hers, and they were soft and warm. "You go on this journey alone," she said, "but I'm here to anchor you to our world. I just hope it's enough to bring you back."

I rolled my neck from shoulder to shoulder, relaxing and letting more of the magic take solace in my body. When I opened my eyes, even the cactus was glowing with the power of the Universe. The simplicity of the plant brought balance to my body and helped ground me from the feeling that I was floating.

"Come forth Alethites, followers of the goddess of truth. Come to me, draw me near," I read.

Nothing happened. I said the line again, louder and still nothing happened. But the connection was growing strong, the magic was there and just waiting to be wielded. It was cascading around me, down my arms and into the palms of my hands, only to evaporate into the ether and start over.

"Come forth Alethites, followers of the goddess of truth. Come to me, draw me near." The candles began to flicker. The shadows cast from the cactus formed unusual shapes on the walls around us.

"Come forth Alethites," I said again, "followers of the goddess of truth. Come to me, draw me near!"

Liv was there, but her figure had become distorted. I saw around her, through her even, to the shadows on the walls. They had broken free from the candle's static hold and circled around us slowly.

"Come forth Alethites." A light chanting filled the room and the shadows moved quicker.

"Come forth Alethites." The chanting was louder, and the shadows moved so fast that I was no longer certain what was moving, them or the room itself. Their figures started to grow and look more human, crouching over themselves to dance along the wall. "Draw me near!"

The shadows pulled themselves off the wall, becoming fully dimensional. Their mouths continued to move with the pace of their chant, and the sounds grew louder with each pulse. They circled around me, like savages dancing around their nightly feast as it roasted on an open fire. If I looked fast enough, I could almost catch a glimpse of eyes forming in the shadowy figures as they closed in on me. When a dark shadow's hand reached out and touched my shoulder, my eyes became heavy and my head dropped to my chest.

When I opened my eyes again, I was standing alone in a forest. Thousands of white birch trees surrounded me and extended as far as the eye could see. Their paper-like bark peeled off the trunks and they were so tall and expansive that they obstructed what little light was coming from the dusky skies.

"Liv?" I called into the silent forest. My voice rolled off the trees and back at me.

In the distance, a figure appeared and started weaving through the trees toward me. "Kevin? What are you doing here?" I asked.

"That's a great question," he said, his voice scratching past my face. "That spell you just cast . . . it called forward a spirit guardian to bring you through The Trials of Truth."

"I'm sorry. I didn't know that it . . ."

He anxiously scratched his chin and the dimple in it wrinkled. "Exactly," he said. "You shouldn't be playing around with things you don't understand. But it's too late now, that spell has pulled me into this, so I don't have a choice."

"How does this work? Should I be . . ."

Kevin held up his free hand to stop me from talking. "I want to help you, Hat. I do, but . . . I have been given strict instructions on my place here and what I'm allowed to say or do during this journey. Follow me." He turned, and I followed him into the trees.

"That spell brought you here in search of answers, but before you can find any, you must complete The Trials of Truth," he said. "It's a statement to the spirits within this place that you're worthy of hearing the answers you seek. The trials you'll face will be the worst truth you know."

"Okay."

"You can stop this at any time by simply telling me to." He held his hand out for mine. "Take my hand when you're ready."

Swallowing hard, I put my hand into his. As soon as I did, the forest disappeared, and I was alone in darkness. I struggled to gain control of my hands, which had been somehow secured above my head.

"Kevin?" I called, pulling at my bonds.

Kevin appeared in the distance holding a small lantern. It illuminated his body and nothing else. "You can't face the future until you can accept your past," he said.

"What does that mean?" Chains rattled above my head as I tried to free my hands. The light from the lantern expanded and I could see the thick black metal that encased my wrists, keeping me close to the stone wall behind me. Chains ran from those cuffs up the wall, attaching to it with oversized rings drilled into the stone.

"What is this?"

A new light opened in the nothingness above us, drowning out the lantern and showing me Kevin's emotionless face. His eyes moved away from me to the base of the light where, out of my reach, a scene started to play out.

Every detail of the room was instantly familiar. A small boy, only about seven, stood alone in the confines of a small library below the light. The boy was looking off into the darkness, unaware of us as we looked on. He slowly circled himself, taking in his surroundings but avoiding touching any of it. Like looking at a picture that someone had taken of me years before, I recognized him as me.

"Hey," I called out. He didn't hear me.

His eyes twitched as they looked over the books pressed against each wall and I shuddered in response.

The library.

It was the library from St. Alberts, my grade school. And it was a room I had seen many times. Its polished wood fixtures and dusty furniture surrounded the boy, making him look smaller than he was, almost toy-like. He was breathing heavy and he pulled on his striped tie. It always did seem too tight around my neck.

What little kid should have to wear those torture devices anyway?

"No discussion, no deviation," said the policy about uniforms there. How insignificant that tie was, I remembered, when a man appeared behind the boy, startling him as he shut the door to the library and locked it behind him.

My heart jumped as if making a desperate attempt to escape my body before what would happen next. I couldn't see the man's face yet, but I didn't need to. I knew who he was. He made his way into the light, looking at the small boy, looking at me as a small boy. I knew what was going to happen.

My head started shaking involuntarily back and forth, and I pulled at the chains with all my strength. With each yank, the chains tightened against the wall, further limiting my movements. I strained every muscle in my arms and back in my hopeless attempt to break free. Sweat started to trickle down my skin, leaving behind a trail of fear and self-loathing that existed to me only inside that school.

"Hey, little buddy," the man said in his stomach-churning voice.

The man slowly walked around the boy. If he had wings, it would look like he was circling his prey.

That library was his hunting ground. As the school's resident priest, it had become his unofficial office, and the perfect place to find unrestricted access and wield his power over the children of the school.

The morbidity of that man's existence started to come back to me, like I was remembering a horrible fairytale a thousand years after I read it. Everything about him crept out from the most disturbed corners of my mind: his voice, the smell of his stank clothing, the way his head naturally rested to the side and forced his eyes up by his forehead when he looked at you.

My body quivered, sending eruptions of acid up from my already uneasy stomach. I could have thrown up right then if I could just have breathed. The boy's skin had gone pale as if to show me that nothing had changed, to show me that he felt the same way I did.

That spell's power was binding, and absolute. I couldn't look away and when I tried to close my eyes, the scene continued unchallenged there. Open or closed, my eyes would force me see what that spell presented.

The scene was all unfolding just like it had before. The boy turned and looked up at the man, the man whose name I refused to say. He wasn't much taller than I was as an adult, but I still saw him as the boy did, a giant in a seven-year-old's eyes.

This isn't happening. Not again.

My panicky eyes dodged back and forth between Kevin and the boy. The man placed his hand firmly on the boy's shoulder and the first tears appeared in the corners of my eyes. Kevin watched me intently but said nothing.

Hat, get it together. You've got this. This isn't real, it's just a memory.

My fingernails dug into my palms, leaving red, crescent-like marks that couldn't distract me from the pain in my heart. *If it was only a memory, why could I feel his hand on my shoulder?*

"It's okay," the man said, kneeling to the boy's eye level and touching his face. That was the moment when the man's malicious yellow eyes would meet the boy's, and he'd lose what little hope he had that someone would find him.

"Stop!" I yelled to him, but he didn't turn around. The cuffs drew blood from my writhing wrists as I struggled frantically to release myself. The blood dripped down my arm, mixing with sweat before soaking into my shirt.

The man had taken off my tie, the boy's tie, and placed it on the room's only table. My tooth dug into my lip as I watched the boy in front of me do the same. It wouldn't matter how hard he or I clamped down, the scene would continue with the same horrifying outcome.

The boy looked out into the nothingness in his small white t-shirt, as the man neatly folded his blue dress shirt and placed it next to the tie. The boy's cheek twitched subtly, so subtly that only I would notice it because mine was doing the same. Next, I knew the twitch would grow gradually, like your very life essence was crawling up through your body and clawing at your skin to get out.

I looked around the darkness helplessly, but I was no more help for myself in that moment than I was in that library almost two decades before.

Someone stop him, the boy and I both thought.

The man's callused hands touched the boy's face again, and I could feel it on my own. Tears broke from my eyes like shards of glass from a weather-torn window. He was a disease, one I'd learned to live with and forget about over the years, but in that moment nothing like that seemed possible for the boy.

I let my body fall limp, my arms stretched from the chains above as they held all my weight. The pain they caused was nothing compared to the pain the boy would be feeling soon.

The boy tried to shrug the man's unwelcome touch, in what would be his one and final act of defiance in that unbalanced battle of wills. The man slapped the boy across his face, and my cheek stung in response. The boy could have cried as the man held him tightly in place, but instead went blank. His mind had escaped the library in refuge, leaving his body to fend for itself. It was a journey he'd take each time he found himself trapped with that man. It was a journey I remembered all too well.

The man's hand moved over the stone-faced boy again, except he was looking at the adult me, chained against the wall. I shook my head faster, as if it would make him stop. I pleaded to the Opalescence's powers to fly from my hands and release me from my bonds to stop him, but they had abandoned me. The man gave a malignant smile as he removed his clothing, to remind me that I was, again, helpless and alone.

In that spell, the boy I was looking at was more than a memory of myself. He was a reflection, and we were linked at a level that even my violent shaking couldn't break. I could feel what he felt, like it was happening to me for the very first time. The fear, the pain, the brute violation one man can cause one child.

And so I screamed; a long unadulterated scream that erupted from the depths of my soul and wouldn't stop until it reached the ears of avenging angels. I had no words and no thoughts, only that raw, primal scream. It moved me past sadness and fear to a place where anger and hatred pulled at your body until it tore you at the middle.

"Enough!" I yelled in agony to Kevin. "Make it stop. Please make it stop." I had to make it end before what would happen next. I had lived through it once, but I was certain I couldn't again.

Kevin nodded slowly, and before my next exasperated groan was finished, the scene was gone.

When I opened my eyes again, I was flat on my back on the floor in Liv's home, at least four or five feet away from where we had first cast that horrible spell. Candles were tipped over, spilling their hot wax onto the floor, and Liv was standing over me with worried eyes.

"Oh my god. Are you okay?" she asked. "You started shaking and screaming and then something threw you across the room. What the hell happened in there?"

Hell. What a perfectly malevolent word. I couldn't respond to her; I had lost the ability to speak. The raging fires of my personal damnation were still swirling all around me, and I was choking on the bitter smoke it left behind. Deserted in a place that cannibalized happiness until all that was left was pain and sorrow. I wasn't sure how or if I could ever speak again.

Chapter 27

I left Liv's that night with barely more than a grunt. I spent the rest of the night lying on my bed like a corpse, motionless and unable to move my eyes from the empty white wall. The searing shambles of memories that the spell had brought up pulled at me like quicksand, and it was only from the fear that whatever was at the bottom was worse that I was able to keep myself from being devoured by it.

The remnants of that spell hung against my soul like cobwebs covered in rain and it took me days of silence in solitude before I could regain any composure. I ate and drank only enough to keep myself alive. At every moment, and just for a moment, I wished I were dead.

The days following my hibernation were enervating as I waded through the marshes of my emotions and avoided anyone and everyone. At work, when I could stand to show up, I was always wherever Liv wasn't. If I saw her, I knew she'd want to talk about that spell, and I couldn't bring myself to tell her what I saw there.

Texts from Max were left unanswered. I couldn't let him see the desolate emptiness in my eyes. He'd want to help me, and I couldn't tell him any part of what caused it. Even if I could have hid all of it from him and pretended everything was normal, I wouldn't have been able to stand having anyone touch me, even him.

Reliving what happened to me as a boy with that priest felt worse than when it first happened. I was older, and I understood so much more of what was happening and how bad it really was. But unlike when I was a boy, that spell held me captive to the experience and made me feel every abhorrent detail with undiluted clarity. It wasn't just a haunting memory, I had no shortage of those. He was victimizing and assaulting me all over again, giving me new memories I'd have to run from.

Slowly, deliberately, and painfully, I packed up all that baggage and locked it away in the same place it had been for most of my life. If I could just avoid it long enough, I knew it would eventually stop reigning over every thought and action in my life, just like the last time. But unlike the last time, I knew that no matter how far away you lock something like that up in the house of your mind, you always know it's there, and can still hear the shrill noises as it fights to escape its confines to haunt you again.

* * * * *

"Side of Veg!" Talia screamed in my ear in the kitchen of the restaurant a few weeks later. The restaurant was busy, and Ms. Monica had decided that any shift she needed help with required both me and Talia to work. Since then, I had developed a deep-down-to-the-core, gut-punching hatred for that place. It was a raspy hate that showed on my face all the time, and it became harder and harder for me to hide or ignore.

That night was especially loathsome because it was Ms. Monica's birthday. That day marked two years since she became a client and I had to start filling in for her staff. It was also a day where she felt she had a free ticket to be extra nasty to everyone around her.

She liked to treat herself and her friends to a nice dinner to celebrate the anniversary of her parents' condom breaking. She would proceed to spend the entire night treating the wait staff like jesters in her royal court, forcing us all to do absurd things to showcase her power over us to her friends.

I drew the short straw, literally, and had to take her table.

"Manhattan, get my girls here some more of that honey butta bread," Ms. Monica called as I passed her table with a completely full, and very heavy tray teetering on my shoulder.

I brought the bread slathered in honey butter over to her table and watched the five of them inhale it like they were at Jabba the Hut's family Thanksgiving. Ms. Monica grabbed my shirt's sleeve as I tried to leave. "Manhattan," she cackled with a full mouth of fresh bread, "you need to be getting me a clean knife, and you tell the kitchen boys that they better not let me catch them puttin' dirty silverware out again."

Talia passed me on my way back to the kitchen with Ms. Monica's knife and I rolled my eyes at her. She shot me a sympathetic grin, but I was too far gone to appreciate it. Ms. Monica was forcing me into a hushed battle for what was left of my sanity, and she was winning.

I was in the kitchen plating up another full tray when Ms. Monica started yelling at some of the other servers to get down on their hands and knees to polish the faux brass fixtures.

Polish the brass fixtures? It was seven o'clock on a busy night. No one had time to polish anything, let alone her ego. I left the kitchen, silently cursing the Wicked Bitch of the West for sitting at the table closest to the door, meaning I'd have to pass her every time I walked to my other tables.

"Manhattan, where's that knife at? And get us some more of that ranch dressing."

I flung the plates from my tray at my table full of customers who were undeserving of my crappy attitude and returned to fetch Ms. Monica's knife and dressing. The five of them had already consumed enough ranch dressing to fill a swimming pool, and I couldn't be certain that I wouldn't stab her with that clean knife when I brought it to her. I licked the blade on both sides and put it on the tray next to the dressing.

I will not stab my boss with this knife. I will not stab my boss with this knife. I will not stab . . .

"I swear to god, if she asks me for one more thing while I'm carrying a tray to another table, I'm going to drop that shit on the floor, and walk the hell out of here," I said to Talia as I passed her at the server's station.

"And where's our coffee at?" Ms. Monica asked when I dropped off the knife. Her harem of equally unpleasant women smiled as they enjoyed the show she was putting on for them.

Did you ask for coffee, you psychotic garbage disposal? No.

I ground my teeth into a smile. "Would you like coffee?"

"That is what I had asked you. Christ, do I have to do everything around here, Manhattan? It's my birthday, and I do not think it is too much to ask for a little service in my own restaurant." Her head weaved and bobbed as she continued berating me. Then she pointed one of her fat fingers at me, the nail so excessively long that it curved at the end and had an everlasting film of dirt underneath it.

"I'll be right back with your coffee, ma'am," I said begrudgingly.

It was getting harder and harder to handle her, and every time I came out of the kitchen and saw her face I'd wish that I had stabbed her with that butter knife in the first place. Talia tried her best to help me by going to their table whenever she was free, but Ms. Monica could still smell a hint of humanity on my breath and had every intention of killing it.

Her gauntlet continued for a solid two hours. My face had turned into clay, molded to whatever emotion I thought would make her speak less. The night was winding down, and when the clock hit nine-thirty, I thought I might actually make it through. Besides the Five Brides of the Apocalypse, I only had one other table. I had broken down into a purely mechanical existence, breathing heavy with every step, exhaling as much disgust and anger from my body as I could before taking another. I took one last, deep breath, and held it before walking past Ms. Monica's table with my last full tray of the night. When I made it past her table I exhaled in relief, but my victory was short-lived.

"Manhattan! We need more Sweet'N Low," she yelled. "*Now.*"

With my other table watching intently as their food steamed from the tray on my shoulder, I stopped in my tracks and swallowed hard.

Stay calm, Hat. You've got this. You've got this.

With another deep breath, I looked up at Talia who shook her head from side to side and mouthed the words "Don't do it."

It was too late.

With a loud smash, the tray and everything on it crashed to the floor below my feet, only an arm's length away from Ms. Monica's table. Everyone in the restaurant jumped and fell silence as the crumbling sound of the plates bounced around the room. I moved casually to the server stand and stood there, meticulously picking out a few Sweet'N Low packets from a basket, counting out two for each of them.

Devoid of emotion and as if I hadn't just dropped $200 worth of food on the floor intentionally, I strolled up to Ms. Monica's table and ignored all of their open-mouthed gapes. No one had yet dared to speak.

I placed the packets between my fingers and ripped off the tops, letting the excess chemical substitute fly across the table, the floor, and everyone sitting there. Then I reached over to each of them and poured a little bit into their cups, not bothering to pull back between them and spilling even more on the table.

The empty packets got tossed on the table belligerently before I took my order pad and pen out of my apron's front pocket, looked up at them like nothing happened, and asked, "Anything else for you ladies tonight?"

I blinked innocently, and they still had no words. "No?" A smirk broke out from my stern face at the first happy thought I had had all night. I turned and walked away, stepping loudly onto the flipped tray, further crumbling the plates beneath it.

In a defiant strut, I made my way to the door. I knew everyone was still watching me, but I didn't bother to look back at them. I didn't care.

I ripped off my ugly, misspelled name tag without unpinning it, letting it tear the fabric of my shirt, and threw it against the wall. Next was my apron, full of the night's cash and receipts, which I nonchalantly dumped by the hostess stand. The two scared little hostesses quivered behind the desk before scurrying to pick up the money as it flew everywhere. Then I pulled at my raggedy shirt, popping all the buttons and letting it fall to the ground behind me. Finally, when I thrust open the front door of the restaurant, it slammed against the outside wall and broke off its already rusted hinges. I walked through it in bittersweet triumph.

* * * * *

My outburst at the restaurant showed me how much I was changing, and the part that felt like a victory mellowed quickly as I returned to hating everyone for the way that I felt. The residue from that spell's consequences was dominating my emotions, and I wondered if I would ever be able to repair the damage I'd done to myself with it, or if the anger that slithered around inside me would ever go away.

That night I drove to St. Alberts, the same place The Trials of Truth took me. It was a place I'd spent six of my younger years surviving, and many of my older years forgetting. Yet this time, the memories of my abuse were forcing themselves to be ever-present.

They sloshed around my mind like sewage, scorning any hope of reprieve. I could still see the sickening body of that priest and what he'd do to me over and over again. I could still smell the room where he condemned me to a future of incongruity and distrust. And I could still feel the serrated sadism he pushed inside me and the immorality that filled the emptiness afterward.

Why I went back to that school, I couldn't tell you. Maybe I thought facing it head-on would help me cleanse the toxicity that spell had brought up, or maybe I was just in that place where you do self-destructive things for the sake of feeling something at all, no matter how bad. I was already acutely aware that life sends you all kinds of explosively painful experiences, so you'd think I would have been equally aware that bringing them on myself was unneeded, if not senseless.

The building was empty by the time I arrived, and it hadn't changed much. Its three dark floors still loomed over the street. Its recessed windows and unwelcoming front doors still made me want to turn away. The only light left on was above the front stoop. It was dirty and flickered erratically, casting monster-like shadows up and down the brick walls.

The street was empty, and the only sound was of thunder building in a distant storm. A half-moon was playing hide and seek between the fast-moving, ominous clouds above me, and I let myself get lost in my thoughts. I don't know how long I was there, staring at that square, menacing building and wrapped in a blanket of self-pity, but at some point the storm moved in and it started to rain heavily. Water tapped against the roof of my car and guided me into a fraught and morose sleep.

The sounds of crushing metal surrounded me, and the sudden jolt of my car told me it wasn't a dream. A large pickup truck had rammed itself into my passenger side door and pushed my car five or six feet from its parked position. Rattled and confused, I couldn't make sense of what was happening before a second truck slammed against the rear of my car, forcing my head violently into the steering wheel.

I blacked out and woke up in rapid intervals. My awareness was fractured, and I was unable to do anything but suffer. The doors from both trucks opened and shut. Then, heavy footsteps thumped toward my battered car.

Seeing two of everything, I struggled to hit the automatic lock on my door's handle. I may have hit it in time, but it didn't matter. Some sort of metal tool crashed through my window, tossing broken glass all over me. I was losing the battle to stay conscious, and I couldn't keep my eyes open long enough to see my attacker's face. The last thing I remember is him reaching for my chest and pulling the Opalescence harshly from my neck.

Chapter 28

"Are you serious right now?" Liv said to me late that night when I arrived at Equinox. She touched and moved my face to get a better look at the bruise forming on the bridge of my nose from where it had hit the steering wheel. At least the swelling had started to go down.

"What?" I asked, taking a sip of Blue Ice.

"You could be seriously hurt. You should be at a hospital, not here at the club," she said with a huff. "You could have a concussion, or internal bleeding, or . . ."

"Relax, will you?" I cut her off and got up to fill my fourth drink. If I'd learned anything today, it was that feeling less was feeling better.

She ignored me actively for the rest of the night. Everyone else, however, went about their lives, and their drinks, as they always did. A man was murdered in that very same room, I doubted they cared very much about a little bruising on my face.

"What?" I asked Liv when she turned away from me on the balcony later.

She didn't take her eyes away from the lower level of the club. "You're an asshole, that's what."

"Could you be any more of a bitch right now? What is your problem?" I turned and walked back to the bar.

She stomped after me, flipped her hair over each shoulder, and titled her head at me while I poured my next drink. "My problem is the fact than you're taking this so lightly. You could have been killed today, and you're not at all bothered by it. What is wrong with you?"

Holding a few ice cubes against my nose, I sipped on a new glass of Blue Ice and tried to will it to be heavier on the vodka that it usually was. "Obviously this sucks, but . . ."

"You okay, baby?" Elle asked as she walked by. She tenderly touched my cheek and frowned.

Liv grimaced. "He's fine," she said. "Go about your business."

Liv walked to the couch and flopped down, exasperated. I followed close behind and sat down next to her on the couch. "Don't make a big deal out of this," I said, finishing off my stronger drink. "It's over. They have what they wanted so let's just forget about it."

"Whatever," she said, crossing her arms and legs and turning away from me again. "I don't know what is up with you, but I don't like it."

"I'm sorry you're upset," I said.

Then she took a deep breath, leaned in close to me, and put her hand on my leg. "Listen, I get it, okay? This place changes everybody. It can make you feel like you own the world, like you can just party and be crazy and do whatever you want without consequence. But it's not really like that in the real world. People get hurt . . . you can get hurt."

I had already gotten hurt and she could see that.

"Justin was murdered right over there," I pointed to the bar, "and you pretend like nothing happened, just like them—so tell me more about how I'm acting like this world doesn't have consequences."

"I don't know what you saw in that spell, but I can see what it's doing to you, and I'm so, so sorry for helping you when I knew you weren't ready. I didn't know it would do this. Please talk to me. Let me help you."

Liv's mind reached out with the lightest touch toward mine and I pulled away violently. I couldn't let her see anything that awaited there.

"I don't know what to say, Liv, but you can't fix this. You can't fix me."

"Then what about the Opalescence? Are you just gonna let them walk away with it?"

I slammed my empty glass down on the table, causing everyone in the room to turn and stare at us. "You know what? They didn't just walk away with it. They hit me with a fucking truck—two trucks actually—and knocked me unconscious with my own god damn steering wheel. Then they stole it from me. Did I smack my own head across my steering wheel and then hand them the fucking necklace? No, I did not."

"So that's it then?"

"Yeah. That's it. I don't care anymore. About that stupid necklace or anything else. As far as I'm concerned, they can fucking have it."

I stood up and walked toward the bar but skipped it and left the room instead. It wasn't until I got outside and started scanning the parking lot that I remembered I didn't have a car anymore.

Liv burst out the door behind me. "Where are you going?"

"Away from the bullshit."

She yanked at my sleeve earnestly, spinning me back around toward her. "Stop! I can see you getting consumed by this and I want you to talk to me." Tears were rolling down her beautiful cheeks.

"You know what I want Liv? I want to forget this ever happened. I want to be just like everyone else up there. Partying, laughing, pretending there aren't bigger things happening around us. That's what I want."

"You're not like them, Hat. You have a bigger responsibility and they couldn't understand that even if they wanted to."

"You didn't seem all that worried about this responsibility before now."

"Well, before now I thought you had it under control. But that didn't mean I wasn't worried. Hell, I am worried. I know that sometimes even I get caught up in the idea that we can just live our lives as free as we want, responsible only to ourselves. But we can't. This is bigger than that. It has to be. Someone has to be the person who stands up to people like that guy who hides his face. And that's you, Hat, whether you like it or not. Fight this, and maybe we can stop accepting murder and violence as a normal part of our lives."

"I don't have any fight left in me." I frowned and walked away without saying anything more. There was nothing I could say to her; because there was so much that I couldn't say to myself. You can't help someone who doesn't want to be helped.

It was well after midnight at that point, but no cabs were waiting on the street, and my house was a long walk from Equinox. When I rounded the corner from the alley, I saw a sleek black motorcycle with Canterbury blue streaks down the side. It was the kind you had to ride leaning in and it looked hotter with its matching helmet and leather jacket, both of which were left on the bike's seat.

The keys were still in the ignition. I wanted to forget every-thing Liv said, and ignore some cosmic duty that she tried to remind me I had. I needed to be free from it all.

Fuck it.

I zipped up the jacket and pushed the helmet down over my head. Inhibitions were a thing of the past, or so I told myself. I straddled the bike and smiled under the helmet as the muffler started roaring.

I had only ridden a bike like this once in my life, but steering around the streets of the city was easy, and almost effortless, when you have very little concern for your safety. My speed increased with each turn, and I passed the street to my house in favor of riding out my magic-induced high. It was a faster, more dangerous version of the treadmill, and if I could just go fast enough, I'd leave everything behind me in the dust.

Blue lights flashing in the small side mirrors of the bike brought my situation back into focus only a few minutes later. I looked down and saw I was doing over sixty on the inner streets. But I kept riding.

The cop swerved around the road to avoid the typical Rhode Island pot holes while trying to catch up to me. I had to make a decision: either stop and face whatever was coming to me or hit the accelerator and take my chances. I looked back at the cop again.

Fuck that.

I ducked closer to the motorcycle's small, tinted windshield and pushed the accelerator down. We had just hit a long stretch of road when the cop started gaining on me. I knew it wouldn't be long before more would join him.

Even though I no longer had it, I could still feel the Opal-escence's power with me. And from it, a radical thought crept into my head, bypassing the part of the brain that controls rational thinking. Slowly I sat up and released my hands from the bike's handles. My eyes focused the Opalescence's powers on the handles and the accelerator, controlling the bike almost better than I had with my hands. I howled into the helmet and looked into the sky, letting my mind control the bike without the aid of my eyes.

Then with my feet secured below the foot pegs, I arched my back completely. I was looking at the cop upside down, and his shock as the bike continued to steer itself was priceless.

"Push it," I said to myself as I continued to concentrate on the handles. It could have been the adrenaline or just my own carelessness which allowed me to manipulate the Opalescence powers like I never had before, even when it was with me. The bike was moving faster, but I couldn't see the speedometer, so I had no idea just how fast.

With my helmet just inches away from the back tire, I extended my hands to either side of the bike. I flicked them back and forth at the cop's car, dumping trash bins into his path with my powers. Any rocks and broken pieces of pavement that I saw flew at his tires too. But it was the loose mailbox that I flung at his windshield that got him to panic and slam on his brakes.

He almost stopped before hitting the speed limit sign, almost. He was out of his car with a gun pointed at me before I had pulled myself back up, but I was too far away for him to do anything.

Then the sounds of the motorcycle faded into the distance as lights and noises attacked me and a cold sweat crawled up my spine.

"Why me?" my mother asked. She was rubbing her eyebrow and pacing around the living room of her house.

"Would you wish it on someone else?" Kevin asked her. He was sitting on her couch and his eyes followed her back and forth in front of him.

"But Victor, he's so young. He needs me alive. And I have another one on the way," my mother said, pointing at her pregnant stomach. *"It's just not fair."*

"I'm sorry Mia. I wish it could have been different. But you know why this happens. You know why you have it."

"I don't want it!" my mother yelled. From inside her shirt, she pulled out the Opalescence and tossed it onto the table. *"I have a family, a life, and this thing can't be part of it."*

"Mia, what do you want from me? I'm dead. I died protecting that stupid thing and I didn't want it any more than you do. But it's our family's responsibility, and we can't just walk away from it. You know what could happen if we don't take care of it."

"Maybe that's just all some story someone made up to force us to do something they wanted us to do."

"Mia, you don't believe that. You know that you have to do what we've all had to do—keep it safe, at all costs."

"And what about after me? What if it ends up with one of my kids? I don't want this life for them."

"I'm going to tell you the same thing that Mom told us our entire lives, sis. Someone has to protect it. Someone has to take the responsibility, because if they didn't, it would be so much worse for everyone else. It's not pretty, it's not fair; it just is."

Through the Opalescence, the three of us were connected emotionally in that vision. From that *connection, I could feel my mother's fear. I could feel Kevin's guilt for having died and caused it. And I could feel the heavy burden that damn necklace put on all of us.*

"I don't want this to ruin my life," my mother said, rubbing her eyebrow.

"Then don't let it. Don't stop living, Mia. Mom had that thing for years without any problems. Maybe it'll be the same way for you. And when it isn't, you'll handle it. Just like I did."

My time in that vision was short, but it was more than enough to make me lose my concentration on the bike. I struggled to retake control with my hands, but it was too late. The front tire was wobbling against the grainy pavement of the bridge I was crossing. I tried to slow down, but the direction of the bike was already too skewed from my stunt, and my battle for control was swiftly lost.

The bike tipped over on its side and slid with my excessive speed across the grooved pavement into the opposite lane, the one I should have been driving in. My leg was pinned between the bike and the ground, and I struggled to grab onto anything that might pull me free from it.

Sparks flew from the metal of the bike scraping against the ground. I wasn't slowing down and had begun spinning in circles across the bridge.

One flimsy guardrail between me and the forty-foot drop to the river below was not enough. Both tires hit the guardrail together, splitting it open and taking me over the edge with the bike. Only after I slid off the bridge, did the bike release my leg, but it was already too late. I fell right behind it, hurtling toward the jagged rocks of the river below.

Chapter 29

They say when you're about to die, your life flashes before your eyes. I don't know what fool ever said that, because the water was approaching so fast that there wasn't enough time to think about anything, even the stupid decisions that got me there in the first place. The bike crashed into the water, and it would only be the smallest fraction of a second before I was next.

I closed my eyes and accepted my fate.

Then a rushing sound slammed into me, and when I opened my eyes I was falling inside the private room at Equinox. I hit the floor with enough force that there wasn't a part of my body that didn't feel it. But I was alive.

"Liv?" I rolled onto my side and pushed off the helmet. My ribs, having taken the brunt of the fall, buckled beneath me as I tried to move. "What happened?"

"You just tried to get yourself killed, that's what happened," she said fiercely. "I think there are more than enough people around who'd be willing to do that for you if that's what you're looking for."

"Fuck." I tried pulling myself up but fell back to the ground in pain. "I was falling into the water . . ."

"I know. I was with you . . . inside your mind. Then I saw that stupid stunt you pulled and cast a spell to transport you back here," she said.

The club must have been closed by then because it was empty except for us. I groaned as I tried to move, my ribs and leg throbbing beyond belief. All I was able to do was prop myself up against the wall.

"Do you even want to try and explain to me how stealing a motorcycle and driving off a damn bridge was going to make anything better?"

"It wasn't exactly intentional," I said, groaning again.

"Damn it, Hat. You're so selfish. Did you think to stop and ask yourself who was going clean up your mess after you got yourself killed?"

"I didn't care. I don't care. I don't want this life anymore. I didn't ask for it and I just want to walk away and try to salvage whatever is left of myself before it's too late."

"I should have just let you die back there if you're just going to give up."

"You should have!" I screamed.

Liv kept talking but I wasn't listening. There was nothing she could say that would help me. I was too far down the hole of pain and misery that I had fallen into, and neither she nor I would find a way to get me out. I meant what I said, too. In that moment, I wished she hadn't saved me and that the motorcycle would have sped me off into the afterlife. It might have been my only path to peace.

* * * * *

The sun was rising by the time I found the strength to drag myself outside and into a cab. I stumbled into my apartment, eyes only half open, and grabbed some ice for my crippled ribs. Beyond that, I couldn't do more than lay on my back in the middle of the floor with the ice pack on top of them. I was slipping in and out of consciousness when someone starting banging on my door.

"What?" I yelled.

More banging.

"Just come in!"

The door opened to reveal a distraught Max on the other side. "Are you alright?" he asked, rushing in and over to me.

I groaned as I tried to sit up. "Yeah, I'm fine, why?"

"Why?" He took a step back and blinked his eyes rapidly. "I've been trying to call you since last night. You didn't show up for dinner, and I was worried something happened to you."

I sat up and held the ice against my aching body. "Well, now you know that I'm fine."

He saw the bruise on my nose from the car attack and gently reached out to touch it, his face crinkling with both fear and surprise.

"Stop," I said, pushing his hand away. It hurt.

"What happened to you?"

"Nothing."

"I don't understand. Why are you acting like this? I haven't seen you in weeks, you stopped returning my texts, and we were supposed to meet up for dinner last night and you didn't show up. Now I come here and see you're clearly hurt, and you're not going to tell me what happened?" Max sat down in my chair, leaned forward on his knees, and rubbed his hands together roughly.

"When did we talk about meeting last night for dinner?" I asked.

"A few weeks ago. Remember? For my birthday. You said you had some surprise planned and told me to meet you for dinner at our favorite place."

"I'm sorry I missed your birthday." Talking hurt more than I expected, and I keeled over to hold my ribs in pain.

"I don't care about my stupid birthday, Hat. Tell me what happened to you."

"I've just had a lot to deal with lately."

"Clearly. Now tell me what happened. Why are you holding your ribs like that?"

"I can't."

"You can't, what?" He waited for me to answer, and when I didn't he asked, "Are you really not going to tell me?"

I shook my head.

"So what am I doing here?" he barked while standing up.

"I don't know, you're the one who just showed up." I pushed my head back against the wall and dodged eye contact with him.

"Don't I have a right to be worried about you? Look at yourself. You look half-dead. Why are you acting like there is something wrong with me for being worried about you?"

Max looked half-dead too, distress spreading across his handsome face. A part of me wanted to tell him everything, to beg for his help, and hope that his help could make a difference. But the other part of me, the broken part that was still sinking in that hole, just wanted him to leave me alone in my suffering.

"You know what, Hat? When I first met you, I thought it was kind of cute how you would run away scared, and how you didn't have any idea what the hell you wanted out of your life," his voice was a little shaky, "but I'm over it now. It's time to grow up and stop running scared from everything. I thought we had something amazing here. Don't we? Don't you know how much I love you?"

"Yes," I said.

"And do you love me? You've never said you do, and I thought you did, but right now, the way you're treating me, it's making me think you don't."

"What do you want from me right now?"

"I don't know, a little honesty maybe? Stop shutting me out."

"You're probably a lot better off just staying away from me."

He came over and sat next to me on the floor, putting his strong arm around me. "No, I won't be. This is part of being an adult. You laugh, and you love, and you get hurt, and you ask people who love you for help to get you through it all. Let me do that for you."

I spat out a few combined expletives and pushed him off me. I pulled myself up using a nearby table, but it was when I started to walk to the kitchen that I noticed I was limping on the leg that had gotten trapped under the motorcycle.

"Hat . . . ?"

"What?" I shouted, holding a new cold pack against my ribs. "Back off, okay? You don't need to get upset about this. It's my life, not yours. Why do you even care?"

Fuck, why did you just say that?

"Are you serious? How many other ways do I have to say it to you? I love you." The toughest guy I'd ever met was starting to tear up.

I sat down at my hand-me-down kitchen table and rubbed my neck. "This isn't about love, Max, or you. Just let it go."

"No, it is about love and it doesn't come around every goddamn day. I've been with other guys before, lots of other guys, but I've never felt this way about anyone. I felt it the first time I met you and watched you tumble all over yourself at the gym. And I've felt it every single moment since then. You have to feel it too. I know you feel it too. That is love. Don't act like it doesn't matter, or that I'm nobody to you. Please."

Love felt like an illusion, like a blanket we wrap ourselves up in so we can pretend we're warm on the outside when we are nothing but cold on the inside. Max was the warmest blanket I could ever hope for, but I didn't want to infect him with the coldness I carried inside me. So, I unwrapped myself from it.

"I can't do this with . . ."

"Fine. I don't know what's making you pull away, but I know it's not because you don't love me. I hope you grow up someday and figure out what the hell you're doing and what you really want, but I'm not waiting around for that to happen."

Max walked through the door and slammed it behind him. It slammed so hard that it knocked over a picture from my dresser in its wake.

It was one of my family, gathered at my mother's house for some everyday event. Everyone looked happy, like we used to be, like I used to be with them. I hobbled over to it and propped it back up in its normal spot and felt a brief moment of hope that it could be like that again. But it was all too brief, because a cold sweat started to form, and I was carried into a vision.

> *The first thing I saw was my mother's dining room table, the center of our family's world when we were growing up. It was built from dark walnut wood, and was worn from hosting countless Walker dinners. Meals were served there, games were played*

there, and tears were shed there. Through it all, that table remained a constant in our lives, a fixed point in time.

"Stop teasing your brother," Sydney yelled from the table. She leaned over in her chair and slapped her son's butt as he ran by, his baby brother running wobbly behind him. "Zoe, come get your brothers and watch TV with them or something," she yelled to Zoe, who sat peacefully at the computer.

"Mom, no," she whined as if her mother were tearing her away from her research in molecular biology.

"Do you know who I saw the other day?" our mom called over from the kitchen as she finished making the last stage of her family-famous lasagna.

"No," I called back, not caring if she was talking to me or not. I had a mouth full and was slapping Finn's hand away from the last piece of garlic bread in the cloth-lined basket at the center of the table. She made the best garlic bread.

Finn slumped down in his chair, crossed his arms, and gave me the same pouty look he would give when he was six years old and didn't get his way. I took the piece of bread out of the basket and threw it on his plate, just like I would have done when he was six years old and gave me that face.

"That guy who used to work at the store down the street, remember? He used to follow you around all the time," she said to Sydney.

"And?" Sydney was uninterested.

"And," our mother said, "I don't know, I thought you'd like to know."

"Yeah, okay." Sydney rolled her eyes to Charley, who giggled quietly. Neither of them saw our mother stealthily coming up behind them.

She glared at them with half serious, half silly eyes. "You're not too old for me to beat you with this spoon," she teased, waving the wooden spoon in her hand as she put down the steaming pan of cheesy lasagna.

"You're single, you should call him," Charley said. She darted her fork around our mother's potholder-covered hand, trying to get a piece of lasagna from the edge of the dish.

Sydney started fork-fighting Charley for a piece of lasagna. "Nah. Not interested," she said.

"What's the matter? Is it the fact that he has a car, a place to live, or a steady job that's stopping you?" Charley asked above my laughter at their antics.

Sydney knew it was true but pretended she didn't and gave a dumbstruck look. Finn missed the entire joke by trying to eat his lasagna and text message at the same time.

The front door opened and knocking followed. That's the way Walkers enter a house, simply implying that they were coming in anyway, but still knocking as a courtesy.

"Hello!" Paige called in a funny, high-pitched voice from the entryway. She walked into the dining room with Damon and his sisters behind her.

"Guess what I did last night?" Damon said, pulling up a chair next to me.

"Or who," I whispered back. That was back when he was younger and was, let's say, brazenly promiscuous.

Damon picked up a fork and made a pass at my plate. "Yeah, who," he said.

"Get your own," I yelled through my mouth full of food and pulling my plate away.

"Pig." He jabbed his fork into the arm I was using to protect my plate.

"Vulture." I kept my plate out of his reach and ate off it. "So, who'd you do?"

"This married chick . . . while her husband was there."

"What!" A little bit of food flew out of my mouth and everyone stopped talking to look at me. Damon punched my leg under the table and gave me a "be cool" look.

"Are you fucking kidding me?" I asked under my cheesy breath.

"Eh . . . he said he wanted someone to have sex with his wife. I said sure. He wanted to watch, he bought me a shot, and the rest kinda played out from there." He took advantage of my shock and moved to the other side of me to get better access to my plate.

"Whore," I said.

He bit into a piece of my lasagna and laughed. "Prude."

Tears were flowing down my face before the lights and noises had subsided. It was such a simple scene from our lives, one that told the story of how we lived them together. It reminded me sadly of a time in the not-so-distant past when things felt normal. That table was normal. The loud conversations and the quirky, yet unbreakable love we had for each other was normal. Me with my family was normal.

Liv was right about me being selfish. How would my family have felt if she had let me die that night? They wouldn't know or understand the reasons that brought me to the brink of self-extinction. And it would be so much worse because it had been so long since I told them how much I loved them.

I still may not have been ready to live for myself, but I needed to live for them. That vision snapped me out of the desperate haze I was in, and I couldn't have been more grateful for it, or my family.

Change isn't always in our control, it's at the behest of the Universe and we just are there to deal with it. But choice. Choice is our point of control. It's our human power. And then and there, I made the choice to not give up.

Chapter 30

"It's never about how bad you fell down," my mother said to me once. "It's about how quickly you get up and how much stronger you are because of it."

There were so many things I had broken in such a short time. I had fallen down and hard, but I wasn't willing to stay down. It was time to get back up, to pull my head out of my own ass, and fix everything I had broken. It wouldn't be easy, but it would be paramount if I was going to fix myself.

"Start at the beginning," my mother said when I asked her how to handle a relatively insignificant problem I had once. "Then take it one step at a time. If you give it a chance, the Universe makes sure everything comes together when it needs to."

Grudgingly parking my lopsided and nearly-totaled car in the parking lot, I showed up at Equinox unannounced that night, hoping to catch Liv. I knew I had to start somewhere, but I took my time going inside, reluctant to jump straight into the confrontation with her that I knew would follow.

"Hat?" Graham yelled to me before I had gotten to the staircase.

I had been out 'sick' far too frequently, carelessly putting my job on the line. I hadn't seen Graham much during that time, and I worried that my outburst at the restaurant was going to be the last straw for him.

"Graham . . . hi, what are you doing here?"

"Just entertaining some clients," he said, pointing his thumb behind him to two people I didn't recognize. "They like it here."

I shuffled a bit and flinched from the lingering pain in my side. "Yeah . . . it's great."

Graham scratched the knuckle under his curved pinky finger and tilted his head at me. "Are you alright, buddy?"

"Yeah. Sorry I missed so much work lately. I've had some family drama going on."

"Everything okay?"

"It should be. Thanks. But don't worry, I'll definitely be in to work on Monday."

He put his hand gently on my shoulder. "Good. You seem to have had a lot of bad luck lately: flat tires, getting sick, family issues. I hope you shake that pretty soon, we're starting to miss you at work." He cleared his throat. "And, I talked to Ms. Monica."

I closed my eyes tight and wished that when I opened them Graham wouldn't be there anymore. "Right. Well, you see, I guess I just had a really rough night, and . . ."

"Don't, please, that woman is a raving bitch," Graham laughed. "Frankly, I'm surprised it took this long for someone to lose it on her. I smoothed it over with her, and everything is fine; I was just more worried about you. I guess we all are."

"I'm good, really, it was just a bad night. It won't happen again."

He patted me on the shoulder sympathetically and returned to his group.

"So this is where a Walker has to go in order to see you," Damon said, standing at a cocktail table by the stairs.

"Hey, stranger," I said hugging him, "I didn't know you came here." The Universe was telling me, in a very straight-forward way, that it would decide which issues I handled and in what order.

"Yeah . . . we like to mix it up," he said. "Paige is here some-where, and Talia said she saw Victor when we first came in," Damon said.

"Wow. Walker party," I said. "I didn't think anyone knew about this place."

"And that's why you've been hanging out here? Talia's been here before, but this is my first time. I told a few people we were coming, they told a few people . . . you know how that works. I think Paige's new boyfriend is even going to make an appearance tonight."

"Oh yeah? Good. I haven't met him yet," I said.

"I don't think anyone has. She's been trying to hide him from us," he said as Talia came up next to us and handed him a drink.

"Are we that scary?" I asked.

"Yes, you are," Talia said. "There are too many of you, I still don't know half your names. That guy has no idea what he's in for."

Damon and I both laughed.

Shit.

"I missed your mom's birthday, didn't I?" I asked, rubbing my forehead.

Damon nodded. "Yeah, ya did, champ. And then we had a big thing for Sydney when she got that teaching job."

Sydney got her teaching degree right before our mom died, and I had no idea she was even looking for a job. I was a bad brother.

"Why didn't someone tell me?"

"Don't look at me," Talia said, sipping on her drink. "I'm not your secretary, and I didn't know about your sister's job."

"You haven't been that easy to get a hold of, you know," Damon said tapping me in the arm with his fist. "You don't hear back after like a hundred text messages and you eventually stop trying."

"I know, I know. I'm sorry. Listen, I need to run upstairs for a sec. I'll be back to say hi to everyone in a few."

Victor was standing at the bar, and I passed him on my way to the staircase. He narrowed his eyes at me but didn't say anything. That was one relationship I wasn't going to be able to salvage tonight. It wasn't even a relationship I was sure was worth salvaging. I looked at him briefly but didn't say anything.

Time to rip off the Band-Aid. No more distractions.

I walked slowly up the stairs and peeked into the room before entering it. When Elle saw me through the doorway, she cheered, and the entire room looked at me and smiled; the entire room, that is, except for Liv. She pretended she didn't see me and walked out to the balcony.

"Hey Coop," I said as I poured a glass of Blue Ice. "How are you?"

"I'm alright, but I suppose the bigger question is how you are," Cooper said.

"I'm sorry about what I said to you in Newport, about flipping out and everything, and I'm sorry I didn't say this sooner. Things have just gotten so screwed up."

"It's a tense world we live in, Hat. I told you before there isn't one of us here that hasn't lost someone important because of magic, so I can understand how that could mess with your head. However, I suspect that I'm not that one you need to be saying this to."

Liv was leaning over the balcony's banister watching the people below when I came up beside her. "Come to apologize?" she asked before she could see me.

"Apologize for what?" I asked back. Liv spun around to face me, and only then did she catch the smile on my face. "I know. I'm an asshole."

She leaned her elbows against the banister and flipped her hair. "And?"

"And stupid."

She flashed her gritted teeth. "And?"

"And I'm sorry."

In that moment, she looked like the most beautiful being in the entire world. The colored lights from the ceiling were making the profile of her face glow more than her natural blush already did, and it glimmered against the sparkly gloss on her lush lips. She moved toward me hesitantly, her aqua colored eyes looking into mine like two large lakes reflecting the sky of a perfect day.

"So, are we okay?" I asked.

"Yeah, I guess we are, if you are. But you can't go off the deep end on me again like that." She leaned in close to my ear. "And just so you know, I have a spell that could give you an unbearable rash for the rest of your life. Seriously. Itchy, red, painful. Don't fuck with me like that again." She finally cracked a smile.

"Aw . . . there's that beautiful smile." I nudged her with my body. "Come on, let's go get a drink."

She followed me back into the main room and I stepped behind the bar. "What would you like to drink, my lady?"

She gave a flat smile and shook her head at me. "Just fill my glass, asshole."

Just as I picked up the pitcher of Blue Ice, a sweat-soaked shiver ran roughly up my back, forcing me to drop the pitcher as a weightlessness took over.

There was a hand. Nothing more. It slowly caressed a wall with tattered, decorative curtains— the same curtains that ran up the walls of Equinox. The hand slowly circled the fabric before it lit on fire, moving away only after the flame engulfed the fabric and ran up the length of the wall.

Yelling started and I couldn't see who the hand belonged to. The giant at the bottom of the staircase abandoned his post to hit the fire with an extinguisher, but it was too late. The flames had already spread the length of the wall, and a stampede for the door ensued.

The mystery hand then touched the cloth that wrapped around the staircase's banister, lighting it with the same vicious fire that was filling the rest of the room with smoke.

"What is it?" Liv asked as I came back from the vision. My feet were soaked with Blue Ice and yelling from downstairs startled us both.

"Oh my god," Elle yelled. "The club's on fire."

A lot of good that vision did.

We all ran toward the stairs, but they were already submerged in the flames. People were scattering around the club, frantically trying to escape. I slammed the door shut to stop the bulk of the billowing smoke from reaching us. The windows of the lounge started darkening from the smoke, and I struggled to look for my family in the crowd, praying they'd make it out unharmed.

"We need to get out of here," I yelled as the sprinklers started spraying from above us. They weren't doing anything to calm the fire below us, and the floor was starting to feel hot, too hot to stand on.

Sirens from approaching fire trucks outside started mixing into the sounds of the crowd. I looked around for validation from someone to tell me that they'd make it to us in time. No one had any false hope to share.

Flames were overtaking the balcony, and Elle fell to the floor from smoke inhalation. Cooper and a few of the others were crouched over her, coughing, trying to wake her up. The glare from the fire's intense orange and yellow lights was reflected in Cooper's eyes as he looked at Elle in worry.

Empty glasses on the bar were starting to fill up with water from the sprinklers. Liv ran to them and grabbed the largest one. "Get over here," she said, slamming the glass down on the center table and pulling Cooper and me to either side of her on the couch. Smoke continued to seep out from below the doors, and our coughing became coarse and maddening.

"This whole room is going to collapse under us," Cooper yelled.

"I know. Shut up. I'm trying to remember the spell," Liv said through the piece of her shirt she held over her mouth. She closed her eyes tight and held her breath. "Give me your hands." She flipped her sopping wet hair out of her face and held out her hands to us. "Concentrate."

The coughing, the sirens, the people screaming below us, all those sounds were deafening and they easily drowned out Liv's voice. With our hands intertwined, Liv yanked on our arms, pulling the three of us close so our heads were nearly touching. Connected by her powers, our focus drifted from the immediate danger of the fire and gradually fixated on the teetering water glass in front of us.

"Water's power fight . . . and save . . . shit. Okay. Water's power rise and fight . . . spread . . . .shit."

"Come on, Liv," Cooper said.

"I know. I know. Just give me a second. Water's power rise and fight . . . spread your wings and save the night, aid us now in this plight, and bring defeat to fire's light," Liv yelled at the glass. Nothing happened.

"A little help here boys," she said.

Our connection with the Universe was strong, and stronger as we approached it together. "Water's power rise and fight, spread your wings and save the night, aid us now in this plight, and bring defeat to fire's light," we said in unison and the glass started to shake.

"Again," Liv said. "Come on. Focus. We don't time."

In unity, our powers amplified each other's as we said the words of the spell again. The water in the glass started to glow as a mighty blue energy expanded into it with our spell. The glass vibrated against the table, before tipping itself over. An endless, growing stream of power-infused water poured out and into the air.

The forceful stream curved as it hit the ceiling, breaking itself off into every possible direction. Taking a near-solid form, the water projected through the windows, shattering them without regard. Like a mammoth-sized octopus with a hundred tentacles, the water attacked the fire below us and around us. It weaved through the black smoke, fighting and smothering the fire at its base until there was nothing left.

"It's a good thing that those pipes burst," I heard a firefighter say outside later, as I desperately waded through the crowd in search of my family. "We wouldn't have been able to get in."

"Damon?" I yelled into the soot-soaked crowd. "Talia?"

"Everybody's fine," Damon said, appearing from behind an obstructively large man in the crowd.

I jumped at him and landed in a hug. "Thank god you're okay. What about Talia? Where is she?"

"She's fine; she said she was going to call her parents."

"What about Paige? Victor?"

"Everyone's fine, Hat" Damon said, holding me steady.

Paige emerged from the crowd with a phone on one ear, and a finger in the other. "No, Mom," she yelled into the phone. "Everyone is accounted for. We're all fine. Uh huh. Uh huh. No. Fine. Yes, fine, hold on. Will you talk to her, please?" she said, handing the phone to Damon.

After a while, the commotion started to die down, and most everyone left. Soaking wet and still a little shaken, I let myself sink to the curb of the street. The thoughts of all the things that could have happened in that fire, but didn't, ran through my head. I wasn't sure if I should feel relieved it didn't happen, scared that it almost did, or both because at any moment it could happen again.

Liv sat down next to me, and the two of us gazed up into the hazardous night sky together. The lights from the fire trucks were flooding out the stars, and stale clouds of smoke still hovered over the building.

"Firemen say they can't tell what started the fire," she said.

I twisted the ends of my sleeves, trying to pry out the dirty water that still soaked them. "I know what started the fire. Or who."

"Do you think that's why he killed Justin, to get that power?" she asked, putting her head onto my wet shoulder.

"Does it matter? He just tried to mass-murder us."

Despite being wet, my phone started ringing. "Hold on," I said to Liv, "It's my sister."

"I'm okay, Syd," I said as I answered. She was sobbing hysterically, and I couldn't make out anything she said. "Syd . . . Syd. It's okay. Everybody's okay. We all made it out. No one's hurt."

She got louder, and through her screaming sobs I could finally make out what she was saying. "No! It's Zoe."

"Zoe?" I started to panic. "What about Zoe? Syd? What's happened?"

She was almost incoherent by then. "She's gone."

A cold sweat emerged from my skin like shards of glass, yanking me into another vision.

> "The Walkers must know how to use this," the man without a face said. He held up the Opalescence, still in my setting, in front of his hidden face. "Or what good is it to have it?"
>
> "I don't see how taking the girl is supposed to help us," the voice of a woman my vision wouldn't show me said. Her voice was muffled, like she was holding her hand in front of her mouth when she spoke.
>
> "She's a Walker, right? And you said she was a Caster," the man without a face said, running his hand through his white hair. "So, we're going to make her tell us how to use it."

The retreat from that vision was violent, as it tossed me around and tried to make sloppy scrambled eggs with my insides.

"I'll be right there," I said to Sydney. I hung up the phone, swallowed hard, and turned to Liv. "He has my niece."

Chapter 31

My car was flying into Sydney's driveway before I took my next breath. Dashing into the house without knocking, I pulled my sister into my arms. She was still sobbing.

"What's going on? What happened?" I asked Charley over Sydney's shoulder.

"She was in bed," Sydney screamed. "She was fine. Everything was fine. And then . . ." she pulled away from me and lit a cigarette, "she wasn't. I heard her scream. I ran to her room, but she was already gone." She put out her cigarette and clasped her hands over her red face.

"The police said they are doing everything they can to find her," Charley said, "but we don't know anything yet."

"The windows were all locked," Sydney said, shaking her head. "In her bedroom, the windows were all locked. They still are. I don't understand how someone could have taken her when I was sitting right here in the living room. How?"

"Where are the boys?" I asked.

"Camille has them downstairs," she said, blowing her nose. "I don't know what to do, Hat." Sydney's face sunk into her chest. "Tell me what to do."

"We're going to find her," I said, rubbing her shoulders. I had entered the house in such a rush that I didn't even notice Finn sitting in the corner, biting his nails and watching yet another Walker crisis unfold. "Where's Victor?" I asked him.

"Dunno," he said between his fingers, "we've been trying to get a hold of him since we heard about the fire."

The door opened in rapid succession as Walkers started to arrive. First Gloria, then Paige, then just about everyone else. They took Sydney into the bathroom to clean her up, but her gut-wrenching wailing bellowed down the hallway behind them.

Charley hugged me, tucking her head under my chin. I rocked us slowly from side to side as she cried into my chest.

"You're all wet . . . and you smell," she said.

"I know," I said. She looked up at me nervously, just for a second. "What is it?" I asked.

"What if she's . . . ," she started crying harder.

"She's not," I said definitively. I knew that I could be wrong about that, but I wouldn't accept any other answer, from myself or from them. "I know she's not." I moved Charley to the couch next to Finn. "Stay here with them. Both of you. Keep everyone together."

"Where are you going?" Finn asked.

"I don't know yet."

On my way out the door, I passed Gloria. She looked at me sideways, but I didn't bother to stop and tell her what I was going to do. There wasn't time for an explanation or for her disapproval.

When I got to my car, Liv was leaning up against it and her car was parked behind me. "What are you doing here?" I asked her.

"I followed you. I couldn't just go home after hearing that. What's going on?"

"No one knows anything, but everyone's panicked," I said. "I wanted to tell them what I knew, but I didn't know how. And I didn't think that it would help anyway. It doesn't matter. I have to find her and get her back before something happens."

"Right," Liv said, handing me the keys to her SUV. "We'll go to my house."

As we sped off my sister's street, swerving around other cars through the city, Liv took hold of my hand. "You're shaking," she said.

"I know."

* * * * *

"Try another one," I spat, pacing back and forth in front of Liv and pressing on my temples. My worry and anger had placed my psyche on unstable ground, and being the only person in front of me, she took the brunt of it.

"Don't yell at me. I'm doing the best I can," she said.

We were at her house, digging through endless stacks of leather bound books and trying any spell that had a chance of finding Zoe. The large steel toolbox that Liv kept all her magical items in was open on the floor, things falling out all around it as she dug into it for something new.

"I know you are. I'm sorry."

She pulled out a small bottle of green paint from inside her toolbox and swished it around. She kept saying "Zoe Walker," over and over to herself before smashing the bottle violently on the coffee table.

I jumped a little as the abrupt sound of breaking glass filled the room. "What is that supposed to do?" I asked.

"Wait for it," Liv said, keeping her focus on the green ink as it slowly spread across the table.

Then the ink stopped moving and started to bubble. It turned slime-like as it condensed into itself, swirling until it looked like a whirlpool. Slowly, the broken glass was sucked up into the center until there was nothing left.

Then a single green bead of slimy ink lifted from the rest and hovered over the table, spinning in the same direction as the whirlpool below it. A sharp snapping sound followed, like bubble wrap being popped, and the bead threw itself against a nearby wall. It was just a tiny bead of ink, but with a powerful impact that shook the paintings right off the wall. More beads formed and pulled themselves up into the air to follow. Thousands of them. The popping noises filled the room as they furiously shot toward the wall.

The beads started to recombine there on the wall and eventually the ink started to form some sort of picture. Over and over it repeated, until there was no ink left on the table. But when it was done, the resulting picture was blurry and nondescript. The spell quickly deflated and the ink dripped down the wall into the carpet below it.

"Damnit," Liv said. "I don't understand why nothing is working. I'm running out of options here."

"What the hell good is magic if we can't even use it to find my niece?"

"You're yelling again."

"I know, I'm sorry. I just can't stand that he has her right now and that I'm the only person who can do anything about it, and I'm not doing anything about it."

Liv was flipping through another book when she stopped and looked up at me. "What if you could get a vision?"

That's a great idea! I was trying not to take out my frustration and fear on her, but with questions like that, she was making it hard.

"Don't you think if I could make these stupid visions show up when I wanted to, I would have already?" I asked.

"No. Stop. Listen," she said, turning the book she was reading around and showing it to me. "This spell is supposed to work just like your powers. I tried it once a long time ago. I don't know if it'll work, or if it even can on you, but it's something, and something is more than we have right now."

I nodded and took the book from her.

She grabbed a potted plant from beside her couch, turned it upside down, and shook out the plant and all the soil in it. "We need a bowl of fire," she explained, shaking the plant free from the soil and putting it back in the pot. She grabbed a stack of unopened mail from an end table and tossed it in the make-shift bowl.

With matches from her toolbox, she lit the contents of the pot on fire. As the flames my mail, she looked at me and said, "You're up."

I held the spellbook in my hands and looked at the fire. *Okay, focus Hat. Focus.*

Liv stood and moved behind me, rubbing my shoulders tenderly. "Relax," she said. "This spell is really specific, so it's important that you keep your focus on what you're trying to get a vision about. Think about the love you have for Zoe, not the anger you feel because she's gone. That'll help."

A picture of Zoe entered my mind and she smiled at me. She had such a wonderful smile, the kind that instilled the confidence that she would grow up to be a simply amazing woman, like her mother and her grandmother. The Universe aligned on the heels of that picture with my urgent need to cast that spell, connecting me to its power through love. I leaned over the flames to call out the spell, and they crackled from deep inside the pot.

"I stand firm on Mother Earth and ask her to take me to the place of peace. Take me, Mother, to a higher plane where all is seen with the mind, and all is understood with the heart. Take me, Mother, to that place at the crossroads of chaos and order, to that place of peace." I closed the book and waited.

It only took a few seconds before bright yellow vapors started to puff intermittently from the bowl. Like yellow clouds above a burning earth, they floated in waiting, growing every second. As the fire dwindled, the clouds combined and forcefully pushed themselves into my nose and mouth.

That was easily the most rank smelling and tasting thing I had ever experienced. It was like dirty feet. Rotting, moldy, dirty feet. I started gagging uncontrollably, holding my stomach and trying to keep myself from throwing up. Unlike my other visions, there were no sweats, no lights or noises, just an immediate presence in the face of the past. It picked up where my last had left off.

> *The man without a face was holding the Opalescence and talking to his unseen companion in the shadows of my sight. Wherever they were, they still had my captive niece with them.*
>
> *"A lot of good that charm of yours is doing to keep him out of our way," he said to the hidden woman.*
>
> *"It's stopping him from using those visions he gets to find out who we are, isn't it?" the woman's muffled voice shot back. "You can thank me for that later."*
>
> *"It's not going to be enough," he said. "I know this family—they won't just lay down and wait while I have her."*

They kept talking, but the vision started to fade away and their voices became distant.

No! Damn it.

I refocused and tried to hold onto the vision to see where they were, but they were both gone. Instead of falling back into the present, like I had with every other vision, I jumped straight into a new one. Moving faster than ever, broken pieces of visions started to overlap, and it was like every corner of the Universe was throwing information at me.

In one vision, Withers was hunched over his workbench at Oddities talking into an old rotary phone.

> *"No, Simone," he said loudly. "No. Listen to me. I have no intention of mixing myself up in the business of Walkers anymore. It's not worth it."*
>
> *A woman's voice started talking back, but I couldn't tell what she was saying. Withers pulled on the phone's cord, stretching it to its limits so he could reach the door. He looked out the window nervously before changing the sign to "closed."*
>
> *"Yes. He just left. Mia's son. The one I was telling you about."*
>
> *The woman's voice on the other end got more urgent.*
>
> *"I don't care about any of that. This isn't for us— we need to get out of here. At least for now."*
>
> *The woman's response was brief.*
>
> *"No. I believe you, but it's not our concern. If the man behind the mask is a Walker, that is for them to deal with and they'll figure it out soon enough.*

In the second, I watched a plump woman I didn't know walk to the front of a large room, filled with people.

She opened a small book and put on reading glasses before saying, "In the beginning, there were five, and in the end there will be five."

Then another vision started before the second had finished.

A woman with bobbed hair and a colorful, ankle-length dress with sleeves sat at a long wooden table. I remembered her from the vision Kevin had forced on me once. Holding the Opalescence in her hand, she smiled as a man approached her.

"This ends now," he said. He held out his hand and fire started to appear, just like I had seen with Justin once before.

The woman started laughing as the colors of the Opalescence started moving freely. She and I were separated by time and space, but somehow I could feel the Opalescence grow cold in her hand. "Take his powers," she said.

That vision started to fade away, but another had already started. I was in the copy room at Cartwright, surrounded by boxes.

"I'm not just being sympathetic, Hat," Kevin said to me. "Once you're connected to the Opalescence, you're connected forever—and that connection doesn't end with death. I can feel it always, just as I can feel you and every other person who has ever worn it. You will, too, with time."

That string of visions was like trying to see which channel the TV was on, while driving past it at seventy miles an hour. It was sickening, and when the fumes finally subsided, I stumbled over to the couch and fell into it.

"You didn't tell me it was going to do that," I croaked, holding my stomach and still gagging.

"Would it have stopped you from doing it?" she asked, shaking her head from side to side. "Did it show you where they are?"

The sickness subsided enough that I could stand again. "Kevin!" I yelled into the air, startling Liv.

"What are you doing?" she asked.

"Kevin, goddammit," I yelled again. "Get your ass down here and help us."

With the Opalescence's power, I tapped into the connection I had with Kevin. I used it to call him—not just verbally, but emotionally too; to send the urgent sense of need I had for him. And even before he arrived, I could feel his dread, fear, and guilt inside me.

"He's blocking you from finding him with spells," Kevin said, appearing from the next room.

"Do you know what that is? Not helpful, that's what that is," I said.

"You're right. I'm sorry," he said.

"You told me once you can always feel the Opalescence. Can you feel it now?"

"Yes."

"Where is it?"

Kevin hesitated for moment and then took a deep breath. Why I'll never know, he was dead. "There's a lumberyard in that industrial park . . . the one in front of the highway. That's where he has it."

"Then that's where I'm going."

"Let's go," Liv said.

"No," I said, holding onto her arm. "I need you to go back to my sister's house and wait there. Do whatever you need to do, but make sure everyone stays there and just . . . just keep them all safe."

"What? Why?"

"Because I can't be in two places at once, and I need someone to look after all of them while I go to that lumberyard. If what I saw is true . . . ," I choked a little, "then we can't trust anyone, not even my family."

Chapter 32

The street in front of the industrial park was still dark and quiet when I arrived. I pulled off the road a few blocks away, shut off my lights, and closed my eyes. Taking a deep breath, I tried not to think too much about what I was about to do or question whether or not I could actually do it.

Once inside the gate, I scanned around the few lit areas for movement. The large wooden sliding door to the lumberyard's office was ajar, and I crept along the wall with a side-step toward it, watching for anyone who might come out of the darkness at me. Once I reached it, I darted through the door and took cover behind a nearby forklift.

Large pallets of countless types of wood were scattered around the room, and they were stacked so high that you couldn't see over them. Together, they created a catacomb draped in midnight's darkness that easily hid everything.

I moved quietly through the tunnels of wood, searching for the source of the one light I could see. As I got closer, I slowed down. I put the heel of my foot out first to lightly touch the ground before rolling my shoe to my toes, gliding into each step to hide any noise my feet might make. The light peeped out from the end of one of the aisles, and I stopped just before it, listening for the owner of the shadow that passed back and forth in front of the light.

I calmed myself as I felt a cold sweat form, and quietly waited for a vision to unfold.

> *The Guido with the pipe, one of the men who had attacked Max and me a few months before, sat lazily on a wobbly folding chair. Next to him, a half-drunk bottle of beer and a dirty can of mace.*
>
> *Illuminated by the room's only light, he sat alone and puffed on a cigarette before throwing it against one of the large stacks of wood. It bounced off the wood, throwing tiny embers all over the cement floor before dissolving and rolling into the darkness. He spit and used the sleeve of his worn sweatshirt to wipe the dribble from his mouth.*

As I opened my eyes, a bent cigarette butt rolled across the dark floor in front of me. I picked up a piece of dowel rod that was leaning against a tier of pellet wood packets beside me. Taking one deep breath and holding it, I jumped out into the light and charged Pipe Guido, who was still perched on the chair wiping his mouth.

"Shit," he yelled before I hit him across the head with the piece of wood.

He was still awake, but painfully awake, holding the lump that was forming on the side of his head with both hands. I took another step forward, but an arm wrapped around my neck from behind. A hand followed and grabbed my wrist to pull it behind my back.

"Ugh," I yelled into the arm.

What the hell? I couldn't have seen both of them in my vision?

316

"Ha!" I growled as I bent my free elbow and thrust it behind me into my attacker's stomach, causing him to drop his arm from my neck.

"Gaaah," I called out, lifting my elbow and striking him in the face with it. After my elbow made contact with his nose, I yanked on the hand still clenched to my wrist. I used all my weight to spin him around to face me, and then pushed him roughly into the wall behind him. He finally let go, and I gave him one swift hit to the stomach before moving away. Finally getting a good look at him, I saw another familiar face, Collar Guido.

"Not bad, fag," he groaned and pulled himself up from my last hit.

I tightened my fists, tucking my thumbs underneath them. "Where's my niece?"

He guffawed at me. "Where's your little boyfriend, huh? You can't take both of us alone."

Before I could do or say anything, his leg was in the air, striking my knee with his foot. I fell hard on that knee, and his fist followed, hitting me in the face with a forceful right hook.

My body contorted and my face landed against the cold and rough cement floor with a smack. He bounced on the balls of his feet a little, like a boxer in a ring, and moved to pick up Pipe Guido from the floor.

"Come on . . . is that it?" he asked.

You have no idea.

The coldness of the Opalescence entered me as I focused on our connection. Without getting up, I slid my arm up from my side toward the canister of mace that lay just a few feet out of my reach. Curling my fingers, I commanded it to come to me, and it quickly rolled up into my open hand. I moved away from the two Guidos and held the mace up at them, letting the top fall back to the ground, and teasing the trigger with my finger.

"You think you can hurt us with that from way over there?"

"No, actually," I said, tossing the canister at them.

Pipe Guido held out his hands to catch it, but before it reached him, I slammed my palms together like I was killing a bug and focused on the canister. It exploded, and the mace sprayed into the air around them. They covered their eyes and screamed out in pain. They couldn't move at first, except to writhe in pain, but when they finally did, a stinging red color had bled out from their eyes and swept across their faces.

Still unable to open his eyes completely, Collar Guido grabbed the piece of wood I had hit his friend with at the start of our scuffle and swung it at his side.

"Oh, hell no," I said, throwing up my hand at him and knocking him away with the Opalescence's power. He flew back about twenty feet and bounced off another stack of wood before flopping to the floor. He made no attempt to get up.

"Where is she?" I approached Pipe Guido, who had fallen to his knees in pain and was still struggling to compose himself from the hit of mace.

When he didn't speak, I pulled my fist into the air and hit him across the face with the back of it. "Where is she?" I asked again.

He still refused to talk. The adrenaline of the situation brought unprecedented control over the Opalescence's powers and my connection to it. I stretched out my hand at him and like I was picking up a cup, I slowly pressed my thumb against my first two fingers and focused on his throat. Without touching him, the Opalescence's powers would close his windpipe, just for a moment, before I released my hold and let him gasp for air.

"I should tell you," I said in between the third and fourth time I cut off his air supply, "every second you test my patience and don't tell me where my niece is, is one more second you're bartering with your own life." I closed his throat a little longer that time for emphasis.

When his face started to turn five shades of indigo, he put out his hand and pointed to the middle of five metal doors behind him. I released him from my magical hold, and then my leg shot up and kicked him in the face with the top of my foot. He twisted and landed on his back, conscious but unaware of me as I stepped over him and ran to the door.

"Zoe?" I called out, yanking open the door. The door led to a long, narrow hallway with another metal door on the other end. Between me and that door, however, was Goatee Guido holding a baseball bat. He started running at me, pulling the bat over his shoulder in preparation to strike.

Running to match his pace, I flicked my hand at him and the Opalescence's power pounded him into one of the hallway's walls. He bounced back quickly, and I followed through by waving my hand again, smacking him into the opposite wall. Stopping a few feet away from him, I concentrated on his mangy black boots and pulled my hands back toward my body in a scooping motion.

Following the force of my hands, his boots pulled out in front of him and he fell backward, dropping the bat and hitting his head. When he didn't try to move again, I pulled my left hand over my right shoulder and focused on his body. With one fluid motion of my arm, his body slid along the floor and through the door I had just come from.

"Zoe, are you here?" I yelled as I made it through the last door. The room was large, dark, and full of grungy, tall machines that made seeing anything impossible.

"Uncle?" a delirious and high-pitched shriek came from the other side of one of the machines. "I'm here!" Zoe yelled with tears in her voice. "Uncle, I'm over here."

I ran through the room with a speed unaided by magic but still as fast as sound itself. Behind the large machine, I found Zoe slouched down in an oversized metal dog cage. Thin metal mesh encased every inch, and a large padlock kept her securely inside.

In less than a second I was on the floor beside her, pushing my fingers into the holes of the cage to meet hers. "I'm here. You're okay," I said confidently. The Opalescence, still in my setting, hung heavily from her neck and clanked against the cage as she lunged for me, all the while choking on her tears.

"He made me wear it," Zoe started to cry harder.

"Who did?" I asked, pulling on the padlock.

"I don't know. He . . . he didn't have a face."

"It's okay, Zoe. It's okay. Just give me a second and I'll get you out of here."

How? I thought, looking around for anything that might help me pry it open.

The Opalescence started to glow as I looked at it. It infused me with its power again, and as if it was telling me what to do next, I took a step back and focused on the corner of the cage's door. With another swift arm movement, the Opalescence's power ripped open the door and flung it to the side.

Zoe pushed through the opening and into my arms, sobbing and digging her fingers into my back.

"I've got you, baby. It's okay," I said, hugging her back tightly and stroking her hair. "But we need to get out of here now."

I felt a slight breeze behind me but before I could turn, a sharp pain tore through my side. I fell to my knees and watched as the faceless man held a blade in my side. I tried to lift my hand to cast the Opalescence's power at him, but he responded by pushing the handle of his blade further into my side, pressing hard on the hilt until it met my shirt. Crying out, I sunk listlessly to the ground.

He pulled the blade from my side and started talking to Zoe as if I wasn't there, mostly because he knew that I soon wouldn't be.

"No," Zoe screamed, pulling herself away from his grip.

"I told you that if you show me how to use that necklace, I'll let you go home," he said gently, moving closer to her. His muffled voice throbbed from under the mask. "Just show me how and no one else has to get hurt."

"Get away from her," I moaned. Blood, my blood, was pouring down my side and soaking into my pants. It drained me, both literally and figuratively. I barely had the strength to wave my hand at him and attempt to push him away with the Opalescence's power.

When nothing happened, he laughed and leaned over my body. "You don't think I know what you can do? I wouldn't have gone through all this only to be unprepared to handle you. You don't take chances when this kind of power is at stake."

He grabbed Zoe's arm and pushed her toward the cage. "No," she yelled before sinking her teeth brutally into his arm. As he staggered backward, she spat a chunk of his own arm back at him. "Uncle! Uncle, are you okay?"

I wasn't okay. I needed to get back up and finish what I went there to do, for her and for myself. I gathered all the strength I had left in me to pull myself up, and then I did, effortlessly. A little too effortlessly.

When I looked down, my body was still lying there in a pool of my own blood, and I quickly realized that my time in that room, and in Zoe's life, was coming to an end.

Chapter 33

Well, that was unexpected, I thought as I looked down at my beaten and bloody body.

Voices started echoing down the corridor outside the room. The man without a face swung his head back and forth between the door and Zoe. I couldn't see his facial expressions, but I could tell he was starting to panic. He crouched, pushed past Zoe's screams to claw at the Opalescence around her neck. He turned, just as the voices breached the hallway behind the door, and then his body rapidly evaporated into ripples of light. A short breeze followed and he was completely gone, with the Opalescence.

At least she's alright, I thought.

My body and everything around it was starting to shift out of focus. Cooper and Liv, the voices from the hallway, ran into the room. Liv held my crying niece in her arms and Cooper looked around for the man without a face. They were saying something, but I couldn't hear them as they slowly drifted away and became nothing more than silhouettes of my past.

So much for destiny.

Or, maybe, dying then and there was my destiny. Maybe the rest of the story was meant to play out without me. Everything was becoming so blurry, and I was overcome with the greatest sense of calm.

"That didn't really work out, did it?" Kevin said, appearing next to me.

"I tried," I said, hardly able to make out anything in the room anymore.

He came up beside me and wrapped his arm around my shoulder. "I know you did," he said.

"Am I dead?"

"No, not yet at least. Death itself can be easy. The pain leading up to death, well, that can be less easy sometimes. I think when the body is dealt more pain than it can handle, you disconnect from it, and you end up here."

"Where is here?" I asked.

"I don't know exactly, but it's sort of a spiritual crossroads. A fold in between the physical and spiritual planes. Most people are only here for the briefest of moments—hardly long enough to notice. They either go back into their bodies or move on. I think staying here is just one more thing our connection to the Opalescence changes."

"So, what now? Do we just wait here until I die?"

"That's really up to you. This won't end with tonight, Hat. He still has the Opalescence, and it's only a matter of time before he figures out how to use it. And when he does, it's going to be a shit storm of problems. We can stand here and wait for you to die, if that's what you want, or you can go back and end this."

"How exactly? You just said I'm practically dead over here. It's over," I yelled. I realized I felt more fear for what I had left behind than what was in front of me. I could welcome death, gladly almost, but I couldn't welcome the havoc the Opalescence could wreak on my family.

"It's not over yet. People can say whatever they want about the Walkers, but there are some things that are core to who we are, and they can't understand it. We're born with this insane tenacity, a way of pulling ourselves up out of the ashes, despite everything and everyone, to keep on fighting. We do it even when we have every right in the world to lie down and give up. Your mother was like that, and so are you."

"I used to think I was a lot like her, but I don't know anymore. I don't think I even knew who she was."

"Secrets have an unfair way of making you feel disconnected from the person who keeps them from you, especially after they die. You may not understand the choices she made, but she was still the mother you knew and loved. Magic was only a small part of her, and not even the best part. You're strong like she was, and you have to believe me that you're enough like her to be able to rise up out of these ashes and end this."

A door appeared in the blurred background as Kevin spoke. "Where does that go?" I asked.

"To some unfinished business. If you are going to end this, you're going to need all the help you can get." The door opened slowly by itself. "That door will lead you back to The Trials of Truth."

"No," I yelled. "I can't. Last time I went there it almost ripped me apart and . . . I won't."

"Maybe you weren't ready the last time you went there, but you still have the same problem—the man without a face. You're not going to be able to stop him with dumb luck, and the fact that you're almost dead right now proves that."

"No," I said flatly. "I almost didn't survive the last time, and . . ."

"Hat, listen to me," my uncle put his large hand on my shoulder. "You're running out of time. It won't be long before he figures out how to use the Opalescence and when he does . . . you won't stand a chance at stopping him. You have the strength to go back there, and find out who he is, and how you're going to stop him. There are answers waiting for you on the other side of this, you just have to be strong enough to get there."

My uncle's love for me was real, but I don't think he had any idea of what he was asking of me, of what it would take to complete the Trials of Truth. If I did have the strength to walk through that door, it didn't mean I would survive what was waiting for me on the other side of it.

On the brink of death, I could choose to walk away or walk forward. I knew I wouldn't have a firm place in my future until I could shake off all the things that pulled on me from my past. Choice—our real power—was waiting to be wielded.

"Okay. We'll just hang out here until you finish dying. It's a pity for Zoe though, isn't it? She shouldn't have to watch her uncle bleed out in front of her. And I wonder what will happen to her, and the rest of the family, once someone else has the Opalescence, I think . . ."

"Stop," I said in a whiney voice. "Fine. Let's do this."

You've got this Hat. You've got this.

I took his hand and we walked through the door together. It returned us to the library, just as we had left it, with me strung up against the wall and Kevin holding a lantern on the outskirts of the hideous scene. I tightened all my muscles, the way you do right before you know someone is about to punch you in the stomach.

The boy's shirt was already neatly folded, with his tie on the table. His face showed me that he had long checked out of that moment and he was nothing more than a breathing mannequin. At the same time, I found a certain respect and understanding for him that I didn't have for myself when I was him—he did the only thing he could do, he survived.

You can do this, I told myself.

The monster of the scene, the tall priest in his drab clothing, was already looking at me against the wall. Like he expected I would crack as quickly as the last time, he strangled me with his leering eyes. Slowly, and without taking his eyes off me, he continued his premeditated invasion of the boy.

I turned my face into the darkness to avoid what I knew he'd do next, forgetting that I could see it there too.

Ahhhh!

"What's the matter?" the priest taunted me. "Scared?"

That's not how this happened, I kept telling myself.

"There's nothing you can do," he said, his treacherous voice booming toward me as he played with the boy's hair. "I have all the power, and you have none. Just like before. Just like when you were him."

The boy's clothes were gone again, and the bent knuckle of the man's finger ran over the boy's arm. The quicksand of memories of what was to come pulled at me from the inside. There would be pain. There would be emptiness. There would be agony. All over again.

"Stop," I yelled, snapping my head back toward him and lifting the side of my lip up into a seething scowl.

"Why?" his voice slithered across his grinning lips. "I don't have to stop. We both know what happens next. There's nothing you can do about it."

That man was the first thing I ever needed to run away from. He was the bringer of discord and anarchy into my life and my mind. But he was also wrong.

I finally stopped fighting the quicksand he created and let myself fall to the bottom. There, I saw that I was just looking at a moment in time, one I didn't exist in. When I was a child, locked in that asylum-like library with him, there was no adult version of me strapped to a wall on the outskirts of the darkness. That spell existed only to scare me with the truth of my own past, a past I had lived through and survived. Realizing all that tipped control of that moment back to me.

"No," I called viciously, pulling at my chains and snarling at the priest. "You don't have the same power over me that you used to."

He tugged on the boy's face and forced him to look at me too. "It seems to me that I have all the power."

"And I'm still standing, damn it," I yelled, rattling my chains. "Despite you, I'm still standing. You can force me to watch this over and over and I'll still be standing, because I've already survived this."

The chains that held me to the wall released and I shook my bonds off easily. The boy's spirit collapsed into a single ball of light and disappeared from the scene, joining my soul and giving me a sense of wholeness I hadn't felt since the priest entered my life. He was the personification of the bleakest point in my life, but it was still my life. If I wanted to own my moments, I had to own all my moments, even the ones as dark as this.

"I can't change the past." I walked closer to the priest, he didn't seem nearly as giant-like as he once did, and said, "but you won't stop my future."

"Where's all your power now?" I asked, grabbing his throat and making him look directly at me. Fear filled his eyes before he too disappeared, dissolved in defeat, and returned to whatever torturous crevice of the Universe's bowels he had first germinated in.

"What now?" I asked Kevin.

He nodded at the floor, where a small hole had opened up between us.

"You're serious? Where's the white rabbit?"

"Just jump in," he said. "The hard part's over."

There wasn't anything The Trials of Truth could throw at me that could be worse than what I had already seen. I sat on the floor and let my legs dangle in the hole. It was just big enough to fit me, and with one large breath in, I slid into it.

When I landed, the ground was unnaturally soft, cushioning my feet from the impact. I was in a cavern of sorts, and other than the hole I had just jumped through, there were no apparent entrances or exits. White flowers of every species covered the ground and all along the base of the walls. I started walking toward a bright light at the end of the cavern.

A sweet melody of soft, operatic voices flowed through the cavern eloquently. An aquatic glow warmed the walls around me. When I touched them, the colors of the iridescent rock billowed beneath my fingertips, creating tiny waves to match the path of my fingers. I followed the path of white flowers until it reached a hearty stone archway, the source of the light, beyond which I could not see.

One more step and I was through the archway into another destination unknown. The light disappeared behind me, and with it the archway.

It landed me in another new cavern. The white flowers exploded around my feet, covering every inch of the ground.

From above, all I could see was water, as if I walked in a cavernous garden below the ocean's translucent bottom. I reached up and touched it. Cold water dripped down my hand, but the magic that kept the water at bay above me was otherwise unaffected by my touch.

"Welcome," a voice said from the other side of the cavern.

A woman sat majestically, and with bizarrely perfect posture, on a large granite bench in the corner of the cavern. She was dressed from head to toe in white satin robes, a gold braided rope tying them together at her waist. She was barefoot, and her skin was as luminous as the cavern around us.

"We should have expected that the next person to make it here would be a Walker," she said. Her voice seemed to echo, like it was being repeated as it came out of her mouth.

From above, I watched as things started falling from the water. They could have been copper pennies, except that as they broke the barrier of water, they floated aimlessly down to the ground like snow. I reached out to catch one, and it hovered in the palm of my hand for the briefest of moments. In my head, I heard "I wish to find love." Then, just as quickly, the penny drifted off my palm like dust in the wind, falling to the ground and disappearing in the beds of the white flowers.

"Where are we?" I asked.

The woman crossed her legs, folded her hands in her lap, and looked up at the sky of water above us. "Someplace warm and beautiful. It is one of our favorite places to create and sit in. You can watch as the coins fall from the top of the wishing well, the hopes and dreams of the lost and lonely falling down and landing at our feet, unanswered. It is an . . . interesting perspective, even for us."

"Who are you?"

"We are carriers of truth," she said, the echo in her voice stronger than before. "Nothing more. People across the ages have called us many things: goddess, spirit, angel, and we are none of those things, but we are all of those things. To many, we are known collectively as Aletheia."

Each time she said "we," I looked around the cavern nervously to see who else might be there.

"The truth is rarely understood from one perspective alone," she said, answering a question I had yet to ask. "We are many voices, speaking as one and telling the story of truth from each of those perspectives collectively."

"Do you know why I'm here?"

"Mortals have such a short life, it makes you rush through everything you do, but time for you stands still right now. It is not easy to pass The Trials of Truth, so sometimes we can go a hundred years without enjoying the company of someone who needs air and water to survive. Let us just enjoy that for a moment."

I sat down on another bench across from her, the stems of little white flowers tickling my ankles as I walked. "Can you tell me who the man without a face is?"

All echoes of Aletheia's voice moaned loudly. "A moment to us must seem like an eternity to you. Why do you ask us questions when you already know the answers?"

"If you're talking about that vision I had, all it told me was that he was a Walker. But that's about as helpful as telling me he's white. I can't just run around my family asking every guy if he happens to own a mask . . . and be a murderer. I need to know who is behind the mask so I can find him."

"We wonder why you ask for daylight when you can already see in the dark," she said, sighing.

"What does that mean?"

Aletheia plucked a flower from her feet and handed it to me. "Is this flower white?" she asked.

"Yeah," I said.

"And you know that to be true?"

"Yeah?"

"Then ask that flower to show you other things and believe them to be true as well."

The sublime simplicity of the white flower absorbed me as I let myself sink into the depths of its petals with my gaze. The textures lining each petal wrapped around me as I fell deeper and deeper into it. Like it was speaking to me through my touch, I knew what I had to do next. When I had finally given myself up to it completely, I whispered, "Show me," and the flower carried me softly to my place of weightlessness and serenity.

> *A red-headed woman I didn't know sat in a lonely hospital room at dusk. In her arms was a tiny newborn, swaddled in a blue striped blanket. Both were crying, but the mother's tears seemed filled with more anger than joy.*
>
> *"He's beautiful," a nurse said to the woman as she looked over her shoulder to the baby. "Do you want me to get his father for you?"*
>
> *"Not unless you can summon the dead," the woman said to the nurse.*
>
> *The nurse's eyes grew big and she stuttered a few words of apology before backing out of the room awkwardly.*
>
> *The woman then began to rock the baby gently in her arms. "It's okay, isn't it little boy? It's okay. My little forgotten Walker. We don't need any of them, do we?"*

My return from the vision was peaceful, soft even, as the petals guided me gently back into the cavern. Then the petals dissolved in my hands until they were nothing more than opulent white grains of sand. Aletheia looked at me and smiled.

"Who was that?" I asked, letting the sand fall from my hands to the ground.

"You asked to see who the man behind the mask was, and you were shown. He is the son of Kevin Walker."

Chapter 34

"My uncle didn't have any children," I said.

"That is what you believe to be true, not what we know to be true," Aletheia said. "Your uncle was taken from your world before he could know his son. But the boy you saw is his nonetheless."

"How do I find him?"

"That truth is perhaps the easiest we have to offer you," she said. "Look up."

The pennies stopped falling and as I looked up into the water above us it turned black, reflecting our image back at us. Then the water rippled, and our reflections dissipated. In their place, the Mask of Apate in a man's hand. As he lifted it to his face, I saw who he really was.

"No," I said aloud.

"Do you not believe the truth?" she asked.

"Not Graham. It couldn't be Graham. I know him, and he wouldn't do all this. Lie. Kill. Steal. No, not him."

"All mortals lie. It's part of who you are and what you do to survive in the world you live in. Your lives are compilations of truths, many of which you cannot see or refuse to accept. The full truth is complex, and with it comes enlightenment and understanding, but also confusion and pain."

"But why? Why would he do this?"

"We know your cousin to be dangerous because his mind has been corrupted, and he fears nothing except the absence of power. The Opalescence, to him, represents the unique opportunity to never have his fears realized. With malevolence, that abundance of power can be destructive, but in his hands, it can be apocalyptic. The truth is clear here, with the Opalescence, he will self-destruct and destroy many things in his path when he does, yourself and your family included."

In just a few seconds, everything in my world was colliding in the most unexpected ways. The man without a face was my boss. My boss was my cousin. My cousin was a killer. A killer was going to destroy everything around me.

The only thing that stood in his way was me, and I was almost dead.

"What do I do?" I asked after pondering for a while longer.

Aletheia said nothing but was looking right at me.

"Are you listening to me?" I asked, waving my hands at her. "I came here for answers."

"No," she snapped. "You came here for the truth, and that is what we have given. We find it bothersome that you continue to ask for things from us that you alone can see the answers to."

"I don't understand. The visions? I can't control when they come or what they show me."

"You too often seek to understand your visions so that you can accept what they are showing you, but in the world of magic, there are many things you must accept first or else you will never understand them. When you fought your visions the hardest, that is when they pulled you apart the most. Only after you started accepting them did the truth of what they were showing you make sense." She plucked another flower roughly from our feet and handed it to me. "Ask and be shown the truth."

"Show me," I whispered to the flower. The soft words pushed against the petals, and one gently fell from the stem. It leisurely swayed back and forth to the floor and guided me to my place of serenity.

A short woman in a floral-patterned, old-fashioned dress sat at a simple table in a small room. She tossed her well-sculpted curls aside and scribbled in a tiny book. Then, she looked up and read:

"To give us strength, the Universe gave us family.

To test that strength, it gave us misfortune.

In that misfortune we found our path to peace.

In peace, we came together with our family."

"It's beautiful, mom" a young man in suit pants and suspenders sitting close to her said. "What is it for?"

"It's a reminder," she said flatly. She was absent-mindedly fidgeting with the Opalescence around her neck. For her, the setting was heart-shaped, with whimsical detailing in the metal around the stone.

"A reminder of what?" the man asked.

"Someday this might be yours, and you'll understand what I'm saying better then, but when you wear the Opalescence, you're connected to it and to every other person who's worn it." She gracefully waved her fingers over the table and the book closed with the power of the Opalescence. "That's how I can do that."

"What do you mean?"

"This doesn't come with instructions, but something about the way the Opalescence absorbs energy means that it keeps a part of us with it, even after we're gone. When you connect with it, you can tap into those powers. The ability to move things with your mind like I just did, that was your grandmother's power."

The woman was calm, and steadfast, but through our connection to the Opalescence I could also feel her attempts to hide the worry that she may someday have to burden her son with it.

"If our family is going to have to protect this thing forever, we're going to have to keep it a secret—even from each other. But I don't want us to forget about that connection we have with it. We might need it someday."

I floated from that vision effortlessly as the next petal pulled itself from the flower, fell quietly to the ground, and guided me into my next vision.

Gloria was pacing back and forth in front of my mother on her deck.

"Did you find out who has it?" my mother asked.

"Not yet," Gloria said back to her.

"I don't understand how someone who has the power to hear anything and everything that's going on can't find just one person."

"I'm trying," Gloria said, looking frustrated. "It's not like tapping a phone line."

"I know. I'm sorry. I'm just anxious to get this spell over with."

"Shit, this hurts," Gloria said, sitting down next to my mother and pointing to the cut on her hand.

"Let me see it." My mother took Gloria's hand in hers and examined the cut. "And this is why you shouldn't put small razor blades in your junk drawer, Gloria."

"Ouch," Gloria yelled as my mother pinched her cut closed and cupped her hand around Gloria's. My mother closed her eyes and a light smile washed over her lips. When she pulled her hand back, the cut was gone.

More petals fell from the flower's stem and floated to the ground as my next vision started.

I was sitting at a kitchen table with Zoe in a house I didn't recognize. She was five, maybe six years older than she was when she was kidnapped. Meticulously, she copied notes from my mother's book into one of her own. She was safe, healthy, and even looked a little happy.

She passed the poem about the Opalescence, stopped, and looked up at me. "Do you think I'll end up with that someday?" she asked.

I gently petted her head and smiled. "I hope not."

"I do. My powers are boring. I want to be able to do all the stuff you can do with it."

"Boring is underrated," I said. "This one," I pointed at a page in the book, "this one I want you to learn by heart."

"Why?" she asked.

"Because it's the only one you'll ever need to keep yourself safe. It creates a sort of safety-net around you, and no one but you can use magic inside of it."

"In this time, and in this place," Zoe started to read the spell out loud.

Coming out of the last vision, I finally understood with Aletheia was saying. As I accepted the visions for what they were, a deeper and more profound understanding of what they were showing me emerged.

"Did I just see the future?" I asked Aletheia. "That's never happened before."

"No one is born with the ability to only walk forward or backward; you must learn how to do both. You have always seen the past because it is easier to see, nothing in it will ever change. Seeing the future is harder, because every choice made shapes or changes that future. But the power to see outcomes, that we know is truly one of the more special gifts the Universe has to give someone like you."

I looked up at the water again, this time seeing my dying body back at the lumberyard. The Opalescence's power surged inside of me and I felt my mother close within it. My body lifted off the ground and spun slowly in front of the others. Tiny tremors of light swirled around the room and pooled above me before taking solace in my body.

"It's time now," Aletheia said. "We have given you everything the truth has to offer."

I closed my eyes and felt the wound in my side finish healing from the powers brought into it by the Opalescence. When I opened them again, I was back in my body, looking at the ceiling. I was damp from laying in my own blood, and sore, but I was alive.

Zoe was attached to my hip and sobbing before I could stand. "It's okay, baby, it's okay," I said stroking her hair. "I thought you were going to stay with my family," I said to Liv.

"I know. I know. I'm sorry. But I was listening in . . . up here." She pointed to her head and wiggled it back and forth. "We had to come when I saw what happened. How did you get back up just now?"

"It's a long story," I said looking down at Zoe. "I'll explain later; we need to bring her home."

Liv drove and I watched over Zoe as she drifted into an exhausted sleep in the back seat. Sunrise was breaking with lustrous hues of pink and purple filling the sky. It poked through the trees around us and cast slivers of light against Zoe's face.

"What are you gonna tell your sister?" Liv asked me.

"I have no idea. I'm not sure that she or anyone else is ready to hear me tell them the truth, or that they could believe me if I did. And what lie could I tell them that would explain all this?"

"From what you've told me about them, I don't think they'll take this lightly," she said.

"No. If I tell them what I know, they'll take up pitch forks and torches and rip this city apart until they find him. And it's just not safe for them."

I looked back at Zoe, her face smashed up against the SUV's window as she slept. "And Zoe," I said, "it's not like she doesn't already know what happened. She might not be able to process it yet, but you don't live through something like that and then just forget about it. Ahhh," I ran my fingers through my hair, massaging my scalp. "Maybe my mother wasn't wrong for wanting to keep us out of this."

"We still could keep them out of it," Liv said. "I can make them all forget that this ever happened; I have a spell I've used before."

"But is it okay for me to do something like that to them, though? Is it my right to make that decision for them?"

"Our lives get messy sometimes and we have to have a way to clean it up. I know how you feel about your family, and all the secrets, but something like this . . . it will change everything for them. There's a plastic bag in my glove compartment, grab it," she said, turning onto Sydney's street. The bag was filled with stalks of blunt smelling sage, tied tightly together with frayed strings of hemp.

Zoe was slowly waking up as the car parked, her face still tear-stained and her eyes distantly searching for an understanding I worried would never come to her. I jumped out of the car and started fishing through the gym bag I kept in my trunk for clothes not soaked with blood.

"Am I doing this?" Liv asked as I changed behind her SUV.

I looked at Zoe again, rubbed my eyebrow with my finger and exhaled uncomfortably. Everyone has a right to their own memories, no matter how bad they are. For Zoe, more than anyone else, I didn't want to rob her of that right, but I also couldn't stomach the thought of letting her live the rest of her life in constant fear of it all being repeated.

"Yes," I said.

Liv pulled a stalk of the sage from its bundle and handed it to me. "Here, hold onto to this so the spell doesn't affect you. I'll take care of the rest." She reached into her purse and pulled out a small tablet computer in a bright red case. I gave her a puzzled looked and giggled.

"What?" she asked. "I can't be carrying around massive books with me wherever I go."

"Okay . . ."

"It's called being a Caster in the digital age, Hat!" she called out after me as Zoe and I made our way toward the house.

"Zoe? Zoe!" Sydney screamed from the doorway. She dropped the phone, and whoever she was talking to on it, to the ground and ran toward us. She latched onto Zoe, and the two of them tumbled into the grass together. The hordes of family that had gathered there started making their way to the doorway to watch with relief as Zoe was reunited with her mother.

"Oh my god! How? Hat, how?" Sydney rocked Zoe in her arms and looked up at me.

In silence, I stood and waited, letting the questions and screams of joy bounce off me, until the smell of sage floated through the air around us. I tilted my head with sad eyes and silently apologized to them, and then to myself, for what I was doing.

The smell of the sage lingered for a minute, casting quiet upon everyone. A breeze followed, and blew it all away, taking with it the memories of everything that had just happened.

Sydney stood up and looked around confused. "Hat?" she said. "Um . . . thanks for dropping Zoe off for me."

"Sure, Syd," I said. "Any time."

"What's wrong?" she asked, looking up into my sad eyes and frowning.

"Just a long night, sis. I've gotta go, but I'll come by soon. I promise."

"Bye, Uncle," Zoe yelled as she playfully ran past the family into the house.

They all looked just as confused as Sydney; like you do when you lose your train of thought and can't remember for the life of you what you were talking about. I had to hope they'd understand and believe that they would have made the same choice I did.

"You did the right thing," Liv said when I approached her SUV. She was wrapping up what was left of the burnt sage and putting it back in her glove compartment.

I looked back at my family as they started to part ways, still unsure of why they were all congregated at Sydney's house in the first place. "You don't know that," I said.

Chapter 35

Liv was trashing yet another set of my bloody clothes when I stepped into the shower at her house. The hot water and pulsating shower head were magic in themselves as they washed the dirt, sweat, and dreadful memories of the night down the drain. I wished that I could have stayed in there forever.

"You were amazing today," Liv said from the other side of the shower curtain.

"Hardly," I said, using some of her shampoo to lather my sore head. "I almost died."

She moved closer to the shower. "But you didn't. You found her, and you got her back, just like you said you were going to. And then you went back to The Trials of Truth. I don't think many people would have done that. I'm not even sure if I would have done that."

The water continued to pour down my face, washing the last of the dried blood off my healed body. "Did I thank you for coming to save me?"

"Sort of. But I didn't actually save you either, did I?" The shower curtain opened smoothly and quietly, and Liv leaned against the wall to watch me.

"Maybe from a life of mediocrity," I said, splashing her with some water, and not worrying that she was seeing me naked again.

"I may not be able to see the future, but I can see a part of people that no one else can. I knew you were someone special the first time I met you, I just didn't know when you'd figure that out for yourself."

It may have been the vibrant feeling of having just beaten death, or the reinvigorating energy from feeling like things were starting to make sense around me, but when Liv slowly stripped off her clothes and joined me in the shower, I didn't stop her.

We kissed gently, and I ran my hands into her magnificent blond hair as streams of water splashed around our faces. When she touched her lips to mine, it was like two souls joining hands and walking down a path of comfort and trust. We were both happy to be alive, and neither of us wanted anything more than that moment had to offer.

Our wet movements were sensual and spontaneous, and each time our bodies touched, I drifted further into a place of relaxation and joy. Sex with her was almost more spiritual than it was physical, a serenity constructed from the safety we felt in each other's arms. Judgment, hesitation, and worry had no place in that shower, and no room to fit between our locked lips, as we owned the moment together.

It was already mid-morning by the time we collapsed into her bed together. We were both wrapped in large bath towels and she rested her head securely on my shoulder as I kissed her forehead.

"It's okay, you know?" she said softly.

"What is?"

"That you don't love me like that."

"But I do love you."

"I know you do, just not the way that could make us any more than this. I don't need my powers to know that I'm not what you really want."

"You're the most perfect woman I've ever met," I said, lightly rubbing the backside of my fingers against her cheek, "and if it makes a difference, you're exactly what I thought I always wanted." I pushed her hair out of her face and kissed her calmly on the lips. "But I think I found someone who showed me that I had no idea what I really needed."

"And where is he now?"

"This is going to shock you, but I may have fucked things up with him pretty good and we haven't talked since."

"Ha. Can't imagine it."

"But you should know that just now, with you, I definitely didn't hate that," I said with a smile, looking back to the shower through the open door from her bedroom to her bathroom.

"Mmmm. Me neither," she said softly, closing her eyes.

Neither of us moved. We didn't need to. I knew that if I couldn't love her like that, then I would likely never love any woman like that, ever. It took sleeping with the perfect woman to remind me just how stupid I had been to let go of the perfect man.

✳ ✳ ✳ ✳ ✳

For the first time since he came to live with me, Cat ignored the food I poured for him. Instead, he waited at my feet, watching every move I made. I was flipping through my mother's book to find everything I'd need, including a way to take back the Opalescence when Graham was unaffected by its powers and able to shift himself between places at will. There was just one ingredient I'd need, and a short call with Liv told me the only place to get it.

Back on Wickenden Street, I looked through the dirty glass and broken blinds at Oddities before tapping my knuckle against the door. "Hello?" The knob was loose and the door opened with a rattle. "Withers?"

The store was nothing but empty shelves and dust. It looked so much bigger than before, with no clutter, no mean old man, and no hope of finding what I was looking for.

I slid down the wall and sat on the warped wooden floor, pushing back against the empty shelves and trying to figure out where to look next.

"What are you doing here?" I asked when the door swung open and an unexpected face came into the room.

Gloria flashed a goofy smile, something I hadn't seen her do since my mother died. "I came to find you," she said, sliding down the wall next to me and flopping out her short legs. "What are you doing sitting here on the dirty floor?"

"Thinking," I said. There was so much I couldn't tell her; there was no time for a lecture. Nothing she could say could change what had to happen next. "I came here for something and with Withers gone, I'm not sure where exactly to get it."

"Ugh," she brushed some of the dust off her shirt, "that windbag is only helpful when he wants to be. If this wasn't the only place in town to get supplies, I doubt anyone would come in here at all. Is this where you got the sage from the other night?"

"How'd you . . ."

"Please," she laughed, "I could smell that spell a mile away."

"I'm still not sure that was the right thing to do, but it's done now, so I'm trying not to overthink it."

She nudged me. "I would have done the same thing."

"Yeah, I know you would have," I let out a little laugh.

She started to speak again, but I cut her off. "I love you, and everything, but I don't have the time or the energy to argue with you about what I'm doing here."

"I'm not here to argue," Gloria said, reaching into her pocket and pulling out a small plastic bag with shiny blue powder in it. "I'm here to give you this."

"Is this what I think it is? You . . . you know what I have to do with this, right?

"Yes."

"Seriously? You're going to help me now, after everything else you've said. Why?"

"Because you need it now. Look, our family is a unique bunch, you know? We have this stubbornness about us, and it tends to make us need to forge our own paths. I love that about us, but I also hate that about us. It means we're not always great at taking guidance or advice when we should. So, you can't always help in the way you'd like."

"Meaning?"

"Sometimes you just have to, we'll say, 'rearrange' the truth so the person hears what you think they need to hear in order to help them get to where they need to go. When you came to me after your mom died, I couldn't just tell you everything that was happening and expect you to understand it. Keeping you in the dark about magic for so long meant that you didn't have the advantage of growing up with your powers like we did, and this world got a lot more dangerous for you once you inherited the Opalescence. So, I told you what I thought you needed to hear in order to get you to prepare yourself for what was coming."

"So you've been helping me by trying to stop me? That makes no sense."

"I needed you to catch up, and fast, and I couldn't carry you the entire way. I knew that if I tried to push you to get here, to embrace this destiny that has been dumped on you, well, you probably would have run away from it. So, I tried the opposite. I tried to push you away from all this, fully expecting that you'd do what your mother would have done in the same situation—the exact opposite of what I was asking you to do."

"So you played me."

"Eh," she gritted her teeth and bobbed her head back and forth, "I like to think of it as nudged you in the right direction. I'd say I'm sorry, but I'm not; it's just what had to be done. I hope you'll understand and forgive me for that one day, but for today that doesn't matter. Today you have bigger things to worry about.

"So you're like what? The Chess Master? And I'm just one of your pawns."

"No, you're not a pawn. If we're using the chess analogy, then I'd say you're the most important piece on the board . . . what is that, the king? Or the queen maybe. Look, I knew that discovering this world on your own was going to be an important step in understanding who you are and why you'd have to do this."

I stood up and started pacing. "Damn it. You can hear everything and you couldn't see how much I was struggling with this? How much I needed your help? I mean, it's one thing to just not help me, but to manipulate me? How do you know I would have run away? You didn't even try. Instead you force some empty promise down my throat about keeping it a secret, and for what?"

"I was . . . I am serious about keeping this a secret. This is a complicated world we live in, and for Casters secrets are like water—they keep us alive. But this secret, the Opalescence, it's bigger than me, or you, or anyone else in our family. I'd love nothing more than for you to be able to walk away from it, but we both know you can't do that."

"Well, seeing you always seem to know so much about what's going on, did you know that when I went to get Zoe back, I got stabbed and practically died? What if I had really died that night and the one thing that could have saved me was your fucking help? How would your plan have worked out then?"

"Hat . . ."

"Fuck," I said to myself, closing my eyes. "Is telling someone the truth ever an option with this family?"

"Come on. Everything I've told you was true. But, our family is complicated, you know that. We decided to suppress your powers because we wanted you safe. The Opalescence should have never been your problem, either. Your mom never wanted that. We've been suffering through the responsibility of that damn thing for so long, and it's brought us nothing but devastation and pain. She spent almost the entire time she had it trying to figure out a way to get rid of it for good so things like this didn't happen. But then she died, and when your powers came back and you got the Opalescence, everything changed. I did what I thought was best to help you through it."

"I know you think that, but it doesn't excuse the endless secrets, and it doesn't make me feel any better about being manipulated. Is this what our family is really about, and I just never knew it?"

"No," she said firmly. "This is what magic does to our family, it brings shit into our lives that we have no control over. Believe me when I tell you that more than anything, we wanted our kids to live the normal lives we never got to have and not have to deal with all the secrets the Walkers keep."

She stood up, crossed her arms, and looked out the window. With a deep frown she pointed at my pocket just before it started vibrating. "You should read that."

"What?" I didn't realize she meant my phone.

A text message from Cooper was flashing across the screen when I pulled it out of my pocket.

"911. COME TO THE HOSPITAL NOW. IT'S LIV."

Chapter 36

"What's happened?" I asked when Cooper met me at the hospital's entrance.

"She was attacked earlier," he said, his hands visibly shaking.

"What? What do you mean attacked? By who? Is she alright?"

"We don't know much," he said, "but I was able to persuade a contact of mine from the police department to tell me what they do know. Whoever attacked her was gone before the police got there, but the witness who called them in the first place said the man that did it didn't have a face. Obviously, the police don't believe that, but that doesn't matter. She was unconscious when they found her and they don't think she's all that badly hurt, but she still hasn't woken up."

When we got to Liv's room, the floor nurse was explaining to Cooper why we couldn't see her. "Sir," she said, "like I told you earlier, only family can go in."

We were forced to watch over her bruised and bandaged body through a window to her room. Her wrist was in a cast, and the opposite arm was in a sling supporting a dislocated shoulder. What's worse, no matter how hard I tried, I couldn't connect with the powers in the Opalescence to try to heal her.

"There is really nothing I can do," the nurse said before walking away.

"Really? Let's see about that," Cooper said, taking a deep breath and fixing his eyes on the back of the nurse's head. She turned and locked eyes with his stare as he started walking toward her.

"What are you doing?" I asked, walking after him and grabbing his shoulder.

"Shut up," Cooper said, shrugging off my hand and moving directly in front of the nurse. She wasn't blinking and her eyes slowly rolled from side-to-side to watch his every move. "So then, how about now? Care to let us in then?"

"I . . . can't," she stammered.

"Are you sure?" he asked.

"I'm sorry," she said, tears starting to fall down her cheeks.

"Cooper . . ." I said.

"Fine," Cooper said, shaking his head. The nurse blinked feverishly before regaining control of her senses and racing off to another room.

"What was that?" I asked. "Mind control?"

"Not really," Cooper said, his body sagging slowly into a chair in the waiting area outside of Liv's room. "I can't force someone to do something, particularly if they don't want to, but I do usually happen to have a bit of influence over them. Clearly not with her." He got up again and pressed his face against the window to Liv's room.

"It's going to be okay," I said to Cooper as he passed in front of me again. "We'll figure out a way in."

"No. We'll make our way in there now," Cooper said, reaching for the door.

"It's locked, Coop. And," I nervously looked around us and whispered, "I don't think forcing it open is going to get us very far with these people. Let's just go get a cup of coffee."

Hospitals must be able to get away with epically bad coffee because everyone who is in there is already in so much pain that no one has the strength to care. Everything smelled like industrial cleaner and death, morbidly sterile, including our cups. On the way back, we passed the steadfast nurse, standing safely behind her shiny and tidy station, talking to a doctor in bright blue scrubs.

"Is this her doctor?" Cooper asked the nurse, leaning over her station.

"Yes. Doctor, these are the gentlemen I was telling you about," the nurse said.

The doctor started to speak, but Cooper got within inches of his face and without blinking, said, "We are as close to Liv as family, and you will let us in to see her."

The doctor didn't fight Cooper's powers. He was either weaker than the nurse, or he honestly wanted to let us in. Either way, Cooper's influence worked and the doctor told the nurse to let us through.

"The door's already open," the nurse said. "Her brother just came back from the cafeteria and I let him in."

We sped down the hallway and when Liv's open door came into view, I could see another set of hands holding hers from the bedside chair.

"Hat?" Max looked up at me in surprise.

"Max? What are you doing here?"

Without letting go of Liv's hands, he gave me an angry scowl. "What are *you* doing here?"

I deserved his aggression and he knew it. "Sorry. She's a friend of mine from work. You're her . . ."

"Brother? Yes." Max didn't look away from Liv as he spoke, as if he was signaling me to leave without saying anything.

"How is she?"

"How does she look, Hat?" he said in a shaky voice. "They can't figure out why she's unconscious. She broke her wrist and . . . ," He stopped talking and started to sniffle.

"I'm sorry," I said.

Max let go of Liv's hand, shot up and hit the wall. "Fuck!"

The nurse scurried into the room in a panic. "Is everything alright?" she asked, looking at me as if I was the one who had hit the wall. I could almost hear her think, "I knew this guy was trouble."

She pulled at the stethoscope around her neck like a ninja would pull at her nunchakus, getting ready to release swirling terror on anyone who crossed her. Max didn't say anything else, he just turned and faced the window, looking out into the cloudy day.

"Sorry ma'am," I said, "everything's fine."

The nurse left and sensing the tension that coursed through the room, Cooper followed, closing the door behind him.

"Everything is not fine," Max yelled at me. "I'm such a fucking jerk. I can't even remember the last time I talked to her. I didn't even know she worked with you. What kind of brother does that make me when I don't know where my own sister works? If she dies thinking I didn't care about her, I'll . . ."

With open arms I walked over to him, but he shrugged me off. "Just leave, Hat. I know you know how."

Screams of silence shot through the air and the awkward moment threw me from the room without saying anything more to him.

Cooper was still transfixed on Liv and was unable to look at me when I came out. "I'll be back," I said to him before walking away and past the deathly stares of our favorite nurse.

I went home long enough to shower, change, and feed Cat again. Max hadn't paused when showing me he wasn't interested in me being at the hospital, but I grabbed some clothes for him anyway. Then I stopped along the way back and picked up a few hospital-living essentials, like a tooth-brush and toothpaste, a razor, and some of the deodorant that I knew he wore . . . the kind that made him smell sexy even when he was sweating.

Cooper had fallen asleep in the waiting room by the time I got back, and Liv still hadn't woken up. Max was in the same place I left him, crumpled up in the chair next to Liv's bed, holding her hand. His face was stubbly, tired-looking and drained of color, and the baseball hat he had on was pulled down so far over his forehead that I couldn't tell if he was awake or not.

"Hey," I said quietly.

"Hi," he grunted in a brittle voice. I handed him a hot cup of non-hospital coffee and the bag filled with everything I had picked up for him.

"What's that?" he snarled, pointing at the bag and taking a slow sip of the coffee. "I'm sorry, I mean thank you for the coffee, and what is that?"

I pulled up a chair next to his and opened the bag, handing him all of the magically non-magical items to make him feel less miserable while he waited for his sister to wake up.

"This is really nice," he said, putting his hand on my knee and looking at me in the eyes for the first time since he stormed out of my apartment. "You didn't have to."

"Yes, I did. You smell," I said, glad I was able to finally pull a little laughter out of him.

He locked himself in the bathroom with my gifts, and I quietly leaned over Liv in her bed. The familiar cold from the Opalescence drifted easily throughout my body. The air went still as I touched her, and tremors of light formed around us. I was awestruck as the light pushed itself into Liv's body, but when the powers subsided, she still didn't wake up.

I fell back into my chair, left with nothing but the hope that the Universe wasn't going to let her die, not after letting me live.

"Better?" Max asked when he emerged from the bathroom a half hour later. He was clean, shaven, and no longer looked like someone who had just pulled themselves out of their own grave. He was so much taller and fitter than I was that the t-shirt I brought him was a little snug, but I didn't mind. He spun around a little, giving me a mock fashion show of my own clothes, and we both laughed again. Then he sat down next to me and leaned in close.

"Can I ask you something?"

"Sure," I said, shrugging.

"How is it that you can be such a complete asshole one minute, and then so nice the next?" He reached over me to grab his coffee, and I took in his smell. Fresh cranberries and leather, somehow.

"Practice," I said.

"I'm serious, Hat." He took a big sip of his coffee and sighed. We were sitting so close that I could smell the liquid of the fresh brewed beans as it poured out into his mouth.

"So am I," I said. "I'm sorry about the other day. I had a lot going on and I should have told you about it. Maybe I've started to think about things differently now. Maybe I'm different now. I can't tell you that I've figured everything out, because I haven't, but I do know that I was just being stupid before. I didn't understand what I had done until you were already gone."

"No," he grumbled, "you didn't. And yes, you should have talked to me." He dragged his chair to face mine and lifted his feet into my lap.

By then, the hospital was nearly still and the road outside the window was lifeless. We sat for a long while, watching Liv like a broken television, hoping and waiting for any twitch in her eye that might mean she was waking up.

Despite Liv's situation, or my own, I couldn't help but stare at Max whenever I thought I could get away with it. Our time apart hadn't changed the way I felt about him, and my attraction for him was doing nothing except getting stronger. I gently rubbed my hand up and down his leg, trying to brush away his worry and offer up any strength I had to give.

"What?" Max asked me when I stood up over him and looked deeply into his eyes—the same way I did before our first time together in his office. His sexy gray saucers looked back at me inquisitively, but I put two of my fingers over his lips before he could say anything more.

Leaning in, I pulled my fingers away and replaced them quickly with my lips, carrying us both into a kiss of such great heights that nothing, not time nor trouble, could touch us.

It was a kiss that spoke for itself. Slow, to let him know I was never letting him go again. Forceful, to remind him of the passion we had whenever we were together. And grateful, to thank him for so many things, not least of all the way he daringly loved me, even when I was too naïve to understand what that kind of love was worth.

"I love you," I said with conviction, pulling him into another kiss that seemed to lift into the air with the intensity of my feelings. "I'm sorry I didn't say that to you before."

"Wait," he said before I could kiss him again.

"Why?" I whispered, our faces almost close enough to touch. I teased his upper lip with mine and said, "I love you," again.

He didn't speak, but he didn't look away either.

"You stubborn jackass, would you just tell him you love him too," Liv's voice croaked from her bed.

Max and I leapt at her bed, hugging and kissing her deliriously. "How are you?" Max asked. "Okay, that's a stupid question. But I'm so glad you're awake. I was so worried about you Livvie."

She gave him a welcoming smile and flinched under the weight of his next hug. "Relax princess," she said to Max, "I'm gonna be okay."

She shuffled her eyes between Max and me, before coughing from a deep chuckle. "We always did have the same taste in men," she said, pinching Max's arm.

"Was it him?" I started to ask Liv when Max left to tell the nurse that she was awake.

Liv nodded but put her finger over her lips to signal my silence. Within another second, doctors, nurses, and Max all came back into the room and hovered over her. She got tired quickly from all the additional tests they ran, and when the doctors finally left her alone, she fell into a deep sleep.

"We need to let her rest," the nurse said a little while later. "You both should go."

"No, thank you," I said without looking at Max. I didn't need to see his face to know he felt the same way I did. "We're fine to stay here."

The nurse started reciting some bitchy, memorized dialog about hospital policies and I stepped in front of Max and gently said, "Ma'am, his sister nearly died today and we're not going to let her be here alone."

"That's just not possible. I don't want to have to call security, but it's unacceptable that . . ."

"Ma'am," I said, interrupting her. "Do you want to know what's really unacceptable? Having someone you love attacked and nearly die. That's unacceptable. Dealing with a nurse who masks her complete lack of empathy as hospital policy. That's unacceptable. So until you're sitting here someday, being asked to walk away from someone you love, don't try to tell anyone what's unacceptable. He's staying. I'm staying. Say whatever you want, call whomever you like, but at the end of it, he and I will still be sitting here. Understood?"

She reluctantly conceded, and we stole a large sofa-like chair from the waiting area and pushed it up against Liv's bed so we could sit there together. We drifted along the edges of sleep, with Max's hand resting comfortably over mine on his chest.

"I love you, too," he said peacefully.

Chapter 37

"Are you there?" Liv asked. We were sitting at a table set with colorful linen napkins, crystal drinking glasses, and pitchers of lemonade with fresh lemon wedges floating along the top. The scent of lemon mixed nicely with the air from the beach in front of us.

"Yeah," I said looking up at her. "But where is here?"

The loose material from her flowery dress flapped with the light breeze behind us. "A quiet corner inside my mind. It's only ever me here, but I thought you might like the view," she said, filling her glass with lemonade.

I looked out at the soft waters and squinted against the setting sun. "I do."

"Our lives are so complicated, aren't they? Why can't we just be normal? Why do we have to fight and get hurt and lose people we love?" she asked.

"How'd you get away from him?"

She took a long sip of her drink and said, "I took him on from inside his own head. It wasn't a pretty place. His mind was . . . broken, that's the best way I can describe it. Tampered with maybe. I don't know. I've never seen anything like it. It was like an ocean, the deeper you go the darker and stranger it gets, until the pressure is so intense that you either have to leave or get crushed by the weight of it. I guess I went too far down and got crushed a little, because the next thing I knew I was in the hospital."

"I'm sorry I wasn't there. I didn't think he'd come after you. I didn't think all my problems would become yours. I just didn't think."

"Hat, stop. I told you that you're not alone in this. I meant it. I knew what the risks of getting involved were, and it was my choice to do it."

"Why'd he attack you instead of me?"

"We weren't exactly chitchatting inside his head, but I don't think he knew I was helping you until after I showed up at that lumberyard. Maybe he was trying to keep me from helping you again, or maybe he thought that killing me would distract you long enough for his plan to play out. I don't know exactly, but I do know that whatever he's got planned with the Opalescence, he's getting close. He knows how it works now, and he's just waiting for the connection to happen. You don't have a lot of time."

I let my eyes drift over the water's reflection of the sun and sipped on my glass of lemonade. "I know."

"Hat, I'm still trying to make sense of everything I saw in his head, but even if you can get the Opalescence back, he's not going to stop. He can't. Whatever it is that's controlling him is just . . . it's just too strong. He's wanted it for a long time, and I don't think that just taking it back is going to be enough."

"I know that too," I said, closing my eyes and trying not to think about what I may need to do to end it. "All the cards have been dealt at this point, and all that's left is me and him, however that plays out."

"I wish you didn't have to go after him. I wish you could just stay here with me forever and look at the beach. There's no drama here. No fighting. Just the water."

"Me too, but can you do something for me?"

"Always."

"If he kills me this time, you know, for real . . . I just want to make sure someone is going to be there to look after my family. He could go after them next, and with the Opalescence, I don't know if they can stop him."

"Okay. But can you do something for me?" Liv asked, taking a sip of her drink.

"Yeah."

"Don't die."

It was funny the way she said it. What was not as funny was how hard it would be to do what she was asking.

"I'm not asking for me, or for your family, but for you. You still have so much left to do in your life, I don't want you to miss out on it. And . . . well, maybe just a little bit, I want you to come back for my brother," she said, giggling to herself. "I don't think I've ever seen him look at anyone the way he looks at you."

The sun was barely awake when I came back from Liv's mind. I rolled over from my stiff position on the couch and yawned. I might as well have slept on a piece of cardboard across the floor for as comfortable as that couch was. If I hadn't been lying against Max, I may not have slept at all.

Noticing me waking up, Max leaned in and kiss me. "I missed waking up to you," he said.

"Who wouldn't?" I said with a laugh. I would never get tired of kissing him. "Listen," I whispered before kissing him again. "I have to go. I . . . I don't know how to explain why, and there isn't really time to, but I don't want you to think I'm not telling you . . ."

"It's okay," Max ran his fingers along my scratchy chin, "she told me everything, you know, in that special way only she can."

"Everything?"

He laughed. "Well I assume it was everything. But we'll have time to talk about anything she missed later, right?"

"Sure," I said, hoping it would be true.

"I'm coming with you," he said. "She told me I couldn't, but I don't care. I don't want you to walk into this alone."

"Mmm. I love you, but you can't come. You have to stay here and make sure nothing else happens to her. Besides, I'm not alone. I have my whole family behind me."

He started to talk again, but I cut him off with a kiss. "I'm sorry that there isn't more time," I said, "but I have to go, and it has to be now. But, you should know that . . . I know I said it last night, but . . . I love you. I'll always love you . . . no matter what."

He grabbed my chin hard, pulling my face up so my eyes met his. "Hey," he said firmly. "Don't you fucking talk like that. I've lost enough people to magic and I'm not losing you too. Don't act like you're not coming back. If it's that dangerous then don't go. It's not worth it. We'll figure something else out."

"I'm sorry. You're right," I said faintly, pulling his hand away from my face.

"Promise me you're coming back."

I kissed him one more time and pulled myself away, walking out of the room without saying anything more. I couldn't promise him that, because I had already learned just how dangerous my life had become, and I knew it would be all too easy for the Universe to decide that I wasn't coming back this time. But there was a certain amount of comfort in the idea that I had a reason, a really handsome and wonderful reason, to fight my way back.

"Thanks," I said to Cooper as he handed me a fresh cup of coffee outside of Liv's room.

"What's next then?" he asked, sipping from his own cup.

"Next, I go after the man who did this."

"Right. When do we leave?"

"I'm leaving now, but you're not."

"Why not? Trust me, mate, I can do much more than persuade people. I can fight head-on when I have to."

"And you may have to. If I don't make it back from this, someone else is going to have to go after him. He won't stop otherwise. It'll have to be you and her; there's no one else."

"But we'll be stronger together, now. We should go at him with everything we have. There's only one . . ."

"No," I said, putting my hand on Cooper's shoulder. "With his powers, it'll be too easy for him to get away if we charge at him. He already thinks he's more powerful than me, and I doubt he'll turn down the opportunity to take me out, so I'm going at him alone."

Cooper looked through the window into Liv's room as she slept, and then back at me. "Call me as soon as it's finished. I'll gather anyone I can find at The Playground and we'll wait for you. If we don't hear from you soon, I'll assume you've . . . I'll assume you need our assistance."

* * * * *

Cars shuffled through the city early the next morning. All the normal people were heading to work on a normal day, oblivious to the clandestine world of magic that lived beneath their own. It was better that way, I think. They didn't need to know how close they were to death and destruction that day.

I texted Talia to find out if Graham was in the office yet, only for her to tell me he was at Storage. The air was stale there from a weekend without the HVAC system running. It was quiet; even the mice that inhabited the place seemed to know what was coming and made themselves scarce.

"Graham! I know you're here," I yelled.

As I walked deeper into the room, something grappled with my ability to stand and I fell over from the weight of nothing. It felt like an invisible brick wall had crumbled on top of me. It was crushing my bones and I was helpless to move.

I'm not off to a good start.

"Gravity is such a simple thing," Talia said, appearing from one of the side rooms. "We take for granted the pure power of it, how it holds us to the Earth, but eases itself enough so we can walk around freely on it."

Her legs crossed over each other as she sauntered toward me. She was twisting her fingers above her head and holding me down with powers I never suspected she had. "Who knew that just a little bit of magic could change all that?"

"Talia?" I yelled as her powers crushed me further into the floor. "What are you doing?"

"Exactly what I was hired to do," she said, tilting her head to enjoy the view of my incapacitated body. "Don't look so pathetic."

"Don't do this."

"Life is pain. I just orchestrate it," she said.

She raised her hand and the invisible bricks lifted, but the severe force of reversed gravity was thrusting me from below, and I shot up to the ceiling, my entire body slamming against the textured popcorn paint.

"Up and down. Up and down," Talia said, twisting her hands back and forth, dropping me ferociously to the ground, only to fling me back up to hit the ceiling again. By the third round, the outline of my body was clearly plastered into the ceiling, along with splatters of blood from my scrapped skin. When I fell to the floor that time, she crushed me harder—so hard that I could practically hear my bones start to buckle and crack under the weight of her gravitational control.

She crouched over me and hiked up her already too-short dress to straddle my stomach. The weight of her body on top of me was nothing compared to the weight of her powers, and my organs shifted to keep from being crushed by the pressure.

The pain was making me dizzy and her weight was the only thing stopping my stomach from exploding out of my throat. "Stop," I pleaded. "Please."

"That's right. Keep begging like a little bitch."

"Talia, this isn't you," I struggled to say. More painful than the crushing effects of her powers were the thoughts behind them. A friend, my closest friend outside my family, was helping the man who killed my mother, and was now trying to kill me.

"But it is, and you have no idea how thankful I am that I can finally stop pretending to give a shit while you carry on with your incessant whining." She bent down closer so our faces were almost touching. Chortling the entire time, she stuck out her tongue and licked my face from chin to forehead. The dribble left in the wake of it was as gross as it was taunting. As she finished, a small vial from around her neck tapped my chin.

"This?" she asked when she saw me looking at it. "Cute, right? It's filled with your hair." She moved it directly over my face and swung it back and forth so it would hit me on the nose each time.

"You can still stop this . . ."

"You know I love your hair, it smells so . . ." She stopped to examine her surroundings before shaking her head eccentrically.

"I took it as a precaution against those visions of yours," she said, and she almost sounded like a normal person again. "Don't you just love the attention? All that work, just for you." The normalcy in her voice dwindled away as she rested one of her long fingernails from her free hand on my lip. Then she giggled maliciously before pulling it back sharply and drawing blood.

"This is all so . . . anticlimactic, don't you think? You came here for the fight of your life and you can't even move underneath my power." She rubbed the blood over my lips before moving her finger to her own mouth and sucking the last of the blood from it. "Mmmm. Tastes sweet, like victory."

Drip. Drip. Drip. Something somewhere was dripping, and the sound of it was getting loud. "What is that?" Talia asked, looking around confused.

Drip. Drip. Drip. The sounds got louder. I followed her eyes and saw black, molasses-like goo dripping down the walls from every corner of the room. We were still there, alone in Storage, but the room was mutating around us as the goo covered and then swallowed everything.

Drip. Drip. Drip. The dripping continued, and color itself was drained from existence. The remaining black and white inverted, making everything distorted like a badly exposed photograph.

"What is this?" She slapped me across the face, and when my face bounced back easily, I realized her powers were no longer holding me down. I pushed her off me and moved behind a broken table.

"How are you doing this?" she yelled, her voice elevated into a full-on shriek.

"Scared of your own mind, Talia?" Liv asked, appearing in the corner. She was still in her hospital robe and she looked tired, too tired to be casting her powers to save me.

"What are you doing?" I asked Liv.

"Shhh . . . it's okay," she whispered.

Talia held out her hand and twisted her fingers at Liv but nothing happened.

"There's no gravity inside your head," Liv said. Her voice bounced playfully around us, but her mouth wasn't moving. She was in control of that moment, and that alone was enough to make Talia pull on her own hair and spin in circles in fear.

The blackened walls of Storage, Talia's mind set in Storage, started to rustle. Outlines of faceless bodies thrust themselves against the paint like it was made of fabric, clawing with their fingers to break free. Moaning followed, and the bodies pushed harder. The walls started closing in, drawing the bodies closer and closer to Talia. She was shrieking again and charging into what little open space was left, desperately hunting for a way out of her own mind.

"Graham's at home. The rest is yours," Liv said to me before disappearing and taking the haunted house of Talia's mind with her.

The color returned to the room, but Talia was still huddled in the corner shaking and shifting her eyes back and forth between the walls to see which monstrous body would break free first.

"Make it stop. Make them stop," she said.

I ripped the vial from around her neck, threw it to the ground and smashed it with my foot. "Why did you do this?" I asked, moving my hand over her throat and holding her down with the power of the Opalescence.

"I know they'll hurt me, I know they will . . . but you won't. You can't. We're friends . . ." Talia babbled in a breathy voice.

"That's right . . . best friends forever," I said, waving my hand at a stack of boxes and walking away as they fell on top of her.

Chapter 38

"All you had to do was walk away," Graham said as I entered his condo.

He was sitting in a tall-backed, beige accent chair in the entryway near the base of the stairs to the second floor. The Opalescence, still safely in my setting, dangled from his neck, and his voice and face were still hidden underneath the Mask of Apate.

"Why bother with the mask, Graham?"

Confidence was exuding out of me in every direction, but it didn't keep him from appearing unthreatened. He casually reached for his face and tugged at the fabric-like whiteness of the mask. It pulled off easily, like putty, and clouds of dust shot up from the ground and followed the whiteness into his hand. When it settled, the mask had morphed back into the golden, decorative form I had seen before. The white hair was gone, and I was looking into the exposed eyes of a murderer.

"It wasn't supposed to be like this," he said, tossing the mask on the ground. "I honestly thought you'd walk away long before any of this happened. I've known you for years

Hat . . . and if there's one thing you're good at, it's walking away."

"But I didn't."

"I guess I underestimated you a lot during all this. I knew who you were when I hired you, who the Walkers really were, but I also knew you didn't have any clue what that meant. I didn't think it would even affect you seeing as you didn't seem to have any powers. But then you suddenly did, somehow, and when I found out you had the Opalescence, I thought you'd walk away from it before it ended like this."

"It doesn't have to Graham. Just stop this. Stop here and we'll both walk away."

"No. I've been waiting for this for too long. The Opalescence is almost mine now, I can feel it. The power is . . . everything they said it would be. You don't even know the extent of what this can do, do you?"

Still sitting, he opened his hand in front of him. Like it was Justin, a ball of fire started to form above his palm. And with one quick flick of his wrist, it was flying at me.

It was slow, though, and I casually crouched down and it brushed over my head.

"Why do all this? That isn't you, is it? You're right, we've known each other for years, and I've always thought you were a little over the top, but I never thought of you as someone who could do this."

"It's all perfectly black and white for you, isn't it?" Graham stirred a bit in his seat, but still hadn't taken a defensive stance against me. "It's never as simple as being right or wrong, or good or bad, Hat. We live in a world built in the gray area, and the only difference between you and me is that I'm not willing to let someone else decide my destiny for me."

With three flicks of my hand, three of his expensive paintings jumped off the wall and hurtled toward his head. He turned, smiled, and then his body dissolved into the ripples of light just before the paintings crashed into the chair.

When he rematerialized, he was at the top of the staircase, a ball of fire hot in his hand. He heaved it at me from above, but I leapt to the ground to avoid it, and it hit the wall behind me, scorching the paint. Another one came flying at me, and I rolled out of its way. It missed me, but little sparks from the flame bounced off the floor and sizzled against the hair on my arm.

"What is power worth when you have to destroy everything and everyone to get it?" I yelled, while reaching into my pocket coyly.

"Great power comes with great sacrifice. You're too weak to understand what makes it worth it, but I'm not. It's my destiny."

"Taken by you, this crime I see," I called up the stairs.

"What?"

"I call back now what belongs to me."

"Stop!" he called down the stairs, realizing what I was doing. He flung another fireball at me from the top of the staircase, but I used my free hand to cast it aside with the power of the Opalescence that was still mine. It landed on a bookshelf and lit the contents ablaze.

"Reverse what's been done, uncross the line." I pulled my hand from my pocket and opened it, revealing a mound of bright blue powder that Gloria had given me. "And return to me what is rightfully mine." As the last words of the spell left my lips, I took a deep breath and blew the powder into the air.

Like a swarm of bees, the specks of powder swirled around me before propelling themselves toward Graham. They created a dense cloud, buzzing between us before attaching to the Opalescence. Graham evaporated again, but the powder had already done its work and sent the necklace back to me.

Two fireballs catapulted from thin air as Graham reappeared behind them. I couldn't raise powers fast enough and both of them hit me, engulfing the arm I lifted in defense. I fell to the ground and rolled to put out the flame, but the skin on my arm had already gone coarse and turned bright red. An immense sting clawed through it, gaining painful momentum with every second that passed. I dropped the Opalescence from the shock of it all, and it rattled to the floor before landing a few feet away from me.

Graham stepped closer to me, the smell of my burning skin making him smile. He put out his hand to form another fireball, but before it could come, I swung my body around and kicked one of his knees from the side, forcing him to drop to the ground with me.

He evaporated quickly and reappeared a few feet away, standing above the Opalescence. I swiped my hand and the Opalescence slid across the floor to the other side of the room.

"Why do all this . . . to your family?" I yelled, holding my crippled arm and trying to hold back from crying out.

"Family?" Graham scoffed, walking toward me. "You're hardly my family."

"We could have been if you had given us the chance."

Another fireball formed in Graham's hand, and it created an eerie glow against his face as its hot orange and red colors swirled in his hand. It grew bigger and swirled faster, joined by the power of his other hand and forming a fiery cyclone between them. "I'm not you, being a Walker means nothing to me."

I threw up my good arm, flinging a chair at Graham and catching him off-guard. It hit him from the side, thrashing him through the banister of the staircase. Without its master, the cyclone of fire spun into the air and evaporated with little pageantry.

"You may have Justin's powers and whoever else's powers you had to kill to get, but you're not getting the Opalescence, and you're not getting me. I'll kill you first, family or not."

Despite the pain of my crippled arm, I raised both of my hands to cast a bombardment of debris at him. From every corner of the room, objects attacked—half burnt books, candles, more art, furniture, and anything else that wasn't bolted down.

He shielded his face with his arms before evaporating again. He reappeared on unsteady footing at the top of the stairs, and I cast a broken piece of the banister at his back. It knocked into him and forced him to tumble down the stairs.

When he landed, he didn't move.

Is he dead?

I picked up the Opalescence and slowly made my way to the base of the stairs. Breathing heavily, I bent down over Graham's reddened face. Before I could react, his eyes sprung open and he grabbed my shirt, pulling me forward and tossing me to the ground above him.

As I tried to get up, he hit me in the stomach with another broken piece of the banister. I let out a long, empty howl and slouched over. Then with both hands holding the banister piece like a baseball bat, he swung hard at my slouched back, driving my body into the floor.

"Keep fighting, Hat . . . it won't matter. I'm stronger than you, and that means I'm the one walking away with the prize." He forced all his weight onto my outstretched, burnt hand to hold me down while he grabbed the Opalescence from the other. As he pried open my fingers, I let the Opalescence go and used the now free hand to yank on his wrist, tipping him off-balance and rolling him shoulder-first onto the ground next to me.

He was starting to evaporate again by the time he'd stood up, but I wasn't going to let him go anywhere. No matter how it was going to end, it was going to end, and even his power wasn't going to stop that. Without thinking, I leapt toward him and grabbed onto his arm just before he vanished.

* * * * *

There were a few brief moments where Graham and I were wrapped up together in his magic, jumping into the ethereal space between two physical places. Our bodies were inconsequential there, but our intertwined consciousness swirled and struggled against each other, fighting for supremacy of direction. When mine won, we reappeared at The Playground, crashing into the bar in an uneasy landing from the sky.

Cooper and the others were all gathered there, and they jumped up and away from us as we wrestled around on the ground. "Stay back," I yelled to them as I rolled away from Graham.

"Damn it," Graham yelled. He was getting ready to use his powers and disappear again when he realized that I'd gotten the Opalescence back from him during our fall, and it was already around my neck. Anger rushed over him, and he pushed out both of his hands and let fire run rampant from them.

The fire streamed out at me like two endless breaths from a dragon's gullet. I held my hands out in defense but couldn't deflect the sheer force of his power. I was able to push back against it with the Opalescence's power, but at the cost of charring my hands. I had to close my eyes to protect them from the heat. The flames were so close that I could smell my eyebrows burning off.

We were locked in that standoff for too long, and my hands sizzled like I'd placed each of them on an unbearably hot stove burner.

"AHHHH!" I called out in pain. Like I was trying to push a boulder away as it rolled downhill toward me, I fought against the fire, moving closer and closer to Graham. The grass wilted and then blackened under our feet. Saliva boiled on my tongue and I could smell nothing but burnt hair. My hands throbbed, but adrenaline pushed me past my pain. Closer and closer, I inched toward him and the backlash of the fire blackened my clothes.

We locked eyes. It was no longer about who was stronger or who had more power, it was a grit-filled battle of wills. One step closer and there were only a few fire-filled feet left between us. Controlling Justin's powers seemed to mean he was immune to the devastation it brought on others, but he wasn't immune to everything.

His expression changed to fear for the first time as the air turned cold around us. Swirling faster than ever, the Opalescence's colors expanded beyond the stone until it was wider than my body. Slowly it started swirling faster and faster until it was just a blend of color. I stood at the fulcrum of the vortex as it sucked all the fire Graham could produce, stopping only when there was nothing left.

Confused, but still not defeated, Graham quickly stood. Before he could evaporate again, I focused on a large shard of broken glass from the bar, casting it at him with my hand. It spun surely through the air before digging into his shin, forcing spurts of blood to spill out around him. He fell back to the ground, unable to focus on anything but the pain.

With his leg still seeping blood, he tried to stand. I kicked the shard of glass still in his leg, causing him to scream out and fall back down. But he wasn't the only one in pain.

My skin was swelling and crisping more with every passing second and felt so tight that I thought at any moment it would tear me apart at my joints. Calling on my mother's powers again, I waited as familiar tremors of light appeared and wrapped around my arm. Then I laughed, and Graham watched in disbelief as the magic healed the severe burns.

The others were yelling something to me from behind, but I wasn't listening. I held out my healed hands, my palms facing the sky, and said, "In this time and in this place, I consecrate this my sacred space."

Two golf-ball-sized blue lights formed in each of my hands. The color was so pristine and dark they almost looked solid—two tiny planets harvesting power within my hands. They shot up, dancing around each other like fireflies in summer before separating and falling to the ground. They splattered like paint balls, spreading their chrome-blue colors across the ground around us. Slowly, their colors spread, and pooled together until we were fully surrounded by their magic. That space, my sacred space, separated us from the others and from reality.

Graham gritted his teeth and held out his hand to me, but no fire came.

"Your powers won't work here," I said to him.

"And now what?" he shouted. "You won't kill me."

"Maybe you're right," I said, "but I don't need to kill you."

Thoughts of my family filled my mind peacefully. They were the Universe's gift of strength, and the source of control over the Opalescence. I could feel every person who ever wore it. I could feel every person who had died for it. Kevin, my mother, countless others. Their emotions amalgamated into one focus—power, which was mine to command.

"Walkers, hear me," I yelled. "Remove this threat from our family. Take his powers and keep them where he can never be tempted by them again."

Whispers filled the circle, and the Opalescence's colors sparkled and moved within the stone freely. One by one, spirits of my family appeared next to me and strengthened the Opalescence's power. The first to come was our grandmother.

"No!" Graham called out as she walked toward him.

She put two fingers to her lips, and then reached out to touch Graham with them. As she pulled away, a bit of his power ripped from his body and when she came to stand by my side, that power funneled into the Opalescence.

The next to come was the woman who wrote the poem. Then her son. Then more women too old for me to have known of.

My mother came too, smiling sweetly at me as she touched Graham and took some of his power. If I could have, I would have stopped everything to have just one moment alone with her. I started to say something, but she shook her head knowingly and took her place with the rest of our family behind me.

The last spirit to appear was Kevin. He looked down upon the son he'd never had the chance to know, and his sadness and grief for him washed into the rest of us through our connection. He whispered something into Graham's ear before taking the last bit of his power.

As Kevin walked back toward me, he and the rest of the family disappeared, the cold of the Opalescence released back into the Universe, and the circle around us broke.

Graham pulled his hand close to his body, and when the fireball he was trying to conjure didn't appear, he laid back in defeat, mourning the loss of his powers.

Cooper and the others crowded around us, looking down at the heap of a once-powerful man.

"What are you doing?" I asked Cooper as he roughly pulled Graham's hands behind his back.

"Don't worry about it," Cooper said without looking at me. "Just be thankful that someone is willing to take him off your hands." Cooper had tied Graham's hands with some kind of cable tie and was moving him toward the door.

"Wait," I said, standing in front of Graham and forcing him to look at me.

It was finally over, and the hatred I had for him as the man without the face, and what he had done as that man, was gone. I felt nothing more than pity, and he could see it drip down my face just from the sight of him. I could still see pieces of the real Graham, or the person I thought was the real Graham, fighting for a place within his dark personality. The generous man, the happy man, the kind man—to him they were masks to wear to sneak into my life, but to me the hate-filled and power-hungry man that almost killed me was the mask, and the rest were just casualties of his actions.

Graham sneered at my outward deliberation. "Is this where you try to help me find redemption?" he asked.

I laughed in his face. "No Graham. This is where I tell you that the next time you come near my family, I will kill you."

For a moment he almost looked disappointed that I hadn't killed him already. "You think you know everything that's happened, but you don't," he said before Cooper started to pull him away again. "You have the power to see . . . so look."

Summoning the control I had felt with the white flowers at the bottom of the well, I calmly said, "Show me."

Lights and sounds came and went without effect or tribulation. In that space between perception and reality, I dove into the primal depths of my soul to enjoy the serenity that waited for me there. And as the weightlessness took over my body, a vision unfolded.

The door to my mother's home office opened quietly. Light from the hallway illuminated the otherwise dark room, casting light over her lifeless body.

Graham entered and stood over her with his cell phone in his ear. Talia drifted in behind him and started riffling through my mother's desk.

"Murder," Graham said into the phone. "They made it look like a heart attack . . . like the others."

"There's nothing in here," Talia said.

"No," Graham continued into the phone, "it's already gone. Whoever killed her must have taken it. Yes. Yes. Fine." He shoved his phone back in his pocket and nodded to the door. "Come on, it's not here. Let's go."

Chapter 39

Change is both cruel and beautiful, inevitable and constant. Whether we admit it or not, it dominates our lives; a common thread in the fabric of our past, a driving force in the actions of our present, and a rippling uncertainty in the outlook of our future. We can yearn for it to come or fight it off with our last breath, but it will be always there, like the dark shadow that follows us through the day and the flickering flame that guides us through the night.

It will always be that way because the Universe will always weave it that way. Close your eyes for a second, and by the time you open them again, things will be different. Sometimes they'll be better, other times they'll be worse, but change itself will be the only thing that remains the same.

In life, my mother taught me not to fear change, and in death, she taught me that change never travels alone. It brings with it companions born from secrets, fear, and struggle, but it also brings a renewed faith in the foundation of what makes you whole—your family, your inner strength, and your trust in the Universe. I accepted the shadows of change as they followed me through the day and thanked that flickering flame for guiding me through the night.

A few quiet weeks later, I stood in an empty room in my mother's house. In one hand, I had a piece of paper, and in the other a lighter. Slowly, the page I had ripped from my mother's book burned away. On it was the spell that had suppressed my powers.

We could no longer be a family that lived in constant fear of being who we were born to be, it was too sharp a contrast to the tenacity and grit that makes the Walkers who they are. We would take care of each other, always and without question, and when change disrupted our world, we would again rise from the ashes and fight on. That is who we are, who they raised me to be.

"Give me that before you burn the damn house down," Max said, taking what was left of the paper into the bathroom.

Summer weather hit the city early that year, and we had just finished clearing out the last of my mother's things from a house I once knew as home. In a few days, the sale would be final, and a new family would move in to start their own memories here.

Max came up behind me and wrapped one of his arms over my shoulder and the other across my chest, clasping his hands together and leaning into me. "Gonna miss it?" he asked quietly.

"I miss her. I guess the rest of this is just an empty box."

There was a certain peace and closure that came with seeing my mother's house empty. Max and I had been talking about it a lot and knowing who killed her wouldn't change her being dead, nor would it change how I felt about her being dead. But it would keep me from moving on. It could also turn me into someone neither of us wanted me to be, someone who lived in constant fear and worry about what the Opalescence would bring into my life.

I twisted around in his grip to look at my favorite feature, those big gray eyes. We kissed and the world around us slowed. I enjoyed another perfect moment with him, learning that I didn't have to be sad when it was over, because with Max, there would never be any shortage of perfect moments.

"You made a mess," Max said, pointing to the ashes on the floor.

As I bent down to sweep up the ashes with my hand, the familiar lights and sounds of my life brought me to my place of weightlessness and a vision unfolded.

> *My mother followed the sounds of knocking to her front door and behind it was Withers.*
>
> *"So, what was so important that I had to come all the way over here, eh?" Withers said as the door opened. He pushed past my mother without invitation and walked into the house.*
>
> *"These," she said, pointing to her coffee table and closing the door. On top of the table were dozens of little totems carved from wood. Each had a unique face, and intricate zigzag markings all over.*
>
> *"And what is it that you plan to do with these, Amelia?" Withers asked.*
>
> *"I need you to help me break them," my mother said.*
>
> *"Pfft. I will do nothing of the sort. It took me months to find that spell for you and countless years off my life."*
>
> *"Things have changed now," my mother said softly, picking up her book of spells. "Test not the force of a Caster's power, but the reach of their heart," she read aloud. She quickly flipped through the pages and held the book up to Withers. "Look at this."*

Wither's squinted as he read the page. "The Trials of Truth? You don't want to go there."

"I already have," she said quietly.

"What would possess you to go to a place like that? What could you have needed so badly that you'd risk that? Hmmm. I always thought you were one of the smarter Walkers, or at least more cautious."

"What I saw in there was . . . big. Bigger than this. And not just for me, not just for you—for all of us. I don't have much time at all. I have to reverse the suppression on the kids' powers before it's too late. And I can't do it without you."

"What of your family, eh? You're lousy with Casters. Pick one of them and leave me out of this."

"My family can't know what I'm doing. They wouldn't understand and there isn't time to explain it all to them. And knowing could hurt them, I think, especially right now."

"You Walkers and your secrets."

"It just happened again, didn't it?" Max asked as he watched me come out of my vision. "What did you see?"

"My mom," was all I said.

"Okay," he said, turning to walk toward the door.

"Hey," I yelled, grabbing onto his shirt and pulling him back to me. I gave him another kiss and felt him laugh a little under my lips. "Love you."

* * * * *

Max and I had a busy day planned. After a quick shower together to wash off a day of acting like moving men, we hauled ourselves to Paige's house for a bigger than usual Walker Family party. In our family, there were simply too many things to celebrate for too many people so parties had to be lumped together. That day we were celebrating two different birthdays, a college graduation, and Paige's engagement to the man she finally decided to introduce to all of us.

"Wanna be my date for a wedding?" I asked Max as we gathered by the table of cakes, plural.

"I better be your date," Max laughed and looked around uneasily at my family. He was still getting used to the sheer quantity of them.

"Know anyone for me?" Damon asked.

"I'm sorry about Talia," I said.

I had told him that Talia quit Cartwright & Company and took off but that she hadn't told anyone where. The truth was no one had seen her since I left her in Storage, and I wasn't expecting that anyone would.

"Wait . . . is he your boyfriend?" Finn pointed to Max and asked me.

Poor Finn. With a family as big as ours, news always traveled fast, but it also always inevitably missed someone along the way. That someone was usually Finn. Laughter erupted from the group as Damon tried to fill Finn in on everything he had missed.

The feeling of eyes watching me pulled me away from the group, and I wandered over to the side of the house to join Gloria. "Hey, Auntie," I said, sitting down in a lawn chair next to her.

"Hi, honey," she said. "You still mad at me?"

"I don't know the answer to that," I said with a smile. "Ask me again later."

"Are you still mad at me?" she asked and we both laughed.

"Things are complicated in this family, that's for sure. And I don't think that's going to change any time soon."

"Probably not," she said, looking off into the throngs of family in the distance. "But either way, I hope you know I'm really proud you. For what you did. And I think your Mom would be too."

"Thanks," I said.

When she noticed me watching Charley as she walked by, she said, "Hat . . ."

I shook my head at Gloria and she stopped talking.

"Hey, can I talk to you?" I asked Charley, pulling her away.

"What's up, Bitch?" she asked. "By the way, I'm glad to see you're still with Hotness over there. I'd hate to hear that you two broke up and he was up for grabs," she licked her lips a little and watched the back of Max's pants tighten as he stuck his hands in his pockets.

"We're close, right?" I asked.

"Mmm hmm," she turned her face toward me but her eyes stayed on Max, "and because we're close . . . we should learn to share better."

I snapped my fingers in front of her face. "Charlotte! Focus."

She finally gave me her attention, animatedly pointing her eyebrows in toward her nose. "Whoa. Why are you full-naming me? And you're being all serious . . . we're never this serious together. What's wrong? Oh god, are you sick?"

"No, I'm not sick, Freak. But, yeah, I guess it is serious. Okay, listen. If I knew something about you that you didn't know, but I wasn't sure that it would make your life better to know, would you want me to tell you?"

"What the hell are you saying?"

"Just answer me."

"I guess so, especially now that you've got me all worried."

"Okay," I pulled a sealed envelope out of my pocket and handed it to her. "Here."

"What does it say?"

"Just read it. I'm hoping it'll be easier to read than hear," I said. She took the envelope and retreated to the house to read it, passing by her mother who was flirting so hard with a man that one of her sisters brought that she didn't even notice Charley.

Max came over to me and rubbed the back of my neck gently. "How do you think she'll take it?"

"I don't know," I said. "If anyone knows how much it sucks to find out stuff so long after the fact, it's me. But even if she doesn't like it, she has the right to know. Right?"

He pulled me into a rough hug. "Right."

"Do save all that for the bedroom," Cooper said. He walked toward us with a stunningly dressed Liv on his arm, both looking happy and rested.

"You made it," I said from Max's shoulder.

Cooper shook my hand and then brushed a chunk of his messy hair back. "Smashing party, really."

"How are you?" Liv asked Max, kissing her brother on the cheek and pulling him a few feet away to start their own conversation.

"The Playground certainly doesn't feel the same these days," Cooper said to me. "You've been avoiding us . . ."

"Not avoiding, just resting. I needed a break from everything. I've been busy finding a place for all my mom's things before her house was sold, and then spending some overdue time with my family."

"The club should reopen soon though. You'll be there?"

"As long as the Blue Ice still pours freely, sure," I joked. "So . . . you and Liv?"

"Right. We thought we might give it another go now that things have settled down a bit."

"Yeah, I'm glad it's all over too."

"For now," he stated with a smile and shifted his eyes.

"We were just saying that the four of us should take a trip together next month," Liv said, coming back with Max to join our conversation.

I took Max's hand in mine and said, "Sounds a little too 'couple-y' for me, but it could be fun."

"Speaking of fun, I have some interesting news for you," Liv said, pulling Cooper's arm around her waist. "I wanted to tell you before we have to go back to work, but . . ."

"The suspense, Liv. The suspense. Haha. Just tell us."

"I'm pregnant," she said.

"Wow," I said, hugging her. "Congratulations!" I reached out and shook Cooper's hand wildly. "You two are having a baby? That's amazing. Congratulations . . . really."

Liv closed her eyes and giggled through her nose as I released her. "No, no," she said quickly, "we are having a baby," she waved her finger in between the both of us.

My neck practically snapped I whipped it so hard to look at Max. His mouth was hanging lower than mine. Neither of us could say anything.

"That's right . . . you and me, a mom and a dad," Liv said.

I shuddered as I felt all the color drain from my face.

Holy shit. Is she serious? How did this happen? Fuck, Hat, you know how this happened . . . you were there. A kid. Me having a kid. Can I handle that?

"I think you can," Liv said out loud.

Acknowledgments

Writing a book is . . . well, hard. But having wonderful people around me makes it worth it. They give my life purpose, perspective, and flavor.

First, there's my family. There can be no question that this book would not exist without them. They provided the inspiration for many of the characters you've met. They're similarly large, loud, and twisted . . . and I love them.

My mother deserves first billing—in fact, this entire book is dedicated to her. She's been my champion, my sounding board, and my friend. She was my first reader, and remains my biggest fan. She taught me how to dream, but more importantly, she raised me to actually believe that dreams can become reality. If I were to ever question these teachings, all I'd have to do is look back at this book.

I have much to be grateful for in my aunt, Donise, and my respect and love for her are deep. She has taken many roles in my life: second parent, confidante, spiritual leader, friend. She gave me a home when I needed it most. And, of course, she was an early reader of this book, looking past the imperfections of a draft to offer encouragement while still asking the tough questions.

Now, if I continue on like this about every family member, you'll need to read another novel (I have more family than Hat Walker). But there are a few others you need to know about.

My brother, Doug, who has a self-confidence and strength that I have always admired and will continue to try to emulate. Without him, I'd have no one to chase after the waitress when our food is taking too long.

My sister (in law and in spirit), Charlene, who is a beautiful person inside and out. Without her, I'd have no one to calm my brother down when the food is taking too long.

My sister-cousin, Rebecca Cheryl, whose friendship spurred some of my favorite dialog in the book. If I were going to jump off a bridge, she'd be the first person I pushed off in front of me.

My cousins, Yvette, Megan, and Dan, who were all early readers of this book but late friends in life. There are no three people I'd rather dig through the trash with.

And all the family who were here with me, offering support (and plugs for characters to be based on them), even if I couldn't always see them. My dad, Aunt Joan, Uncle Kenny, and Lucky.

Then there're my friends.

The first you need to know about is Lisa, who has been the most involved in this book's creation, production, re-creation, and re-production. She has been my accountability partner, my grammar consultant, my business strategist, and the mediator for the voices in my head. Her support in this process has meant everything to me, but her opinions and insights have meant everything to this book. When the person who doubted the story the most was me, she was the one that gave me the perspective I needed to shut up, get working, and get better. I could not be more thankful.

Rebecca "Lemon" Lambertstein is both a close friend and this book's proofreader (if you find a typo, her email is on the next page . . .) She is my partner-in-crime and the perfect currency when bartering for freedom in a random city.

I'm going to get gushy about my friends if I don't stop. But before I do, I have to thank a few others for being amazing. Claudine, Leah, Andrew, Monique, Kristine, Travis, Mike, Sara (but not Sarah), Jackie, Jen, Carson, Tim, and Chris.

And, I'm not done yet. There are also so many others who have contributed meaningful things to this project.

Kimberly Peticolas, my editor and publishing consultant, who didn't try to kill me for using British-English words or constantly changing my mind about formatting.

CJ Anaya, my writing/publishing consultant, who ended up becoming a mentor (whether she wanted to or not), talked me through some of my crazier 'author' moments, and taught me to trust my gut.

Fiona Jayde, my cover designer, who held up in the face of my intense distaste for all things normal or standard, and created unique artwork that gave Hat Walker form.

My cat, Cat (yes, that's his name), who reminds me daily about the powers of persistence, relaxation, and humor.

Tom Sommerfield, who gave me the tools and patience (his . . . I don't have any of that) to tackle tough areas of the book.

Michelle Ciccaglione, who took on the role of my spiritual sherpa without begrudging it and is helping me navigate the pothole-filled journey of my life.

Brené Brown, the researcher/storyteller who showed me why creativity cannot exist without vulnerability. Even though we haven't met (yet—hey Brené, call me!), I am certain that without her work I never would have, in her words, stepped into the ring.

Gary John Bishop, the author of *Unfuck Yourself*, whose book emerged from a sea of mostly bland and homogeneous self-development material to become my unofficial guide to life (I have it in print, digital, and audio).

Lastly, and most importantly, I have to thank one more person. It's that person I didn't forget, but whose name I didn't add here, and is reading this going, "What the hell, man?" This is for you.

No, really.

JM

CPSIA information can be obtained
at www.ICGtesting.com
Printed in the USA
LVHW010309180119
604375LV00007B/185/P